For an American Warrior!
God bless, Austin!

Ps. 97

The
Warrior
Spy

A Thriller

Dony Jay

MHP
Merry Hill Publishing

Merry Hill Publishing

This book is a work of fiction. Any references to historical events, real people, or real places are used fictitiously. Other names, characters, places, and events are products of the author's imagination, and any resemblance to actual events or places or persons living or dead is entirely coincidental.

The Warrior Spy

Copyright © 2015 by Dony Jay

Scripture taken from the New King James Version®. Copyright © 1982 by Thomas Nelson. Used by permission. All rights reserved.

Cover design by Damonza

For more information visit the author's website at DonyJayBooks.com

ISBN 978-0-9969270-0-0
ISBN 978-0-9969270-1-7 (mobi)
ISBN 978-0-9969270-2-4 (epub)

To Jill, Claire and Jackson—
for your support, encouragement,
patience and prayer.
You are my everything.

And to all the warrior spies out there,
protecting and defending freedom and liberty,
and the families that support them.
You are my inspiration.

For he is God's minister to you for good. But if you do evil, be afraid; for he does not bear the sword in vain; for he is God's minister, an avenger to execute wrath on him who practices evil.

Romans 13:4

PROLOGUE

Jariyan Al Batnah Province, Qatar
10 Miles from the Saudi Border

BULLETS snapped by his head like popcorn on a stove. Reagan Rainey crouched behind a low-slung stone wall, at least what was left of it. They were everywhere, men with AK-47s shouting angrily in Arabic, far more than what original intelligence estimates had indicated. Several rounds jack-hammered against the exposed engine block of an old Land Rover behind him, throwing a brilliant shower of sparks into the obsidian darkness.

"Frag out!"

Rainey hurled the grenade into the swarm of terrorists pouring toward him and his team. His voice was nearly drowned out by the cacophony of gunfire. The resulting explosion rattled the mud brick structures all around them, pocking walls and shredding bodies. As Rainey's team began to push forward, a man appeared on their right, shouldering an RPG. But just before the terrorist could fire upon them, his head exploded.

Thank you, Wizard.

The Delta Force sniper in the overwatch position had just saved their butts.

America's shadow warriors, games faces on, swiftly curled inside the first structure on the west side of the compound and advanced down a short featureless corridor carved into the sun-baked, wasteland of southern Qatar. Reaching the first corner, Rainey and his stack of guys stopped in quiet chorus, remained still. Except for their eyes, which continued scanning for threats.

Several sporadic cracks of gunfire coughed in the distance, muffled by the earthen walls. Somewhere on the other side of the compound the guys from Blue Team were still taking names and doing so with extreme prejudice.

Then all was quiet. Eerily so.

His radio clicked. Rainey clicked back a response, then a voice came alive in his earpiece: "Bronco, we're clear on this side of the compound. He's not over here. Got a few phones, a laptop, and some digital media though." Rainey clicked his radio in acknowledgment as the sweat trickled down his back beneath his gear-heavy vest.

Rainey knelt along the blind corner, dug into a pouch on his vest. Behind a mask of coal-black face paint, he studied a tiny, telescoping mirror for threats and danger zones, for booby traps. There was a long hallway that descended into the bowels of the compound now transformed into hues of green and gray by his helmet-mounted NODs (night optical devices). He quietly stood, gave several hand signals, then readied his rifle and fell back in line behind his fellow operator, Mouse.

Rainey took a breath. *Protect us, Lord.* He reached out and squeezed Mouse's shoulder, wordlessly signaling that he was ready to move.

The "empty" corridor suddenly came alive, men appearing from everywhere with muzzles breathing fire. Rounds ripped into the walls on either side of them as the team pressed forward returning fire for fire. Unlike their enemy, Rainey and his mates were well-disciplined. And they did not miss. Terrorists leaning out of doorways twisted and fell. The voice from an injured terrorist wailed loudly for a few seconds until it grew weaker and finally died.

Again...a loud silence.

The thick cloud of gun smoke stung the back of his throat like seawater. Rainey dropped the empty magazine from his HK416, slammed home a fresh one, and brought the weapon back into battery. His four-man team had just dispatched eight men in less than three seconds.

To look at them they were each a mix of supreme alertness, professionalism, lethality. America's elite fighters on the modern front lines of war with an enemy that had no compunction for mercy, for reason, for peace, for anything but what was evil in its truest sense. This was an unqualified fight between good and evil.

Treading with resolve and purpose, Rainey's team moved deeper into the compound where, based on their intel, a member of the American diplomatic corps—in actuality, a high-level CIA operative—was being held captive. Nearly three days ago, the ambassador's residence in Doha, Qatar, had been attacked. By whom exactly and for what purpose was still unclear. The ambassador had been out of the country at the time, but several others hadn't been so lucky. Eight Americans including two members of the Diplomatic Security Service had valiantly lost their lives; two more had been seriously wounded. One man, Lonnie Conover, had been taken captive. Conover had been ripped from the ambassador's residence after being brutally beaten—all of this evidenced on the home's surveillance footage. Conover, a senior CIA officer with an incredible knowledge of Agency operations and personnel, was a man who had been operating in country for the past several years under a cover position within the State Department. Due to the information and skills he possessed, his loss was catastrophic.

Working with its other Five Eyes SIGINT (signals intelligence) partners—Canada, Britain, Australia, and New Zealand—the Central Intelligence Agency tracked down the man's whereabouts to this remote windswept encampment in southern Qatar. The intel had been deemed actionable and Rainey, part of a package of CIA and Delta Force special operators, had been tasked with bringing the action.

Rainey, call sign Bronco, wiped the sweat from his forehead with the back of his gloved hand and re-adjusted his NODs before giving the signal to move on. He knew this battle had only just begun.

Suddenly, a man appeared in front of them with an AK tucked under his arm. In perfect synchronicity, Rainey and Mouse directed their muzzles on him and fired. Two to the chest, one to the head. The six rounds drilled through the man's body, pitting the wall behind him. He sloughed to the ground like a rag doll.

Rainey and his team cleared rooms as they went, leapfrogging each other in pairs, greedily consuming undefended real estate. As they rendered each room safe, they remained attentive for signs that would reveal where Conover was being held. He was definitely here somewhere. They just had to find him. Hopefully, they weren't already too late.

As they rounded the next corner in the tunnel network, a hail of gunfire came alive from further down the corridor. Each man stepped backward out of the line of fire pulling the man in front of him. Rainey glanced down as something bounced against his boot. Without hesitation, he scooped up the object and threw it back toward the enemy.

"Grenade!"

A nanosecond after the explosion, Rainey scrambled forward, leaned out with his rifle aimed down the tunnel and scanned for more threats. As the hot dust settled, he could see a pockmarked metal door behind the scattered bodies of several dead terrorists. He motioned to his men, and they eased onward. Stepping through the carnage, Rainey suddenly detected movement from one of the terrorists at his feet. A hand sliding toward a pistol. *Nice try.* Rainey shot the man in the center of the forehead.

Without a word said amongst them, the four-man team approached the battered metal door. It was locked. Rainey and Mouse stepped out of the way, giving Monster—another teammate—access to the door, where he attached a thin, linear charge. As soon as it blew, Mouse tossed in a stun grenade and the men quickly pushed inside. They had barely cleared the threshold when more automatic gunfire greeted them.

Rainey heard the grunt behind him. One of his guys had been hit. Then it registered: the white hot burning sensation in his left thigh. He'd been hit, too.

He gritted his teeth and ignored the pain as he quickly moved to cover. Once there, he palpated the wound with his support hand. No arterial spurt. That was good. No major blood vessels had been hit. Though hunched over, he found that he could still put weight on his leg, too, so there was no major structural damage either. He gripped his carbine again with both hands.

Rainey fired, moved, got behind cover. He did this several more times, surgically plinking terrorists as they popped out from behind stacks of wooden crates—the room was chock full of them. His teammates likewise did the same.

There was a chorus of "Clear!" when all the threats had been neutralized.

Now the air was rank with the odor of cordite and the coppery smell of blood. Rainey, Mouse, and Tonka—the fourth man on the team—maneuvered to the end of the room and stacked up outside another door. This one was old and wooden, secured only with a shiny metal hasp and a fat, new padlock. Rainey gave Mouse and Tonka a silent three-count before he launched his boot into the door. The dilapidated wood splintered and crashed to the dirt floor beyond. The doorway issued into what could only be described as a prison cell that probably dated back to the seventh century. The small room reeked of body odor and body fluids. In the middle of the room were a solitary chair, some rope, and several pools of dried blood and urine that had caked the dirt. Lying in a heap in the shadowy corner, bound and gagged, was Lonnie Conover.

"Bronc, you've been hit," said Tonka, as they all lowered their guns. The big team medic was pointing to the dark, wet spot on Rainey's left leg.

"We're all hit. Go check on Monster." It was true. They all had dark, wet spots on their pants and sleeves in varying sizes.

"On it, boss." Tonka was already racing out of the room.

Pushing up their NODs, Rainey and Mouse clicked on flashlights and peered at the horrifically brutalized CIA officer. He was naked, beaten beyond comprehension and nearly any semblance of recognition. His face literally looked like raw meat, was crusted with dried blood, swollen in places, and covered with nasty shades of purple and red. It was obvious that the bones in his legs had been savagely pulverized, probably with a sledge hammer, judging from the circular wound patterns. He had several other ugly burns, cuts and lacerations about his battered body that were showing clear signs of infection.

"Are we too late?" asked Mouse.

Rainey unslung his rifle, handed it to Mouse. He knelt beside the unconscious man and gently checked his vitals. "He's alive but not by much." As Rainey pulled the gag out and continued taking stock of his injuries, the man involuntarily quivered. Then a wince and a moan. Conover attempted to open his right eye, a slit in puffy, raw flesh. It seemed to take an incredible amount of effort to do so. "Hang in there, sir. We're gonna take you home." Rainey keyed his mic. "Sandstorm, this is Red Team Leader. Capital is secure. I repeat, Capital is secure."

"Copy that, Bronco. Confirm status, over."

"Sandstorm, Capital is alive but needs immediate medevac, over."

"Sandstorm copies, birds are on the way. Will be on your station in five mikes. I repeat. Birds on your station in five."

"Copy that." Rainey cradled the man's limp hand. "Hold on, sir. Just a little longer." He looked up at Mouse and then Tonka, who was just now returning. As the big Native American medic knelt down beside the wounded Lonnie Conover and began providing care, Rainey asked, "How's Monster?"

Tonka dragged the back of his gloved hand across his face, took a deep breath. With moist eyes and a runny nose, he slowly shook his head. "He's gone, boss."

Rainey clenched his jaw and swallowed the emotion of the moment which had sublimated itself into a thick knot deep in his throat. He looked back at the horrifically beaten Agency man. Did anyone back home truly comprehend, truly appreciate the unbelievable sacrifice he and his mates as well as all of those within the intelligence and special operations communities at large were willing to make for their nation, for each other, for all that was right and good? This was the brutal reality of the world in which he and his fellow shadow warriors operated day in and day out all around the globe.

A fight between good and evil.

1

Langley, VA
Two Months Later

"WHAT is happening to this agency?" boomed CIA Director Ken Thompson. Only minutes ago, the head of his Clandestine Service, Sean Vajda had informed him about the loss of yet another covert operative and thus the impetus for the hastily arranged meeting. "Where was it this time?"

"Spain. Catalonia," said Vajda. He passed around a series of photographs that had been sent from his people who were doggedly working with their Spanish counterparts in country. "He'd been working a cell of radical Islamists there for the past six months or so."

"Four. FOUR!!" He pounded the armrest of his leather chair. Director Thompson had heard this horrific news now for the fourth time and by any director's standard it was four times too many.

Kenneth Thompson was a tall and lanky man with steely gray eyes and a horseshoe-shaped patch of reddish brown hair, that he fastidiously kept cropped no longer than an eighth of an inch from his scalp. He had a banker's knack with numbers and a robust aptitude for inductive and deductive reasoning. Overall, he was well-liked by both the politicians in D.C. and his charge of subordinates at

Langley and abroad. Thompson's usually stoic, unflappable demeanor was rarely ever shaken, but on those few occasions when it
was, his face filled with blood and took on varying shades of red.
Right now, his face was as bright as a chili pepper.

"Would someone please tell me how in the world our people
keep turning up dead?" He paused and scowled across his polished
walnut desk at the individuals seated before him. "Anybody?!"
Thompson's ire was obvious and well-understood. Since August,
four of the Agency's top covert operatives had been mysteriously
exterminated abroad. "This is absolutely unacceptable! This is the
Central Intelligence Agency and yet we have *no* intelligence!" He
glared at each person in the room. In addition to Vajda, several other
heads of the various Agency directorates were seated around the
room. Notably among them were Director of Intelligence Stan Timmons, Deputy Director Franklin Gettle, and Rebecca Swalgin—a
tough-as-nails former field operative who was now in charge of
Agency counterintelligence. Then there was Curt Keller—head of
Agency security—a man with a bullet-shaped head and a physique
that was still rock hard. Keller had a long, impressive resume that
included some of the most dangerous Agency operations in the Middle East over the past thirty years. Several of their trusted aides stood
quietly on the perimeter.

"What about the FBI, NSA? They have anything?" Thompson
posed the question to the group, but looked at the man seated to the
right of him.

"No, sir," said Timmons shaking his head. "Nothing."

"DHS. Are their people hearing anything?"

Again Timmons responded in the negative.

Thompson stared at Gettle, who was beginning to fidget in his
chair. The man was trying to repress an urge to voice his opinion.
"What? What is it, Frank? For heaven's sake, man, spit it out!"

Gettle subtly rocked back and forth in the winged back chair, a
yellow legal pad in his lap. "I think there's no question that we have
a real problem, sir. We've got a leak."

"Really? D'ya think?!" barked Thompson. "Thanks for stating
the obvious. Well, at least Frank's up to speed and on the record,
now." If you looked closely enough, it was almost possible to dis-
cern a fleeting cloud of steam escaping from either side of Thompson's head. "First off, people, this is not a leak. Do not call this a
leak. There is a traitor among us. A *traitor*.

"Secondly, everything we've tried so far to identify who is behind these assassinations has failed. I don't care what it takes. I want solutions. Do you understand me?! I'm tired of making this speech! I don't care how you do it. I don't care what you have to do. I want the traitor or traitors caught and hung by their testicles. Do I make myself clear?"

Melvin Pope, a nervous, little man from the Office of General Counsel, shook his head and was about to speak, when Thompson abruptly turned and snapped, "Zip it, Mel." He asked again, this time in a slow, deep growl. "Do I make myself clear?"

They all nodded, except for Pope.

Thompson turned toward the window, hands on his hips. After several long seconds, he turned back around. "While everyone is here, what about this thing in Montreal? Any reports about this DARPA scientist? How long has he been missing now, nine days?"

"Ten, sir." Timmons's eyes darted back and forth and then returned to his notepad. He shook his head. "We have some bits and pieces, but it's still too soon for anything concrete. Pentagon is working it hard, too, sir."

"Is there any link to what is happening to our people? I find it vaguely curious that Nelly was killed in Montreal." Keith Nelson was the third CIA operative who had been assassinated.

Timmons clicked his pen twice as was his well-established habit. "Anything is possible, sir, but I'm afraid it's just too soon to tell. Our Canadian friends are assisting where they can, but they haven't turned up anything useful yet either. Hopefully, we'll know more soon."

"All right. Stay on top of it people."

"Yessir," Timmons quickly answered for the group.

Thompson adjourned the meeting and stood, giving Vajda a subtle look that translated to words meant "hold on." Vajda waited behind while everyone else quietly filed out of the seventh-floor suite. When they were finally alone, Thompson turned to his Clandestine Service director. "Remember what we talked about before?"

"Yes, sir."

"I've given Job's shop the green light. That stays between us, you hear? Utmost secrecy."

Vajda nodded. "Understood, sir."

"And Sean. Eyes and ears...you know?"

"I hear ya, sir."

After Vajda had gone, Thompson closed the door and locked it. He wound his way across the office to a door on the far side of the room. He tapped his knuckles on the thick wood and said, "They're gone."

The door opened and another man stepped into the room.

Thompson regarded him with a look of exhaustion. "I hope this plan of yours works."

"Me, too. Kenny. Me, too."

"How much will you tell them?"

Job Jackson handed him some files, gave them a soft pat. "Only what they need to know."

Thompson frowned. "They're not gonna like that...if they ever find out."

"I know. But if they were in my shoes, I'm sure they would see it how I see it. Remember the SAS motto: 'Who dares wins.' We need to get to the bottom of this, Ken. Before we lose any more. Who knows what other damage has already been done."

"Yes." Thompson leaned back in his leather chair and rubbed his forehead. He'd been with the Agency since the late seventies. "I don't want a long protracted mole hunt. I don't think our intelligence community will be able to bear it, least of all now." There was a time in the mid-eighties during which the CIA had lost a number of valuable agents to the KGB. These agents, all Soviets who had been secretly spying for the CIA, were inexplicably rolled up and executed. This felt strangely similar to that period save for the fact that the men and women now being targeted and assassinated were full-fledged American CIA operatives. To be sure, there was a fox in the hen house. They needed to flush him out, before anyone else ended up dead.

"I've given you a lot of latitude, Job, please don't let me down. Don't let this Agency down."

"I'll do my best, sir."

Thompson lowered his head slightly and with dark resolve looked directly into Job's eyes. "Get 'em."

2

"NICE and easy, Georgia. Easy does it. Those muscles are warm, but you don't want to overdo it. By the way, I really liked what I saw out of you today. You're doing a lot better with your base. I can tell you've been paying close attention and are working hard at it." Madison Rainey walked slowly between the lines of students as they were finishing up their end-of-class stretches.

"Everyone, listen up. You've heard me say this a thousand times by now. But it's very important. What I'm teaching you guys is useless unless your mind is in it. You just might be forced to defend yourself one day. If you expect the unexpected you'll be better off. If you expect your attacker, you'll have the advantage over him. Expect it when you're *least* expecting it. Be ready at all times. At all times! Does everyone understand?" Maddie stressed this key element to her warrior mindset at the end of every class.

"Yes, Master Rainey!!" The class responded in unison.

Maddie leaned down and whispered into the ear of a strapping man in the back row, "Especially *you*." Her boyfriend of eight months grinned despite the strain he was currently putting on his hamstrings.

"Okay, remember there is no class next week, so I'll see ya next
year. All of you have a very merry Christmas." Maddie dismissed
the class which consisted of both guys and gals, varying in ages from
14 to 57.

"Master Rainey?"

"Yes, Georgia."

"When I grow up I want to be just like you."

Maddie smiled. "That's very sweet of you. Thank you. If I ever
have a daughter, I want her to be just like you, Georgia." Maddie
waved at the ninth grader's father as the girl slung her thick winter
coat over her shoulders and plodded off, ponytail bouncing happily.

Madison Rainey was a high school freshman, too, when she'd
begun seriously studying martial arts. Her purpose being, at least at
first, to send a message to a big bully at school named Chip. He'd
made a habit of beating up kids after class. Maddie liked this one
particular boy at the time who had been constantly getting knocked
around by the much bigger junior class punk. Until one day, after
learning a few things from a man by the name of Job Jackson,
Maddie put an end to it for good. A broken nose tends to do that to
a bully, especially when the person who causes it is a girl—and a
girl half his size and two years his junior, at that. Despite the one-
week school suspension, the tale of Maddie Rainey beating up the
arrogant bully became legend.

Throughout the rest of her high school and college years, Maddie's passion grew. She'd studied a variety of disciplines, soaking
everything up like a sponge and soon began participating in and
summarily winning competition after competition. She was a natural. Athletic and quick with a big brother on which to practice each
new technique, each new talent. She was so good, in fact, that during winter break of her sophomore year at American University,
with some help and advice from Job and encouragement from her
mom and brother, she decided to open her very own martial arts
studio. It didn't take long for word to spread about the chick who
could hold her own against men twice her size. In no time, her studio became a rousing success.

Now 27, Maddie possessed a black belt in both Muay Thai and
Judo. Even more incredibly though, Maddie had just reached the E-5
expert level of proficiency in a fighting discipline known as Krav
Maga.

This was her specialty. In some unspoken, shadowy circles, she was highly regarded and deservedly revered.

In stark contrast to her interest and abilities in the martial arts world, Maddie was a self-admitted computer geek. She had earned herself a computer science degree at AU and right out of school had been hired by the United States Library of Congress as an IT specialist. But her heart remained in her studio. She dreamed of one day being able to teach her own brand of martial arts full-time.

Despite her relatively diminutive five-foot-seven-inch frame, she could be a real spitfire when she wanted to be. Maddie had straight brown locks and the most intriguing eyes of amber. By all accounts, she had inherited her mother's elegant beauty and her father's feisty take-no-B.S.-from-anyone attitude. She ran five times a week and had the sleek athletic figure to prove it.

Maddie's martial arts classes, taught only in the evenings, were mostly made up of young professionals from the D.C. area who wanted to learn practical skills for personal protection. After all, D.C. was one of the most crime-ridden cities in America. On Tuesdays and Thursdays from six to eight, classes were restricted to law-enforcement and military personnel, the only exception being made for her boyfriend, Wes.

They came from all levels of government, too. About every other week or so, a new cop or federal agent would waltz in wanting to scope out the class, kick the tires, see if it was right for them. This evening had been one of those times. A fresh-faced man with a buzz cut, a military bearing, and a large colorful tattoo on his left arm had come in. He was tall and muscular with a loud attitude to go with it. A DHS agent and former Marine, she'd heard from one of the D.C. cops in the class.

During the warm-ups, she'd caught bits and pieces of him referring to the "hottie up front" and some of the graphic things he'd like to do to her. Maddie let it go at first. But when he began interrupting the class with his comments, she'd finally had enough.

She walked over to him and calmly said, "Are you sure you're in the right place?"

The big guy eyeballed her up and down. "Uh, I must not be cuz I heard this place was taught by an unbelievably-gifted fighter, which you most certainly can't be. I mean look at you. Don't get me wrong, I wouldn't mind taking you out sometime, but you? A fighter? C'mon."

Maddie blandly smiled. "Tell you what. How about a simple little one-on-one, *full-contact* sparring match. I'll avoid your eyes and nuts if you will agree to give me your best shot and not hold anything back. Whaddya say?"

He chuckled, his manhood now challenged. "All right, doll face, but I don't want you suing me over this."

"I won't if you won't."

Maddie and the loud-mouthed guy moved to the center of the room onto a large blue mat as the rest of the class spread out along the walls, each student jockeying for a good view. A brief buzz erupted amongst them as they surely sensed what was about to happen. Next came shushing and finally complete silence.

Then it began.

Then it was over.

Twelve seconds later, the guy came to. He was on his back staring up at the fluorescent lights in the ceiling. He slowly sat up. Guy had to have a splitting headache, judging from the size of the knot on his forehead. As he tried to stand, a small trickle of blood began running from his nose down across his lips.

If the DHS man had bothered to ask around, he might have learned that like her big brother, Maddie possessed an affinity for a challenge, for danger. Both she and Reagan were true artisans of how to inflict damage to the human body, death even, if the situation called for it.

At the spectacle, some students grimaced, some chuckled, some just shook their heads as the federal agent staggered to his feet. He offered Maddie a curt apology and admitted he was sold on her talents. Maddie bowed, accepted the apology, and directed her assistant—ice pack already in hand—to help the man wash up. The burly guy vacantly walked off, rubbing his forehead and cursing to himself.

Waiting for the class to get back in position, she caught Wes's attention and winked.

Wes shook his head and mouthed the words, "You're incorrigible."

3

WESLEY Ruehle, a handsome brute with soft eyes and an easy smile, watched the latest victim trudge off and again shook his head but this time for another reason. *That man deserved it.* Wes still marveled at the technique, the speed. Maddie was an invisible bear trap. He was grateful that he and Maddie had met under vastly different circumstances.

Wes recalled the first time he'd laid eyes on this little firecracker. He had been heading back to his apartment at The Ellington, when to his delight, a goddess, obviously just back from her morning run, joined him in the elevator. Her lustrous brown shoulder length hair was pulled back in a sporty ponytail, her forehead glistened with sweat. With his eyes, he'd clumsily traced her ear buds to the iPod strapped on her toned left arm then to her attractive neckline. He'd quickly averted his eyes in embarrassment after realizing she was noticing him noticing her. Maddie had just smiled. He'd missed his floor because of it. That bright, warm smile made his heart nearly pound out of his chest. To this day, her smile was the most disarming quality about her. It could literally make a man forget his own name. Then in the next instant, Maddie could go complete warrior chick on you without blinking an eye.

That very next evening he had serendipitously found himself in her martial arts class down the block. He'd attended on a whim after there had been some daytime muggings in the area. It was his first real martial arts class; he wanted to learn some effective self-defense moves, that was all. Wes had had no idea Maddie was the instructor. She probably knew some moves, but he doubted he'd learn anything useful from a bombshell like this. Maddie didn't have that female body builder look; she was toned and thin. Considering he stood six foot three and outweighed her by a good ninety pounds, he thought he would endure the class then check out another studio nearby he'd found on Google.

Wes had reconsidered after that first class. And after a month of vigilant attendance and no intimation of a boyfriend, he asked Maddie out while they were once again sharing an elevator on their way to class. She smiled, her cheeks blushed, and those marvelous honey-colored eyes fluttered excitedly as she acquiesced, clearly but pleasantly caught off guard. The rest, as they say, was history.

* * *

"So was I too tough on that guy, today?" Maddie asked as she began cleaning up.

"No, he asked for it and he got exactly what he deserved. You didn't hear some of the things he was saying about you early on. I was actually hoping you would teach him a lesson and you definitely taught him a lesson. That elbow strike to the forehead was nasty. I'm sure you did a number on his federal-agent ego, too. After all it's not every day that a guy from the Department of Homeland Security gets his butt whooped by someone looking like you."

"All right, but I hope he comes back. He's got potential."

"Well at least he can remember what happened to him. You know José still can't remember what you did to him. But the others sure like reminding him." José was the previous one to undergo a Maddie Rainey initiation.

Maddie looked at him with puppy dog eyes and coquettishly smiled, "Who me?"

"Yeah you little lady. Hey, you hungry?"

"Starved."

"Me, too. How 'bout that new place down by Dupont Circle? One of the guys at work has been raving about it."

"Sounds good to me. And while we eat, you can tell me what you got me for Christmas."

Wes deadpanned. "Coal. I got you coal."

"Funny. I can't wait. You know this year, Ray's going to be home for Christmas. I'm so looking forward to it."

"Cool. So everyone will be there? All the men in your life in one place." A pause. "So, what is it that Ray does again?"

"He's some kind of instructor or adviser, I forget exactly."

"You said he once worked at Fort Bragg, right? My luck, he's probably one of those hot-shot ninja warrior dudes you hear about. Or should I say *don't* hear about. If he doesn't like what I got him, he'll probably fold me up into a pretzel. Tell me, and this is important, have you ever knocked him out?"

Maddie jabbed Wes in the stomach with her elbow and smiled.

"Easy, girl."

"Hey, what if we head over to my mom's tonight? We can grab a bite to eat on the way."

"Honey, I can't tonight. Remember…my editor? I gotta be in his office first thing tomorrow morning. I'm guessing he wants to see me about a story on the upcoming swearing-in ceremony. I've done a lot of research and written extensively on several incoming senators and congressmen. Things are going to change in Washington, that's for sure."

"I'll believe it when I see it."

"Yeah, I know." Wes assessed the foot traffic on the sidewalk as Maddie locked the front door. "You can go tonight if you want to. I'll come by tomorrow after my meeting."

"No. I'll wait. I want us to go together."

Wes put his arm around her as they walked, pulled her close and kissed her forehead. "Thanks, babe."

4

Aldie, VA

JOB Jackson stepped out of the sedan and looked around at what winter had inflicted upon the rolling pastures, the wooded landscape since he'd last been here. Other than a few patches of yellow-green here and there, it was an endless sea of boring browns and grays.

He took a deep drag of the fresh air and instantly recognized a familiar stew of olfactory flavors: burning coal, molten iron, the faint hint of horse manure. Job waved for his bodyguard to stay put then trotted through the front gate, which squeaked as it opened and softly clanged behind him. He ascended the porch steps and approached the wide front door, affixed to which was a handsome, homemade wreath and crimson bow. Though he had a key and was always welcome inside, he rang the doorbell.

The original house, a large Adam Federal—the entire farm in fact—dated back to the late 1700s. In spite of several obvious alterations and additions aimed at modernity, the homestead still looked the part. The whole house had been completely restored, its structural integrity beefed up to withstand a hurricane. A fresh coat of white paint had been added within the last year or so. The windows and casings were dressed with custom-made wooden shutters—black, of course—that visually matched the originals right down to the last detail. A sturdy lamppost stood like a sentry beside the flagstone path which led from the drive—a small parking lot, really—to the front door. The lamppost was trimmed with wrought iron as was the gate he had just cleared. The iron work was all new, forged by the very hands of the current property owner. Incidentally, that also had something to do with the odors that permeated the air here today.

Job rang the doorbell again and rubbed his hands together in the cold air as he waited. Finally, the heavy wooden door swung open and a man who looked to be in his mid- to late-seventies, wearing jeans and a long-sleeved, flannel shirt and a dark gray turtleneck, emerged.

"Hi, Pappy. I need to talk to Ray."

Saul "Pappy" Baker was an old-school Agency man. He had a brilliant mind for espionage and covert action which he had used mercilessly against the Soviets throughout the Cold War. Though he no longer worked for the Agency, he still kept in contact with countless sources at Langley and within the intelligence community at large. Job Jackson was something of a protégé to the man and came to him often for advice or just to bring him up to speed with the latest Agency news.

This was originally Pappy's farm; it had been in his family for generations. In fact, it was Baker family lore that Pappy's ancestors had been close friends with America's first president. After his wife died, Pappy had initially considered putting the farm on the market. After all, his kids didn't want it. Indeed, they wanted nothing to do with him. One day, during one of Job's visits, the conversation turned to their late Agency colleague, Ben Rainey, and then his son, Reagan. Job had been regaling Pappy with Reagan's growing reputation within the special operations and intelligence communities, specifically outlining the prospects of his future with the Agency, when Pappy posited the idea of selling the farm to Rainey. And that's what happened. Pappy sold it to him for next to nothing with only a few mutually agreed upon stipulations. He would get to stay for as long as he was alive; Rainey would have to help him with improvements, renovations, that type of thing; and the farm could only ever be re-sold to someone within the Rainey family or at least to someone else from the Agency that he loved so dearly.

Rainey had had a few stipulations of his own: he would be allowed to resurrect the old blacksmith shop behind the house and at
some point rebuild the big, dilapidated barn next to the horse pas-
ture, and most importantly make some much-needed security and
technological enhancements about the property. It had been a win-
win for both men.

Pappy squinted past Job toward the sedan in the driveway. Then
his eyes instinctively scanned the terrain beyond. "No 'Merry
Christmas?'"

Job apologized for the oversight. "Merry Christmas."

"That's better. Come on in. I was just making some tea. Care for
a cup?"

Job followed the old intelligence man through the house. He always liked coming here. It had an unapologetic flare of tribute to the
American Revolution and the nation's budding existence. There was
also no mistaking Pappy's and Ray's love of the Founding Fathers,
no one any more so than George Washington. There were at least
twenty books about the man in the bookcase on the far wall. The
house was decorated with care and precision, but was also functional
and practical. The interior had been further renovated since he'd last
been here. Ray's doing, of course.

Pappy led him past the robust fireplace, logs burning and crackling within. Job's eyes tracked up to several handsome, old muzzle-
loaders over the mantle then to a table with standing picture frames.
A mosaic of family moments frozen in time. They walked across the
large handmade rug spread over the tongue-and-groove floorboards.

*This place feels like a home. Safe. Warm. Secure. As a home
should feel.*

Job closed his eyes as the intoxicating aroma of cinnamon, or
maybe it was apple pie, struck him. Suddenly, his mind was flooded
with memories of his childhood, his grandparents' old place in Pennsylvania. *Grandma always did make the best apple pie.*

"No thanks, Pappy. I just need to talk to Ray."

"He's out back, in the shop. Let me know if you change your
mind."

"All right. Thanks."

Job made his way through the kitchen, out the back door and
across the winterized grass. He walked the fifty yards to the shop
and was greeted only by the firelight cast off by the furnace within,
flickering against the windows. His head tilted upward as he reached

for the door handle. Smoke from the chimney slithered into the winter sky like a slow-moving snake.

Ping. Ping. Ping. The telltale sound of hammer and anvil.

He opened the door and stepped inside. There was music playing, the volume turned up, but not necessarily loud. Who was it this time? Bach? Brahms? Maybe Mozart. Job sighed. He was clueless when it came to classical music. Now jazz on the other hand...

For a minute, he just stood there mesmerized. The man before him, *his* man—his warrior spy, wearing a black apron over thick Carhart pants, shirtsleeves rolled up, sweat beaded on his forehead—was deep in concentration. Job watched as he pounded a slab of iron with careful calculation. The philosophical and metaphorical aspects were apparent. The precise, targeted and intense violence of action. The perfect marriage of intellect and brute force. These were just some of the qualities that made Reagan Rainey such a valuable asset in America's arsenal.

Ping. Ping. A pause. *Ping. Ping. Ping.*

Job shuffled his feet as he moved closer, still studying Rainey's mannerisms. It was obvious, the parallel between the way in which Rainey worked the iron, his tools, the way he labored with efficiency and economy—no wasted movements, and that of how he conducted himself during a complicated, well-coordinated intelligence operation. Or likewise a delicate, deniable terrorist kill mission. This man was the best he'd ever known, perhaps the best in the world. Thank God for Reagan Rainey. He belonged in the Agency, or to be more precise, in the Directorate.

Technically, Directorate Twelve (D12)—often just referred to as the Directorate—was a sort of CIA within the CIA, however, its Agency affiliation was a well-kept secret. Its place, its people were all hidden within a well-established cover organization known as the Greenbriar Foundation.

The Directorate's people were stringently recruited. Most came from active and non-active duty military and intelligence circles, others from law enforcement. There was a civilian staff element as well, culled from the realms of academia, scientific and research communities, or other specialized arenas of knowledge or expertise. The Directorate also utilized key personnel from various divisions within the Agency: Special Activities and National Resources, to cite two examples. On extremely rare occasions, people from DHS, FBI, NSA or other agencies would cycle through its doors on temporary duty assignments depending on various operational or intelligence requirements.

Through various means, the Directorate had established its own black budget funding streams. Cover NGOs and businesses, seized terrorist network funds, to name a few. The Greenbriar Foundation and its network of partners and cover ventures, made it possible for Directorate personnel to easily move about the globe without the least bit of scrutiny.

Rainey's powerful arms flexed as he brought down the hammer on the red-hot metal yet again. Job swelled with pride at the sight of the man, a man whom he'd always thought of like a son. A man with unquestionable integrity, character, lethality. The ultimate force for good. The elite of the elite. A warrior's warrior. An American warrior.

"Why do I get the impression that I'm going to be spending Christmas abroad this year?" said the thirty year-old with his back still toward his interloper.

"It's important, Ray."

Rainey pounded on the metal a few more times with precision until the bright red color gradually faded to gray, then stabbed the rod into a bucket of water. There was a sizzling sound, like steak on a grill. A cloud of steam instantly rose from the bucket. He examined his handiwork carefully. Then after several seconds, he laid down the rod, removed his thick gloves and safety glasses and stepped over to Job—his boss and surrogate father. "It always is, isn't it?"

Job shrugged and nodded as he stepped backward allowing Rainey space to brush past him.

Rainey quietly went about turning off the CD player and packing his tools away. When he was finished closing down the shop, he stopped, turned and gave it one last glance. "Let me wash up."

5

WHILE Rainey took a quick shower, Job indulged himself with a piece of apple pie and a cup of piping hot coffee, which Pappy had brewed at Rainey's request. Soon, the two of them were seated in the living room in front of the raging fireplace.

"How's the leg by the way?"

Rainey shrugged. "Fine."

"Good. Your teammates are still out of commission, but I suspect the doctors will give them the green light soon." Job was referring to Mouse and Tonka. Both men were still recovering from the wounds that they'd sustained in Qatar. Job purposely didn't bring up the loss of Monster. It was a tough subject to broach. Even now. And he needed Rainey to focus. America had lost one of its best warriors in the Conover rescue op; Monster had been a supremely gifted operator. And an even better man. But more than any of that, Monster had been Ray's best friend.

Job uncrossed his legs and dug into his pants pocket. He pulled out his vibrating phone and frowned at the screen.

* * *

Rainey studied Job's face. Something was bothering him. He'd known Job for as long as he could remember. Job and his father had been childhood chums. They'd attended Duke together, joined the CIA together. Two friends couldn't be tighter. They'd even built houses next to one another so their wives wouldn't have to be alone when they were away on assignment. Their history had taken an unexpected and painful turn in the mid-nineties though when just two weeks after Ray's eleventh birthday, Ben was killed in a plane crash during an Agency operation in South America.

Rainey sipped his coffee and set his mug down next to an old family portrait. His gaze fell upon the faces in the photograph. Mom, Dad, him and Maddie. All of them smiling happily. All of them full of life. His eyes began to glaze over, his mind began to drift. He didn't blink for nearly a minute. The hypnotizing orange glow from the fireplace danced in his dark eyes.

Was it ever like this for Dad? Did he *ever grow tired of being the one everyone turned to?*

He could still picture it as if it were yesterday, when he and his family were told the news about his father. He remembered, his mother falling to her knees and sobbing uncontrollably. His little sister clinging to her for dear life as the Agency men tried their best to console them. Job had been overseas on assignment, but Iris, had rushed over immediately when she'd heard. She and Sarah were like sisters.

But young Reagan had been unusually stoic in the face of the terrible news. In reality, he hadn't wanted anyone to see him crying. He eventually ran off into the woods, to the fort he and his dad had built together before he finally let himself go. There, he cried his eyes out, punched and kicked the big oak tree by the fort till his fists bled. He'd had so many questions for God. Why had He allowed this to happen? Why to his dad, such a good man, such a faithful believer? Two things happened that day: 1) Ray's childhood as he knew it had ended; and 2) he became the man of the house.

Since then, Ray had taken it upon himself to protect and defend his mom and kid sister with primal ferocity. He'd gotten into scrapes and scuffles on their behalf at times, but nothing at all serious. Except for one particular fight—and that's exactly what it was, a fight—when a pack of cruel teenagers had decided to malign the memory of his father, particularly with respect to his faithfulness to his mother. That was one fight in which young Reagan Rainey had sent a number of kids to the hospital and the police to his mother's doorstep. But in the end, the victims' parents had mercifully declined to press charges.

Through those challenging times, Job and his wife had become an even bigger part of the Rainey family. Rainey considered how Job had become the father figure he and Maddie desperately needed back then. He learned many things from him over the years, too. Valuable survival skills for all aspects of life. The value of hard work and delayed gratification. The virtue of seeking to do what was right even when no one was watching. The responsibility of being honorable stewards of the freedoms all Americans share.

"Sorry about that."

Rainey cleared his throat, snapping out of his reverie. "So what's up?"

"I need you to go to Montreal."

"Montreal?"

Job nodded. "To look for this man." He handed Rainey a photograph. "He's a DARPA scientist and has been missing now for...tomorrow will be eleven days. Name's Dr. Edward Horst."

"What was he working on?"

"Well, you're getting ahead of me, but... High-energy lasers, specifically the man-portable variety. I understand he's come up with a concept that is similar in platform—size and weight—to an M4. He was in Montreal visiting extended family for the holidays when he disappeared. We think he was abducted."

"Why? What makes you think so?"

Job passed him several still images from what was obviously surveillance footage. The footage was date-stamped the same day Horst was determined to have gone missing. The photos showed the scientist walking past an ATM. There was a female several paces behind him in each frame. "We found this after carefully retracing his steps. Only we know about this."

"I don't understand. Who's the broad? You think she was involved somehow." It was a declaration, not an interrogative.

"Her name is Nika Aleksandrovna Chernikova. Born in Israel. Grew up in Ashdod with her Jewish mother. Later moved to Herzliya when mom married step-dad, a Frenchman. Real dad's unknown but believed to be Russian or maybe Ukrainian. She's former Mossad, Ray. Kidon. Special recruit, I'm told." The Kidon group was a highly secretive unit within the Mossad—Israel's Institute for Intelligence and Special Operations. Little was publicly known about it, but its members were generally regarded as elite assassins. "Based on what my sources in Tel Aviv tell me, she left the Mossad a few years back—*deserted* were their words—to search for a man by the name of Vladislav Kozlov. Him we know a little better. It's all in your packet there. It's unclear why the sudden interest in Kozlov or what the connection to him might be.

"Vladislav Kozlov. Former Russian Armed Forces. Spent some time in the GRU (Russian military intelligence). Went off the radar about five years ago. No records on him since then exist, none that we've been able to uncover, that is. I suspect he's never left the game. Unconfirmed reports have him being mixed up with Russian organized crime in some capacity, but nothing more specific than that, I'm afraid."

"How do you know when Horst was abducted? Or even that he was abducted?"

Job scratched his wrist beneath his watch. "When he passed by that ATM, he was on his way to meet his uncle for dinner. Horst never showed. We traced his likely route from his hotel to the restaurant. That's how we found this footage. We also found this." He showed him some more photos. "In a Dumpster along the same route, we found his wallet—money still inside, his passport, and his phone, which had been powered off, the SIM card removed."

"So he obviously wasn't robbed."

"Correct. He was taken for some other reason. Beyond that we know nothing. But we suspect it has something to do with his work at DARPA. We've already been through his hotel room, his home, office, computers, bank accounts, and nothing has come up to suggest anything else. Nothing to suggest he defected either."

"I see," said Rainey taking a sip of coffee. "What else do you have?"

"I have a three-man surveillance team sitting on the girl's apartment. They've been monitoring her movements for the past three days. She's been using an alias—Isidora Khan. Based on records associated with that name, she's been in country for the last ten years, but we obviously already know that to be false. From what the team has reported thus far, she seems to be working at a small travel agency a few blocks from her building. Could be a front or just a good backstop for travel abroad. That's about all we have at this point on her. She's obviously very clever and extremely lethal."

"So you want me to interrogate the apartment?"

"With the aim of finding out what became of the scientist, yes. And who is behind his abduction."

"Of course," said Rainey matter-of-factly.

"You speak Russian, French, *and* Hebrew. I have no idea what you might encounter there, but I want someone who can interpret anything found on the spot. I need you, Ray. Go sniff around, see what you can turn up."

Rainey looked into the fire then after some deliberation said, "This wouldn't have anything to do with what's been going on within the Agency would it? The assassinations…"

Job raised an eyebrow. "Anything's possible. I will tell you this, Ray: Keith Nelson was the Agency's foremost expert on the Russian mafia in Canada. If that's relevant, I don't know. Let's just say, it certainly can't be ruled out." Nelson was the third CIA operative killed in the recent string of Agency assassinations.

"When do I leave?"

"Plane is on standby at Leesburg. Ray, I don't have to tell you this, but please be careful."

Rainey swallowed the rest of his coffee and stood. "Always, Job. Always."

6

ROMAN Lerner sat behind his desk gazing at his computer screen, intently reading his daily string of e-mails. The Agency had as a whole been on edge for the past few months; he was no exception. Four dead. Four assassinated. Conover could have made it five, should have made it five, if only his handler would have listened to him and thus utilized the right people to do the deed and not some local group of terrorist screw-ups. Those idiots apparently had no concept of operational security. The Agency had found them easily and worse yet, found Lonnie Conover.

Alive.

Lerner had no idea what the endgame was, but allowing the man to live was going to be trouble. He knew that deep within his soul. If it had been up to him, he would have made sure that after the interrogation, Conover was dead. His assassination would have blended into the others which after all, as he understood it, was the plan. At least Conover had slipped into a coma and had minimal prospects of ever regaining consciousness. If he ever did though, Lerner's environment would instantly become incredibly dangerous. Being one of Russia's most prized American agents offered plenty of risk already, but if his nation ever found out he was the one feeding the Russians information about America's best spies, he would meet a quick and painful death. Of this he was one hundred percent certain.

An hour ago, Lerner had spoken with his Russian handler about the usual Agency business. More importantly, Lerner had also related that he sensed something was up. Yes, something was already in the works. It was nearly impossible to believe anyone might be on to him, but from the scraps of information he was able to garner from his loyal friends within the Agency, there was definitely some kind of operation underway. The look Thompson had given Vajda yesterday in the director's office was very telling. Very telling, indeed.

Lerner was still waiting on a phone call from one of his faithful contacts in Montreal. So far, the investigation into the Horst affair was going nowhere and he didn't anticipate that changing unless... Unless it was being kept quiet on purpose. Lerner rocked back in his chair and allowed his mind to work. What he lacked in patriotism for his homeland, he made up for in mental prowess. Staying off the molehunters' radar to this point had been no easy feat.

Who at the Agency would know if such a covert operation was ongoing, who he could trust? And how would the Agency go about such an operation to begin with, how would he go about it if he were in the director's shoes?

Lerner sifted through his e-mail some more, his right hand on the computer mouse, his left tapping the arm of his desk chair. He froze, looked at his watch. He needed to meet his handler again, needed to warn him. Needed to tell him to put his people on full alert. It was entirely possible the Agency was already on to them.

7

Leesburg, VA

AS the Agency jet gained altitude, Rainey interlaced his fingers in his lap and closed his eyes. He began to pray, asking God for wisdom and clarity, for success and safety.

He took a deep breath and exhaled slowly. From head to toe, he tried to relax every muscle in his body and sleep. It was always advisable to grab a few pre-op winks whenever possible, because ops had a way of being unpredictable no matter how much planning and preparation were put into them. Usually, falling asleep was as simple as closing his eyes and willing himself to do so. But this time was different. As much as he tried to nap, the gears of his mind continued to spin.

The operation in Qatar. Lonnie Conover, his savagely beaten body. The media accounts after the story finally broke. It was everywhere at once, yet no one knew what had really happened, who had pulled the man to safety, or even who Lonnie Conover was, despite the rampant speculation. Ever since, Conover had been at Walter Reed lying in a coma. The doctors were not optimistic he'd ever come out of it. Even if by some miracle he would, Conover faced long odds at any semblance of recovery.

There was a different reality for others, however. Some had already paid the ultimate price. Some had already given all they had to give. Despite the limited information available, the media had learned about and covered the somber ceremony at Joint Base Andrews, where the flag-draped transfer cases containing the bodies of several of Conover's fellow countrymen, including Monster, had been brought before a quiet, tearful group of loved ones for what was known as the dignified transfer of remains.

Rainey opened his eyes as the jet was just breaching a blanket of thick clouds. The muscles in his jaw flexed as he ground his teeth and choked back emotions. It should have been him. He should have been the one to take the bullet. He was the man in charge. Instead, it was Monster—Cole Isaiah Everett. The service at Arlington was in many ways no different than any of the others he'd been to during his career, except for the fact that this one broke him completely.

Monster. Gone.

Many of the same questions he'd had when his father died plagued him yet again. *Why him? Why such a faithful man of God? Why God? WHY?!*

The two of them had been together since the beginning—the very beginning—from boot camp all the way through Special Forces and Delta, until this past spring, when they'd both been attached via temporary duty assignment to the Joint Services Group within the CIA's mysterious Directorate Twelve. Through it all, they had developed a very close friendship. It was an agonizing reality of their profession. Friends sometimes got hurt, sometimes worse. Monster, especially, had been one of those guys who even though he was a trained killer had a huge heart for people, particularly for kids. A warrior by definition—fearless, strong in body, stronger in mind and strongest in heart—yet he was always the first guy out of the Humvee to help some little Iraqi or Afghan kid frozen by the horrors of war. He was also the type of guy who never passed up an opportunity to share his faith. Though he was this big, dangerous dude, he had a remarkably compassionate side. And his teammates loved him even more because of it.

How on earth did people without a strong relationship with Jesus Christ, ever manage to deal with such overwhelming grief? At least Monster's now in a much better place. But he's going to be missed dearly.

Christmas was going to be incredibly difficult for his family this year. The first Christmas after his dad died was. Excruciating didn't even begin to explain it. It had been that way for all of them—Mom, Maddie, Job, Iris.

For once, the prospect of spending Christmas at home this year with the family had looked to be quite real. And very well-timed. Wes was close to proposing to Maddie. A week ago, he'd called, asked to meet. It was then that Wes had asked for his blessing which made Ray like and respect the guy even more than he already did. Maddie had found the right guy after all.

Wes was doubtless planning to propose on Christmas day when they were all together, Job and Iris included.

So much for spending the holidays at home this year.

Before catching his flight, Rainey had called his mom and sis and explained that he had to go out of town on Foundation business. No one, including them, actually knew what he really did for a living. In those times, when someone did exhibit anything more than a modicum of curiosity about his occupation, Rainey would draw in a long controlled breath and then very matter-of-factly launch into a dry monologue about his important work as an adviser or consultant or advocate or some such equally boring title at the ubiquitous, in effect, quasi-governmental construct known as the Greenbriar Foundation. The intent was that the inquirer would conclude that he was nothing more than some mid-level functionary, a wannabe-government so-and-so whose importance was entirely self-aggrandized. On those rare occasions when anyone dared to press him still further, Rainey would meekly grin and recount in mind-numbing detail his list of pre-established duties within the Foundation, to include his rigorous efforts toward instituting programs aimed at developing stringent standards of policy review for the Office of Compliance, Office of Government Ethics, and other seemingly inconsequential, administrative vagaries within the behemoth of bureaucracy that was today's federal government. By now, Rainey had this speech worked out right down to his choice of words, which were designed to leave the listener either running for the door or contracting a sudden case of narcolepsy. So far, no one had made it anywhere near the coma-inducing end.

Rainey opened his eyes again and sighed. He sat up straight, picked up the briefing packet Job had given him and began to read. Dr. Edward Horst worked for a company called Grumhold-Bern Technologies; it had been under contract with DARPA—Defense Advanced Research Projects Agency—for the past several years. The company was involved in many facets of defense-related materials and products, however, Horst's expertise was in high-energy lasers.

Horst had developed a man-portable prototype, something called an L-97X. Rainey perused the attached photos. Impressive. Testing wasn't complete, but if it worked, it could change everything. There were detailed notes about its capabilities: how the weapon could cut through heavy armor, steel, concrete, but also be throttled down in order to be used as a typical light infantry weapon. The theory behind the L-97X could radically change the dynamics not only in ground force combat, but ultimately U.S. military strategy and tactics as a whole. The implications for war, for terrorism, for the global balance of power were both endless and enormous in scale.

8

"HOWS'S she coming?" asked Pyotr Kupchenko stepping into the oversized garage bay.

"Good. Two more days and we will be done."

Kupchenko paced around the vehicle, his hands clasped behind his back. "Excellent work, Gregor. Just superb." He peered inside the open driver-side window careful not to touch anything. "Well done. Let me know the minute you're finished."

"Yes, sir," replied the workman.

Kupchenko walked next door. He stripped out of his clothes and poured himself a glass of red wine as he began studying the contents of several dossiers he'd just received. This was a new wrinkle but not really all that surprising. His CIA source had said that the molehunters were everywhere. CIA, DOD, FBI, DHS. There was chaos brewing in America's ranks. The assassinations had obviously been highly successful in that regard. There was still much to be done though, much that lay ahead.

Pyotr Sergeyevich Kupchenko was an officer within the Russian foreign intelligence service, *Sluzhba Vneshney Razvedki*, otherwise known as the SVR. But Pyotr Kupchenko was no ordinary intelligence man. Rather, he had been hand-picked by his boss to act as a liaison between the SVR and the shadowy and unforgiving world of a particular brand of Russian organized crime. And he did exceedingly well at just that. The dirty little secret: at the very top of the organizational food chain for both entities was the same man—Russia's own director of foreign intelligence, Levka Borovsky—an extremely dangerous and cunning man, indeed. So cunning was he, in fact, that no one knew he was actually the one running one of the world's most ruthless Russian mafia networks, because largely he did so from the shroud of his government post. And his tentacles were everywhere.

Kupchenko had just returned from a meeting with Sentinel, one of his nation's most prized and highly placed American agents. Sentinel had provided him with the dossiers of several men—candidates, really—who, based on his knowledge and access of Directorate Twelve, limited as it was, were likely to be utilized in the event an operation, aimed at locating the missing DARPA scientist, were to be launched. Sentinel though had already fingered the man who was considered by large margin the best of them. Thus, it was this man whom Sentinel was betting on to be tasked to find out what had become of the scientist.

Kupchenko smirked as he ran his fingers over the man's name in the dossier. Reagan Rainey. *Reagan.* Oh, how he loathed that name. For his country's and his own pride's sake. *Could this really be the man they are sending? Please let it be so.*

He placed the file folders on the bathroom sink while he dialed Levka Borovsky. The call was made using a series of digital cut-outs such that it made the call untraceable. After he updated Borovsky with the latest, Kupchenko slipped into the roomy hot tub and fired up a cigarette. Taking long deliberate drags, he carefully read each man's dossier from beginning to end. As the smoke filled his lungs and impregnated the room, Kupchenko allowed his mind to digest the information contained within the pages. But mainly because of the name, he couldn't help but to focus on the Reagan Rainey dossier. He squinted, took another long, deep drag on the cigarette and exhaled the smoke slowly as he flipped open the man's dossier again and studied the contents once more. There was a color photo attached to the inside flap of the folder with a paperclip. He sucked on the cigarette again deeply, then without taking his eyes from the photo, ground the butt into the porcelain ashtray on the edge of the hot tub.

He quickly relit another and read on.

There was a section on Rainey's childhood years, most had been spent abroad. Homeschooled until ninth grade. Graduated from Annapolis High School with academic honors. Declined scholarship offers to Harvard, Yale, and a number of other prestigious universities in order to attend Duke. Double-majored in political science and history. Minored in Asian and Middle Eastern studies. Played men's varsity soccer. Voted All-American and ACC Offensive Player of the Year…as a freshman.

Interesting.

Rainey's academic adviser's computerized notes highlighted his plans to attend Duke Law. Kupchenko flipped to the next page. Dropped out of school in the fall of his sophomore year…to join the Army. *Wonder what prompted that?*

Kupchenko continued sifting through the pages of highly classified information. He came to the details of the man's military career. Countless citations, awards. He ran his finger down the list which ran onto the subsequent page. *Impressive.* Purple Hearts. Bronze Stars. Silver Stars. Distinguished Service Cross. Several meritorious citations from foreign governments. Medal of Honor. *Medal of Honor?* A note indicated that it had been purposefully kept quiet and classified.

This guy might be trouble.

Kupchenko stopped for a few seconds and stared down into the froth and bubbles while contemplating his own people's merits. He wiped the beads of water—Or were they beads of sweat?—from his forehead.

Where was he, now? Ah, there: Rainey's linguistic abilities. Fluent in eight languages—French, German, Russian, Hebrew, Arabic, the list went on. Kupchenko flipped back to the page about Rainey's early childhood and ticked off the list of countries in which he'd lived at one time or another. There seemed to be some correlation.

When he was finished reading, Kupchenko climbed out of the hot tub and wrapped himself with a plush yellow towel. He quickly scanned the photos of each man—each candidate—and the first few pages of each dossier into his laptop, then forwarded the intel to Kozlov and his team. He then sent the same intel to another man—a man so secretive, so invisible, that there was no known record of his existence anywhere on earth.

For one full minute, Kupchenko just stood there wringing his hands as the screen stared back at him. Finally, he turned, eyed himself in the mirror for a few seconds, and in one quick motion, threw off the towel. Water dripping from his naked frame, he squared his shoulders, lifted his chin, and flexed his lean chest muscles. He leaned forward, drawing his face rather close to his fogged-up reflection. There was a sparkle in his eye that bespoke the fact that he welcomed a challenge.

Please let it be so.

With an air of self-satisfaction, he padded back to the hot tub and reclaimed his seat. Kupchenko's thin lips gradually formed into a prideful smile. It was still on his face when he submerged himself into the foamy, chlorinated water.

You're dead.

9

Montreal, Quebec

RAINEY continued reading the briefing packet that Job had given him back at the farm. He'd been through the files once already, but wanted to run through them again and did so, looking up only to steal glances out the window. There, on the western horizon, was an august sky that shimmered in varying pastels. Orange, pink and purple. Lurking, too, in the colorful panorama were rows of cirrus clouds. A pair of tire tracks from an old John Deere. Rainey marveled as his eyes drifted upward to the darker shades of God's heavenly design. Indigo and violet. Like far-off stadium lights, the stars were beginning to come alive, growing in intensity with each passing second. Some of the larger specks of light appeared to pulse in a steady rhythm like that of a tiny, new heartbeat inside a mother's womb. Nightfall was nigh.

Rainey thumbed through the file on Nika Chernikova again, studied the photo therein. She was extremely attractive. Doubtless that factored into her lethality. Moving on, Rainey flipped through the briefing packet until he found the files on Vladislav Kozlov. His eyes rolled over an out-of-date, black and white photo of the man. There was an obvious air of confidence about him. The lethal aspect of a military man, but not just any military man. Russian Special Forces. *Spetsnaz.* The piercing eyes, the tight jaw-line, a jagged little scar on the cheekbone under his right eye.

What did Job say about being careful?

After plowing through the files yet again, he looked up through the reflection in the window. Dusk had passed. The sky had now gone black. He shielded the glare from the interior cabin light and peered deeper through the window. The stars appeared dilated now, their bright glow piercing the darkness. Just like God's glory and power and love penetrate the darkest dark. The darkness of death, even. God was speaking to him, albeit through a metaphor: *"I am here. Trust in Me."* Even amidst the blackest storm clouds, when stars are impossible to see by human eyes, the Hand of Almighty God is present, His voice at times loud as a hurricane, other times soft as a whisper. No matter what, the God of the universe—his God—would be right there beside him, always in control, always faithful.

Thank you, Lord.

"Two minutes and we'll start our descent," advised the pilot over the speaker.

* * *

Situated in the middle of Lakeview Memorial Gardens in Pointe-Claire, Quebec, was an ornate monument constructed of pure Elberton Granite, one of the hardest, commercially utilized natural stones in existence. At its base was a perfectly carved pedestal six feet square and four feet high. The polished veneer was smooth to the touch and cold. Oh, so cold. Dr. Edward Horst dragged his hand across its face. There was some kind of inscription, but it was too dark to read without the use of a flashlight.

"Out of the way!" hissed Vladislav Kozlov as he shouldered the recently "commissioned" prototype. Kozlov pointed the high-energy laser gun at the granite pedestal. "Good?"

Horst leaned over and with a small penlight examined the gun's settings. He nodded. "Yes."

Kozlov squeezed the trigger. After about five seconds, a perfect circular gash appeared in the slab of granite.

The putrid smell of burnt rock stung his nose, though Horst was ecstatic if not outwardly so. His laser gun had performed to perfection. Just like it had in his lab back in the States. But that one he'd built with his staff, from research notes and meticulous specifications. This one he'd made on the fly… From memory.

Kozlov and his teammate, Gavril Udovin, stood there both with big grins on their muscled faces. "Good work, you. I'm impressed with the— Oww!"

"What is it, boss?"

"Stinkin' thing burned my hand. Feel it. It's red hot."

Udovin touched the gun's frame. "Wow, I'd say! Will it hold up for the—?"

"Shh! Do not say it!"

Horst looked on, his elation juxtaposed with a queer, unsettling sense of error. Then dread.

Kozlov held the weapon up and glared at him. "It needs to do more than make a tiny hole. Will it hold up for, say, a full minute, maybe two or even three?"

Horst nervously regarded his mental calculations and the composition of the laser gun, its structure, its component parts. He inspected the weapon with his blue-beamed LED penlight then Kozlov's gloved hand. The palm side of the glove had been burned almost completely through.

"I know what needs to be done. Some minor adjustments, internally. But this is viable."

"How long will it take?" pressed Kozlov.

"Maybe another twenty-four hours or so."

"You have half that. Clock starts as soon as we get back."

Udovin grinned at his boss's implied threat. The Kedr PP-91 submachine gun strapped around his chest only seemed to add unnecessary emphasis to his wordless regard.

How in the world did people ever develop Stockholm syndrome? Horst obediently nodded. *Just survive. That's all that matters.*

* * *

Despite the minor setback and added delay of actually having a finished product, Kozlov was thrilled. They would still be ahead of schedule even if it took the scientist another day or two, but he would keep the pressure on regardless. The laser gun had made easy work of the hunk of granite, but what about its other capabilities?

Kozlov's eyes narrowed. He turned toward Udovin and whispered something. The brusque Russian team leader then looked at the DARPA scientist, "What is the effective range of this thing?"

Horst yanked the zipper of his coat up past his chin, drew his shoulders in and bent his spine into a letter C. He continued shivering. "Well, some like to say, 'Line of sight, line of light,' but that's not entirely accurate. This particular laser's range is very effective to within a mile, two tops, but after that certain conditions can affect its accuracy, notwithstanding the beam concentration and operator settings. Mostly weather-related but there are other dynamic factors that can come into play, too."

Kozlov grinned. "I see." The weapon had cooled somewhat. He shouldered it like the professional soldier he was and pointed it into the inky, black sky. "How about on a night like tonight? Cold and clear."

The rumble of an approaching jet penetrated the otherwise silent night.

"Oh, no! You can't! Please! I beg you."

Gavril Udovin jabbed his gun barrel into Horst's abdomen causing him to double over in pain. His eyes swelled with tears.

As the jet appeared in the eyepiece aperture, Kozlov flipped the selector switch down with his thumb. He took a breath and let it out halfway then squeezed the trigger, his countenance full of unmitigated, violent resolve.

10

A FTER Rainey had committed to memory the contents of the briefing packet, he slid it back into his briefcase. He would burn it at the safe house. He looked out the window again. In the distance, runway lights converged into a single point. Snow had recently fallen over the city. Just how cold was it down there?

Suddenly, Rainey snapped his head to the left, as if someone had just yelled his name from the other side of the glass. He cupped his hands against the window. Nothing there. Then, a reflection. A flash of bright light.

No. A spark.

Then another.

In the very next second, there was a thunderous blast. He nearly came out of his seat. If he hadn't been wearing his seatbelt, he would have. The pilot must have jumped, too, because the plane jolted abruptly toward the starboard.

An aircraft not far off in the distance to the west erupted into a blinding fireball. Rainey looked on in helpless horror. An instant later, a second explosion ripped the plane in half.

"What the heck was that?!" yelled Rainey to the pilot.

"I don't know!"

As if in slow motion, the fractured tail section of the doomed plane sank into the darkness below. The remaining portion of the fuselage, fully engulfed in a kaleidoscopic fire, one wing still intact, began violently spiraling downward leaving behind a trail of thick acrid smoke. As what was left of the splintered plane slammed into the ice and water below, another explosion though muted by the distance seemed to punctuate the event with raw morbidity.

Rainey's eyes were wide, pasted to the window.

"You okay back there?" asked the pilot with a spice of tension in his voice.

"Yeah, fine."

"Touchdown in thirty seconds."

Welcome to Montreal, Ray.

* * *

Horst heard the gut-wrenching explosions and watched the flaming parts of the condemned plane clap into Lac St-Louis. His body quivered as the horror of what he'd just witnessed assaulted his conscience. He was mortified. A tidal wave of nausea and bile came rushing up from his abdomen causing him to involuntarily vomit.

As his captors shoved him into the back of the SUV, his head began to spin. He'd never in his life believed there was a God in heaven. He was a scientist; it just didn't seem logical. But right now as his body trembled with fear and despair, he silently rendered with contrition and supplication, his very first prayer.

Save me, Jesus!

As they hit the highway, Horst looked as if a calm had washed over him. His eyes relaxed, as did his heartrate. Alone in the backseat, he slowly slipped an object out of his coat pocket and began manipulating it with great care.

Steady. Steady, now.

When he was finished, he placed the object back in his pocket as subtly as he'd extracted it.

Someday, hopefully soon, these despicable men would be caught. When that happened, he would see to it that they'd be thrown into the deepest, darkest prison cell known to man.

11

SIRENS screamed as emergency vehicles swarmed the coastal areas. Following a crude path of burning debris, rescue crews set out across the frozen surface of Lac St-Louis toward the dark foreboding chasm that punctuated the lake's white crust of snow and ice. Small fires flickered within the dismal darkness. From the shoreline all the way into the normally pristine, wintry landscape lay the solemn and tragic countenance of freshly sown battlespace.

Rainey descended from the jet and made his way to the back of the private hangar where a delegation of one awaited him.

Mark Alcott was six feet tall and had a rangy athletic build. He had a handsome face that possessed an intelligent bearing, but one that could just as easily be quickly forgotten. A valuable attribute for an intelligence officer. Affixed under a crop of brown hair, were a set of inscrutable eyes, which alternated between varying shades of blue and green, depending on how the light hit them. The former DIA man wore a thick, puffy jacket under which Rainey assumed he carried a pistol, maybe two.

Rainey had the deepest respect for Alcott and it wasn't just because Alcott had been his detachment commander in the 3rd Special Forces Group. It was because of who Mark Alcott was as a person.

He was a devoted husband and father, always talking with the troops about his wife and kids. Blessed with a magnetic personality, he was a gifted leader, a real thinker, and his work ethic was unmatched. Alcott was the type of guy that other men wanted to be. And when it came time to fight the evils of this world, everyone lined up to follow him into battle. No questions asked.

Mark Alcott had come to Directorate Twelve after spending several years in the Defense Intelligence Agency, where he'd served as a senior intel ops officer. It was vaguely amusing: the fact that Alcott now supported him. This was the exact opposite of how it had been back in the ODA when he was Alcott's 18F (detachment intelligence sergeant).

Rainey strode over to his old friend and mentor.

Alcott popped open the trunk of a navy blue Audi Q5 into which Rainey dumped his briefcase and carry-on. *"Bienvenue à Montréal,"* said Alcott as he extended his hand.

"Merci."

"You know how to make an entrance."

"Yeah, how 'bout it. That was sure close. Any news on what the heck happened up there?" Rainey glanced over his shoulder as he climbed into the front seat.

"The only thing being reported thus far is that the plane had been in no apparent distress, no indication of hijacking or terrorist involvement, what have you. Truth? Nobody knows yet."

Alcott headed toward the safe house. En route, he made several turns, negotiating the city terrain in such a way as to expose anyone who might be following them. At the same time he put forth his best effort to avoid spiking any unseen pursuers' sensibilities.

"All right. Looks like we're clean."

"So what's the latest?" asked Rainey.

"Drummy and Bobo are set up on the apartment. So far it's been quiet and predictable. She leaves in the morning a little before seven. Walks to work—a travel agency a few blocks away—then comes home. Made one stop yesterday…bought some tea. That's about it. So far, nothing all that exciting. But then again we've only been here for a little more than three days now."

Rainey nodded. "Blueprints?"

"Yep. Everything's back at the safe house. We're all set."

"All right. I want everyone to be in position before traffic dies down too much. Come morning when she leaves for work, we'll hit it."

Alcott checked his rearview, then looked at Rainey, smiled. "Roger, that."

* * *

"Plenty of escape routes. Good." Rainey and Alcott each cradled a cup of coffee and were hunched over the kitchen table in the safe house reviewing photos, maps, and blueprints of the apartment building. The safe house was a luxury fifth-floor apartment in the 300 block of the rue St-Paul Ouest with polished wood floors, red brick walls and elevated ceilings. The Directorate's support staff kept the place well-stocked, too, with everything from food and bottled water to high-tech communications gear, weaponry and ammunition.

Alcott patted a stack of photocopies. "Here are the records we found in the manager's office. Not much here for Nika's apartment except dead ends."

"Not surprising. With this chick's pedigree, I would expect as much."

"Agreed." A few minutes ago, Alcott had checked in with the men watching Nika's apartment and learned that there was still nothing to report, which was in essence something to report.

Rainey rubbed his eyes. "So, what's the deal with these assassinations? You have any theories?"

"Not yet. I've been thinking about it a lot, believe me. But I haven't been able to come up with anything that makes much sense aside from the obvious. I know the Agency is sphinchtered up pretty good right now. And that goes for Job and the whole of the Directorate, too. There's a traitor in our ranks, Ray."

"You're definitely right about that."

"Seriously. Watch your back."

12

ALL four men were in constant radio communication, but kept their traffic to a minimum. The status quo continued with every update: nothing to report. The girl hadn't left the apartment since returning home from work.

Rainey and Alcott had rotated into their respective positions allowing the others time to catch a few hours of sleep. Drummond and Boyd, the first team members in the city, had been at it for over three days. They needed a break, but it wouldn't be a long one.

Nika Chernikova was indeed playing it cool, assuming she was involved in the abduction of Dr. Horst.

Rainey had armed himself back at the safe house with a suppressed FNP-9 and extra magazines to go with it. It was among a stock of eight pistols kept in the secret arsenal typical of all Directorate Twelve safe houses worldwide. He carried it in a shoulder holster under his left arm, still easily accessible despite the heavy winter coat he was wearing.

It was now 11:45 p.m. After monitoring the apartment building and street outside for several hours, getting a feel for the rhythms of the neighborhood, Rainey slipped into the back seat of the tinted-out Toyota minivan, just as Drummond climbed into the driver's seat.

They were parked on the rue Durocher, a one-way street, a few doors down from Nika's building.

"Feeling rested?"

"Not really. But hopefully the caffeine pills will soon kick in," said Drummond yawning.

At one time, Jim Drummond and Bob Boyd had both served in the Army's Intelligence Support Activity, but—like Alcott—now worked exclusively for Job within the Directorate. Rainey had come to know them over the years, mostly during his time in Afghanistan. The ISA guys regularly performed what was known in military parlance as "operational preparation of the battlespace." Rainey had worked hand-in-hand with the ISA people at times. He regarded ISA operators as top-notch and as brave as they come.

Drummond yawned again.

"So much for the caffeine pills."

"It's a shame about Monster, man. He was a great guy."

"The best," Rainey said, the muscles in his jaw and temples flexing.

"Listen, why don't you catch some winks and I'll wake you if there's any activity."

Rainey tried to sleep for what seemed like hours, but couldn't stop thinking about Monster now and his family, the military funeral, how he'd been to far too many already. Somehow he knew that he hadn't seen his last. Finally, though, his mind relaxed and he drifted off.

* * *

The sun slowly peeked over the horizon, throwing full, radiant beams of glimmering light into the cold winter sky. Several slowly dissipating contrails high above Montreal appeared to luminesce in a magnificent display.

Reagan Rainey sat in the back of the minivan diagonally from Drummond who had his seat almost fully reclined. From this very spot, they could easily see the windows of Nika's third-floor apartment. Just before 4:00 a.m., Rainey had startled awake and then couldn't get back to sleep. Since then he'd gone over everything in his head again: the briefing packet Job had given him, the intel Alcott had provided at the safe house, his objectives, myriad what-ifs. What if the apartment was under surveillance by another agency? What if the apartment housed a small army of men? What if a gunfight broke out? What if the safe house was booby-trapped? What if, what if, what if…?

Nika's building was attractive in a functional kind of way. It was an older model high-rise, with wide windows on the front and small balconies on the back. No one would confuse its design as an attempt at opulence or even indulgence, for that matter. The building's security seemed to be relatively lax, too, which was a plus for men like Rainey. A lone surveillance camera hung above the building's entrance. Likewise, one was bolted onto the back of the building over a rear entrance. Both were maybe twenty years old.

"Mornin', nancies," said Alcott over the radio.

Rainey twisted and stretched his neck and back until they popped as his eyes swept back and forth from Nika's apartment to the activity on the street.

"Anything from overnight?"

Boyd keyed up from his position on the back of the building. "Well, at about oh three hundred this guy slipped in the service entrance, could have been Kozlov, don't know—"

"What?!" exclaimed Alcott.

"Relax, Shepherd. Just yanking your chain. Nothing happened."

Rainey and Drummond looked at each other and grinned.

"Drummy, anything on your end?"

"Nada. But then again, we just woke up."

Alcott shook his head. "All right, ladies, look alive. Time to put your game faces on."

Each of them had his own proprietary call sign. Alcott was Shepherd. Boyd was Bobo and Drummond, Drummy. Rounding out the group was Rainey who'd been Bronco for as long as he could remember. His namesake could be attributed to his father's old '89 Ford Bronco Eddie Bauer Edition, which he'd driven proudly ever since his junior year in high school.

It was now 6:00 a.m. on the dot. Rainey and Drummond both intently focused on the apartment. Lights inside flickered to life and a lithe silhouette crisscrossed back and forth behind the thin black curtains that veiled the apartment to spectators. Based on the succession of lights going on and off in the apartment, it was obvious she was getting ready for work.

"Anything different compared to the past few days?"

"Nope. Carbon copy," replied Drummond.

At 6:15, Alcott initiated one last comms check with each man. Then he stepped out of his car which was parked a block down the street in the opposite direction from Drummond and Rainey's location. He entered a café, where he could observe the street and begin to blend in with the sleepy pedestrian traffic. Alcott bought a coffee and easily assumed the lazy-eyed workday morning visage as was common the world over.

After another forty minutes or so, a slim, attractive woman in her late twenties, with straight golden locks pulled back into a ponytail, exited the front door of the apartment building. She pulled her winter headband over her ears, tucked her chin into a gray scarf and headed off in the direction opposite him. *Wow.* Nika appeared to be in exquisite physical shape. Her gait was familiar. Intrepid, aware. Like she could take care of herself. *Yes. Maddie's got the same walk.*

"Okay, Shepherd, Oriole's on the move. Heading your way," said Drummond. The team had given Nika the operational code name Oriole; it was Boyd's idea since he was a Baltimore native and a diehard Orioles fan.

"Copy that. I see her," said Alcott behind his tall coffee cup.

Rainey and Drummond watched as Nika moved away from their position. As she paced by the small café, bustling with the morning Montreal regulars, a man stepped out and casually turned to follow her.

Alcott.

As he did so, Rainey and Drummond paid careful attention to survey if he, in turn, was being followed.

"Shepherd, you're clean," said Drummond hopping out and walking to the opposite side of the street. He would take up a staggered position, keeping eyes on both Nika and Alcott.

"Copy that. Bronco, you guys are up."

Boyd had already slipped into the building through the service entrance. He looked like a cable TV repair man, complete with toolbox and uniform. He would take the service elevator to Nika's floor and meet Rainey there.

Rainey exited the van, walked across the street and made his way into the lobby of the apartment building, conscious of the camera mounted high above. He kept his head down under the bill of his Montreal Canadiens ball cap until he was inside the old wooden door. The lobby was well-lit and cozy. A plain gray elevator door was off to the left directly across from a grid of brass-trimmed, wooden mailboxes, which were neatly recessed into the wall. There at the far end of the lobby was a sturdy metal door that led to the stairs.

13

RAINEY took the stairs two at a time. When he reached the third floor, he paused behind the door which led out into the hallway. He peered through the slim, vertical window in the door. The hall was empty and quiet but for the muffled sounds here and there of people moving about inside their apartments.

Apartment 3C was two-thirds of the way down the hall on the right. He slid the key into the lock—the key that Alcott had already cut for him from the mold taken during the team's advance recce work. He was in in less than two seconds flat. If anyone stopped him and asked, he was the building owner's son and wasn't happy about having to come in and cover for the absent manager today. Seemed the guy had two flat tires this morning when he'd woken up and wouldn't be in until who knows when, if at all today. Alcott's doing.

Rainey stood just inside the apartment door. With the bill of his cap still pulled down, he meticulously scanned the room. Warm air spilled out of a floor register nearby, adding a soft, droning timbre to the otherwise dead silence. It was as if he'd stepped into a museum after closing. Everything was set in a neat, spectacular display. The three remotes on the coffee table were equidistant from each other and patently positioned at right angles to the inlay design on the surface of the table. Books on the shelves were arranged in alphabetical order by author. The mat under his feet was perfectly square with the lines in the wooden plank floor.

He advanced further into the apartment, through a small living room and nook before twisting into the kitchen, which was a model of order and cleanliness. Pots and pans hung in perfect symmetry above the blue and white tiled island countertop. A wooden block of knives was set at an exact forty-five-degree angle in the corner of the counter. The metal toaster next to it looked like a mirror. Not a smudge on it.

Rainey's eyes continued searching, while his face yielded no emotion. A small, slender form softly encroached behind him, stopped. Rainey whipped around, bringing his silenced 9mm pistol up in a blur.

A calico gingerly sauntered up to him rubbing against his pant leg, the pads of its feet barely making a sound.

Stupid cat. Ray sighed, holstered his gun.

He stepped over the silent spectator and resumed his search. Nothing probative in the living room or kitchen. Rainey ambled into the hallway stopping at an elegant bathroom on his right. He peered inside without turning on the lights. Three towels in cascading order according to size hung on a wrought iron rail evenly spaced an inch apart. On the lavish vanity was a magenta-colored, rectangular candle garnished with a mix of potpourri. And nary a drop of water on the floor...or in the sink. He checked the usual hiding places, but discovered nothing out of the ordinary, nothing hidden.

Rainey approached the end of the hall, where the bedroom was situated. The door was closed. He gripped the knob in his left hand, turned it counterclockwise slowly and steadily with his pistol in the other. He held the gun close to his ribs, but canted away from his body so in the event he had to fire, the gun's slide wouldn't catch on his coat or punch him in the gut, which would cause the gun to improperly cycle and jam. Or more importantly miss his target.

He slipped into the room without a sound. A candle had been recently extinguished; its fragrance still hung in the air. There was something else, too. Another scent. This one exotic. Expensive perfume. Had to be. The heavenly amalgam of aromas rekindled memories of a small village in the Tegharghar Mountains in northeast Mali. It was a kill mission, plain and simple. A high-value target—a terrorist cell leader affiliated with al-Qaeda in the Islamic Maghreb. The operation was insanely audacious in concept and perhaps for that reason alone had been a rousing success. To this day, the entire thing remains a virtual mystery to anyone not involved.

"Bobo, where're you at?" Rainey spoke in a clear yet hushed voice into his lapel mic.

"Be there in a sec."

"The apartment's ours. Shake a leg."

"On my way."

Rainey walked back down the hallway, across the living room and leaned toward the door of the apartment. He spied Boyd through the peephole traipsing up the hallway, toolbox swinging, metal clipboard tucked under his arm. As he approached the door, Rainey quickly swung it open and hurried him inside. "What happened?"

"Sorry. Some old guy flagged me down in the hallway and wanted me to service his cable. Wouldn't take no for an answer. Figured I'd better keep up the pretense, so I popped in quick and actually fixed his problem. Just needed new batteries in his remote," he said with the smile of a used car salesman.

"Get started, but be careful. This broad must have OCD." Rainey then disappeared back into the bedroom. He inspected the cherry wood dresser, but found nothing save some expensive French undergarments, some hosiery and an assortment of clothing: sweaters, turtlenecks and rolled-up blue jeans. He took a quick peak behind the mirror. Nothing.

The closet contained a rather impressive array of pant suits, designer shirts, slacks, jackets and coats, but yielded nothing of any consequence.

An imposing armoire stood along the one wall. In the corner of the room, was an ornately, hand-crafted antique desk that matched the armoire in both style and finish. A four poster bed, dressed in exquisite care—like something out of a catalog—was positioned in the center of the room.

There was nothing in the armoire, under the bed, or between the mattresses.

Rainey maneuvered over to the desk. He flipped through a few neatly assembled stacks of paper and a blank notepad before turning his attention to the drawers. He furtively examined the contents of each one save for the top drawer. It was locked. With no key in sight, he carefully picked the lock, so as not to leave any scratches in the metal. The old lock was one of those types that require a skeleton key. The mechanism was stiff but eventually relented with a soft *click*.

The warped, wooden drawer squeaked as he slid it open. Inside was an assortment of papers with travel agency letterhead, a small notepad and a red-brown leather portfolio. It made little logical sense to have these items under lock and key. For a few moments, Rainey seemed to be studying the desk, its lines, its construction. Over the years, he'd developed more than a passing interest in woodworking to complement his blacksmith tinkering. Just one of several pursuits that could actually take his mind off his work.

He took on the appearance of someone sensing they might be on to something. Rainey began removing the desk drawers, slowly at first, then with increasing efficiency. As he pulled each drawer out, he checked its underside for anything that might be taped there. When he had all the drawers neatly lined up on the bed, he stuck his head inside the voids of the desk. With a small flashlight, he scrutinized its undercarriage, the careful carpentry. He swept the light back and forth slowly.

There.

A glint of light reflected from the scratched head of a screw. It was this sole incongruence that betrayed such a magnificent hiding place.

14

HE pulled out his Leatherman and worked at the screw until it finally fell into his gloved hand. Rainey wiggled the drop-panel free from its slots, slid out the secret hide which was about twice the size of a cigar box and then extricated himself from beneath the desk.

Opening the wooden container, he first found an album chock full of photos, some black and white with yellowed edges. More recent images were tucked inside the back cover. In one of them, Nika, probably around age seventeen or eighteen, stood facing the camera. Her hair was shorn close to her scalp. She was wearing a prison jumpsuit. She bore hate-filled eyes and a recalcitrant snarl. The epitome of rebelliousness. The stenciling on the left breast of her jumpsuit was in Hebrew. *Hebrew? An Israeli prisoner? Thought she was Mossad.*

He continued flipping through the photos, some creased, some stuck together, mostly all including Nika in various stages of her youth. He'd seen none of this rage in the woman on the street just a few minutes ago. Intelligence, confidence, absolutely, but nothing that even closely resembled rage. Tucked between some papers, he found a gray-white envelope addressed to Nika, when she'd apparently been living in Herzliya. There was no return address. Rainey pulled out the contents. More photos. In each of them: Vladislav Kozlov. Him playing hockey, climbing trees, standing bare-chested in a large creek, its banks covered in snow and ice. The last several appeared to chronicle his development as a soldier. The man's face grew increasingly intense in each photo. The final one in the stack showed Kozlov with a twelve-man Spetsnaz team. Commandos armed to the teeth dressed in winter camo, standing around and sitting on a Russian BTR-82A.

Rainey pinched his nose in an attempt to fight off a sneeze caused by the dusty old papers. He then resumed shuffling through Nika's effects. His fingers stopped at a second envelope, identical to the first. This one contained a three-page handwritten missive. When he opened the letter, two photographs fell out. In the first, was a man he didn't recognize and an attractive brunette with long wavy hair that shimmered in the sunlight. They were sitting together outside a Paris café smiling, seemingly lost in each other's embrace. There was a faint resemblance between the woman in the photo and Nika.

Nika's mom and dad?

The second photo was starkly different. No doubt about it, it contained a version of the same man, but here he was older and alone. He wore a Soviet military dress uniform and appeared absolutely devoid of any emotion. As if he were frozen.

Rainey turned the photos over in his hand, examined them carefully. Scribbled on the back of the first was a date: *October 19, 1987.* The second photo had no markings whatsoever.

The letter was written in Cyrillic text, its prose emotional and at the same time informative, though there were sections in which the author seemed to ramble. Some lines contained unfinished thoughts, or perhaps thoughts too painful to put into words.

The author was clearly Nika's father.

And Vladislav Kozlov's father.

The same man, in fact. It was an undeniable link.

This must be what had driven Nika to walk away from Mossad. The letter explained in detail the existence of an older brother—a half-brother. His location was either unknown to the author or else simply withheld from the letter. Rainey followed the Cyrillic text with the tip of his finger. Nika and Vladislav had been born of different mothers. Over and over, Nika's father urged her to seek him out. Find him, get to know him. After all, family is family.

As he read on, Rainey pictured a sickly man sitting at a desk, maybe this very desk, in a dreary room on a dreary day in Moscow. A man writing with a shaky hand and a seemingly shattered hope for his own fate. It was obvious that her father was mourning some kind of dreadful realization. Like that of man who'd suddenly found himself out of time. Tucked away in the meandering prose was a poorly articulated attempt at acknowledging his failure as a father.

Rainey shook his head. The man had made an unforgivable error. He'd neglected his only daughter and now—as the letter continued—it was far too late for him to do anything about it. He had ignored Nika's existence since birth, in favor of his only legitimate child: his son, Vladislav.

This revelation now cast a slightly different light on Nika, colored his understanding of her. Somehow, he felt a strange connection with her, as he knelt there on the floor reading. They'd both grown up without a father.

At the end of the letter, there was a curt apology for his life's work and his "final act of cowardice," what Rainey assumed referred to an intended suicide. He could no longer deal with the grief racking his mind and conscience, even more than the constant pain that ravaged his withered body. He'd contracted some type of aggressive cancer, apparently. Rainey gathered that he had worked in some capacity with chemical or biological agents.

The letter was signed, "With Deepest Regret, Your Loving Father."

Rainey picked through the remnants of the box nearing the bottom. An aged manila envelope caught his attention. He quickly opened it and withdrew a single piece of parchment that revealed Nika's full name. Her real name.

Nika Aleksandrovna Kozlova.

Rainey snapped some quick pics of the photos with his camera phone along with the handwritten letter and various other scraps of paper.

He rolled back on his heels, leaned against the bed. The box was still heavy in his hands, heavier than it should be. Rainey turned it over and gave it a tap. A flat piece of wood—the bottom previously—fell out and exposed a spy's bounty. There were five passports, each contained a different name, but the same woman in every photo: Nika Chernikova, er, Nika Kozlova. Three banded bricks of $100 bills—ten thousand dollars apiece—and several similar bricks of various foreign currencies in equal amounts. A rubber-banded block of pre-paid VISA cards. A brand new disposable cell phone and a total of ten SIM cards to go with it. Lastly, shrouded inside a blue velour pouch, was a Kahr P380—a handsome little handgun with a stainless steel slide and a textured black polymer frame and two spare magazines. Rainey dropped the magazine from the gun and eased the slide partially back, eyeballing the ejection port. The mag was topped off and there was a round in the chamber.

Suddenly Alcott's voice came alive in his earpiece: "Bronco, Oriole's heading your way."

"What? I thought she was going to work."

"Me, too. You two need to get moving. *Now.*"

"How much time do we have?"

"She just left her office, so I figure you have about five minutes till she reaches her building."

"Copy that."

Rainey poked his head around the open door, peered down the hall into the living room at Boyd. "Hustle, bro."

The travel agency *Bon Voyage!* was only a short walk from Nika's building. But with the temperature and wind chill what they were, a five-minute walk could easily become a three-minute trot.

Hurriedly, Rainey placed everything back inside the secret compartment just as he'd found it, then carefully slid it back into its home. He zipped the screw into the drop panel and then pushed each desk drawer back in place. A collection of wood dust had accumulated on the floor in front of the desk where he had removed each drawer. He leaned down and blew it into oblivion then worked his way toward the bedroom door.

He quickly turned back. The desk drawer was locked. *Duh!* After another five seconds, the lock clicked back into position. Rainey smoothed out Nika's bedspread and gave the room one last glance. *Like I was never here.*

He clipped down the hall, padded across the living room just as Boyd was putting the last of his tools back into his toolbox. Rainey helped the surveillance man fold up his special polymer ladder, then looked on as Boyd slid it into the base of his toolbox. "We good?"

"We're good," replied Boyd.

Rainey checked the peephole as he reached for the doorknob. "It's clear. Let's go."

Boyd picked up his toolbox and stood up. The abrupt motion must have spooked the cat from wherever it had been hiding. In a flash, the calico sprinted under the coffee table and leapt onto a narrow shelf, knocking over a small glass figurine of a woman ice-skating, which in turn fell to the hardwood floor and shattered into a million pieces.

"Crap!"

"What is it?" asked Alcott in his ear.

Rainey ignored the question. Should he leave the mess? The cat would doubtless be blamed. But would Nika deduce something might have spooked the cat? *There's no time! Gotta make a decision.*

"Go. Go now," he instructed Boyd in a hushed voice.

"Approaching the front door," Alcott advised. Then a few seconds later: "She's in the lobby."

"I'll call the elevator up, Bronc. Give you a few more seconds," said Boyd exiting the apartment.

Sweat beaded on his brow. Rainey swept up the shards of glass into his gloved hands and stuffed them into his coat pocket. With a hearty breath he whisked off all of the glass dust he could see. He looked around one last time then stood up.

Yanking his ball cap down low on his forehead, Rainey left the apartment. He re-locked the door and fast-walked down the hallway. Just as he made it through the door to the stairs, the elevator yawned open at the opposite end of the corridor. Rainey watched carefully through the slender window in the door as Nika stepped from the elevator and walked to her apartment. He swallowed hard, his throat as dry as Death Valley.

He waited until she was inside then made his way down to the lobby and casually walked out the front door.

* * *

Nika set her handbag down on the chair just inside the door and dropped her keys into a brass dish on the adjacent end table. A computer bag draped over her shoulder, she continued into the kitchen, removing her tobacco brown Sorel Joan of Arctic boots en route. She set the bag down on a stool then filled a kettle with water from the tap and set it on the stove to boil.

She slid a laptop from her bag and placed it on the island. A car horn clamored outside which diverted her eyes for only a second.

Nika lifted the lid of the computer and saddled up behind it. While the machine was booting up, she hopped back down. She needed her purse. Inside was a secure thumb drive, which she used religiously to add an impregnable layer of encryption to all her e-mails.

"Oooh, *Lyutik* (Buttercup)," she said making kissing sounds.

The calico bounded toward her as she made her way to her purse. She bent down to pet it; the cat purred lovingly in response.

Nika retrieved her purse and turned to head back into the kitchen, when something bit the bottom of her foot.

She barked out a curse word in Russian as she drew up her foot to inspect the source of the pain. A look of bewilderment on her face, Nika focused her eyes on the jagged triangular shard of glass about a half inch long sticking out of her heel, blood steadily oozing out around it and soaking her thick sock. She earnestly scanned the room for the origin of the broken glass as she tore off her sock. Holding her bare foot in her hand, both now replete with crimson, she made a startling discovery.

Her ice dancer was gone.

15

Directorate Twelve Headquarters
Arlington, VA

JOB Jackson sat in his office sipping his strong morning brew. He was staring out his window at a flock of geese flying toward the Potomac, but his attention was entirely focused on the mission at hand. The weight of recent events continued to loom heavily on him. He hadn't slept well in what seemed like months and the added stress of the current operation only added to his anxiety. He was on pins and needles as he waited for the call. Finally, his secure phone chirped. "Yes?" He straightened in his chair at the sound of Rainey's voice. "How'd you make out?"

"We'll see. She's certainly no travel agent. That's for sure."

"Whaddya mean?" asked Job.

"I found quite a little stash. A bunch of phony passports—good quality stuff, too—bricks of cash, a clean phone, and a cute little piece for those James Bond-type cocktail parties."

"Yeah?"

Rainey related what he'd discovered.

"So that explains why she's been trying to track down Kozlov."

"Exactly. Mark is sending this stuff to you now," said Rainey as he stroked his smooth face where a months-old beard had been the day before. He paced around the room as Alcott punched away on his laptop, then nodded. "You should have it in a second or two."

"Just got 'em. Nice! Well, this is our confirmation that Nika *is* tied to Kozlov. And that goes a little further toward circumstantially implicating Kozlov in the abduction of Edward Horst. All right. Anything else?"

"We got two bugs installed, so we'll see how it goes." Rainey took a breath then let it out slowly. "Bad news is... She has this cat. Right as we were about to leave, the stinkin' thing jumped up and knocked over some glass knick-knack thingy that shattered into a billion pieces. I chose to clean it up, but obviously..."

"You think she'll notice?"

"This babe? Yes, I do. Mark agrees. She might not notice right away, but this is one compulsive broad. Honestly, it wouldn't surprise me if she walks in and discovers that it's missing almost immediately."

Job sighed, which came out a little louder than he'd intended. "Yeah."

"Okay. Well, let's just hope for now that she doesn't notice. Good job. Tell the others I said so. You hear me?"

"I hear ya."

"We still have eyes on the girl, right?"

"Affirmative. Cagney and Lacey are on it. Mark's here with me. He's monitoring the feeds from the apartment. You have any further instructions?"

"Just sit tight for now. I want to explore a few things in light of this new information. Call me if anything changes. I'll be in touch."

16

Montreal, Quebec

ER foot now cleaned and bandaged with white gauze, Nika sat on the edge of her bed. She checked the tube of her pearl-handled SIG Sauer P232, a pistol she always kept with her. She steeled herself, suppressing her nerves although outwardly you would be hard-pressed to see any signs of anxiety, because there were none.

Gun in hand, she padded back into the kitchen to check the feed from the tiny camera she had painstakingly hidden in the living room of her apartment several months ago. She set the gun down next to her laptop and swiped her finger across the touchpad coaxing the screen out of dormancy. A few seconds later, she frowned into the glow of the screen. The footage was not there. There was nothing. Not even from a week ago. She walked to where the camera was se-creted. The tiny cable supplying the unit with power had been chewed completely through. She turned and cursed at the calico be-fore quickly returning to the laptop and closing the lid.

Donning a quiet pair of flats, Nika tucked the pistol into her waistband, pulled her sweater down over it and gave herself a once-over in the bedroom mirror. She considered the past several weeks in

Montreal and what lay ahead. She needed to be extra cautious now. There was just too much on the line.

A renewed confidence in her sea foam green eyes, Nika took the elevator down to the lobby and paraded over to the wall of mailboxes. Just as she did every day, she inserted her key, opened the tiny square door and yanked out a handful of mail. The only difference between her usual daily routine and now, was that she did not open the mailbox assigned to her apartment. Instead, she opened the mailbox directly beside hers; it was assigned to another apartment in the building rented under an entirely different identity. This mailbox contained a tiny pinhole camera with a self-contained digital video recorder (DVR). The lens of the camera had been aimed through the small glass window in the mailbox door. The high-tech device was quite remarkable. It held a tiny self-charging battery that could last for 20 years.

Nika pulled out the device with an assortment of mail—mail she herself had placed there for the sole purpose of camouflaging the camera. Acting as if she were perusing unsavory bills and tired junk mail, she headed back upstairs and into her apartment.

She stuck the DVR device directly into the USB port of her laptop. A few clicks on the touchpad and the video viewer was up and ready to go. The DVR had been pre-programmed to record each day in a real-time 24-hour loop.

Nika held a mug up to her lips, blew across the surface of the tea, making tiny waves in the hot liquid. Her eyes narrowed in concentration as the file for today loaded in the viewer. She skipped ahead to the time just before she'd left for work and then slowed the video down. The time stamp showed 06:59:12 as she left through the front door of the apartment building. Nika drew closer to the screen. Almost a full minute later, at 07:00:10, he appeared: a man in a black and green hooded North Face parka and a worn Montreal Canadiens ball cap pulled down tightly over his brow. His face was mostly hidden, but this much she could tell: he was Caucasian, the lower half of his face was tan and lacked any trace of facial hair. He had a strong, athletic build and walked with a deliberate pace, like a man who had high regard for punctuality. There were sixty-three other tenants in the building, most she'd seen and even casually greeted at one time or another. This man was not one of them.

She tracked him with her eyes as he strode through the lobby and took the stairs. Her pulse quickened.

Again, she hit the double arrow and skipped ahead. Fifteen minutes later on the DVR's time stamp, Nika appeared on the screen again. She moved past the camera shaking off the raw chill of Montreal air and stamping the salt from her boots. She disappeared into the elevator. The doors closed. After about a minute, the mysterious figure in the black and green parka returned to the lobby through the metal door that led to the stairs. Goose bumps formed on her arms and an electric charge shot down her spine.

It was him.

Reagan Rainey.

Nika pulled off the ponytail holder and let her lustrous golden locks fall over the nape of her neck as she pinched the phone between her cheek and shoulder.

"Yes?" A man's voice.

"It's me. We need to talk."

17

Washington, D.C.

SHE and Wes emerged from the elevator and walked down the bustling hall. This was the first time she had ever actually been inside *Washington Post* headquarters. Buoyed by the Christmas season, Maddie beamed as Wes led the way to his editor's office.

A middle-aged man, his shirtsleeves rolled up and necktie long ago discarded, was on the phone. He noticed their approach and waved them inside through the windowed door. Wes held the door for Maddie and when they were inside, closed it muffling the clamor outside of phones ringing, computer keyboards clicking, file cabinets opening and closing.

Maddie inspected the editor's office from right to left and back again. Files, books, notepads were everywhere. It was organized chaos.

When the man finally hung up the phone, Wes offered a polite, "Morning, boss. You wanted to see me?"

"First things first. You must introduce me to your gorgeous little friend, here."

"Of course, how foolish of me. Oliver Marcone, meet Madison Rainey...my girlfriend. Maddie works over at the Library of Congress."

"Oh, is that so?" slobbered the editor eagerly skirting around his desk. He took Maddie's hand and in a show of prideless predation, pressed his lips against it, allowing them to linger longer than what was clearly defined by social mores as appropriate. "Mmmhuh."

Maddie smiled awkwardly.

"Wes, why haven't I seen this deliciously beautiful young woman in the office before?" He winked at Maddie. "You are ravishing, my dear."

Wes opened his lips and was about to speak, but Maddie beat him to the punch. Still wiping her hand on the back of her pant leg, she said, "He's been busy."

"I'll bet he has." He winked at Wes this time and grinned slyly.

"You know, I'm having a New Year's Eve party at my place this year. Gonna be huge. Gonna be wild. I mean *really* wild. Why don't you bring Wes? Or not." He smiled lustfully.

"As good as that sounds, people my age don't really play pinochle." She winked at him with subtle mockery.

A queer look registered on Marcone's face. Maddie had an innate knack for being an instigator, a quality she'd honed on her older brother throughout childhood.

Marcone's puckered face relaxed into a chuckle. "Oh, you're kidding. You're a spry one, Miss Rainey. You hang on to this one, Wes, or else I just might... Mmm." Marcone licked his lips as he voraciously eyed Maddie up and down, his eyes lastly focusing on her chest. Then, with a hint of conceit in his voice, said, "I'm sorry my dear, could you excuse us for a few minutes?"

Maddie looked at Wes. "Sure."

* * *

Wes was already seething with contempt for his boss's behavior. He waited till Maddie was gone before he let him have it. "What the heck was that?!"

"I'm sorry?" Marcone said the words as if he didn't have the slightest clue as to what Wes was talking about.

"You know darn well what I mean."

"Calm down, Wes. You should be flattered. She's quite a looker. If you ever tire of her, let me know, because I would love to—"

"You know, I've had just about all I can take of you. In fact, I loathe you. For many reasons, really, but probably none more so than the way in which you treat women around here. I've bit my tongue so many times in the past, I've gotta have scars. But I can't do it anymore. I won't. After the way you just treated Maddie... That woman is the love of my life, the best thing that has ever happened to me. And I refuse to stand idly by while you disrespect her like that. I'm done. I'm out. I can't work for you anymore. You and your smug misogynous grins, your lurid stories make me want to puke!"

Marcone stood there flummoxed, mouth agape. Never had anyone stood up to him before.

"I'm done here." Wes turned toward the door.

"You're done everywhere! Get out of my office this instant!" Marcone had a habit of blinking repeatedly when he was angry. Right now it looked as if two hummingbirds had taken up residence on either side of his face. He was twitching and blinking, face maroon with rage.

"Gladly. Because I can no longer stand the sight of you." And with that Wes walked out, letting the door swing as he did so. It banged loudly against the wall. An exclamation point to his exit. Everyone in every cubicle stopped what they were doing and stared. A few women began to clap.

Wes didn't stick around to bask in the moment, he wanted to find Maddie and get the heck out of there. But that didn't take much effort because she was standing by a water cooler, an arm's length away.

She'd heard everything.

Wes blushed a little then softly said, "Let's go. Meeting's over."

Maddie followed Wes silently to the elevator. Once they were inside, she spun him toward her and planted a big one right on Wes's lips. It was long and passionate. Never before had a man publicly stood up for her like that. Finally, they parted. She beamed from ear to ear. "Thank you, Wesley."

Wes looked into her dazzling amber eyes. "You are so worth it. It's true what I said in there, you know. You are the love of my life."

Maddie, her heart racing, latched on to him and squeezed tightly. A tear of joy slipped out of her left eye. "And you are the love of mine, sweetie."

He was still amped up. "I just couldn't let it go. You know, I've actually been thinking about leaving the *Post* for a while now. I'm sure you've noticed that the brass and I don't believe in a lot of the same things. It's been weighing on my mind a lot recently. Most of all, I love you more than anything or anyone. Standing here with you—right here, right now—know that I will do anything to protect you and your honor." He appeared confident in his resolution then slyly smiled. "Even if you can kick my butt."

"That is the nicest thing anyone has ever done for me. But, Wes, your job…"

"That news organization doesn't care a lick about me. And Marcone doesn't scare me one bit either. There are plenty of things I can do. Plenty of jobs out there. I'll dig ditches if I have to. As long as I have you. Besides, just because I'm not working at the *Post*, doesn't mean I have to give up journalism or writing altogether. Regardless, God will show me what He wants me to do.

"You know what would be great? Finally working with someone who believes in the things I believe in. Who knows, maybe I'll write a book. You never know."

"And what do you believe in, Wesley?" Maddie said coyly, her eyes going back and forth, studying his.

He smiled. "You know what I believe in, sweetie. I've just not been as vocal about it as I perhaps should have been. But that is all going to change." He brought her head to his chest as they embraced. He was at a crossroads in his life in more ways than one. "I believe in the same things you believe in, Maddie: integrity, honor, and accountability, humility, freedom, dedication to the Constitution and the American way of life. The rule of law. I believe in the One True God." He softly stroked her arm as a vision for his future entered his mind's eye. It was a beautiful vision. Center stage was Madison Rainey. "I believe in us."

"Maybe you should run for office." Maddie smiled, her bright, intelligent eyes sparkling like little pools of liquid honey.

"Maybe I will."

"I love you, Wesley." She squeezed him again warmly and then endowed him with another affectionate kiss on the lips. This one tender and soft. "You know how wonderful it is for a woman to know that the man she loves has principles? Thank you."

His eyes met hers and he naturally smiled back, standing there helplessly captivated in her uncontrived radiance. The exotic fragrance she wore teased playfully with his senses, and when coupled with the thoughts of kissing her again, caused his body to spark with stimulation. Her stunning beauty, not only that on the outside but also that on the inside—her remarkable character, her fortitude, her unyielding zest for truth and the zeal to hold people to it, penetrated his entire being. It was in this moment, in this very second, that he knew he was going to ask this woman to marry him.

And soon.

* * *

Maddie giggled. Here, standing in this cathedral of liberal thought, this monument to leftist group think, Wes was holding fast to his principles and demonstrating the strong character to which she was so attracted. Again, she giggled, this time the evidence all over her face. In the dimples in her cheeks, the tiny laugh wrinkles by her eyes. Without equivocation, she knew this was the man with whom she was going to spend the rest of her life.

18

Montreal, Quebec

PERSISTENT shards of sunlight penetrated tiny cracks and crevices in the tightly pulled blinds. They knifed their way far into the room, exposing the intricate wood grain texture of each plank in the floor. It was quite a spectacle within the safe house, as clusters of clouds outside drifted in front of, then past, the sun. The invading light would quickly dim and disappear, then in an instant, return with ferocity. Each time, the sunlight seemed more intense as it splintered into a latticework of squares, rectangles, and trapezoids across the floor.

Now, a little more than three hours since they'd been in Nika's apartment, Rainey sat in a lumpy, cappuccino-colored recliner. His eyes were fixed on the Fox News Channel's footage of the salvage effort taking place along Lac St-Louis. Including the crew, all 215 people aboard Flight 612 had perished last night in one inexplicable instant. Rainey shook his head as he took in the carnage being hauled up onto barges and flatbed trucks. A small army of people clad in red search and rescue gear spanned the panorama.

"Any word on what caused it?" inquired Alcott from behind his laptop.

"No. Just a lot of speculation."

"Well, now," said Alcott.

"What?"

"I just got an update from Job about that phone call Nika made."

"And?"

"Number comes back to a pre-paid assigned to Telus Mobility. Metadata puts the phone in the same general area where Horst was taken. Date and time fit, too. And get this... The phone is still active. It's hitting off a tower in the St-Lèonard area of the city as we speak. Job has it narrowed down to a specific address. It's about twenty minutes from here."

"So what's the plan?"

Alcott stood up. "He wants you and me to go recon the location. Drummy and Bobo are to stay on the girl for the time being. I've requested some more people. For us to properly tail one person, let alone two, we're going to need them. He said he'll get back to me. It's your call. What do you want to do? You wanna wait?"

Rainey shook his head. "No. We can't. Intel's perishable. We might lose our lead in the meantime. No, we do what we're told. We go to the address and develop the situation."

"My thoughts exactly. Let's do it."

19

A freight train rumbled down the tracks, howling into the frigid, late morning air like a rabid wolf in search of prey. A bone-chilling wind every bit as ferocious had picked up and now raged across the Rivière des Prairies.

The rue Pascal-Gagnon was a dead end street in the heart of an industrial area of Montreal well past its prime. Mark Alcott pulled to the curb and went through his countersurveillance checklist. It was quiet here. The target location was, gauging from the sign affixed to the crumbling, red-brick facade, a local hub for a truck transport firm, or at least what was left of it. He parked on the small pock-marked street and carefully assessed his surroundings. Behind a pair of dark sunglasses, he sized up the drab, characterless warehouse in the crook of the cul-de-sac down the street.

He and Rainey had left Drummond and Boyd to keep tabs on Nika while they reconned the warehouse. Their counterparts would let them know if the girl left or anyone showed up at the apartment. Two minutes ago, Alcott had dropped Rainey off on the Boulevard des Grandes-Prairies. He would come in from the front, Rainey the rear.

"How's it look?" Alcott studied the front of the large building occasionally checking his surroundings.

"So far so good. I'll soon be at the back door. Stand by.

* * *

Rainey cautiously worked his way on foot along a ragged line of tangled weeds and decaying refuse. He steadily eased toward the warehouse from the south, earnestly searching for any signs of activity at the expansive, austere complex. This could very well be a trap. But then again, someone could be here. Maybe Dr. Horst. In fact, that's what he and Alcott were hoping.

The warehouse appeared dormant, abandoned. As Rainey approached, he checked the exterior for surveillance cameras, motion sensors and any other type of visible security measures. There were no signs of such, nor was anyone lurking about that suggested an active or even passive patrol.

Rainey straddled a heap of scrap metal and moved closer. He crept up behind a chipped concrete wall of an adjacent warehouse of similar design and disrepair, strategically shielding himself from view while he eyeballed the target location.

All was quiet.

Stealthily, he maneuvered to the building and up a flight of concrete steps leading to a severely dented metal door to the left of two rusty overhead loading dock doors. They were covered in graffiti. Putting his ear against the door, he listened for any sounds inside.

Silence.

He tried the knob. It was in need of some oil, but it was unlocked.

Rainey whispered into his mic, "Back door's unlocked. Everything's quiet so far. Stay put until I'm inside."

"Roger that. Be careful."

With his FNP-9 indexed in front of him, Rainey quietly cracked the door and slipped inside, where he ducked behind a dusty stack of wooden pallets. He eased upward and scanned the cavernous warehouse. Save for a few old flattened cardboard boxes and rusty metal bands scattered about, the place was largely bare inside.

Rainey edged out from behind the pile of debris. There were three other exits within eyesight, the closest being about fifty yards away down the length of wall to his left. The front door was further away to his right. Above him, there was a ring of windows that ran the entire circumference of the building, some shattered—the apparent victims of mischief. The weathered cement floor beneath his feet

was smooth, shiny at spots. Other sections of the floor across the
vast interior were fragmented from decades of abuse, a network of
little fault lines.

"Shepherd, looks clear. Go ahead and make entry. I'll cover
you."

"Roger, that. Entering now."

Rainey scanned for threats while Alcott made his way inside. As
the door squeaked open and closed, a long wedge of sunlight raced
into the darkness then just as quickly disappeared. Alcott skirted
along the wall to his right.

"Come toward me. I'm on your ten."

Once Alcott had made it to Rainey's location, both men studied
the warehouse together.

"I don't like this," said Rainey. "Something's not right."

"I'm tracking."

Rainey was completely still save for his eyes, which scanned
every nook and cranny of the interior. "I'm gonna make my way
over there. Cover me. Watch that roof. Once I'm in position, I'll signal you over."

Alcott wiped a spider web from his goatee. "All right."

Straight ahead, situated for the most part dead center, there was
what appeared to be a small building within the building, the walls
of which were windowless, constructed of painted cinder block rising ten feet high.

Rainey, gun ready, stepped out and quickly but quietly dashed
off into the dimly lit behemoth, his eyes darting back and forth to the
danger zones, areas in front of him where threats could be hiding and
waiting to jump out.

Approximately halfway to the shoebox-shaped structure, he
came upon a deep channel that ran all the way from the front of the
building to the rear, where it disappeared under a set of huge, wide-
mouth bay doors. The void had been boarded up long ago. The
channel was about four feet deep and ten feet across. Inside the wide
culvert was a worn pair of metal rails where at some point long ago
in the warehouse's assuredly long, colorful history, train cars were
brought in for the loading and unloading of freight.

Rainey eased down into the channel, stepped over the rails and
then peeked up over the other side. He studied the inner building.
Could Job's information be wrong? This place looked deserted. There

was total silence except for dripping sounds that echoed from some place far off and the occasional rummaging of birds in the upper recesses of the warehouse.

Vaulting himself up and out of the far side of the channel, Rainey stalked over to the windowless building and carefully paced its circumference. When he'd finally deemed it safe, he signaled Alcott, who quickly joined him. Rainey pointed to the tattered sign in the middle of the door denoting the obvious: OFFICE.

Alcott nodded.

Rainey noted the position of the doorknob, the locking mechanism then placed his left hand flat against the door feeling for any vibrations that would indicate someone might be inside. Carefully, he checked for signs that showed the door might be booby-trapped but found nothing.

Crouching low on the knob side of the door, his back against the wall, Rainey threw the door open and sucked backward, avoiding the "fatal funnel" of the doorway in case someone was lying in wait inside, ready to cut them down with a hail of machine gun fire.

When nothing happened, Rainey edged cautiously around the doorframe with his gun at eye level. The void within was alive with darkness. Reaching into his coat pocket, he pulled out a light stick. He cracked it and then tossed it inside. The stick emitted a haunting green glow that illuminated the room with an eerie gloom.

He peered in. There was an outer office area and a short hallway with two doors further back. In the outer room were a lone metal desk and three chairs, one laying on the floor on its side, a beat-up pair of file cabinets and a small folding table atop which was an ancient, abandoned fax machine. Several outdated employee advisories were still pinned to a dusty corkboard on the wall.

Gripping his flashlight in one hand and his gun in the other, Rainey tilted his head toward Alcott but kept his eyes downrange. Alcott tactically drew up against Rainey's back then squeezed him on the right shoulder indicating he was ready to move. They'd done this loads of times together in Iraq and Afghanistan back in the ODA.

Rainey and Alcott quickly penetrated the first room sweeping their pistols and flashlights back and forth, up and down then likewise cleared the other two rooms, a break room, and an employee bathroom. Once it was evident they were alone, they lowered their pistols and walked back to the front office area where they began examining the room in more detail. Tiny dust particles floated in the beams of their bright flashlights. The air was stale and smelled of mold and mildew, paper slowly rotting with time.

"You see that?" Rainey said.

"What?"

"There in the dust, you see those? Shoe prints. They're not ours."

Alcott changed the angle of his flashlight. Now he could see them. On the floor, there was a trail of shoe prints in the thin film of dust mingled with their own. They were roughly a men's size thirteen.

Rainey's sixth sense screamed. He shined his light up and down on the file cabinets. He inched out the top drawer slowly and immediately a pulse of adrenaline shot through his body. "I've got a phone here."

Alcott who was warily searching through the desk drawers and a stack of papers he'd found in one of them looked up with urgency.

A generic-looking cell phone blandly stared up at Rainey from the middle of the file cabinet drawer. "It's powered on." He threw his light around the room, now saw more shoe prints leading out of the office door, around the corner and toward the back of the warehouse. There, inside a cage of chain-link fence, were two 500-pound propane tanks.

They both noticed it at the same time. The gate to the cage was standing open. Their eyes widened with alarm as the split-second realization set in.

"IED!!" yelled Rainey.

Both men turned on their heels and took off out of the room. They ran as fast as they could for the only place there was to go.

The exploding tanks of propane loosed near simultaneous cracks of thunder; it was deafening. The entire structure erupted into a gigantic fireball. Showers of deadly projectiles screamed through the air in all directions. Jagged pieces of pulverized metal and cement showered down indiscriminately. The earth within a four-mile radius trembled.

Out on the nearby Boulevard Henri-Bourassa, vehicles collided as the shockwave blasted across the heavily trafficked expressway. Buildings all around the warehouse were now littered with broken windows and debris from the enormous blowout.

* * *

Leering behind a pair of binoculars from the rooftop of a cookie-cutter apartment building off the rue Renoir, a man studied the wreckage of the monstrous blast as he placed the remote back inside his coat. From his vantage point, he had a clear view of both approaches to the building, front and back. He had seen a man—one of his new targets—enter the warehouse at the rear just minutes prior. From the intelligence he'd received earlier he knew his name to be Reagan Rainey. Rainey was soon joined by the other man, Alcott was his name. Mark Alcott.

He'd given them time to move deep inside before detonating his little surprise. Satisfied with his handiwork, the man punched out a text message for Kupchenko and hit SEND. Thirty seconds later, a reply came with some added instructions. The assassin texted back that he understood.

He watched for a minute more until a choir of sirens began to sing loudly. Descending down to the street, the assassin slipped into a forgetful-looking sedan and casually drove off.

Two down, two to go.

20

TWO full minutes after the explosion had leveled the warehouse, Rainey came to. At first, he had no idea where he was. It was Iraq all over again. An IED... Steadily, he regained his bearings and fought his way out of the heap of debris that covered him. If the railway channel wouldn't have been there, he would undoubtedly be dead. Rainey had just managed to leap into its relative safety when the propane tanks, rigged with a powerful explosive charge, blew.

Something screamed in his left shoulder. His ears...not functioning. Rainey kicked his right foot free from a conglomeration of rusted metal and detritus. He slowly rose to his feet and took stock of himself. There was a shiny piece of metal jutting out whence the blistering pain in his left shoulder was emanating. He ran his hands over his face. Only a few minor cuts and abrasions. He moved his hand north of his right eyebrow and over a goony on his forehead that appeared as if a golf ball had been surgically implanted under his scalp. Then, he drew his attention to the warm blood running down his leg. Being that his pants had been all but shredded, the small gash in his left leg was plain to see. It was just above the scar he'd picked up in Qatar. This would need to be addressed in time. But not life-threatening. All in all, nothing serious considering a building had just blown up on top of him. For now, he would leave the piece of metal shrapnel in his shoulder until he could attend to it properly in a safe environment. It felt like the devil himself was stabbing a finger into his shoulder, but the metal shard would not cause any additional damage in the meantime. In fact, pulling it out now might actually do more harm than good.

He rooted around in the rubble, located his gun and that's when he heard them. Muffled screams.

Shepherd!

Rainey spun in circles trying to pinpoint the man's location. After digging frantically in several areas, he finally found him. Urgently, he burrowed down into the wreckage. There under a big hunk of roof blanketed by broken cinder blocks and other junk was Mark Alcott.

Was he alive? How could he be? His entire lower body appeared to have been crushed. But, wait. No. The piece of roof that covered him from his hips down was supported by a metal I-beam.

Alcott's eyes fluttered, tears of anguish streamed down his face, which was caked in dust and grime. He moaned.

"Shepherd! Hang on, brother!" Rainey threw piece after piece of metal and cinder block away with reckless abandon. Once he had him uncovered as best he could, he gripped the man by his trouser legs and slid him out.

Alcott grunted and grimaced, as if suppressing the natural urge to scream.

Now he could fully triage the man's injuries. It was obvious. Alcott's chest cavity had been pierced. Probably from that long metal rod, slick with crimson, sticking out of the rubble in the very spot Alcott had been pinned. No telltale hissing or sucking sounds. Air infiltrating Alcott's chest cavity was going in but not coming back out. *A tension pneumothorax.* It was causing his right lung to collapse. Alcott's breathing was labored and shallow, the veins in his neck distended. Simply put, the guy was in a lot pain. If he didn't get immediate care, he would die.

Rainey ripped open Alcott's shirt, what was left of it, and noticed that several ribs were cracked as well.

He opened a small combat med kit he carried in his coat pocket. "You're gonna make it, Shep. Just gimme a sec."

Alcott choked back the pain, gritted his teeth.

"This is gonna pinch." Rainey wiped the area with an alcohol swab just under Alcott's collarbone on the same side as the injury. Next, he took the 14-gauge needle and catheter unit and tore the wrapper off. "I know it hurts, but try to hold still." Carefully, at a 90-degree angle to his skin, Rainey pushed the needle in just above Alcott's third rib, at the midpoint of his collarbone. Slowly he applied pressure until finally he felt a *pop*. Immediately, the trapped air escaped from Alcott's chest cavity with a *shhh* sound.

"Ahhh! Thanks. I needed that." The relief was instantaneous. Alcott's breathing returned to a more normal state, considering.

"Almost done here." Rainey quickly taped down the hub of the catheter and made sure it was going to stay put. "Okay, all finished. Now we gotta jet. Can you walk?"

"I think so."

Rainey holstered his gun and pocketed Alcott's before he helped the man up.

Alcott tried to put weight on his legs but his right ankle was either broken or dislocated.

Rainey instantly grabbed his fellow warrior around the waist. "I got you. I got you. We gotta go. Now."

"Bronc, we gotta get word to the others. Immediately. The team's been compromised. Drummy and Bobo are in a world of danger."

Rainey tried to radio them, but it was no use. They'd lost comms. He tried using Alcott's radio, but that didn't work either. Probably damaged in the blast. Rainey pulled out his phone, but it came out in pieces. And Alcott's phone was nowhere to be found. Somewhere lost in the rubble.

Please guys, be paying attention. God, please keep them safe!

21

BEHIND the heavily tinted windows of the minivan, Drummond assessed the condition of the foot traffic on the street. Not much had changed. People were quickly whisking to and fro, shielding themselves from the brutal gusts of wind. "Anything new out back?"

"No. Unless you count the garbage now swirling around the lot. It's like a wind tunnel back here."

"Still no word from Bronco or Shep. Wonder how they're making out."

"Yeah. Hope they find the doc so we can get the heck outta here. Gonna surprise the wife with a trip to the Caribbean in a couple weeks. Can't wait to get out of this rotten cold."

"Stand by. I got someone approaching me." Drummond pulled his pistol and put it beside his right leg as he scrutinized the man walking toward him.

Just a local beat cop. A sergeant judging from the stripes on his shoulder.

The officer locked eyes with him and wagged his finger impatiently for him to lower the window.

Drummond cracked the window, but the officer repeated his nonverbal order indicating he wanted the window opened further.

Drummond complied. "What can I do for you, officer?" he asked in French.

The policeman leaned over. "We've got some complaints about this vehicle. Neighbors are concerned there are drugs being dealt out of it or something."

"Just waiting on a friend. He should be out soon," Drummond said with a friendly smile.

The uniformed man nodded. "Fine, but I must take down your name and information. Department rules, you see." He reached inside his jacket to ostensibly pull out his pad and pen, but instead extracted a 9mm pistol. Before Drummond could go for his own, the assassin fired three quick and accurate shots into his head, the last one catching the top edge of the lowered window. He stepped closer to the car, reached into his coat pocket and tossed several bundles of heroin into the vehicle. Then he immediately turned and sprinted away.

* * *

"What was that? Drummy, you good? What the heck?" But Boyd knew exactly what it was. He knew the sound of gunfire. When Drummond failed to respond, he decided to act. He sprinted down the alley toward the front of Nika's building, gun in hand. His immediate thoughts were prescient and few: the op was blown and now the only thing that mattered was getting everyone to safety.

A policeman wearing a thick black coat and a Taslon hat with fur-trimmed ear flaps suddenly stepped out of the shadows in front of him, squared off and began firing.

Boyd took three rounds to the chest before he knew what was happening. He tumbled face first onto the blacktop.

Focus on your breathing. Focus! Can't move. Breathe. Breathe.

A dark shadow fell over him.

The cop was now standing directly over him with a smirk of disdain on his face. He was about to say something, but when a bystander screamed, he turned and fled.

Seconds later, a small crowd began to encircle him, some coming closer than others. Most simply stood there like they were watching it on TV. No one offered him aid. A few had their cell phones up and were filming.

A wave of nausea quickly washed over him. He was lightheaded. He went to reach for the radio on his hip, but his fingers didn't respond. His mind caught up with events. He'd been shot. He looked down upon his chest and the rapidly blossoming flowers of crimson.

This is bad. This is very bad.

Air whistled through his lungs with each labored gasp. A round had to have hit him in the spine, because he was paralyzed, couldn't feel a thing from the neck down.

It was funny really, in a dark kind of way, the things now going through his mind as he lay there dying. The mass of people now gathering, camera phones out taking pictures and video of him.

Help me! Somebody, please help me!

He blinked, sucked air into his open mouth. His head pressed against the cold, hard surface, he continued leaking into the layer of salt and muck, the veneer of the street.

It was madness, the way the onlookers with their desensitized faces scrutinized every pained grunt, every phlegmy gasp, which were now becoming more and more shallow. The theater of death. His eyes blinked lazily. He could see their mouths moving. Why couldn't he hear them? For a few seconds, he studied the cloudy puffs of exhalation, wisps of steam rising out of his open wounds. He closed his eyes. It took him several seconds to open them. The light seemed dimmer, foggier. The air colder.

Lips feel dry. So dry. Where's my Chapstick? Pocket. It's in my pocket.

Boyd looked at his hand, a mere eight inches from his face. Useless. He willed himself to move. *MOVE!* But alas, the only movement that came was the almost imperceptible by now rising and falling of his own chest.

Why?

The assassin. He'd struck again.

His wife's face appeared. It was their wedding day and she was standing at the altar waiting for his reply of "I do." He closed his eyes, envisioned himself before God and witnesses, reaching out and embracing her delicate hand, placing the ring on her finger.

Without warning his mind flashed to another scene, this one in the future. There were men on his doorstep, breaking the news to his wife that he wouldn't be coming home this time. He wanted to console her, explain to her somehow that he was sorry. The news would surely devastate her, turn her life irrevocably upside down. She was pregnant after all. Their first. His eyes became moist as he considered the child he would never know. A tear streaked down his face and splashed onto the street. Urgently, he tried to focus. What would his precious little boy's face look like? What kind of man would he be without a father? Would he be proud of his dad? The agony. He would miss everything. Miss the joy of being a father for the first time. Unable to move, he lay there and motionlessly wept.

God, whoever you are, wherever you are, please watch over my family, protect them, comfort them.

If only he weren't feeling so tired. He fought the urge to sleep. He fought it with everything he had inside him. Then a warm sensation came over him and he passed over to the other side.

22

RAINEY had found a pay phone and dialed a number only to be used in case of emergency. A duty officer at Directorate Twelve headquarters had answered and quickly forwarded his call to Job. Without delay, Job had rattled off very specific instructions then immediately tried reaching Drummond and Boyd. But they'd failed to respond. He'd promised to keep trying.

Per Job's instructions, Rainey had then met a local support staff operative named, Georges-Henri Danvers, at a small office in the city center. Danvers had arranged for clandestine medical care with a small team of professionals who could be trusted to keep things quiet. Alcott was now out of commission, but he was alive.

Before racing off, Rainey had promised his old friend that he'd check in later. Alcott understood, of course. He had to get to the others, warn them. Before it was too late.

His shoulder was screaming. One of the doctors had pulled out the piece of metal and stitched the wound. Stitched up his leg, too, and given him some antibiotics to ward off infection. The seams had been neatly done but the pain had no regard for the doctor's handiwork. Hopefully, the painkillers would soon kick in. Until then he, too, would be grateful with just being alive.

Having left the Audi with Danvers to dispose of, Rainey now drove a silver Jeep Commander that had been arranged for his use. After all, the Audi was surely blown. Danvers had also provided him with a change of clothes to include a thick knit hat, which suited the purpose of hiding the big lump on his forehead.

Rainey parked the Jeep two blocks away and proceeded cautiously down the sidewalk along the rue Durocher. As he drew closer to Nika's building, his fears were validated.

He was too late.

Policemen swarmed the area. The streets around the apartment building were blocked off. There was a large crowd bellied up behind long bands of yellow crime scene tape, which ran up and down the block.

No!

Two bodies had been covered with white sheets. One in a car— Drummy's car. The other in the alley just around the corner of the building. No doubt about it. Drummond and Boyd had been assassinated. The team had been compromised.

The operation was a complete disaster.

23

THICK winter clouds the color of galvanized steel were steadily beginning to encroach upon the brightness of the day. Flurries, barely perceptible specks of white really, began to fall.

Reagan Rainey sat in the café just down the street from the grim scene in front of Nika's building, reviewing his options; there weren't many. He'd not yet returned to the safe house. He wasn't sure he could at this point. He and Alcott were doubtless presumed to be dead, but that would soon be dispelled when the news broke about how there'd been no bodies found in the warehouse ruins.

The items left in the safe house though could be damning. Would point right to Nika's building. A thorough investigation would yield something much more than a mere random act of violence. His laptop and team's collection of intel, if found, would open the flood gates. It would be all over the news: Americans illegally operating on Canadian soil. There would be a stink. A big one. It would create a major international incident. America would suffer. The Directorate would suffer. And right at the heart of it all, would be Job Jackson. He would be blamed for everything.

Rainey drank down his second bottle of water and worked to temper his righteous rage. He brightened though not outwardly. The bugs. Were they still operational? Or had they, too, been compromised? If they were still functioning, had they recorded anything useful? Didn't seem that the cops had stumbled onto Boyd's van yet, the equipment inside. But they would in time. It was time to tidy up.

It was time to be bold.

After slipping into Nika's building by way of Boyd's cable man routine, he was able to confirm what he already knew to be the case: Nika was long gone. Her place was cleaned out, the secret hide had been dumped, the empty box lay there on the mussed bedspread.

He found some balled-up tissues, some white gauze soaked with what appeared to be dried blood, and an empty vinyl Ziploc bag in the trash can in the kitchen. Rainey extracted the bag from the can and gave it a once-over. According to the small retailer's sticker, the bag had contained some weird-named green tea. He pushed it into Boyd's toolbox.

Rainey then checked the status of the electronic eavesdropping devices Boyd had planted. Miraculously, they were still intact. Apparently, they'd not been discovered. He removed them, placed them in the toolbox and took a moment to say a prayer for Drummy's and Boyd's families. Both men had given their lives for their country, but their families, too, had now sacrificed a large part of theirs as well. Boyd's wife was expecting, she would be crushed with the news. The swell of emotions, the fierce rage boiling within he again pressed deep down inside. He would save it until the time was right to let it loose. Rainey resolved himself to honor these men by not allowing the mission to fail. He would not quit on it, especially now. At all costs, he would press on.

Rainey looked both ways in the hallway before stepping out of the apartment. As he turned to walk down the hall, an old woman emerged from the room directly across the hall from Nika's. Her face was puckered and weathered. She looked to be in her late eighties. Her clothing was frumpy and threadbare. She was holding a calico tenderly in her arms. The same dang calico that he'd crossed paths with previously in Nika's apartment.

"Excusez-moi madame."

The woman cautiously eyed him up and down. There was no equivocation in the woman's body language. She was clearly suspicious of the strange man despite his cable man appearance. She was hesitant, withdrawing halfway back across the threshold.

Rainey seized on trying to put her mind at ease. "Yes, I understand, I must look absolutely dreadful." He pulled off his hat, exposing his forehead.

The woman's suspicious eyes instantly relaxed. She asked him with legitimate sympathy, "Are you okay child? That looks painful."

"Believe me, it is." He nodded back toward Nika's door. "See, I'm trying to find your neighbor across the hall. It's kind of important. There's a problem with her *wiring* and..." Rainey pointed to the cat. "Ah, I see you are tending her cat. You must rate pretty high with her."

The woman grinned and nodded her head. "Isidora was here, but she left. Just a few moments ago, actually. Asked me to look after her Buttercup while she is gone."

"Gone?"

"Yes. She said she is heading out of town again on another trip. I try to help her when I can as we are both single women, living alone in this city. Ah, she works at a travel agency—"

"I guess with all the fuss outside today, she forgot that I was coming." Rainey smiled and then winced while touching his head delicately, purposefully trying to appeal to the lady's sympathetic nature as much as possible. "Manager gave me the key, but I'd like to call her, let her know what's going on before we get to work. We're gonna have to move some things, it's gonna get messy. Do you have any way of contacting her? Maybe a cell phone number? We can't have those wires in there starting a fire. Yep, yep. Definitely need to take one of her walls apart. Ugh! What a mess."

The woman hesitated for only an instant. "I'm sorry, child." The old woman then just stood there, staring at Rainey's forehead as if it were an enigma.

"Okay. Well, thanks. I appreciate your help. Have a good day."

The woman smiled. "You, too."

* * *

When her phone rang, she looked at the display. She knew the number immediately. It belonged to the woman tending her cat. The same woman she had instructed to call should anyone come around asking questions. The old woman had obviously taken great care to remember what the inquisitor looked like. She described him as tall and dressed like a cable TV fix-it man. He was nice and polite, ruggedly good-looking with a warm, friendly smile and eyes the color of milk chocolate. His face was tan and devoid of facial hair.

But this was no cable TV fix-it man. It was him. It was Reagan Rainey.

After the brief conversation with the old lady, Nika punched out a number on another phone. A clean phone. She waited for the man on the other end to answer. When he finally did, she listened patiently for several long seconds. When the man was done talking, Nika said, "Okay." Then, without drawing attention to herself, she calmly separated the phone from its battery and joined the current of people descending into Bonaventure Station. As she descended the platform, she discreetly slipped the phone and battery into a folded newspaper and dropped it into a trash bin.

Finally, as the metro lurched forward, Nika sat down and took up what seemed a random conversation with an older gentleman in a Wool Stirling Parka without acting the least bit concerned about her enterprise.

24

A tall man wearing a long, black wool overcoat and expensive leather loafers set his suitcase down and bought a bottle of cranberry-pomegranate iced tea. He twisted the cap off and brought the bottle up to his mouth. Just above his upper lip, was a tiny scar that stood vertical just left of center—a souvenir from his youth. He took a chug then lit up a cigarette.

The man had the ostensible appearance of a tired executive on the last leg of an exhausting business trip abroad. But, in fact, he was not an executive and he never tired. The identification and credit card he had used to pay for his hotel room indicated his name was Vittorio Pugliano. But like his masterful Italian accent, his name was a dutiful fiction.

At this point in his life, Demyan Rostov was well-accustomed to using assumed identities. Strange as it was, his real name wasn't even real.

Born in the North Caucasus region of Dagestan, outside the city of Khasavyurt along the border of Chechnya, Rostov had no memory of his real name. But there were things he did remember. Like fear, horror, and despair. Rostov remembered at the tender age of four watching a group of Chechen rebels brutally murder his entire family after labeling them Russian spies. In actuality nothing could have been further from the truth. Yet somehow they'd been fingered as such and despite the desperate pleadings from the village elders to the contrary, the bloodthirsty savages could not be convinced otherwise. For reason was not necessary when it came to rooting out Russian spies.

Rostov was an ethnic Dargin yet grew up hating Islam, hating all religion. It was religion, he believed, that killed his family. Demyan Rostov, had grown to be tall and slender, handsome, in fact, with dark hair, coal black eyes, and white skin that tanned easily. He was perfect in his benefactor's eyes.

When the young Russian intelligence officer had found him, he was destitute and nutritionally deficient, doomed to a premature death. But Levka Borovsky and those to whom he answered, changed all that. They might not have loved him in the traditional sense, but they cared for him, gave him a purpose for living.

Rostov was raised in the secret training camp until his eighteenth birthday. It was a place few knew even existed, even among Russia's tightest intelligence circles. A place where he and some others—he didn't actually know how many there were in total—had been trained exceedingly well. Trained in all sorts of disciplines. Espionage, linguistics, communications. Above all, they were trained to be secret, invisible killers.

Assassins.

Initially, Borovsky and his bosses had planned to use Rostov and the others to infiltrate the Chechen forces, but Demyan Rostov in particular, with his special features and special talents, had proved himself far too valuable for that.

It was ironic that Rostov's family had been murdered for being falsely accused of being Russian spies, since in a sense, he now was one. A creation of their paranoia and hatred.

After exiting the hotel, his business in Montreal concluded, he hailed a cab. While en route to the train station, his phone vibrated inside his pocket. A new text message. He read it without emotion then quickly thumbed opened the DRAFTS folder in the e-mail account through which he and Kupchenko communicated. He carefully read the e-mail before deleting it. After he was finished, he slipped the phone back into the inner breast pocket of his coat.

Rostov coughed. Must have picked up something. He leaned forward to the cabbie and with a thick Italian accent calmly implored,

"*Signore*, change of plans, I'm afraid. If you would be so kind to re-route me to the rue Saint Paul, *per favore*. Business calls yet again."

"No problem," huffed the heavy-set man behind the wheel.

The assassin relaxed back in his seat after extinguishing his cigarette in the ashtray of the cab door. He exhaled a final cloud of blue smoke and then popped a cough drop into his mouth. As the cool eucalyptus began to clear his sinuses, his mind drifted back to the woman he'd bedded outside Barcelona three weeks prior.

What was her name? Candela?

Yes. Candela. That's it.

25

IT was extremely risky. If the team had been compromised, the safe house might have been, too, but he had to take the chance. Everything he needed was there. Plus he needed to cover the team's tracks. From the news report he'd just heard on the car stereo, emergency responders were still digging through the warehouse remains. Thus the presumption that he and Alcott were dead was still viable.

Rainey blamed himself for everything that had gone wrong. And that stupid cat. Nika knew they were on to her and she'd set them up. Maybe even killed Drummond and Boyd herself. She was Kidon after all.

Rainey parked a block away from the apartment complex in which the safe house was situated. For several minutes, he analyzed the likely observation posts of a surveillance detail. If anyone were keeping an eye on the place they were doing a phenomenal job of staying out of sight.

He made his way up the spiral wrought-iron staircase on the back of the building and entered the apartment without making a sound. He stopped the moment it struck him. The faint odor of eucalyptus like that from a cough drop mingled with cigarettes.

Someone had been here. Might even still be here.

Rainey drew his gun and tactically began clearing each room one by one. When he reached the master bedroom, he paused.

The door was closed.

He thrust his foot into the door and swung into the room, sweeping his gun back and forth. From out of nowhere, a lightning fast arm lashed out snapping down across the top of his wrists. The shocking pain caused the gun to fall from his grip. The pistol bounced off the bedframe with a loud clang before it thudded to the floor. The assailant quickly swept the gun away, shuffled his feet and prepared to lunge.

Rainey caught a glimpse of a shiny blade in the bedroom mirror. It must have been ten inches long, maybe more. With absolute fury, the intruder swung it in a wide, horizontal arc. Rainey managed to push off and dodge out of the way before it could flay open his abdomen. The knife chinked against the metal drawer handle of the dresser behind him throwing off a spark.

Rainey countered by moving in fast and closing the distance. With his left hand, he grabbed the intruder's wrist just above the knife and at the same time drove his right fist into the other man's jaw. Continuing as if in one motion, Rainey immediately latched onto the man's torso, spun, and executed a judo throw. The man slammed into the nightstand across the room. A lamp shattered as it hit the floor. Rainey grabbed the alarm clock from the bed stand and threw a fastball at the man's head, but the man moved his head to the side at the last second and the clock shattered the window behind him and fell to the street below.

For a brief moment, they stood there squared off at each other, their eyes locked. Neither man showed an ounce of fear. Each bore the look of a dangerous predator.

Rainey reached over and snatched up the standing lamp and with a quick tug, ripped the cord from the wall. He swiped the shade off and held it like a staff. The men stalked each other, circling, waiting for the other to make the first move. Rainey was patient and did not react to several of the other man's feints. The man lunged again with the knife. Rainey blocked it with the top of the lampstand then countered by swinging the base upward in a roundhouse-type move from left to right. It caught the assassin square on the chin, but the man shrugged it off and just smiled.

"You are good, my friend." The man took a breath then jumped forward with the speed of a cheetah. With even more force than before, he slashed upward with the knife.

Rainey deflected the knife away with the lampstand again, this time following up with a push kick to create space. The warm, wet sensation on his leg was immediate. The assassin had drawn blood. Unless he disarmed this guy soon, he'd draw a lot more.

Again the intruder lunged with the blade. This time though Rainey threw the lampstand into the man's face and with both of his hands immediately locked onto the knife hand at the wrist. He also delivered a right knee hard to the groin. The man grunted loudly. Seizing on the split-second distraction, Rainey quickly rotated the knife hand clockwise then counterclockwise trying to lock out the man's elbow.

In a flash, Rainey executed another judo throw and both men went sprawling to the floor. But the other man pulled off a crafty reverse. Both still locked together—a two-man scrum for the knife— the assailant now had the top position. The knife was squarely pointed down at Rainey's face.

. The assassin began to push slowly and steadily downward using his body weight, literally inching the knife closer and closer to Rainey's right eye. Rainey resisted against the powerful force with everything in him.

The man hissed through gritted teeth, spittle in the corners of his mouth. "Well, Mr. Rainey, are you ready to die this time?"

Rainey snarled as he pressed upward with all his strength. His arm and shoulder muscles burned. His whole upper body now was starving for oxygen.

Demyan Rostov smiled despite the strained muscles in his face and neck. He sucked a quick breath of air. "You've caused me a great deal of embarrassment. This time I will *watch* you die."

Rainey remained focused and said nothing as he continued to counter the man's downward force. No question about it, this man was very powerful. How much more did he have in the tank before this guy, whoever he was, plunged the blade through his eye socket and into his brain? He had faced mortal danger plenty of times on the battlefield in Iraq and Afghanistan and other places and often considered the stark reality of a warrior's death. But this was not how he wanted to die—in a CIA safe house in Canada of all places.

No.

No!

I am not going to die today.

He had only two things left: willpower and rage. Although the former was considerable, it was the latter that fueled him to go on. Rage from the depths of his existence. Now was the time to let it out.

Rainey shifted his hips rapidly and at the same time threw up his right leg across the other man's face and quickly locked his ankles together. In the same motion, he twisted the man's knife hand so the tip of the blade was pointed away from him, then pulled the hand against his chest with both arms, trapping it there with his wrists. Keeping his ankles hooked together, he stretched out both legs while driving his hips forward. Rainey had the man in a jiu-jitsu move called an arm bar. It was one that put an enormous amount of pressure on the trapped arm, particularly at the elbow joint.

Rainey pulled back hard, then harder yet. He continued to wrench the arm as far back as he could. There were crunching sounds in the man's elbow as tendons and bones gave way. The man screamed in agony. Forced to react or suffer more damage to his arm, the man violently writhed and bucked. His free hand somehow managed to land on Rainey's gun and he quickly claimed it off the floor.

CRACK! CRACK!

Two rounds slammed into the wall just above Rainey's forehead. He released his grip on the man's left arm and kicked at the gun. It flew in the air and clattered against the baseboard on the far corner of the room. All of this allowed the assassin to wriggle his badly injured arm free after which he rolled over and delivered a hammer fist to Rainey's face. Then in an instant, he was on his feet and sprinting out of the room.

Rainey's eyes were watering, his nose bleeding profusely but that didn't stop him from giving chase to his assailant. When he hit the dark street outside, the man was already half a block away.

The man dodged through oncoming traffic. Horns blared. Tires screeched. People yelled curses. Rainey pursued him for two full city blocks. Even with a bad arm, the guy was lightning fast. Rainey lost sight of him after he'd entered a crowd of people. It was no use.

The guy was gone.

26

RAINEY returned to the apartment. He had just cheated death. Again. Going back to the safe house had been a really dumb move and it had nearly cost him his life.

Thank you, Lord. Thank you.

He retrieved his gun from the bedroom and the rest of his gear including his laptop and files that Alcott had hidden in the safe house safe. He also grabbed an HK UMP and several mags of ammo. Throwing everything into the Jeep, he pulled out and sped off. He cast a furtive glance in the rearview mirror. He looked like a savage. His nose wasn't broken but it sure was a mess. Using his shirt sleeves, he wiped the blood from his face.

After a few miles, he pulled into a mall parking lot to think and to clean up. Fifteen minutes later, he pulled out the burner phone he'd brought from the safe house. He dialed a number at Directorate Twelve headquarters and waited.

"Hello?"

"It's me."

Job hesitated, then said, "You know this line isn't secure."

"Yeah, I know. But we're past that at this point. The team's been compromised. I don't know how or by whom, but we're blown. The safe house, everything."

"I don't understand how that's possible."

"Nevertheless, two men are dead. My old buddy and yours truly almost suffered the same fate."

"What do you need?"

"I need to know if there were any calls from the number I'm about to give you, and if so, I want to know where to, who to, the works." Rainey rattled off the phone number for the old woman across the hall from Nika. He'd found it in the intel Alcott had acquired prior to his arrival in Montreal. It was perhaps a long shot, but a long shot was all he had at this point. He'd already scanned the recordings from the bugs in Nika's room and found nothing more than the ten-second call that Boyd had picked up after the team hit the apartment. From that call, they'd gotten the phone number/phone that led them to the warehouse. They'd been set up and Nika was the one responsible. All because of that stupid cat.

"I'll see what I can do."

"And send someone for our boys, too."

"Absolutely. I—"

Click. The phone went dead.

Thirty minutes later, Job called back on a secure line. He relayed what he'd found out: the old lady had made one call to a number to this point unknown. A series of checks had been run on this mystery number. Job related how this mystery number was linked to several incoming and outgoing calls and text messages belonging to another number though that number was no longer active. It was a goat trail of digital breadcrumbs. Metadata put the phone connected to that number in an area about 160 miles northwest of Montreal, in a town called Sainte-Anne-du-Lac.

"I'm sending some people your way to deal with our friends. They'll be in Montreal in an hour."

"Good."

"I hope you're not gonna do what I think you're planning to do."

There was a pause. "I'll be in touch." Rainey disconnected the call, removed the battery and SIM card.

* * *

He sifted through recent events as he drove. He had the distinct feeling that he was being hunted now. They knew the location of the safe house for crying out loud. It was glaringly obvious: the Montreal team had been sold out by someone within the Agency or even within the Directorate. Though the latter was difficult to comprehend, anything was possible. Without question, the Agency assassinations were linked to Montreal, to the abduction of Dr. Horst but how? And why? His mind was swirling.

He needed to find Nika. That was the only way he was going to uncover the answers to the questions ricocheting around inside his head.

Turning onto the Laurentian Autoroute, Rainey checked his mirrors, gripped the steering wheel and punched the gas pedal to the floor.

The hunt was on.

27

JOB sat in his office, mulling over Rainey's call and the developments in Montreal. If there was anything he knew for sure, especially now, it was the fact that Rainey would hunt those responsible regardless of what he had to say about it. He knew Reagan Rainey to the core. It was pointless to argue with him right now, and besides, he himself was boiling with anger. Truth be told, he wanted Rainey set loose on whoever was betraying America. They had no idea who was coming for them.

He paced around his office. He didn't want to believe it, but what else could explain it? Very few people outside of D12 knew about the Montreal team. Could Ken Thompson or Sean Vajda be the mole? Or was it someone actually within the Directorate? He didn't want to even begin contemplating that. Rainey would find answers. He must. If the past were a predictor of the future, his surrogate son—hands down America's best warrior spy—would not rest until he did. The Directorate and America were counting on him to do just that.

God be with him.

28

Northwest of Montreal

THE more he thought about it, the angrier he became. And likewise the angrier he became, the faster he drove. Vladislav Kozlov banged the dash with a hammer fist and swore loudly, the thoughts in his mind swirling as he tried to make sense of everything.

A bevy of bifurcated lines ran long and deep across Kozlov's forehead and on either side of his dark eyes. His robust, muscular shoulders were drawn together in a vice-like fashion holding within their fibers his internalized white hot rage that contradicted his usually cold, calculating demeanor. His face bore it, too—nose snarled, lips pulled taut, utter anxiety radiating across his jawline. From what Kupchenko had related to him, he knew in his gut this Delta guy was going to be trouble and trouble was the last thing he needed right now. The team had to move ASAP. He couldn't jeopardize all the hard work they had put into the mission thus far.

Kozlov checked his rearview mirror, caught a glimpse of himself, the worry in his eyes. It was a look that angered him even more. He couldn't shake the feeling that they were being followed even though there was clearly no one behind them. He silently looked over at Nika. She back at him.

"What? What is it?" she probed.

"Nothing. We leave Canada tonight."

Nika nodded. "Good."

The truck's powerful V-8 engine roared as they passed another motorist and forged on chasing the horizon. After this operation was over, he would disappear for a while. Norway or Finland. As long as it was cold like back home. He was desperate to return to his homeland, to Mother Russia, but there was just no way that was ever going to be possible. A memory of his youth back in Murmansk trickled like a mountain stream through his mind bringing with it a serenity, a calm. For a few seconds the intensity in his face softened. The moment was fleeting, however, as he forced himself back to the task at hand and his previous granite glare returned to its full glory.

29

Sainte-Anne-du-Lac, Quebec

THE terrain consisted of a thick forest of conifers and rocky outcroppings of various sizes, some as big as a car, others barely visible. They jutted out at all manner of angles, too. Everything here was covered with a fresh layer of heavy snow and ice.

He'd left the main road twenty minutes ago. Aided by the illumination of a gleaming sickle moon against the bright snow, he followed a gravel track without the use of his headlights. A lake lay beneath the ridge on which he now precariously climbed. He drove deep into the snowy wilderness. This place brought back memories of a certain lake in the Adirondacks, where he and his family vacationed years ago.

Stay focused, Ray.

Approximately half a mile from where Job had digitally pinpointed the phone, Rainey pulled over and covered the Jeep as best he could. He would traverse the rest of the way on foot. Before heading off through the dense coniferous foliage, he quickly examined a map of the area via his laptop. It was a perfect place to hide someone. It was literally the middle of nowhere. Probably have to put that on the shipping label to have something delivered out here.

He kitted up, strapping to his chest a suppressed HK UMP 9. His pistol was now holstered on his right hip. Rainey jammed a handful of extra magazines for both guns into the pockets of his jacket then adjusted the neckline of his soft-shell bulletproof vest. As he cinched up his tactical gloves, he studied the landscape like a predator. He checked his six then gently closed the trunk, careful not to make a sound.

Rainey began walking. Magnified by the snow, the moonlight made it relatively easy to trek through the woods without the use of night optics. His footsteps fell nearly silent save for little crunching sounds as he moved across the new layer of powder that blanketed the forest floor.

Just shy of a quarter mile into the woods, he crept up to a rocky ridge that lay under a canopy of low-hanging conifer branches. There in the distance, maybe three hundred yards away, was a rather large chalet. Parked beside it were two four-wheel-drive vehicles. Beyond them, a quartet of snowmobiles. Through the trees far below, a long flat expanse: Lac L'Allier. It's frozen surface was covered in an unadulterated sheet of the whitest snow. The picture of serenity.

Rainey extracted an ATN Voyager 5-3P night vision binocular from his rucksack, popped the lens cap and for a few minutes surveyed the building and the possible routes of ingress and egress. His attention quickly turned to two men. Sentries. They were patrolling the area surrounding the chalet—one near the front and one deeper into the woods. Each man held a tricked-out SIG SG-552 Commando assault rifle and wore a vest chock full of extra magazines and other gear. The one closest to him was smoking. Between drags on his cigarette, the man blew large clouds of warm second-hand smoke into the air which easily gave away his position. This guy was not a pro. Or else he was a pro who had grown lazy with boredom.

Rainey tactically withdrew and quietly weaved his way through the ragged branches and undergrowth, circling his way around to the other side of the chalet. A garage had been cut right into the side of the mountain. A small, shed-type building was tucked away into the fringe of the tree line.

Moving further around to the back of the chalet, Rainey tucked into a tight little crevice in a rocky outcropping betwixt two pines. He paid special attention to the aptitude of the security element. Another man soon came into view, moseying through the woods without much care. He was smoking, too.

These guys are probably bored out of their minds out here.

Rainey scanned the span of the chalet, back and forth, every window, every ledge. Nothing went unnoticed. Then something, nay, someone caught his eye. He darted the binocular back to the window and adjusted its focus.

Movement in a second-floor window.

The light in the room was dim but it was clearly a silhouette of a man. He adjusted his focus again. The man's face. Just can't make—
A light flicked on inside the room. Rainey's eyes widened with elation. There, framed in the window, was the missing scientist, Dr. Edward Horst. He looked no worse for the wear, save a swelled, black and blue shiner on the right side of his face. Otherwise he appeared in decent shape.

And there. There, too, was...

Vladislav Kozlov.

The big man was standing in front of Horst; he looked seriously pissed off. The former Russian Spetsnaz soldier slapped the scientist hard across the face then grabbed him by the neck. He then pulled a gun and pressed it against Horst's forehead, held it there while another man plunged a syringe into his right arm.

Rainey's natural instincts were to fall back. Call it in and wait for numbers. But even if he did that, how could he be sure the intel wouldn't be intercepted somehow by whomever had put the assassin with the coal black eyes onto the team's trail back in Montreal? Drummond and Boyd were dead and Alcott, based on his last check, had used up eight of his nine lives. He was the only option left. It was after all his butt on the line out here. And this was his domain. His sanctuary. The scientist was alive, but for how much longer he couldn't be sure.

Besides, it was far better to apologize after the fact than to ask for permission and be told to stand down. And be compromised at the same time.

No. He would proceed.

Alone.

30

CROUCHED down behind a truck-size rock only ten yards away from the back door of the chalet, Rainey held still as the sentry nearest him stopped, fired up a fresh cigarette and gave it a long deep drag. The man's left hand lazily rested on the hilt of his rifle, its barrel now slouched toward the ground. He was smoking with his strong hand, too. His gun hand. Bad move.

With one last check of the area, Rainey took a step forward but quickly pulled back as a familiar noise broke the silence.

The sentry bolted upright, flicked his cig into the snow. The man put his left finger to his ear and looked skyward. His lips were moving. It was difficult to make out what he was saying through the clouds of hot breath. After his radio transmission, the sentry murmured something to himself—a curse word—rather loudly. In Russian.

Splitting his attention between the sentry and the growing clamor, Rainey located its source. The chopper was coming in from the east. Rainey swiveled around, his back now against the large gray rock. The helicopter set down in a clearing about three hundred yards in the distance, directly north of his position. The rotors kept spinning. Whoever just arrived did not intend to stay long.

Rainey maintained his perfect silence. After a few minutes, there was rustling in the forest. A pair of men appeared, walking at a fast clip down a narrow trail. The first man was a large and husky brute, armed with an AKS-74U. Looked like the bodyguard type. The man behind him was tall and thin and older. The bodyguard lit the space in front of them with a small blue LED light obviously with a mind for tactics. The older guy impatiently pushed ahead. He was armed with one of those big D-cell flashlights with the halogen bulb, its bright cone of light sweeping back and forth against black tree trunks with each step.

"Come on, Ivan! There is nothing to worry about out here. Move it," said the older man in a vapid, Russian groan.

Rainey ducked down and froze, holding his breath, so not even a cloud of condensed air would give him away. He waited as both men passed, no more than ten yards away. After they were by him, Rainey poked his head up slowly. The sentry opened the back door and the two new arrivals entered without saying a word.

From his position, Rainey didn't get a clean view of the new-comers' faces. But for the older guy to have an armed personal escort, he had to be someone of considerable import in the broader picture. Maybe someone to whom Kozlov answered.

This could be big.

Rainey crept out from behind the rock, turned so that his back was about two inches off the stone wall of the house and stealthily approached the sentry now posted on the back door. Like a tiger stalking its prey, Rainey stepped with great care, inching closer and closer. And then in an instant, he was on him. All in one motion, he clamped his left hand over the sentry's mouth while at the same time he raked his knife deep across the man's exposed throat from left to right. The sentry tensed for a brief moment. Blood shot into the air in a wide arc. Careful to stay out of its path, Rainey quietly forced the dying man to the ground and knelt on top of him, till he was completely still.

He plucked the radio off the man's vest, the earpiece from his ear. He quickly inserted the earpiece into his own ear. He remained still for several seconds, crouched down along the chalet listening for radio traffic. But there was none. The only sound was the rhythm of his own slightly elevated heartbeat.

Rainey scooped up the lifeless man and placed him behind a near-by rock, then with his boot, swept snow over the fresh deposits of blood.

Throwing his sub-gun around to his back, Rainey used the sturdy metal spouting and brackets on the stone wall like a ladder. He climbed quietly, paused on a ledge that jutted out just above the second floor. Like a mountain goat, Rainey eased upward until he was high enough to peek over the ledge. Another sentry stood by a weathered wooden door on a landing that ran the length of the building. He seemed to be playing a game on his cell phone or maybe he was texting someone. In any case, he had his head down. Rainey lowered himself back down over the ledge. These guys' TTPs (tactics, techniques, and procedures) were horribly sloppy.

He pulled his silenced 9mm pistol from his holster and gripped it in his gloved right hand. The toes of his boots gripping a bracket on the wall, he balanced himself and then rose back up gently over the ledge using his leg muscles and holding the spouting with only his left hand. He brought the pistol up smoothly and aimed at the guard's head.

The gun kicked in his hand. There was a subtle splashing sound just before the man fell over into a freshly shoveled pile of snow.

* * *

"Sasha, that you?" The sentry in the woods knew he'd heard something—a metallic clicking sound. He turned his attention toward the back of the chalet, while at the same time furtively readying his rifle.

No response.

He leaned around the corner of the building and began to scan for Sasha.

Probably snuck off to take a leak.

Better find him though. The Colonel was here. If he or Vlad found the back of the house unprotected, the whole security force would suffer mightily.

* * *

Rainey heard the hushed Russian tongue checking on his buddy through the earpiece.

He slinked along the landing and edged out over the lip of gray stone. The man had his gun shouldered, but still wasn't ready for a fight. And he paid for it with his life. Rainey fired one round from his

UMP into the man's face and then quickly did the same to another sentry who had also come to investigate the alien clicking sound.

He prepared for a barrage of well-armed commandos to come vomiting out of the chalet, but instead there was only silence.

He had to move quickly now, before the dead sentries were discovered. He returned to the back of the house and mapped out in his mind where he had seen Horst and how it correlated with the likely layout of the interior of the building. Without a sound, he approached the heavy wooden door that led out onto the landing. It was unlocked. He stepped inside with extreme caution, his eyes scanning. Just inside the door was an alcove that led into a grand hallway. He turned left, in the direction of the room in which he'd seen the DARPA scientist minutes ago.

Swiftly, he moved down the hallway. When he reached the room, he swept in smoothly. His gun up and ready to fire controlled bursts, he was prepared for a storm of violence. Instead, he found the scientist sitting peacefully by himself. His right sleeve was unbuttoned and disheveled from having been pushed up on his arm. Horst looked up with lazy eyes. He was rocking back and forth a little, as if he were about to doze off.

"Doctor Horst." Rainey whispered.

There was a glimmer of recognition from the man at the mention of his name.

"Doctor Edward Horst, I'm an American and I've come to get you outta here."

Horst looked confused, his eyes unfocused. He grinned. Every movement slugglish.

"Doctor Horst!"

"Laser… Plane… *Boom*." The man was apparently under the influence of a powerful narcotic.

Rainey spun at the sound of voices—Russian voices—echoing down the hall.

Someone was coming.

He leaned toward the doorway. It was difficult to make out what they were saying, but— Wait. They were discussing Horst. *He'd been drugged… The chopper… They were going to move him.*

Rainey crept forward and peeked around the doorway. Suddenly, there was movement in his peripheral vision. A man had just emerged from a room to his right. The man's eyes jolted wide open at the sight of him; he instantly went for the pistol on his hip.

Rainey quickly brought up his UMP and pulled the trigger. Two suppressed rounds bore into the man's chest, dropping him to the floor.

He quickly looked back to his left and saw two men now running toward him. One of them yelled something.

Then all hell broke loose.

31

KOZLOV briskly walked down the hall with the Colonel, at his side. He filled the older man in with what had transpired thus far in Montreal. He also vented about the assassin's failures.

"The American should be dead by now!"

"I can't argue with you there," said Vasili Tupitsyn. "But I don't have time for that. That's within Pyotr's purview. The chopper is probably already drawing attention. We need to get moving."

Vasili Tupitsyn, aka the Colonel, was an officer with the GRU—Russian military intelligence. Normally stationed in the Russian embassy in Ottawa as a military attaché, he'd been conscripted by Levka Borovsky to collect the scientist and his work product and bring them back to Moscow.

"He's been prepped. Should be good to go now. He'll be docile for around twenty hours or so." Kozlov handed Tupitsyn a small duffel bag. "His notes and calculations."

Tupitsyn glanced inside, seeing several spiral-bound notebooks and computer discs. Satisfied, he zipped up the bag. "I want nothing left behind. When you clear out, I want there to be no evidence of any kind. Do you understand? Nothing."

"*Da.* I will see to it personally."

In unison, the two men stopped in their tracks. It was a sound they each knew well. They pressed on carefully to the corner of the large hall.

Kozlov took a target glance. He saw a man peeking out of the room in which Horst was being staged. The shock of it all though didn't trespass into his muscle memory. He immediately broke into a sprint while drawing his sidearm and began firing.

Tupitsyn did the same.

* * *

As rounds snapped off the stone wall around him, Rainey dove into an alcove and quickly got to a kneeling position. He fired several suppressive rounds then looked across the hall. The door to the landing was directly across from him. He quickly leaned out and ripped off a few more bursts at the two men advancing toward him. His two targets dodged for cover. It was only a glance, but… The man on the left. Definitely Kozlov.

A sentry armed with a carbine, came running toward him from down the hall in the opposite direction. He was pinned down now from both sides. In the middle of a gunfight, it was normally very ill-advised to move from a position of good cover, but in this case he had to. He couldn't stay here. He had maybe a handful of seconds until more men would likely race to the area and finish him off with superior firepower.

The earpiece suddenly came alive. Men were yelling urgently in Russian.

Have to move. Now.

Rainey burst from the alcove, raced across the hall for the door leading outside. As he did so, the sentry tracked his movement with the muzzle of his carbine. Gunfire raked the wood and stone inches behind him. High-velocity rounds whirred and whined, ricocheting down the hall. A spray of splintered wood and chipped rock showered him as he made it through the door and back out onto the icy landing. He pulled the door shut behind him which made a loud *whomp*.

"Watch your crossfire!" Kozlov began barking commands to his people over the radio. "Everyone! We move. Now! Ivan, get him out of here!"

Ivan. The bodyguard? Him. The older guy? Or Horst. The chopper. They're going to exfil to the chopper.

Rainey rushed out onto the landing, looked both ways. He hustled over a few yards to the left, turned and knelt just as the door he'd just exited flew open. He fired two three-shot bursts into the sentry. The man tumbled into the ice and snow that had been pushed along either side of the doorway.

What to do.

Can't leave. Horst is here. Won't leave him behind. But they have numbers. Gotta retreat for now. Need a plan.

Rainey stepped up on a knee-wall that ran the length of the landing. The snow had already been brushed off so he didn't have to worry about leaving footprints to betray his escape route. With his chest to the wall, he reached up and over his head until he had a firm grip on the green, oxidized copper spouting. Then, while pushing off of the wall with his boot, he pulled himself up onto the roof of the portico. Once he'd gained leverage, he shimmied quickly back from the edge. He was now on the roof looking down on the rear of the chalet.

The door banged open. There were angry grunts and heavy breathing below. Boots shuffling on the stone slab landing. They were searching for him. Men ran to the edge of the landing and peered over.

Rainey turned his attention to a line of fast-moving silhouettes now hurrying away through the woods. Several of them were heavily armed. One had a ponytail. They were headed toward the helicopter, flashlights whipping back and forth as they ran. The chopper's blades were already spinning up faster now.

When the train of people were a safe distance away, a series of floodlights came alive that lit up the area around the chalet bright as day. He whipped back from the edge just as enemy rounds began penetrating the portico beside him. He'd been spotted.

Rainey scurried backward out of the line of fire. He stood up and glanced around, searching for a way out.

There.

A tree approximately thirty inches in diameter and ten feet from the side of the chalet, beckoned. Rainey swung his submachine gun around to his back and darted right for it. Planting his foot just shy of the edge, he jumped with all his might. He sailed through the air into the murky shadows that skirted the looming building. When he slammed into the tree, he hugged it tightly, digging his fingertips into the cold tree bark, like a koala bear. Ignoring the impact to his groin, he quickly slid to the ground using the tree like an improvised fireman's pole.

* * *

Kozlov continued shouting orders over the radio to the three sentries left behind to deal with the Delta Force man. "Make sure he's dead and destroy everything. Everything! Your lives depend on it."

When they reached the helicopter, Kozlov slammed his fist into the seat in front of him. *How did he find us?!* His blood boiled with rage. He'd lost a good man tonight. Andrei Zukov was one of his best. He stared down onto the landscape awash in floodlights. He knew the Colonel was seething with rage as well. Everything they'd work so long and so hard for had nearly gone up in smoke.

* * *

Rainey crouched behind one of the snowmobiles. He was helpless to do anything about Kozlov and the others getting away. He shook his head as the chopper rose up and then Dopplered away over the treetops.

A stick snapped in the woods off to his left. Rainey held perfectly still, shielding the glare of the floodlights from his eyes. He squinted into the darkness. There. Between the trees. A shadow appeared then was gone just as quickly. Then the floodlights flicked off. That could only mean one thing: these guys had night vision capability.

Crap!

Rainey fingered the earpiece. A man was whispering over the radio, updating the others, instructing them to make their way around to his side of the chalet. "We'll pinch him. Let me know when you're in position."

Thank God for the earpiece. Time to move.

Rainey slid over behind a big tree and sneaked a peek. At that very moment, chunks of the tree exploded next to his head. Shards of the pulverized bark bit at his face.

He leaned out, fired off a return volley then immediately dodged off as a sentry let loose with his carbine. The man's voice over the radio was booming and raspy. The man shouted for the others to give chase. They would push him to the shoreline, where their interloper would run out of real estate and trees and rocks to hide behind.

Think, Ray! Think!

Bullets snapped at his heels, kicking up dirt and sullying snow. Rainey gripped his sub-gun with both hands, pointed it over his left shoulder and fired. After two rounds, it clicked empty.

* * *

The three sentries joined up and pressed on at a dangerous pace, pushing their prey further and further to the lake's edge. Suddenly, there was a loud racket in the woods ahead, like a large tree had fallen.

The lead sentry smiled.

We got him.

32

RAINEY could feel them on his heels, hear their grunts, their heavy panting. Black bears crashing through the forest. They were leading him into a trap. Soon he'd have no place to go. He had to come up with a way to use that against them. But how?

With his pursuers closing the distance, Rainey hit the magazine release on the side of his gun and retrieved a fresh one from his pocket. Scampering through the undergrowth, he slammed the mag into his gun and hit the bolt catch. He pivoted to fire. But as he did, his foot skidded several inches then caught a rock causing him to stumble awkwardly backward. Rainey toppled, banged against a tree and began cart-wheeling down the sharp descent, which progressively grew steeper and steeper. He pawed for something, anything as he picked up speed. He was completely out of control.

The lake loomed closer and closer as he tumbled. In a few seconds, he'd reach the shoreline where there was a drop-off of about ten feet. Rainey sprawled wildly. With true urgency, he reached out for something to grab on to. A branch. A rock. Anything. He was simply going too fast.

And that's when they fired. Again and again.

The shock of the icy cold water almost made him gasp. If he had though his lungs would now be full of 38-degree water. He'd crashed right through the frozen surface and was now trapped beneath it.

More shots.

An angry downpour of bullets probed the ice and water leaving little white streaks of air bubbles in their wake. Several hit him. However, due to the scientific characteristics of distance and density, the water absorbed much of the rounds' momentum. Thus even though it stung, the tiny lead torpedoes did no real damage. Kind of like being pelted by rocks. But the sheer volume of gunfire was unrelenting.

Swimming in water at this temperature, he had maybe a minute before his fine motor skills were gone, but he wasn't just swimming; he was underwater. The situation was dire. The brain could only endure so much. His cognitive abilities would decline in mere seconds. And of course, he had to hold his breath, too.

Rainey swam deep at first, avoiding the gunfire, then paralleled the shore. When far enough away from the hole he'd created with his body, he swam toward the rocky coast. Clumsily, his feet struck bottom.

The pounding in his eyes was almost unbearable, the icy water on them excruciating. His brain actually hurt. His body was already trembling. He wasn't going to last long like this. He had to get out before it was too late.

33

THE three men stood over the gaping hole in the ice. They continued firing into the abyss, sweeping back and forth from jagged edge to jagged edge. The effects of the cold water on the human body were obvious. If the American wasn't already dead, he would have to surface soon. And when he did, they would riddle him with bullets.

After ten seconds of continuous fire, they quieted their weapons and waited. The undulating inky water settled to a sheet of black glass. There was now complete silence. The man in charge smiled. Finally satisfied their prey was dead, one way or the other, he patted his subordinates on the shoulder and jerked his head back toward the chalet. They had to work quickly. There would soon be swarms of police descending upon the whole area.

* * *

The gunfire had stopped. There was silence above the ice but a raging storm inside his head and now his lungs. He had already begun to lose sensation in his fingers. The extreme pain in his eyes was nearly unbearable. They felt as if they were literally going to explode. He had to take the chance. Now. If he were killed in the process, so be it. Better a result of action than inaction.

His hands clumsily retrieved the knife from the Kydex sheath on his left leg. The SOG SEAL Pup was all black, the blade nearly five inches long. In fact, he had just used it minutes ago to kill the first sentry. He'd used knives many times in his career. A good knife could truly be a lifesaver in his business, but he'd never envisioned ever using one quite like this.

Mentally forcing the numbness from his limbs, Rainey stood squarely on the bottom of the lake while he positioned the tip of the blade against the ice. He pushed upward with a controlled motion then began pounding his palm against the hilt. Feverishly, he punched a hole in the ice the diameter of his knife.

Not big enough. Can't breathe.

He raced to unscrew the silencer on his UMP. He stuck one end in his mouth and the other he inched up through the hole. Using it like a snorkel, he blew out the standing water then took a few gulps of oxygen.

Beautiful, heavenly oxygen.

The cold air stung his lungs. After he sucked in another breath, he spit out the silencer and urgently punched out a hole big enough for his head to fit through. The extreme temperature of the water made it feel as if his head were in a vice—a vice that was getting tighter and tighter. He'd never been so cold.

A loud voice from years ago in training: *"Get out of my pool!"*

His body responded sluggishly. Its natural responses to conserve heat were causing him to lose command of his fine motor skills and his mental focus.

Rainey stuck his head through the hole, cleared the water. He gasped for air.

Get control! You're good. You're sitting by a fire. It's summer in the desert. It's hot... Not working. It's freezing!

He took small controlled breaths. Under normal conditions, he could stay like this for maybe twenty minutes if he had to. He wouldn't like it, of course, and the odds for hypothermia setting in increased exponentially with each passing second, but he could do it. However, in this case, his head was wet and the water was already beginning to freeze in his hair and on his eyelashes.

He searched the coastline in earnest. Were they still there, standing on the beach with their weapons ready to shred him? Praise God, they were gone. Were they hiding in the woods, lying in wait for him to appear from the water? No. They had the upper hand directly over the hole in the ice. There would be no better practical strategy than that.

It's safe.

Rainey finished carving away the ice until he had made a hole large enough for his entire frame to fit through. He reached out through the hole and dug the blade of the knife into the snow-covered ice. With both hands wrapped around the hilt, he jumped up and pulled himself out of the icy water. He lay there for several seconds on the frozen surface like a beached whale.

His face was a mask of exasperation. He had to get warm. The best way to do that was to strip naked and start a fire. Warm himself and dry his clothes at the same time.

He crawled to his feet, stepped onto solid ground. Water ran off of him, spotting the pristine snow all around him. Bent over, hands on his knees, he looked up. An ironic smile briefly flashed on his face. He chuckled to himself. No point in starting a fire now.

The chalet was ablaze.

34

SHIVERING his way up through the woods, Rainey discovered the two vehicles that had been parked outside the chalet were now gone. The night air was thick with the aroma of woodsmoke. Sounds of glass breaking, loud snapping and crackling—freakish sounds of a gluttonous fire greedily feasting on the mammoth house—echoed across the mountain and down into the valley below.

The front door was wide open. Should he chance it? There was a distinct possibility that something inside might be of use in finding Kozlov and his people. Why else would they set fire to the place?

Rainey sprinted inside and up to the second floor. Red-orange flames licked the walls all around him. Thick acrid smoke flowed along the ceiling. The pungent odor of accelerant was apparent. Hunched over, he ran down the hall in which just twenty minutes prior he'd shot it out with Kozlov and his goons.

Before stepping over the dead man in the hall, he knelt down and looked into his face. Even now, in the man's glazed over eyes, there was derision. Anger. The man had no identification on him, no pocket litter of any consequence. Rainey started as a small explosion erupted from somewhere down below. He pressed into the room in which he'd seen Horst. Hot black smoke began to billow all around him. Funny. A minute ago, he'd nearly been a human Popsicle. Now he was on the verge of being cooked alive.

He hugged the floor as he pulled his wet jacket up over his nose and mouth. *Oh, no.* There beneath the thick smoke lay the lifeless body of Dr. Edward Horst, still strapped to the chair, which had been knocked over on its side. He was quite obviously dead. Shot twice in the head at close range. Dark red blood was still slowly pooling on the floor around his body. They'd killed him in haste.

Rainey slid closer in the intense heat. He could barely take it any longer. He was about to withdraw when something caught his attention. He reached over and pulled up the man's left sleeve.

Unreal. Un...freakin'...real!

Coughing uncontrollably, he escaped the room and probed the rest of the house—the rest that was not yet fully engulfed in flames, that is.

Finally, he raced out the back of the chalet and up through the woods, his mind a jumble of rage, shock, fear, and foreboding. He stopped when he reached the small clearing where the helicopter had been, turned around and, still coughing, fell to his knees. There in the snow, he helplessly watched the huge raging firestorm. Literally, the fire roared. The previously picturesque chalet was completely engulfed in intense flames, its timbers cracking and beginning to shift. The stone structure formed a natural oven allowing the temperature of the heat within to grow extremely high. Several blasts echoed into the air. Soon a wall collapsed. There was a rumble then another wall fell. The chalet was now nothing more than a huge pile of burning rubble

Maybe his mind was just playing tricks on him, but he swore he could still hear the rotor noise fading in the distance. And with it all hope of finding Kozlov or Nika and whoever else ever again.

35

Washington, D.C.

LIGHTS flickered and danced across the undulating crests of the Potomac. From a speaker somewhere above them came a serene romantic melody. Violins, cellos. The smooth chamber music danced about in the raw air, its only competition the sound of the water licking at the hull of the *Spirit of Washington*.

Maddie snuggled beneath Wes's chin, her back pressed into his chest. His arms were wrapped around her in an effort to shield her from the cutting breeze whipped up by the boat's momentum down the river.

"This is so romantic. I've never seen D.C. like this," she said, flecks of the city's lights reflecting in her honey-colored eyes.

Wes smiled and squeezed her tightly, drawing her closer, if that were even possible. The idea of a New Year's Eve cruise on the Potomac had been a spark of spontaneity. The time and place couldn't be better. He had originally planned to do this at the Rainey house, in front of everyone. But when Ray had called about having to run out of town to take care of an emergency at work, they all decided to delay their Christmas until they could celebrate it together. Hopefully, Ray would be back soon, but if the past were any indication of the future, it could be days or even weeks till they heard something. So far, it had been an unforgettable night. It was about to become even more so.

"Kind of gives you a new perspective, doesn't it?" he said.

"It's just so lovely. Makes you forget about the other side of the city. The ugly side. I love how the lights kind of dance and wiggle on the water."

"Yeah, that's pretty cool. The stars, too… Look."

"Pulsing like tiny Christmas lights."

Wes smiled. "Like diamonds frozen in a pool of the blackest ink. Watch carefully and you'll swear they are moving."

Maddie giggled as she studied the heavens. "Yeah, you're right."

Wes made a show of reaching into the air and pinching his fingers together. "Gotcha."

After a second, she quizzically turned to him, a look of confusion, anticipation on her face.

Wes stepped back and knelt on one knee, a serious though joyful glimmer in his eyes. In his hand, he held a two-carat, emerald-cut diamond ring as if he'd just plucked it out of the sky. She covered her mouth with her gloved hands. Her eyes began to melt, a wide smile radiating across her chilled, rosy cheeks.

Wes reached out and gently took her left hand. He looked up into her wide, glowing eyes. "Maddie, I love you with all my heart. You are the one woman on God's green earth with whom I want to spend the rest of my life…if you'll have me. I wanted to do this in front of your family, but I can't go on another minute longer without knowing… Madison Elizabeth Rainey… Will you marry me?"

She giggled involuntarily and wiped a tear from her cheek. "Yes! Oh, yes!"

Wes gingerly slipped the glove off her left hand and slid the ring on her icy finger.

"I love you, darling," he said standing up and looking deep into her eyes.

"I love you, Wesley!" She kissed him excitedly and bear-hugged him. "Oh, I'm so happy."

Some of the passengers nearby who had been quietly looking on, broke out in congratulatory applause.

"Happy New Year!" whispered Wes, looking up just as fireworks rocketed into the sky over Washington, D.C.

"Happy New Year!"

36

Arlington, VA

IT was late at Directorate Twelve headquarters. And quiet. From up here on the twenty-fourth floor, the sound of New Year's revelers was non-existent. Job gazed out his office window facing the Potomac as CIA Director Ken Thompson continued. "I don't get it. How did they know? You're sure it's not someone here?"

Job studied the river curling around Theodore Roosevelt Island far below. "I don't know anymore. I hope not."

"What of our suspect list?"

"Nothing yet on any of them. But they're gonna make a mistake, Kenny. I don't know how, but I can sense it. We have to be ready for when they do or we might miss our chance. We must be ready to act."

Thompson massaged his temples. "I'm tired, Job. I'm getting all kinds of pressure from above. President's gonna soon pull the plug. He's not happy about the way things turned out in Montreal. Tell you the truth, he doesn't care much for the Directorate in the first place."

"Yeah, well, I'm not happy about Montreal either. But we have to let this play out." Job stared across the river to the cityscape of Washington, D.C. "I've sent Ray to Iraq."

Thompson brightened a bit. "Good. I tell you, my friend, this whole thing scares the crap out of me. We still have no idea what Kozlov is up to or to whom he answers. It feels like we're playing with fire on this one."

"Yes, I know. And that's why it's critical we find out whether or not the intel from Iraq connects. And if it does, how. Are the Russians really behind this or is Kozlov's team some kind of mercenaries-for-hire group working for something or someone really nasty?"

"My money's on the Russians."

Job nodded. "I tend to agree. But what if it's both?"

Thompson cringed as both men regarded each other. "Just make sure your man succeeds."

"Kenny, I have complete confidence that he won't stop or won't *be* stopped until he does."

"I hope you're right about that."

Both men strolled to the private elevator.

"Any news on Lonnie?"

"No," said Thompson looking down. "There's been no change. And I don't know that there ever will be."

Job patted the older man on the shoulder. "Well, let's keep praying. If there's one thing I've learned over the years, it's that there is always hope in the power of prayer."

37

Somewhere Over the Atlantic

HOW? That was the question that had been nagging at him for the past three hours. How was the Horst abduction tied to the Agency assassinations? Just as important, was why? He was exhausted and sore. He tried to think, but his mind just couldn't make the connection. At least not yet. Could something else be going on under the surface? Definitely possible. But what?

Rainey squirmed in his seat, thought back to what he'd seen in the basement of the chalet. A make-shift lab. Work tables, discarded materials, machined parts. Kozlov had obviously forced Horst to build him a laser gun. And now the dangerous Russian was out there somewhere with it.

How could he have lost them?

Rainey went over the phone call again in his mind—the call he'd made to Job after leaving the spectacle of the burning chalet. He'd told him everything. It was only after he'd recounted verbatim the scrawled writing on the dead scientist's arm that Job had issued the curt instruction to get to the airport ASAP. Indeed, Dr. Edward Horst had courage. His collected bits of intel were huge and also vexing:

Jet shot down w/L
Neeka
André
Olezka
Gavril
Vlad = Leader
ATVs
Mtg w/2 Arabs in US??
Jamil
Fayyad

During the phone call, Job had related that something urgent had come up that could very well link to Montreal. He was to go to Iraq and find out if it did. Before the call was through, Rainey had given Job the best lead yet about the person believed to be assassinating CIA operatives over the past year or so. He related how he had seen him, looked into his eyes. He'd provided a physical description of the man and promised to develop a composite using Agency software tools as time permitted in Iraq. It was a start, but if the guy was a professional, he had probably already changed his appearance.

Rainey now sat there with nothing to do but think. It didn't take a genius to put it together: the plane that exploded over Montreal had been shot down with the newly minted laser gun. Neeka: Nika Chernikova/Nika Kozlova. Vlad: Vladislav Kozlov, clearly the group's leader. Job would run the other names and get back to him with anything fruitful. As for the reference to ATVs and the notation of a meeting with two Arabs in the U.S., that was still as of yet unclear, but alarming nonetheless. More pieces to a puzzle that was just impossible to solve at this point.

One thing was abundantly clear despite the myriad questions. He was headed back to familiar territory. He was headed back to Iraq with Job's parting words still echoing in his mind: *"Do what you do best: get results. Gloves are off, Ray. Whatever it takes."*

38

ROMAN Lerner followed his boss, Sean Vajda, down the hall, staring at the back of his head, trying to decipher what was going on inside. What valuable bits of information were being kept from him? And why? Were they on to him? No, not possible. Still, best to be cautious. He was playing a very dangerous game.

This could be big. Whatever it was, something was about to be revealed to him. Perhaps he was about to be read in on the secret operation he knew was already well underway. He was desperately curious to say the least. Clearly, Vajda had reservations about the rapidly developing situation in Iraq. Could that be a factor now? When they'd first reviewed the latest intel reports from Baghdad Station, Sean Vajda's follow-on questions were entirely linear. But that had all changed with the added layer of context recently received from their Directorate Twelve liaison.

The D12 intel had of course been scrubbed of names, sources, and other proprietary information, but the nuts and bolts of it were clear. Someone now had a man-portable high-energy laser gun capable of taking down a plane. The list of new American vulnerabilities went on and on. It was deeply concerning. Scary, in fact.

Lerner had never actually been assigned to the Directorate, but he knew people who had been and some who still were. He'd begun right away, working his contacts, massaging them carefully for relevant information without arousing suspicion from the Agency mole-hunters. From what he'd been able to cull, he was now fully aware that there had indeed been a secret Agency operation in Montreal with D12's Joint Services Group being the central player.

Twenty minutes later, he and Vajda emerged from the private meeting. He was absolutely miffed. Nothing remotely related to the laser gun or Montreal or even the latest intel from Iraq had been discussed with him. In a way, it was validation for what he'd already passed on to Pyotr Kupchenko earlier this morning. And the resulting string of events that he knew were about to be set into motion. Reagan Rainey would have a surprise waiting for him this time.

A big one.

39

Erbil, Iraq

RAINEY'S plane touched down at Erbil International Airport without the excitement of Montreal. He spotted him right away—his Agency contact—but decided to hang back and make sure this wasn't another trap. He hated being paranoid, but it was necessary for survival, especially these days and with this particular assignment. After studying the man for close to fifteen minutes, he was satisfied there were no hostiles monitoring the man's movements.

The dark-haired man was about fifty or so. Beneath his coffee bean eyes, he bore a trimmed beard which contained an army of persistent gray flecks, especially around his chin. He looked very much the part; he actually looked like an Iraqi. He wore a powder blue *thawb*, a robe-like garment that ran to the floor. In his left hand, he carried a tan leather briefcase scarred with a prominent V-shaped tear—the signal Job had told him to look for in order to identify his Agency contact.

Rainey approached the man. *"Salaam alaikum."* Peace be upon you—a common greeting among Muslims.

"Alaikum salaam." And peace be unto you. The man's right eye

tightened, he was on edge, as he should be if he worked for the CIA these days. "Mr. Renaud?"

"Please. Max." Rainey nodded politely.

"Yes. Well, Max, we need to go quickly."

Ezra Gold was a CIA operative who had been covertly working within the Iraqi Ministry of Oil in Mosul when the brutal insurgency calling themselves the Islamic State—also known by such names as ISIS, ISIL and Daesh, but commonly referred to in military and intelligence circles as ISIL (Islamic State in Iraq and the Levant)—began their siege. Gold had developed a solid, but small network of spies in and around the city during his time in Iraq. Some of his agents had since fled to Erbil or other refugee areas, some had been killed, some had just disappeared altogether. One of his most valuable spies, perhaps the most valuable in light of recent developments, was a man named, Raji Fayyad. Only yesterday, Gold had learned that the man was still alive. But his whereabouts were still something of a mystery, that is until about an hour ago.

ISIL forces had him.

They didn't have much time if the Agency was going to try to save him. Gold had adamantly advocated for Langley to do everything in its power to do so. This time, the Agency was in full agreement and promised to put a rescue package together from available resources in the region.

Both men walked casually across the airport. They made their way free of the other passengers roaming about. While keeping his face forward and eyes alert, but not obviously so, Gold asked, "Any problems along the way?"

Rainey regarded the man, who looked convincingly native, with nonchalance. "No." They continued steadily toward the parking lot. "Which car?"

"That one over there. The brown Toyota." Ezra pointed with a smile still keeping up the pretenses in case anyone were watching.

When they had reached the relative security of the parked car, Gold seemed to relax a little and only then spoke in English. He leaned forward and opened the glove box and pointed to a SIG Sauer 9mm. "Here. Just in case. There's an MP7 in the door, just pull up and out on the armrest. And a sawed-off here between the seats." Gold flipped up the center console revealing a pistol-grip shotgun with a fourteen-inch barrel. "The blanket on the back seat is Kevlar."

"For those *really* hot dates, I presume." Rainey checked the pistol's chamber then slid it into his waistband. "I like what you've done with the place."

"You can never be too careful in Iraq these days. ISIL is everywhere and their brutality is unlike anything I've ever seen. They are intent on consuming the entire country, the world really. Many here have fled from Mosul. They've lost loved ones, their homes, everything to those barbarians." Gold eased into traffic then filled him in on the latest developments in country. "So, Langley says you've got some tangible intel…"

Rainey quickly explained what he'd uncovered thus far.

"*Jamil*. He is the link." Gold massaged the steering wheel with both hands.

"I'm not sure I completely understand. What do you have going on here?"

Gold checked his mirrors then said, "For about a year or so now, I've been working an Iraqi intelligence official in Mosul, named Raji Fayyad. He's piped in pretty good. I was supposed to meet him about a month ago, here in Erbil. But that meeting was postponed due to recent ISIL activity. In the meantime, I lost contact with him. Tell you the truth, I thought he was dead. But then just yesterday, I learned from another source that Fayyad is very much alive. Fast-forward to about an hour ago… I got word that he's been captured by ISIL. Langley is working on a hasty rescue op, but there's no telling if it will be in time."

"Why is this guy so important?"

"Because at our last meeting, he confided that he's heard some things about a terrorist plot. He's got a source in a Russian embassy. That source apparently has expressed knowledge about a large terrorist plot to strike the homeland. So far, my guy's only been able to get me bits and pieces. A name is really all I have at this point. *Jamil*. Jamil ibn Hasan. What's worrisome is that Langley has nothing on him, this Jamil. Fayyad was to have met with his source since. He promised to have a lot more specific intel for me. It's critical that we find out what he's learned. About Jamil and this plot."

It now made sense why he'd been sent to Iraq. "So…," Rainey mused. "This stuff is all related. Horst, Montreal, the Agency assassinations, this pending plot to hit America."

Gold shrugged his shoulders and scanned his surroundings. "Certainly seems that way."

"So now what?"

"I know where my Iraqi friend is being held. I'm just waiting on word from Langley about their plan to rescue him. I do know this: if Fayyad isn't pulled out soon, he's a dead man, if he's not dead already. The ramifications couldn't be more dire, Max. We're talking about another nine-eleven here."

Half an hour after they had reached the Erbil safe house, he received word from Langley. Gold passed the message on to Rainey. "They're gonna go get him. There's a five-man team of Delta operators that's already inside Mosul. Jonah Team is what they're calling themselves. They're moving into the area where Fayyad's being held, but...they're sorely outnumbered."

He hated standing on the sidelines especially in a time like this, when his brothers clearly needed extra bodies. Rainey leaned forward. "Can you get me in?"

Gold looked up at him, his forehead wrinkled in confusion. "No. It's too dangerous. I—"

"I need you to get me in. It's not up for debate."

"You don't understand, Max. I'm telling you, it's too dangerous. We get caught out there and we're dead. They'll cut our freaking heads off and put it on the Internet."

"Then we won't get caught."

Gold shook his head in silent protest.

"Listen, I'm not asking you to go with me. Just get me in."

When Gold realized he was not going to talk this guy out of his death wish, he sighed and said, "Let me make some calls."

Twenty minutes later, he came back into the room. "Okay. It's gonna be a bit dicey, but I have a way for you to get into the city. Have you ever worn a burqa?"

"Sure, who hasn't?" Rainey said deadpan.

But Gold apparently wasn't in the mood for operator humor. "Good. We leave in fifteen minutes."

40

Mosul, Iraq

GOLD wasn't kidding about the trip being dicey. They traveled quickly along several desolate roads filled with nothing but potholes and craters from exploded IEDs. Duct-taped to the trunk of the car was an IR strobe which had been placed there so they could be identified from the air. When they approached the first signs of an ISIL patrol, Gold punched a number into his cell phone and said, "Hold on...and you might want to cover your ears." In the next few minutes, a U.S.-led coalition bombing campaign suddenly rocked the landscape. It was this way six or seven more times until they were close enough for Rainey to jump out and hoof it. He soon melted into the dangerous, ancient cityscape.

A beat-up, old Toyota Corolla was waiting for him on the fringe of a particular souk. Climbing into the unlocked sedan, he found the keys above the visor, care of one of Gold's trusted spies. The next bit was incredibly dangerous. Under ISIL oppression, women were not permitted to drive. It was a big risk to drive with the burqa on, but with what hung in the balance, it was a risk he was willing to take. If he were actually stopped by ISIL soldiers, they would be surprised to learn about the arsenal he carried beneath his long, loose robe. Quite.

It took him twenty-two minutes to reach his destination, a small dusty building in the heart of Mosul—the heart of ISIL-controlled territory. He quickly dialed Gold to let him know that he'd arrived safely then sent a text message to a different number as instructed. As he waited, Rainey scanned his surroundings. The Tigris River was off to the east. Swarms of seagulls littered the balconies of the ancient architecture all around him. Their screeching was relentless but also peaceful in a way. His eyes followed one of them as it landed on a latticework of wires that hung loosely from a high wall. On the roof of the next house over—a house that seemed to have been ravaged by centuries of weather and war—was a brand new satellite dish. *How nice.*

When the door of the run-down building swung open, Rainey entered quickly and immediately smiled at the bearded faces that greeted him. "Fig. Babe. Man they're scraping the bottom of the barrel on this one," said Ray as he shook hands with each rugged American warrior.

"Nice threads," said Fig. "Where's your sister?"

Angel "Fig" Figueroa and Justin "Babe" Ruth were both fellow D-boys but not from Rainey's squadron. Fig and Rainey had gone through Delta selection at the same time. Fig excelled in hand-to-hand combat tactics and was perhaps the most skilled, unarmed fighter in the entire American military. He was absolutely phenomenal. Over the years, he'd helped Rainey and other operators hone their craft, employing various disciplines of martial arts such as Krav Maga, Brazilian Jiu-Jitsu, Judo, Savate, and others. Strange as it was, Rainey's sister, Maddie, had actually trained with Fig in Israel two years back, though at the time she had no clue what Fig really did for a living. It was a topic of conversation Fig constantly brought up with Ray and incessantly teased him about.

Babe on the other hand was a Delta progeny. Big and physically imposing, he appeared as if he'd been chiseled out of sheer rock. Set within his handsome, tanned face were a pair of merry eyes that missed nothing. Babe was one of the naturally strongest guys in the Unit and routinely demonstrated such when his mates would offer up new and unique challenges, which was often. Babe had been an All-American slugger in college, even been drafted into the Majors. Nevertheless, his dad had been a Delta operator back in the Charlie Beckwith days, so after college Babe decided to join the Army and follow suit.

"Hey look at this guy. Wassup, Bronco?" Phil "Jazz" Weather-ford, was another Delta mate from Fig and Babe's squadron.

"Jazz! How you been, brah?"

"Can't complain, can't complain." Jazz turned around. "Hey Boost! Look who decided to crash the party."

Booster looked up from across the room and smiled. "Oh, yeah. It's *on* now."

Fig patted Rainey on the shoulder. "Follow me, brother." He proceeded down some steps into a relatively large, well-lit room. Here, the Delta Force commandos began making final checks of their equipment.

Fig led the way across the room to the Jonah Team leader, Shane "Dino" Cassel. Cassel was leaning on his palms behind a table which was set up like a desk. A rugged-looking computer tablet was positioned in front of him. He swiped his finger across the screen several times in succession, cycling through an array of photos of their target location, which had just been taken a few minutes prior. He maximized a window that showed a live overhead feed from the MQ-9 Reaper circling high above the city.

Cassel looked up. "Bronco. Good. Now we can finally get this show on the road. Well, Bronc, you're in luck. Word from the spooks is that Fayyad is still there." Cassel pointed to the screen. "But God only knows how long he's got till those ISIL pukes make him famous by putting him in one of those stinking propaganda videos. Command says we're good to go whenever we see fit. Birds are staging, they just need to know when we decide to move."

Rainey threw off the burqa and now looked like the rest of the warfighters. "Dino, I'm ready when you are."

"Look at you...all dressed for the prom. Okay. Good deal."

Twelve minutes later, the team was just about ready to launch. Gold had already prepped Rainey on the operation specifics while they were dodging their way across northern Iraq. Jonah Team would hit the building where the Iraqi intelligence official, Raji Fayyad, was being held. Once Fayyad was secured, the team would race out of the city to a pre-determined location. From there, they'd be extracted by a specially modified MH-60 Black Hawk helicopter accompanied by a tandem of AH-64D Apache Longbows and flown to a secure CIA base east of Kirkuk. One of Gold's Agency colleagues was already en route from Baghdad Station for the debrief.

"Any questions?"

"Nope, I'm good," said Rainey.

"All right, this is gonna go off in concert with another coalition bombing run. So those ISIL turds will have plenty to worry about while we do our thing."

"Got it."

"Just be ready to flex. This is gonna be very fluid."

"Fluid I can handle. It's seat-of-your-pants that concerns me."

"Understood. I'm gonna call it in. We move in five."

Rainey shifted the tan load-bearing vest fitted with armor plates. Gold had hooked him up pretty good back in Erbil. Of course, Rainey had to reposition some of the MOLLE pouches to where he was used to them being, but it hadn't taken long. Muscle memory was a crazy thing. When the nasty hit the fan, he didn't want to be reaching for a magazine and find he was yanking on a blowout kit. Mistakes like that got you or, worse yet, one of your buddies killed.

He was armed with a suppressed Heckler & Koch 416 rifle out-fitted with top-notch optics and an HK USP SD 9mm pistol which he wore in a thigh rig on his right leg. He made several last-minute checks to his gear as Cassel reviewed the key mission objectives, radio frequencies, and op-specific vernacular.

Booster paced over when Cassel was finished. He strapped on his helmet then racked the bolt of his rifle, an FN SCAR MK 17 CQC. Booster could have passed for a young Denzel Washington; they both had the same charming, toothy smile. Like his fellow D-boys, Booster was extremely intelligent and built like a professional athlete. "Looks like you're with me, Bronc. We got external security."

"Roger that." In his mind, Rainey was going over again the maps he'd just been shown. The areas circled and marked in red ink: the target location, zone assignments, exfiltration routes and primary, secondary, and tertiary extraction points.

"You good?"

"I'm all set. Let's get it on."

"Okay, everyone listen up!" said Cassel, walking back into the room. "We roll in two. FYI, SIGINT picked up cell traffic a few minutes ago that indicates several roving patrols are moving into our area of operation. This could get ugly. But we do what we gotta do. Head on a swivel, men.

"As noted before, intel indicates that the compound is not heavily-fortified or very well-guarded and that still stands. But like always, we're not gonna take any chances. If everything goes smoothly, by my calculation we'll be in and out, in about three minutes tops after which we'll exfil to primary extract. If conditions deteriorate quickly, as they sometimes do in this business, we get the principal out of Dodge any way we can. Understood?

"Bronco, you and Booster watch our backsides. Your area of responsibility is the street outside the entry/exit point. Now…"

Booster slapped Rainey on the back as they powered on their radios.

Cassel stepped forward, his rifle strapped across his barrel chest. "There's been a good bit of vehicular traffic around the compound, so we're just gonna ride right up onto the target. Anybody have any questions?" No one responded. After Cassel had them all perform a quick comms check, he said, "Okay, let's move out."

41

HE had never failed an assignment before, let alone twice. So when Demyan Rostov was given the opportunity to redeem himself he vowed that he would do whatever it took to succeed. He'd been out of commission only a couple of days since the Delta operator had nearly destroyed his left elbow in Montreal. By now though he had already seen a doctor who had provided him with some strong painkillers and a mechanical brace that would help to support the injured joint until he could find the occasion to undergo surgery. If only he had another chance to kill the man responsible, he would surely make him pay. But alas, Rostov had been sent here, to Iraq, for another assignment. Another target. This other man would have to do for now, a man upon which he would visit vengeance by proxy. From what Kupchenko had said, he was a man who posed an enormous threat to the cause. A man named Raji Fayyad.

Rostov cinched up the bulky brace on his left arm and walked out to view the target location, looked at his watch. Anytime now. At that precise moment, his disposable cell phone vibrated. "Yes?"

"Dinner's in eight minutes, don't be late." Then the line went dead.

Rostov pushed the phone back into his pocket. Eight minutes. *Perfect.*

* * *

"There's a truck parked out front now. Four guys with AKs are hovering around it. They seem anxious," said the drone operator—call sign Red Robin. Red Robin was a uniformed woman seated behind a console in a non-descript, air-conditioned trailer across the Kuwaiti border at a U.S. military base called Camp Buehring.

From the front passenger-seat of the lead vehicle, Cassel keyed his radio. "Victor One. Copy."

Rainey readjusted his earpiece then placed his hand back on the fore grip of his rifle. It felt good having a long gun strapped around him again; it was very much an extension of his own body. He looked over at Booster who was tightening the Velcro straps on his tactical gloves. He was intense yet calm. They all were. Switched on and ready to take care of business.

Victor One (Cassel): "Jonah's a block out. Charlie Two, let her rip." Charlie 2 was their command and control—the JSOC liaison to the US-led coalition assembled to battle ISIL. He'd been waiting at Buehring for the precise moment to order up the bomb drops and Hellfire missile strikes on known ISIL emplacements while the Fayyad rescue operation simultaneously occurred. This was designed to distract and confuse ISIL personnel in the area, draw them away from the target compound.

With that, several blasts thundered in the distance, each one growing progressively closer…and louder. ISIL strongholds on the outskirts of the city were suddenly being decimated.

Victor One: "Jonah Team, engage on my count. In three, two, one. Execute. Execute. Execute."

The two vehicles moved quickly and efficiently to the target building in tight formation. On Cassel's command they drew even closer together. They shot off the main road into the narrow street that ran past the plain-looking, pocked-marked complex. The fast-moving vehicles were now less than eighteen inches apart. There were more loud blasts off to the left and further ahead. The keys to the mission's success were precision timing, speed and violence of action.

As Jonah Team rolled up to the building, one of the ISIL men stationed out front started urgently shouting commands to the others. He shouldered his AK-47 and was about to fire. Two of the Delta operators fired simultaneously, drilling him with silenced 5.56mm rounds. The man spun and fell over dead. His three associates were quickly dispatched in like manner.

* * *

Demyan Rostov had just checked his watch. Three minutes and fifteen seconds left. He peered through his binoculars. A man appeared on the other side of the louvered window he was studying. His orders were to aim for that very room. Just beyond the far wall was where Raji Fayyad was being held, according to the intel Kupchenko had passed on to him. The man in the window seemed to be engaged in a tense phone conversation. Then suddenly he became erect and quickly picked up a nearby rifle. Rostov watched as the man threw open the window and glowered toward the dusty street below. Rostov lowered the binoculars to see what had so urgently captivated the man's attention.

It couldn't be.

Rostov blinked and refocused the binos.

A chance for redemption.

There he was, the American—Reagan Rainey. He and several other men, all dressed in similar fashion, had just leapt from a dirt-caked Toyota Hilux. *Deltas. Have to be.* He looked on as the fast-moving Americans surgically dispatched the ISIL quartet guarding the building.

Rostov licked his lips as he checked his watch again, his heartrate quickening. He brought the binos back up. The Americans hesitated for a second, then disappeared around the corner of the building, where the front door was located. It was obvious they were going to storm the complex. The emphatic report of a stun grenade punctuated his thesis.

He smiled as he picked up the object on the floor next to him and drew in a relaxed breath of air. For close to a minute, he waited, anxiously enduring sporadic cracks of gunfire from across the way. He didn't bother to check his watch anymore.

Close enough.

* * *

When the fast moving convoy came to a halt, the highly skilled, keyed-up men jumped out and executed their assigned duties with flawless precision and discipline. This was their real estate now.

Rainey and Booster fanned out taking up security posts, scanning for threats. Meanwhile, the four assaulters made hard entry through the front door, smashing it open and tossing in a stun grenade. A half-second after the diversionary device exploded, they pushed inside. Several ISIL men went scrambling for their weapons but were quickly put down.

When the first floor was clear and secure, Jonah Team moved up. On the second floor, they encountered three rather feisty militants, two wielding Zastava M-70s, the other a Chinese AK knock-off. A gun battle ensued. But the ISIL men were just no match for Deltas. It was over in a matter of seconds.

They found Raji Fayyad handcuffed to a file cabinet in a room loaded with wooden crates. Identifying themselves quickly as Americans, they hustled the stunned Iraqi intelligence official downstairs. The operators were just about to exit to the street when someone outside yelled, "RPG!"

The voice was drowned out as the earth suddenly trembled and a cataclysmic clap of thunder rocked the street. The entire compound erupted in a series of violent explosions and then began crumbling like a sand castle.

* * *

There was nothing quite so haunting or horrific as the screams on a battlefield, where men lay ripped open and torn apart, writhing for the relief only death can bring. Body parts strewn about. Air thick with the stench of shed blood, internal organs and cordite. And so was the scene here. Rostov hadn't known that ISIL militants had placed stockpiles of high explosives, rockets and ammunition in the room with Fayyad. The same room into which his RPG-7V2 round had just slammed. But someone apparently had.

Demyan Rostov assessed his handiwork with pride and satisfaction. He waited a few more seconds, studying the billowing clouds of dust and cordite, the carnage before gathering up his things. He smiled broadly, as an electric shock of exhilaration charged through him.

Redemption cometh.

42

RAINEY and Booster were each posted up behind cover as they scanned the streets with eyes of predation.

"Friendlies coming out!" yelled Cassel.

"You're clear!" Rainey's eyes darted back and forth. The first two crossed the threshold. Rainey began to move backward toward them, toward the vehicles still scanning for threats.

Booster's voice. "RPG!"

Then sudden heat, concussed air. The powerful blast mule-kicked him from behind with such a violent force it was like being hit by a train. Rainey went soaring through the air and across the narrow alleyway where he slammed into the wall of a computer shop.

Ignoring the ringing in his ears, he wiped the dust and grime from his eyes and quickly glanced back at the giant burning pile of rubble. Thick black plumes of smoke were billowing upward. Red-orange flames licked at the sky. Rounds were beginning to cook off, popping and fizzing like firecrackers on the fourth of July.

For a moment everything seemed to be in slow motion, as if time itself had been wounded and needed a chance to catch its breath. Then without warning, the real-time chaos resumed with a contemporaneous chorus of car alarms, ear-splitting screams from injured bystanders, panicked shouts in Arabic for help, for mercy.

Rainey climbed to his feet, checked himself for missing limbs, serious injuries while scanning the area for an explanation to the madness. How was he still alive or not seriously wounded? Ten yards away to his right, Booster lay perfectly still, folded over in a pool of blood that was growing at an alarming rate. Rainey raced over to his buddy. Booster was bloodied and unconscious...but breathing. His right shoulder was badly injured—quite obviously dislocated—and there was a deep gash across his left forearm. Streams of crimson were pumping from his arm in rhythm with his heart.

Rainey sat him upright and ripped the tourniquet from the quick eject carrier on Booster's vest, looped it around the man's left arm and pushed it to the top of his bicep. Once he had it clamped tight enough to stop the spurting blood, he locked it in place and continued to assess Booster for injuries. Rainey was in the middle of palpating for broken bones when Booster sputtered out an expletive and angrily came to.

"What the— What happened?!" Then the pain registered. He growled in agony.

"FUBAR, Boost. We gotta move. Your legs work?"

"Think so," he barked with a grimace.

Rainey grabbed Booster and hoisted him up to his feet. "Jonah Team, Red Robin. Anyone copy? I repeat. Jonah Team, Red Robin! Anyone copy? Over."

"Victor Three. I copy. Bronco, that you?" said Fig coughing.

"Roger that. Booster's hurt, but ambulatory. He needs a medevac, toot sweet."

"What's your pos?"

"Across the street. Southeast from the front door."

"Roger that. What happened, man?"

"I don't know. I—" Rainey's head snapped to movement in the street directly in front of the compound.

Cassel.

Rainey darted over to him as Booster limped behind, holding his rifle in a one-hand grip. The injured Delta operator tucked himself behind the closest team vehicle—a Nissan Frontier—ready to provide Rainey and his mates cover.

Cassel was mortally wounded, his body nearly blown in half. "Fay...yad!" A gasp for air. "GO!"

Then he was gone.

Rainey spotted Fayyad who had been launched face-first through the Toyota's front passenger-side window. His face was bloody, but he was alive, squirming, attempting to free himself. Rainey keyed his mic. "Fig, where are you guys?!"

Fig and Jazz both came chugging out of the entrance of the compound behind Babe. The big Delta man was bulldozing a path through the rubble. All had a variety of scrapes and cuts on their dust-covered faces. Jazz was limping badly. Babe's pants had been all but blown off. Fragments of fabric still clinging beneath his belt and thigh rig flapped in the breeze as he approached.

Rainey yelled for Fig to radio the drone operator and the inbound choppers as he and the others got Booster, Fayyad, and Cassel's torn body loaded into the Nissan. When they were all inside, Fig stomped on the gas.

A crackle of gunfire erupted from down the street as an ISIL patrol responding to the blast site spotted them. An army of black-hooded soldiers appeared out of thin air. In a flash, men in load-bearing vests with AK-47s were everywhere, swarming the area like locusts. An RPG round whooshed past, missing them by mere inches. Then another. This one slammed into the Toyota left behind and exploded on impact.

* * *

They sped haphazardly through the city, zig-zagging around cars, trucks, people, anything and everything that lay in their path. Rainey sat in the back seat on the left side of the truck next to Raji Fayyad, who was squeezed in the middle. Rainey was wide-eyed, squared up behind his rifle as Fig negotiated obstacles like an Indy car driver. Jazz rode shotgun with Booster directly behind him. Babe sat facing backward in the bed of the truck beside Cassel's body, safeguarding their six.

Fayyad seemed oddly at ease, cradling his broken left arm in his lap. "Thank you," he said in a meek voice.

Firing several bursts through the open window, Rainey yelled over his shoulder to the Iraqi intelligence officer. "We're not out of the woods yet! Stay down. And hang on!"

"You do God's work. The God of Israel. The God of my wife and son. Only by His grace and mercy have you gotten this far."

"He's my God, too." He fired off a volley. "How 'bout you? He can be your God, too, you know. Desperately wants to be."

"Afraid I have done many evil things. *Many*. I'm just not worthy."

"No one is. That's the point. Jesus Christ died on the cross to save you from all those evil things, all that sin." Bullets whizzed through the open windows, making little snapping sounds. "His blood washes us white as snow. He rose from the dead, defeated death so that we, you and me, might have eternal life through Him. Otherwise we could never be worthy, no matter how much good we did. All you gotta do is accept Him into your life. Believe in Him and what I just said. Only then will you be saved. Only by the blood of Jesus."

Fayyad sucked in a gulp of air, looked at Reagan Rainey beside him, patted him on the leg. "Yes. Yes! I believe! I believe in Jesus Christ! I accept Him as my savior. Praise God. Praise His holy name."

"Roger that," said Rainey. "Congratulations, sir. You now belong to Him!"

It came out of nowhere: "I wanna believe, too, Bronco, I *do* believe. I accept Him as my savior, too," yelled Booster across the cabin, bullets still flying.

"Awesome, Boost! Proud of you, man. Proud of you both." The way in which God worked was amazing. They were in the middle of a nasty gunfight in possibly the most dangerous city on the planet, yet God through the Holy Spirit was right here convicting hearts.

Amazing grace, indeed.

* * *

Fayyad smiled, looked down at his mangled limb, knowing in his soul what God had just done. He could feel His presence. God—the One True God, had changed his heart and now he was saved.

Saved by grace.

It had taken his capture and subsequent rescue—a clear act of God, a miracle—for him to want to tear down the wall of pride and defiance that surrounded his heart. But it had been the brave, young missionary woman who had come to Iraq long ago, who had first planted the seed. A seed that had been cared for and nourished by his faithful wife and son for years despite his loud protests. Both had accepted Jesus as their Lord and Savior back then. But he'd laughed at them, ridiculed them. He'd had the hardest of hearts and unflinchingly refused to abandon Islam. But when the savage ISIL troops had come and taken his wife and son, brutally killed them right in front of him for refusing to deny their faith, that little seed began to grow and flourish.

Fayyad began to cry. They would be so proud of him. Now there was the promise of seeing them again someday beyond heaven's gate.

Praise God! Praise His holy name.

Fayyad smiled through his tears, offered up a silent prayer. When he was finished, he closed his eyes. Then he passed out.

43

Kingston Park
East of Kirkuk

AFTER crossing the Tigris River they had continued in a southerly direction at insane speeds. They'd been forced to pick their way through the ISIL-infested streets and bombed-out terrain. The extraction had been relatively uneventful except for a sliver of time in which a persistent band of militants had decided to fire up toward them with small arms fire. Big mistake. The Apaches had responded by raining down Hellfire missiles and 2.75-inch Hydra 70 rockets.

As extreme as the violence and chaos had been back in Mosul, so now was the silence and peacefulness here at Kingston Park—a secret CIA base situated on a crooked spine of mountains east of Kirkuk and south of the Kurdish city of Chamchamal. It was here, behind a stony wall that could have been built in the time of the Sassanids, where Rainey restlessly stood. He stared off into the distance, into the rugged mountains of western Iran. A number of Special Forces soldiers assigned to the base moved about, giving aid to their Delta Force brethren.

Cassel's remains had already been placed into a black body bag for transport to Buehring. Talk amongst the fierce warriors was now limited to task-oriented dialogue. A pall of loss hung in the air like an opaque fog. Some of them were quiet, while some seethed with anger. Others went off by themselves to mourn the loss of their brother in solitude. The operators took turns, each of them spending a few private minutes alone with Shane "Dino" Cassel before it was time to move out.

Rainey gazed out over God's creation, lost in his thoughts. What happened? Why did everything go so badly, so quickly?

Woodsmoke from a far-off mountain campfire drifted skyward. Shane Cassel was another good one gone. He was a rough man, fierce and unflappable. A quintessential American warrior. He was a strong leader, who enjoyed much popularity within the special operations community.

Rainey flipped a stone in his hand, threw it to the ground. Just like the warehouse back in Montreal. They'd been set up. Someone was playing a game—a brutal game—with rules that didn't make any sense.

"Mr. Renaud," a voice called out over the drone of generators.

Rainey broke from his reverie, turned. Christofer Bracks, the man who'd been sent from Baghdad Station, stood there waving his hand. Dressed in khakis and a starched white dress shirt, no tie, Bracks was a man who appeared out of place. Too clean and neat to be out here rubbing elbows with the likes of Rainey and his buddies.

"Fayyad's awake."

"And?"

"And...he refuses to talk unless you are present. Seems he's formed some sort of connection with you. If you have a minute...," said Bracks sarcastically.

Rainey followed Bracks into one of the four modular, tent-like buildings, known in military parlance as temporary deployable accommodations, which constituted the secret base.

A Special Forces medic looked at them as they entered. Rainey patted him on the shoulder and asked him to come back in twenty minutes. He assented without complaint. Rainey watched as he gathered his things and disappeared out of the room. When Rainey was sure he was out of earshot, he gave Bracks a thumbs up.

Raji Fayyad was lying on a rudimentary hospital bed, his broken arm now set in a cast, his face cleaned up and bandaged. Fayyad offered a meager smile at the sight of Rainey. "Ah. There he is. My brother in Christ."

Rainey walked to the Iraqi intelligence officer's side. "How ya feeling, sir?"

"Sore. But I'm alive. I'm sorry for the loss of your comrade."

"Thank you. He will be greatly missed."

"Did he have a wife?"

"Yes."

"And children?"

Rainey's eyes fell to the floor. It came out a whisper: "Twin girls."

Fayyad sighed. "I will pray for them."

Rainey nodded. "Me, too."

Bracks stepped forward. "Mr. Fayyad, I don't mean to be rude, but like I said before... My name is Steve (an Agency cover name). Bill (Ezra Gold's Agency cover name) and I are colleagues. We've been working together on the intel you've been providing the Agency. Now, Bill said that you have some critical information to pass on to us. Let me just say that Bill cares a great deal for you. I know you've taken some incredible risks to work with us in the past. I thank you for that. Unfortunately, due to some logistical constraints, Bill is unable to be here, though he certainly wanted to be. You should know that he was instrumental in your rescue." Bracks paused. "Now, please don't mistake my haste for rudeness..."

Fayyad assessed Bracks with unease before he responded. "I understand. Forgive me if I appear overly cautious."

"No, I understand completely. An unfamiliar face and all. You and Bill have built a bond of mutual trust. I get it. But that being said, and with all due respect, I need you to fill me in on exactly what you had intended to tell him," said Bracks. "Lives are at stake."

Fayyad's eyes nervously flicked to Rainey.

Rainey offered a small, empathetic nod.

Fayyad took a deep breath, let it out, then began. "I have a source at the Russian embassy in Qatar." He hesitated, looked at his injured arm. "In Doha. For years, this man has provided me with information. Sometimes significant, sometimes not so much. Always credible. This information I would in turn pass on to the CIA, to Mr. Bill. Only recently my source had obtained knowledge of a plot—a diabolical plot." Fayyad closed his eyes. *"Diabolical,"* he whispered.

"Who is this source?"

Rainey shifted his weight to his left foot, crossed his arms. The question seemed a little premature, but then again he wasn't running the show here. Bracks was. Rainey studied the Agency man, as if taking minor satisfaction in the fact that Fayyad completely ignored the interrogative.

"My source has learned that there is an attack coming to America, but there is..." He seemed to be searching for the right words. "Everything is not as it seems...or will seem. The attack will appear to be instigated by Iran, evidence will lead to the plot's mastermind—a Quds Force officer by the name of Jamil ibn Hasan."

"When? Where?" probed Bracks.

"My source didn't know, but he made mention of...Mexico and...*Carnicero.*" His lips carefully formed the word. "He said two martyrs have already been selected to carry out the attack. They are to be traveling together to Mexico on orders from this Jamil." Fayyad shook his head.

"What is it, sir?" said Rainey gently.

Fayyad inclined his head to Rainey, stared into his eyes. "This Iranian man...he does not exist. Jamil ibn Hasan is a fabrication."

44

RAINEY was confused and tired. His body ached. As he stood there and listened to Fayyad relay the rest of what was known about this *diabolical* plot, a fire within him stirred. Into his mind crept the images and sounds of 9/11. Horrific displays of hopelessness and tumult. Americans jumping to their deaths. Stunned faces caked with dust and detritus. Cops and firefighters bravely running toward and into the danger. The Towers collapsing. Fast-moving dust clouds chasing terror-stricken men, women, and children through a city-size maze. America after she'd been sucker-punched in the face. Hard.

For him, like so many other Americans, 9/11 had been a turning point. A galvanizing moment in time. It put everything into perspective, even for a kid in the tenth grade. After graduation, he'd struggled with the idea of going off to college, while others his age went off to war. To fight for their country.

In the fall of 2004, another one of those galvanizing moments came. His college roommate's brother—a highly decorated Special Forces soldier—was killed in a gun battle in Afghanistan. For Rainey, that was it. The last straw. No more standing on the sidelines. The War on Terror became his war. His fight. And no Rainey ever ran from a fight. The very next day, he'd left school and gone to his local

Army recruiter's office to enlist. It was his turn to fight. His turn to stand up and be counted.

The muscles in his jaw flexed involuntarily. His eyes bespoke raw and righteous purpose. Someone was going to hit America. He could not let that happen. He would give anything and everything it took to prevent another 9/11. His life, if need be. In that moment, his body became alive with energy.

It was during Rainey's quiet reverie that Christofer Bracks pulled out a pistol and took aim at Fayyad's face. Rainey flinched at the sudden and familiar sound, that of a suppressed, semi-automatic pistol spitting its first round.

The spray from Fayyad's head wound painted a bright crimson Rorschach pattern on the white sheets and olive drab wall beyond. The Iraqi man's head jerked back violently, then fell slowly to the pillow, his eyes wide with surprise.

Rainey lunged, grabbed for the gun, but Bracks was ready for him. He twisted away, took a step back and prepared to shoot again, this time at Rainey.

It was instinct, muscle memory that now dominated his every fiber. Rainey quickly launched himself forward, closing the gap between himself and the man intent on killing him. Rainey's left hand brushed against the stubby snout of the pistol, as he clamped down over the weapon's slide and pushed it away. At the same time, he drove the palm of his right hand into Bracks's jaw. Rainey torqued the gun, still in Bracks's grasp, 180 degrees. Bracks yelped and swung at him with a meaty fist. But Rainey slid his head out of harm's way just in time and Bracks whiffed. Rainey stepped around the outside of Bracks's right leg, leaned into him. Both men, still locked together, went to the floor with a thud, Rainey on top. Bracks squirmed like a fish out of water. Rainey applied constant pressure on Bracks's wrist and finger, which was still trapped inside the trigger guard.

Pfft!

The expelled round sliced upward through Bracks's neck, entering just below his chin. His body jolted, then relaxed.

He was dead.

Silence flooded the room. Rainey's shirt was covered in blood, his heart nearly beating out of his chest. Had anyone heard what just happened? He peaked out of the room and down the corridor in either direction.

Empty.

Dashing across the narrow hallway into another room, he quickly stripped off the bloody shirt and washed himself up with a bottle of water. As he toweled off his face, chest and arms, he located a stack of fresh olive drab Under Armour T-shirts. He wrestled into one. Outside, the Black Hawk was winding up, preparing to take off. The D-boys with Cassel's remains en route to Camp Buehring.

Now or never.

Rainey jogged outside to the helo and jumped in.

Behind a dark pair of Oakleys, Fig regarded him with a look of "What gives?"

Rainey shrugged his shoulders. "Change of plans."

45

Camp Buehring, Kuwait

FAYYAD'S words reverberated in his mind like shouts in an echo chamber. Rainey was lost to himself, trying to dissect each thought as it came to him. He felt alone, betrayed. He had to keep pressing on though, even if he had to do so by himself. It was painfully apparent that he could trust no one right now...at least no one at CIA. And that included Directorate Twelve.

There was no doubt. Whoever was behind the Agency assassinations was linked to the business in Montreal, to the Horst abduction. Somehow that bore significance to what had happened back there in Iraq, to Fayyad and his source. Why else kill Fayyad?

His head hurt.

As soon as they touched down, Rainey quickly lost himself in the commotion of the bustling, rapidly growing military installation. He dropped his cell phone into a trash can and drifted across the base to a barracks alive with young Marines. With a friendly smile, he bummed a ride from a trio headed into Kuwait City to burn off steam the way young military men do when they are far from home. Rainey hopped into the back seat and closed his eyes. If he slept, he wouldn't have to engage in conversation.

* * *

"Where's your buddy?" barked the base commander. He had a salt-and-pepper brush cut beneath his cover and a powerful, I'm-in-charge look about him. He also had a pair of MPs in tow and he was absolutely livid.

"My *buddy?*" Fig walked down the hallway in a restricted section of the base, a place reserved for only Special Forces troops and other JSOC elements staging for deployment into Iraq. "What buddy?"

"Don't play games with me, soldier. Bronco. Didn't he fly back with you guys from Kingston Park?"

"Bronco? Yeah. He's right..." Fig spun around but Rainey was gone. "Well, he's here somewhere. Why? What's up?"

"He murdered two men up there. He's to be taken into custody immediately. You see him, you report it. You hear me, Sergeant?" With that the base commander stormed off.

Fig turned to Babe who was just now drifting out of the briefing room.

"What's up, bro? You look like you've just seen a ghost."

"They say Bronco murdered two people back at KP."

Babe's jaw dropped. "Say what?"

46

Kuwait City, Kuwait

THE Marines dropped him off outside the Marina Mall in the Salmiya District. They offered to drive him back to base later, but Rainey politely declined. He wasn't going back, but didn't bother mentioning that to them.

Wanting to shed his soldier look, Rainey made his way to the American Eagle Outfitters store, where he bought a fresh outfit that consisted of a plain, collarless button-down shirt, khakis, and a pair of boat shoes. He bought a cell phone at the X-cite store, then sat down in a quiet corner of the mall and dialed a number from memory.

"Bonjour?" Georges-Henri Danvers said dryly.

Rainey spoke in French. "I need to speak to my friend. How's he doing? Can he talk?"

"One moment."

"Yes?" Alcott yawned into the receiver. He was groggy, but then again Montreal time was eight hours behind Kuwait time. It was morning there.

"It's me."

"Bronco?"

"How you feeling, brother? They taking good care of you?"

"I'm feeling a bit better, and yes, I'm being very well-cared for. What's up? Is everything okay?"

"No. Everything's not okay. I can't talk about it on an unsecure line, but I need a favor."

"Name it."

"I need you to wire me some money and fast. Five K should do it."

"Five thousand bucks? What's going on? Where are you?"

"Kuwait City. Can you wire me the money or not?"

There was a pause. "Call me back in five minutes."

* * *

This time when Rainey called, Alcott answered the phone. He explained that he'd just made the arrangements for the money to be wired per Rainey's particular instructions, then with sincerity asked, "Bronco, are you in trouble? What the heck's going on? I heard about our two friends."

"That's what I'm trying to figure out, Shep. Appreciate the help. Get better. I'll be in touch." Then the line went dead.

* * *

Rainey was seated behind a workstation at an Internet café on Salem Al Mubarak St. punching away on a keyboard as Raji Fayyad's voice played over and over in his mind. He typed the word "Carnicero" into the computer's Web browser and hit ENTER. There were several hits. According to a Spanish-to-English online dictionary, the word meant butcher. He scanned the remaining results, but nothing else seemed to make much sense.

He then punched into the search box "Primer Sol Energías." Fayyad had mentioned that Carnicero was somehow involved with a corporation by this name. Rainey stared at the screen. There were 4,289 hits. The first several of which were links to the same website: www.primersolenergias.com. He clicked on the hyperlink and was taken to the company's homepage. It could be viewed in several languages. He clicked the one for English. He then scrolled over to the ABOUT tab and clicked again. Primer Sol Energías was actually a conglomerate of companies all playing a part in the growing industry of the development and application of "green energy." Solar panels, wind-powered turbines, electric cars, the list went on.

He moved the cursor up to the CONTACT US tab and clicked. There were 27 listings of various offices around the world. The closest was in Greece. According to the site, the corporate offices were located in Mexico City.

Mexico. The border.

Could explain how the two martyrs would enter the country. It seemed logical. Hezbollah and other terrorist organizations were already developing footholds in Mexico and other nations south of the border. The loopholes there were abundant. Most politicians back home didn't really want to talk about securing the border. It didn't sit well with Hispanic voters. Or so they reasoned.

He needed to talk to someone who just might be able to put this new information in context. *Worth a shot.*

Rainey punched in a new search string and hit ENTER. The website for the Drug Enforcement Administration popped up. He pulled up the listing of offices. There were over 200 DEA offices in the U.S., but none of the domestic ones interested him. Instead, he clicked on one of the 86 foreign offices, specifically the one in Rome. Rainey mentally noted the phone number and shut down his workstation. He dialed the number while he exited through the back of the café.

"Hello, Drug Enforcement Administration. To whom may I direct your call?"

"Doug Creighton, please."

"Who shall I say is calling?"

Rainey chewed on his bottom lip for a second, then said, "Edmond Dantès."

The receptionist cleared her throat. "Hold, please, Mr. Dantès. I'll see if he's in."

Rainey sat down on a bench, paying careful attention to anyone within earshot. He hated to admit it, even to himself, but he was absolutely exhausted. His body ached and he was in serious need of sleep. But there would be time for that later. This was far too important.

As he waited on hold, the lilting voice of the muezzin calling the faithful to prayer blared from a local mosque. It was time for *Maghrib*—sunset prayer.

"Thank you for holding, Mr. Dantès. Agent Creighton has stepped out for a bit, but if you would like to leave a message for him I can put you through to his voice mail."

"Do you know when he'll be back? It's urgent."

"I'm sorry, sir, but I really can't say. Would you like to leave him a message?"

"Are you able to page him or reach him on his cell?"

"I can try, but I can't make any promises."

"I'd appreciate it. If you are able to raise him, please have him call me at this number." Rainey spouted off the number for the phone he was using.

"Yes, I will try."

"Thanks."

"Good day, sir."

Rainey went across the street and collected his prepaid Master-Card loaded with five thousand dollars from the Al Muzaini Exchange Company. Then he walked back to the Marina Mall and bought a fashionable pin-striped suit, a crisp white dress shirt, trendy necktie and expensive leather shoes. He also purchased a cheap pair of drugstore variety reading glasses. With his shopping done, he paid for a room at the Ibis Kuwait Salmiya Hotel but didn't plan on spending the night. Instead, he used the room to shower and shave and to don his new attire, the idea being that he would be all the more inconspicuous if he took on the visage of a successful businessman, especially considering his plan to travel abroad.

Creighton still hadn't called. Rainey sat down on the bed and willed the muscles in his neck and shoulders to relax. Through the window, his eyes followed the coast of the Kuwait Bay and the wake of a freighter as it lumbered out into the Gulf. He'd always loved watching the ships. He used to watch them as a boy as he fished the waters of the Chesapeake. There was something incredibly peaceful about a boat that big drifting across the horizon.

Memories of Mom, Dad and Maddie, Christmas and home, came into view. Warm feelings of nostalgia, too. He ached to be with them, ached to be home. The tune from *O Holy Night* seeped into his mind. Then without warning, his phone came alive.

47

"**D**ANTÉS."

"Ah, the Count of Monte Cristo," chuckled the DEA agent. "It's been a long time, my friend."

Rainey had met Doug Creighton in southern Afghanistan a couple of years back. At the time, Creighton had been assigned to one of the DEA's Foreign-deployed Advisory and Support Teams. The FAST team's helicopter had been forced down with mechanical problems on a Taliban-infested mountain, and Rainey and his Delta mates were called upon to get them out. It had taken three hair-raising days just to get to them. For anyone else, it would have been a suicide mission. But Deltas were an altogether different breed.

There'd been a gunfight—a nasty one—during which Creighton took a mortar blast to his right leg. His recovery had been long, but eventually he was able to return to full duty, complete with a shiny new prosthesis. During the lengthy recuperation, Rainey had made sure his DEA buddy had a steady supply of books to keep his mind off the pangs of boredom. The very first novel he'd sent was *The Count of Monte Cristo* by Alexandre Dumas.

But the reason Rainey had called Creighton today wasn't to discuss old books or old times, it was because Doug Creighton like many of his fellow FAST teamers had a military background. Creighton's in particular was in naval intelligence.

"Doug, buddy. It's great to hear your voice."

"Lois said it's urgent. What can I do for ya?"

"I need your help, brother."

"Well, considering what you did for me and my guys in the 'Stan, I'm all ears."

"Are you somewhere you can talk?"

Creighton lowered the phone and looked around. "Yeah. I'm alone in my office. Why?"

"Doug, I'm in a bit of a pickle. I'm in the Gulf and need to get back to the States quietly."

"How quietly?"

"Extremely. But I'd also like to talk to you in person first. There is something I need to discuss that is too sensitive for the airwaves if you get my drift."

Creighton was silent.

"Can you help me?"

After a second, Creighton replied, "Absolutely. But let me call you right back."

Ten minutes later, Rainey's phone vibrated. "Yeah."

"Where are you right now?"

"Kuwait City."

There were several seconds of silence. Then Creighton said, "Okay. Listen to me very carefully."

48

Rome, Italy

ONCE on the plane heading out of Kuwait, Rainey kicked off his shoes and tried to relax. He'd been on edge the entire time he was at the airport. Surely whoever knew he was still alive would be waiting for him there. There were few other options for getting out of the country fast, especially under the circumstances. Thus his altered appearance. His hair was now spiked. He wore dark sunglasses and a designer suit, carried an expensive leather briefcase he'd purchased on his way to the airport. He could be a hedge fund manager, a high-profile attorney, an oil magnate. No one would ever figure him to be a rugged American warrior spy.

For a little more than two hours, Rainey had dozed off more than a dozen times only to be startled awake by the loud jovialities of the two men seated in front of him. He urgently needed to focus on connecting the dots, to think, but more so, he needed sleep. Deep sleep. His seemingly endless reserves of energy were nearly depleted. This time, when he awoke, it was on approach into Rome Fiumicino Airport. He stretched out his legs and arms, slipped his shoes back on. Rainey yawned. Man was he tired. Maybe even more so now than before the cat nap.

He managed to make it through passport control and customs unmolested. Shuffling through another security chokepoint, he headed for a specific row of chairs in Terminal Three. With his eyes, he counted five over from the left and sat down. To anyone watching him, Rainey was just another busy traveler, sitting down for a spell to check some papers in the hectic terminal. After a few minutes of rummaging through the contents of the briefcase, Rainey subtly reached under the seat and pulled a short strip of duct tape from its underside. In the middle of the tape were a key fob remote and a single key though his eyes went nowhere near them.

Rainey made his way to the lot, where he pressed the key fob remote and watched for flashing headlights or taillights to respond. He finally located the small rented Opel Corsa and squeezed inside. He started the car before opening the glove box. Smiling, he pulled out the contents. On top was a paperback novel: an Italian language copy of *The Count of Monte Cristo*. A handwritten note with a local address was tucked inside the cover. Beneath the book was an envelope that contained $5,000 USD along with another prepaid Master-Card. A tiny Post-it note had been stuck to the card, which delineated the same amount.

Doug was indeed a good friend.

The directions led Rainey to a restaurant not far from the airport. Douglass Creighton was seated in the rear with his back to the wall, a cagey smile on his face.

Rainey placed the book on the table as he took his seat. "Nice touch."

"I assumed you didn't have an Italian edition. Well, now you do." Creighton patted the cover of the paperback and then shook the Delta man's hand, all the while keeping his eyes in casual scan mode. Creighton ordered each of them a plate of fettuccine Alfredo and a cup of caffé Americano—a strong Italian coffee. "So, how're you doin'? I like the new look."

"Sorry to have to get right to the point, Doug, but time is of the essence." Rainey scooched his chair in and took a sip of his coffee. "I'm on TDY. I'm afraid you'll just have to trust me."

"Enough said, Ray. What's up?"

Rainey set his cup down. "Have you ever heard of the name *Carnicero*? Specifically in the context of the Mexican border. It's Spanish for—"

"Butcher." He lowered his head and his voice. "The answer is yes, I have. Carnicero is the nickname of a man named Devonte Reyes."

"Devonte Reyes? Yeah, I've heard of him. Windmills, eco-this, eco-that."

"Precisely what I was getting to. You wouldn't know it, but Devonte Reyes secretly runs the Sinaloa Cartel, one of the most ruthless drug cartels on the planet, yet publicly he is known as a stalwart crusader of the alternative energy movement. He's got his hands in a lot of crap. Done very well in his PR campaign. He's a brilliant businessman, and is well-loved in Mexico and around the world for his philanthropy. But make no mistake," Creighton lowered his voice, "Reyes is a ruthless murderer, a cold-hearted savage who distributes illegal narcotics all around the world, but to no country more so than the good ol' U. S. of A.

"For years, the DEA has been wanting to get their hands on him. He's been extremely elusive for us to nail though. Knows how to play the game. Been at it for a long time and no one, I mean no one, rats on him. He snaps his fingers and you and your family are dead. Plain and simple. He pretty much owns the Mexican government—at least the part that matters anyway. Reyes makes old Pablo Escobar look like a choir boy."

"But I thought Joaquin Guzman ran the Sinaloas. You know, *El Chapo.*"

"You and most of the world." Creighton shook his head. "No, Reyes is the real kingpin."

"That explains a lot." Rainey polished off his pasta and wiped his chin with a napkin.

"This is strictly confidential…I know I can trust you. I know of a handful of agents in our Tucson office who are far more knowledgeable on Reyes and his operation. If you'd like, I can make some quiet inquiries and get you more info. Why the sudden interest in Carnicero? If you don't mind my asking."

"I'm doing an exposé for Nat Geo," said Rainey deadpan.

The DEA man smiled and shook his head.

"All I can say is, it's important. And germane to my TDY."

Creighton studied Rainey's face as he devoured a fork full of pasta.

"Don't worry, your name is completely off the radar and I intend to keep it that way."

The DEA man squinted, scratched his chin. "You mentioned that you need to get back to the States...*quietly*..."

Rainey discreetly slid the Canadian passport across the table. "I need a new passport. And it can't be in my name of course."

"Of course," Creighton said dryly. "Anything else?"

"Another plane ticket."

"Where to this time?"

Rainey sipped his coffee again, breathed in the intoxicating aroma, then smiled. "Tucson. Where else?"

"This has something to do with what happened in Mosul, doesn't it? Al Jazeera's already reporting that some kind of American covert operation has taken place there. Something terrible must have gone wrong, huh? At least it seems that way from the images I've seen so far...bodies being pulled from a pile of rubble. Looked to me like a bombed-out building of some sort."

Rainey said nothing. He just looked at his friend, blankly masking the rage brewing within. "You're gonna have to trust me, Doug. I don't have a lot of time."

Creighton sat back and seemed to be thinking as he finished his fettuccine. After nearly a minute, he leaned in. "I may know someone who can help, but it's not going to be cheap, especially with it being a rush job."

"It's extremely important, Doug. I can assure you that it is vital to our national security."

Creighton fished a cell phone out of his jacket pocket. "Don't worry, Edmond, I'm sorry, *Count*," he quipped in a French accent. "There are few people in this world I would dare say this about these days, but...I know I can trust you without condition. And don't worry by the way, I'll front whatever the cost is going to be. You can pay me back later. I know you're good for it."

Rainey winked. "You can *count* on it."

"Oh, that was bad."

Both men shook hands, drained the last of the coffee from their cups and left one at a time.

49

Westbound Over the Atlantic

TWO hours and thirty-four minutes later, *Luke Dalton* was airborne en route to Tucson, Arizona with two scheduled layovers along the way, one in Philadelphia and the other in Dallas. Rainey had a carry-on containing clothes as well as some used toiletry items. Creighton had also come through with a garment bag in which were two Brooks Brothers suits in order to further legitimize Rainey's newly acquired cover, that of a soccer-loving—er, football-loving—Brit on a business trip abroad. His business: books. Acquisitions, publishing, you name it. Creighton had even scraped up some rather convincing pocket litter in order to authenticate the hurried legend. There was an assortment of business cards he might have picked up at a meeting or two in London. He had his own stack of cards, too. If anyone bothered to call the number thereon, they'd reach a voice mail greeting on a disposable cell phone telling them that Luke Dalton was out of the office and would return to work the following week. Rainey also carried a rumpled pack of Treasurer Luxury Menthol cigarettes—exactly two left—and a creased calfskin wallet, inside which was a worn ticket stub from a year-old match between Man U and Tottenham. And just for good measure, in addition to the 500 dollars-worth of pound notes, Creighton had produced a wallet-size photo of someone's smiling little one-month-old. He obviously still had some very good connections.

The flight back across the Atlantic was a long one and gave Rainey a chance to get some much-needed sleep and plan his next steps.

While waiting for his source to obtain the new passport and other bona fides, Creighton had done some digging. Rainey was sure going to owe him big time. Amazingly, Creighton had managed to arrange a meeting with one of the agents who had intimate knowledge of Reyes's organization. What's more, this very DEA agent was the point of contact—the handler—for a deep-cover DEA operative who was even now secretly working within the cartel. Using his influence and relative celebrity within the DEA, Creighton had asked that the handler only be told the meeting was with an important "fellow federal agent."

What should he say during the meeting? Should the approach be direct or subtle?

His phone vibrated. It was an e-mail reply from Pappy Baker about some of the items he was looking to acquire without going through the normal channels. Pappy was still an Agency legend after all, and despite being retired, he maintained a global network of loyal contacts. More importantly right now, Pappy could be trusted.

Rainey read the e-mail and grinned. The order was intact. Everything could be ready and staged within four hours of notice. All he had to do was tell Pappy where.

With tired eyes, Rainey stared into a pristine sky. It was a bright cobalt and clear. So clear. Set against the horizon far in the distance was a familiar cityscape. The Big Apple.

What would another 9/11 look like? No. Can't let that happen.

Gloves are off, Ray. Whatever it takes.

50

Philadelphia, PA

MAKING it through passport control and customs without incident, Rainey synchronized his movement with that of a group of weary-looking international business travelers. He struck up a conversation with one of them—a German man, as it turned out. He and his colleagues were here to negotiate a tech company merger. Rainey took the man's card with a smile and a handshake. Luke Dalton lived for cutting edge technology and was always looking for innovative, new ways through which to grow his business. After all, competition in the book biz was fierce.

With some time to kill until his departing flight to Dallas, Rainey ventured into some of the airport stores. Luke Dalton, the businessman, was about to vanish into thin air.

In one shop, Rainey picked up a backpack. In another, he purchased a long-sleeved T-shirt, a gray hoodie, a pair of blue jeans, a leather belt, some new socks and underwear, and a pair of hikers. Finally, he bought a Philadelphia Eagles ball cap and a pair of Arnette shades then slipped into a restroom to change. On his way out, he stuffed his old clothes into a trash can. In another, he disposed of the cell phone he'd been using since Kuwait, having already separated it from the SIM card and battery. Then he walked to the Best Buy kiosk, from which he bought a new phone and a pair of earbuds.

Rainey settled into a chair overlooking the tarmac, tugged the bill of his cap down and pushed his new earbuds into his ears. Like most young men these days with time to kill, he was blissfully oblivious to everything going on around him. Or so it seemed. Rainey grabbed a newspaper which had been left on the seat next to him and read it from beginning to end. When it was time, he tucked the folded paper under his arm, ambled back through the terminal and boarded his flight to Dallas.

The trip there was uneventful. The layover, too. Soon he was in the sky again, headed on to Tucson.

A heavyset woman next to him bumped him with her arm nearly jolting him from his reverie. In his polite way, he grinned and accepted the woman's apology. Then drifted back to his musings.

The assassinations, the abduction of Dr. Horst. Nika. Kozlov. The Russians in Montreal. Where was it all headed? Why did they need a laser gun built? They could have had that done back in Russia. Much safer to do it there. Why keep Horst around and have him build it in Montreal. What was the hurry? And how did that connect with Fayyad's shocking revelation. This diabolical plot. This fictitious Jamil ibn Hasan character.

Ugh! Please, God, give me time. Help me stop them before it's too late.

Rainey thought about contacting Job, relaying everything he had learned; he trusted him without equivocation. But how could he trust that the message wouldn't be intercepted? Was there a traitor at Directorate Twelve?

Rainey thought about that for a moment, thought about what had happened to Fayyad at Kingston Park. Someone inside knew about the Jonah Team's rescue op. They also knew about Kingston Park. Was Fayyad the target in Mosul or was it the Jonah Team? He wanted to call Job, but… No. For now he would keep pressing on. He had to find out what these two tools of terror were up to, or at least who they were and/or where they were headed.

As the wheels chirped down in Tucson, there was one singular phrase pounding inside his head.

Failure is not an option.

51

Arlington, VA

"WHERE is he?" Job demanded as he moved about the Operations Center, his eyes scanning the bank of large wall-mounted monitors in front of him. "Run it again."

Each of the specialists behind him was saddled up to a trio of computer screens in an ultra-secure, temperature-controlled room six floors below ground at Directorate Twelve headquarters, known publicly by its signage as the Greenbriar Foundation Home Office. At their disposal were some of the most sophisticated intelligence databases and networks on the planet.

Here, they monitored various situations and operations around the globe via an array of classified systems and secure communication portals. It was a literal hub of up-to-the-minute intelligence activity.

The Directorate Twelve Operations Center, or 12OC, was very much like its sister, the Agency's vaunted Global Operations Center, save for the fact that the 12OC staff was without a doubt an even more irreverent crowd, especially with regard to the bureaucracy of intelligence.

There was one other notable difference. The 12OC had an access point to COIL—Computerized Organ for Intelligent Linkage—a complex construct of computer systems, a digital marriage of software and hardware. In many ways, COIL could actually think for itself. Amazing stuff. A force multiplier to be sure.

"Yes, sir." One of the specialists pounded away at her keyboard. "Here, sir. I've got him. Looks like he did catch a flight out of Kuwait. Seems the computers had some difficulty with his altered appearance." She pushed the contents of her screen to the middle monitor on the wall in front of Job.

Standing in his smart black suit, hands on his hips, the spymaster stared at the frozen image, the glow of the monitors illuminating his face, reflecting ominously in his pupils. He shook his head. "Two million dollars for this software and it missed him on its first pass. Unreal. Okay. Where was he headed?"

She nodded in agreement. "Algorithms might need tweaked a bit." The specialist played the surveillance footage at double, then triple speed. They followed Rainey to the ticket counter and across the terminal. More sounds of computer keys clicking. "Rome, sir. Used the Maxim Renaud passport."

"Rome?" said Job. His mind was already crunching its own data matrix. "All right, do this for me: run all outgoing calls from Kuwait City—ones connecting to Italy—in the last fourteen hours. Then isolate the calls to Rome."

"Doing it now, sir." When the search was complete, the bespectacled specialist pushed the results to the screen beside the monitor displaying the Kuwait International Airport surveillance footage.

While Job studied the list of phone numbers and accompanying data, he asked over his shoulder, "Find out who paid for the ticket to Rome."

"Already done, sir."

Job moved his eyes to the screen below the phone data. "Hmm. Interesting. Okay. Who do we have in theater?"

After a few mouse clicks and some more typing, the specialist replied, "We have Janis and Zhaki, sir."

"Send Zhaki. See if he can get a bead on him. We have to find him, people. We have to find Reagan Rainey."

* * *

Two Hours and Forty-Nine Minutes Later

"Zhaki just reported in, sir."

"Whaddya got, Kelly?"

"Seems Rainey made contact with a DEA agent by the name of Douglass Creighton. Currently works out of the Rome office. Looks like he served in Afghanistan on a DEA FAST team. Several notable operations in country. Former United States Naval Intelligence. Sir?"

"Creighton. Creighton." The spymaster's head tilted back, his eyes were closed. When his mind had finally zeroed in on the man's face, he opened his eyes. The same face was now on the screen in front of him. "Yes. Okay. Run his calls, texts, e-mails. Office, cell, home. Everything. Do it now." Job turned to one of the other specialists. "Mikey, what do you have from Fiumicino?"

"Surveillance is ready to go. Playing it now."

Job watched his warrior spy pace through the terminal. The 12OC specialist toggled between the various camera feeds without missing a beat. It was during the fourth time through the footage, Job all at once belted out, "There! Zoom in on that, please." He drew closer to the screen.

You are good, Ray. You are good.

Job was silent as he watched Rainey pull something from the underside of the chair on which he was seated, palm it and casually embark.

"Where does he go from here?"

"Parking lot. Here. This car, here. Tag's not visible due to the angle of the camera. He drives off northbound. That's as good as we've got."

"Who loaded the drop?"

The thirty-one year-old specialist reset his cursor several times until he had the footage pegged at the right spot. "Here, sir. This man right here."

"Okay. That there is Doug Creighton. Same person who bought the plane ticket out of Kuwait City. All right." Job turned back to the young woman beside him. "Zhaki?"

"He followed Creighton to the Metropole. Creighton made a brush pass with another man in the lobby there. Zhaki snapped a photo of the other man with his cell phone. Then Creighton returned to his office. He made a few calls to his wife from his cell and...that's about it, sir."

Job nodded. "Let's see it." When the image Zhaki had captured with his cell phone appeared on the screen, Job took a deep breath and let it out slowly.

"This is interesting."

"What is?" asked Job.

The female specialist followed the information she was reading on her monitor with the tip of her index finger. "Records indicate Douglass Creighton isn't married."

But Job was already thinking way ahead.

"Shall I have Zhaki make contact, sir?"

Job ignored the question, still studying the man's face in the digital photo. "Run through the passenger manifests of all flights out of Rome—and then cross-reference that with anyone flying on a British passport. I think I may know what Mr. Rainey is up to."

Ten minutes later, the 12OC specialists had their confirmation that the Luke Dalton passport was indeed a fake. One of the specialists turned to her boss. "Do you want me to flag it, sir?"

With his hand massaging his forehead, Job shook his head. "No. Leave it in play. And arrange a flight for me to Tucson. Wheels up ASAP."

52

Hills of West Virginia

QUIETLY tucked away under thousands of tons of rock and earth, the Strathcona Research Facility was a highly secure installation that served as a laboratory for some of the most secretive and forward thinking projects known to mankind. Most, if not all, had some type of defense-related or national security application. Built directly into three contiguous mountains several decades ago, Strathcona's only access points were few and only known to a handful of people, most notably the DOD bus drivers who transported the facility's staff here each day from nearby Raleigh County Memorial Airport. Everyone who worked here was under the most stringent of security clearances such that even the security clearance itself was ultra-secret. Area 51 sans the notoriety.

Each day, the blacked-out buses lumbered up County Route 25, eventually turning onto an innocuous gravel road somewhere between Claremont and Thayer where they seemed to just vanish into the woods. Entry to the facility was made through a gigantic hydraulic door perfectly disguised to look like part of the mountainside. Spread across the terrain was a network of invisible intrusion detection systems. There were myriad, infrared cameras secreted in trees and rocks,

a gridwork of pressure plates, infrared beams and other highly sensitive electronic equipment that blanketed the landscape. All this so
Strathcona's vitally important existence would stay secret.

Supplementing these security measures was a cadre of heavily
armed and superbly camouflaged men in hidden posts at strategic locations across the expansive topography. The entire area was posted
with signs that plainly read, "No Trespassing—Private Property."
Anything otherwise, for instance the kind that proclaim U.S. government ownership, would only draw attention and unwanted suspicion.
If anyone had, in fact, ever stumbled upon this secret piece of real estate, there were no records anywhere to show for it.

In a quarantined storage area of the subterranean complex, sat a
pallet of one of the latest experimental materials conceived by America's brightest thinkers. Developed by an all-star team of physicists,
chemists, engineers and others contracted to the Department of Defense, more specifically to DARPA, TRB-80 was an explosive compound with such destructive capability that it paralleled that of a nuclear fission bomb. Yet what made TRB-80—affectionately dubbed
Turbo—special was that it had none of the detectable radioactive sig-
natures of a nuclear device. TRB-80 would allow the United States to
maintain its stellar military force capability amidst the constant calls
within the international community for nuclear disarmament. But
there were still more tests to be done at places like the Nevada Test
Site and others in the coming weeks and months.

The pallet was tightly wrapped in an opaque, tan, vinyl skin that
outwardly might easily be confused for a crate of foodstuffs. It rested
safely cordoned off in a separate, restricted area of the Strathcona facility that was comparable to a bank vault on steroids. With only one
door, a massive slab of steel close to twenty inches thick, the room
and the entire Strathcona facility at large, was nothing short of a well-
fortified bunker.

* * *

"Here. This is the spot." Kozlov killed the engine of his ATV.

Based on the maps, detailed specs and other intel that had been
passed along to him, the mine shaft was right in front of them, though
there was no visible evidence of it. The shaft had been sealed off to
the outside world decades ago. Ever since, the mountain had steadily
swallowed up all signs to indicate it had ever been there.

Kozlov and his team covered their ATVs with brush. They all wore camouflage BDUs and balaclavas.

"Give it to me," said Kozlov after scraping back the twigs and foliage—nature's curtain.

Gavril Udovin unzipped the large pack he had strapped to the back of his ATV and extracted the prototype they had forced Dr. Horst to build. "Here."

By now, Kozlov could operate the thing with his eyes closed. With precision, he set about cutting a hole into the reinforced concrete and rock wall that sealed off the mine shaft—a hole just big enough to crawl through. The high-energy laser beam made short work of the fortified barrier. Like sticking a finger into a wall of peanut butter.

When he was finished, he handed the laser gun back to Udovin who slid it into his pack with a grunt.

Nika nestled into the brush just outside the shaft. Her job: watch for interlopers. For security reasons, none of them save for Kozlov actually knew what they were there to steal. The original plan had called for her and Zukov to work as a tandem out here, but he'd been killed at the chalet outside Montreal. Now, she alone would operate as the team's external security as the others pushed deep into the mountain. "Good luck," she whispered.

* * *

Olezka Antipov gave her a wink. "Be right back." He'd been enamored with her ever since the first time he'd laid eyes on her, in large part because of her drop-dead looks. But when he'd learned about her very unique abilities and how they far surpassed his own, currents of testosterone raged within him. She was a mystery. A gorgeous, dangerous mystery. But he kept his feelings for her in check for fear of how Vlad would react if he ever found out. He still couldn't believe that Nika and Vlad were brother and sister.

* * *

For more than an hour, the three men trekked along the deserted mine, following a set of old rail lines by way of their night-vision goggles and Kozlov's keen military bearing. As suddenly as they'd begun, the rail lines stopped. Now the mine curved off to the right and descended at a considerably steeper grade; it also became much more narrow. The trio forged onward through a tight space created by a pile of dusty old bracing timbers. Finally, Kozlov broke the silence with a whisper. "O, you stay here."

After another two hundred yards or so of carefully descending into the guts of the mountain, the pair came to the end of the mine shaft, a natural wall of cold, damp rock. Kozlov checked a handheld sensor. Nothing. He powered off the device and slid it back into his pack then removed two slim sticks. He cracked the Cyalume ChemLights and dropped them at his feet then pulled off his NVGs. Udovin did likewise.

"Laser," he said while glancing back toward where they'd left Antipov. From the green glow of the ChemLights came an ominous unease in the cramped space.

Udovin let his SMG hang from his chest, unhitched from his pack. As he fought with the zipper, Kozlov visually examined the shaft. Everything about this pointed to a foreboding of lethal consequence. It wouldn't take much to set off a cave-in. But then again with what he had in mind that was also very encouraging.

Udovin handed Kozlov the laser, gripped his gun and paced back a few yards, keeping his muzzle trained on the rock wall that would soon be gone.

It took Kozlov a little less than a minute to carve a hole in the wall. He smiled as light from within bled onto him. The intel, geo cords and corresponding maps that their man inside DARPA had provided were absolutely spot on.

Udovin stepped forward, but Kozlov snapped his arm out, held him back. He shoved the laser gun into Udovin's hands then slithered through the newly created burrow, the edges of which were still smoldering. In a matter of seconds, he was inside the secure storage room staring at the pallet of TRB-80.

He extracted a Zero Tolerance 0400 Scavenger knife from his pants pocket and flicked out its black blade. Quietly, he sliced an X across the shrink wrap then clipped the knife back inside his pocket. Kozlov slid out one of the metal boxes; it was roughly the size of two cinder blocks sitting side by side.

He opened it.

Inside were twelve tubular gel packs, each about two inches in diameter and close to a foot long. They were couched in a strange type of insulation that protected them from heat and impact despite their chemical stability. Kozlov reached inside and touched one, gave it a squeeze. The outer casing was clear, some type of cellulose. The blue gel within was soft yet kind of stiff, like toothpaste that had been refrigerated.

Kozlov closed the box and pushed it through the hole to Udovin, then pushed himself through as well. He whipped out an empty duffel bag he'd brought with him and held it open as Udovin placed the box carefully inside. Kozlov slung the bag on his back and motioned for Udovin to head toward the surface. As Udovin was negotiating the slippery, damp shaft, Kozlov pulled something from his leg pocket and slapped it against the rock wall, above the hole through which he'd just wiggled.

Soon they met back up with Antipov. After a few minutes of fast walking, Kozlov checked his watch. He allowed Antipov and Udovin to continue on ahead of him for several seconds then removed a wallet-size remote from his coat pocket. He took a deep breath, steeled himself.

Then began to run.

53

RED lights on the security control panel lit up almost immediately and a speaker built into its face began to clamor with a shrill, tinny beeping. The terminal operator touched the computer screen in the area that was flashing red. A specific grid instantly appeared on the screen—an array of four camera feeds from the large secure storage bay where the TRB-80 was awaiting shipment. The operator touched each block in the grid, one by one, which enlarged the frame to full screen. At the top of each individual frame in white text was the camera number, date and time, along with a coded title for its designated zone within the complex.

Cam1. Good.

Cam2. Nothing.

Cam3…

"What the—" Something was off. He zoomed in on the large crate and rotated the camera a few degrees to the left. He zoomed in further yet and saw a half-moon-shaped blemish in the wall behind the pallet of TRB-80. A curse word escaped his lips as he pawed at his base station mic. "Tower to Utah Three Seven, please respond urgent to Zone Six Zero Zero and report back immediately."

"Roger, Tower. Utah Three Seven en route."

Utah Team was the moniker for the cadre of men whose responsibility it was to provide armed security for the entire facility inside and out. They were all specially-trained United States Marine commandos. Utah 37 was the designation of the specific Marine assigned to the zone in which the storage bay containing the TRB-80 was located.

In less than thirty seconds, Utah 37, now joined by two of his cadre mates who had heard the transmission and responded to assist, had the metal door open and was surging inside the expansive, sterile room. At first nothing seemed amiss, but as they spread out along the walls, they discovered with horror what had happened.

"Utah Three Seven to Tower, we have a breach! I repeat. We have a breach! Alert Maximum! Alert Maximum!"

The entire complex launched into complete security shutdown mode. Doors closed and locked, sirens wailed, bright red lights flashed. Alert Maximum also meant that a FLASH message, code word Iroquois, was to be immediately sent from the Strathcona Tower duty officer to various watch desks at the Pentagon, White House Situation Room, CIA, FBI, DOE and a small number of other agencies within the American government. It was the highest alert in existence at Strathcona, and to date, save for monthly emergency preparedness drills, had never been utilized.

Quickly, Utah 37 barked out orders to the other Marines while more of them sprinted to the area. "You three with me. Joe, you and Cal stay here. Get someone down here to do an inventory."

"Roger that."

Utah 37 probed the hole in the wall with the flashlight attached to his Colt M4. Then successively, he and the other three commandos squirted through it. As the men from Utah Team stormed into the mine shaft and pursued whoever or whatever had made the hole, they reported back to the Tower by radio. But their efforts were in vain. The sudden blast quickly cut off their transmissions and any chance they had at seeing daylight or anything else ever again.

* * *

Kozlov threw the remote to the ground and pushed Udovin from behind as they sprinted up the mine shaft using only their NVGs. The explosion had effectively closed them off from their pursuers, whoever among them wasn't already dead, but in doing so had given rise to an altogether different problem, albeit just as potentially damning. Dust and bits of rock began falling from the ceiling of the shaft. Larger rocks started to fragment and fall.

Kozlov yelled at his men to run. They needed to move or they would all be swallowed up by the collapsing old mine.

Antipov was ten yards ahead. He slowed to step over some fallen rocks. Just as he was straddling them, a large mass of dolomite sheared off from the ceiling and struck him square in the head, crushing his skull. Kozlov and Udovin didn't bother to stop and check their friend. He was clearly dead. Both men slithered past and ran as fast and furiously as they could now.

The earth violently shook. Udovin lost his footing. He went down hard on the old metal rail line. He was almost back up when another falling rock easily weighing more than a ton crashed down on him at the waist. His entire lower body was pinned beneath its crushing weight. He screamed out in pain. Through gritted teeth, eyes blurry with tears, he yelled to his comrade. "VLAD! VLAD! Help! I'm stuck! I can't move!"

Kozlov, who himself had been knocked to the ground by the rumbling, now sat facing the writhing man, presented with the daunting choice of helping his old friend and jeopardizing the mission or leaving him behind and getting out alive with the TRB-80. He knew what he had to do. Kozlov swung his sub-gun around and fired a single shot into his friend's head.

At least he's out of his misery.

He scrambled back to his feet and ran.

* * *

Nika felt the ground beneath her quake. A long, low rumble from deep inside the mountain, a continuous guttural growl as if an angry beast somewhere within had been rousted from a long hibernation. She wrapped her gloved fingers tightly around her submachine gun and hunkered down even closer to the ground. Before long, the noise grew louder, like thunder rolling across the sky during a violent summer storm.

The earth visibly shook.

She was about to break radio silence when suddenly Kozlov shot out of the mine shaft.

"Poekhali! Poekhali!" Let's go! Let's go!

"What about the others?"

"They're dead. Mountain got 'em. We need to hurry."

Kozlov was already uncovering his ATV as Nika cast a worried look back into the abyss of the mine. He was right. The Americans would soon be swarming the area with extreme prejudice.

Nika swept the brush off her ATV, pushed it away from an ancient oak tree and jumped on. She started the engine and raced off after Kozlov who was now a good fifty yards away.

Soon they hit an old fire lane and were traveling upward of forty mph. When they reached a certain fallen log—a landmark of sorts—they turned and edged down through the trees to the bottom of a valley. Negotiating into a shallow creek, they forged downstream as fast as the ATVs could maneuver. Ice cold mountain water splashed up on them from every angle. Eventually, they reached a dilapidated, little-used bridge under which they rapidly dismounted, then ascended the rocky embankment to an old gravel road.

"Get in!" barked Kozlov as he popped the back gate of a Chevy Tahoe that to any unsuspecting passersby appeared to have suffered an untimely flat tire, its driver presumably gone off in search of help. "Watch my back."

Gun up and ready, Nika stole a glance over her shoulder, watched him throw open a hidden compartment in the back of the vehicle. The lid now blocked her view of him.

After seven or eight seconds, Kozlov closed the lid with a *whomp* and scurried around to the flat tire.

Nika studied the landscape then glimpsed Kozlov in the mirror on the driver's door.

He looked up at her.

She averted her eyes quickly and continued scanning for threats. "We're still good. All clear. You need any help back there?"

"Stay put." Kozlov was workman-like. He moved quickly, but did not seem flustered, didn't rush. He crouched by the flat tire, pulled out a small can of compressed air. He connected its protruding nipple to the valve stem of the flat tire and squeezed the nozzle trigger. In less than three seconds, the tire was re-inflated. Without comment, Kozlov climbed back inside the SUV and dropped it into gear.

Nika brought her carbine to a low ready. "Now what?"

Kozlov brooded. "Now we drive."

54

Arlington, VA

NOEL Patterson waited until he was right beside his car before chirping the alarm off and unlocking the doors with his key fob remote. The leather seat was cold and stiff. He slid the key into the ignition and turned it, cranked up the heat. Not waiting for the car to warm up, he slipped it into gear and pulled out. In that moment, fleeting as it was, everything he'd been doing for the past five years flashed before him. He was afraid. An unfamiliar sense of guilt now crept into his mind.

For the last five years, Noel Patterson, via his post at the Defense Advanced Research Projects Agency (DARPA)—the R&D arm of the United States Department of Defense—had been selling some of his nation's most closely guarded secrets to a man he knew next to nothing about. Even his name was a mystery. Never before had Patterson given his betrayal a second thought.

Until now.

The man he knew only as Mr. P had just called, said that they needed to meet. Something was wrong. Mr. P was nice. Mr. P was never nice.

Patterson agreed, though he never intended to do anything but disappear. He had a friend in Florida with whom he could stay for a little while, maybe a few months, until he could set up his new life abroad. He'd already bought a plane ticket and had just left the Hilton in Arlington, where he'd stayed last night, just to be safe.

He was sitting at the red light at N. George Mason Dr., one hand on the wheel, the other playing with his bottom lip. His eyes were open, but he saw nothing but flashes of future events. What if they found him? What would happen? What if they knew where he was already? Mr. P was an intelligent man, he would not tip his hand unless...

Dread gripped him, wouldn't let go.

He glanced in the rearview mirror. Instantly, terror shot through him like a sniper's bullet. The man driving the car behind him was wearing a ski mask.

* * *

"Wait... Wait... Now!"

As soon as Kupchenko gave the command, Yuri Pershin dropped his radio on the seat next to him and rammed his vehicle into the back of Patterson's BMW. A fraction of second later Kupchenko, in a vehicle directly in front of Patterson's, accelerated backward. Patterson's car was effectively pinched.

Leaving his sedan in gear, Pershin jumped out and ran up along the driver's side of Patterson's Beemer, wielding a big .45 in his right hand.

* * *

He screamed involuntarily as the near simultaneous collisions occurred. Frantically, he jammed his car into reverse and stomped on the accelerator. At first, his tires only chirped and spun, but within a second, his vehicle was able to push the car behind him backward. The first bullet hit him just as he was throwing the car back into drive. He stomped on the gas as a white hot pain quickly streaked down his left side. The bullet had taken a big bite out of his left shoulder just above the bicep and made a ragged hole in his coat that was now wet with blood. The fingers in his left hand began to tingle, but the adrenaline coursing through him masked the true pain that was yet to come.

With just enough room to navigate out of the pincer maneuver undoubtedly orchestrated by Mr. P and his people, Patterson swerved, sideswiping the back end of the car in front of him and the masked man approaching from behind. His vehicle now free, he sped off at a reckless pace.

* * *

Pershin got off a total of five rounds as the big BMW lunged at him, an angry bull busting out of a bucking chute.

He swore loudly as the powerful Beemer slammed into him at the hip. As he twisted away, the back left tire ran over his right foot and violently torqued his ankle and knee.

Kupchenko had just exited his car, when Patterson's sedan broke free. He barely had time to dive back into his open door. He dropped the car into drive, yelling and cursing at Pershin to get in.

Dragging his damaged right leg behind him, Pershin hustled around to the passenger-side door, yanked it open and fell inside. He ripped off his sweat-soaked ski mask and bellowed out in soliloquy, the most vile curse words he knew.

Kupchenko peeled out in hot pursuit, and as he did so, Pershin's door slammed shut. "You idiot! You let him get away!"

* * *

He was driving way too fast. But he had to get away. If he didn't, he was a dead man. Patterson gripped the steering wheel tightly. His face scrunched up as he braced himself for impact. He blew through a red light at N. Pershing Dr. Miraculously, he made it through un-scathed, but so did his pursuers. He managed to make a hard left turn onto Arlington Blvd., but after doing so, realized he was now going in the wrong direction. Horns blared. Oncoming traffic swerved dangerously close to him on both sides. He didn't care. He had to get away.

Patterson raced down the off-ramp, causing a box truck coming toward him to whip into the grass and nearly tip over. Still, wide-eyed and panting heavily, he pressed on. He raced up the ramp onto N. Glebe Rd., pumped the brakes. *Going too fast!* Somehow, he pulled off an unbelievable slide—one he knew he could never repeat.

Near the end of the long, sideways skid, the BMW's wheels gained traction and Patterson stomped the accelerator.

* * *

"Move! MOVE!" Kupchenko yelled between honking and cursing. How Patterson hadn't wrecked yet was a miracle.

"Sorry, boss."

"Shut up!"

Pershin's face was covered with sweat, his hair mussed. He finally buckled his seatbelt when they turned onto Arlington and began chasing the BMW against oncoming traffic.

"Hold on!" Kupchenko replicated Patterson's sliding turn onto Glebe, straightened out and accelerated again. The faint sound of police sirens in the distance began to compete with the roar of the car's engine. But steadily, with Kupchenko's superior driving ability, they began to gain on their prey.

* * *

Patterson fought to keep his car under control. Somehow, he'd managed to make two more incredible turns, first onto N. Quincy then a second onto Wilson Blvd. As he screamed down Wilson, there were a few seconds in which he thought he just might get away. The light was red at 10th St., but there was no oncoming traffic, so he swerved around the cars stopped in front of him.

That's when his luck began to run out.

A large SUV turned northbound onto Wilson from westbound 10th just as he entered the intersection. Patterson swerved to avoid a collision and quickly lost control, oversteering into a long, wild skid. He shot up onto the curb, folding over a row of street signs like they were blades of grass. Trying to steer the car back onto the street only made things worse at that speed. The Beemer hurricaned across the street and into a storefront shattering a large plate glass window. Behind the window, sat the store manager who was busy on the phone, completely unaware of the fate she was about to meet. The weaponized car crushed everything in its path until it finally came to rest against the back wall of the office in a heap of bricks, drywall and ceiling tiles.

Noel Patterson's entire body shook with adrenaline. Tiny particulates from the exploded airbags pervaded the air and filled his lungs, forcing him to cough uncontrollably. He reached for his nose which was now throbbing in pain. With convulsing hands, he felt the deformity. His nose was pushed in and to the side, obviously broken. Then he looked down at his right wrist which felt as though someone had just hit it with a sledge hammer. When he saw the unnatural S-curve in his arm, he immediately had the urge to vomit.

In the confusion of the crash, it didn't quite register when the first shot thudded into the dash. But after the next one pierced the passenger-side head rest and nipped at his right ear, a renewed sense of panic consumed him.

Patterson ducked down and crawled over the center console into the front passenger seat. He suppressed the sharp pain in his damaged right arm and pawed at the door handle with his left. The door jutted open slightly, but was blocked by debris. He pushed and pulled it several times, each time more frantically, then finally swung his legs around and kicked it open, forcing the splintered desk and pile of bricks back far enough for him to slither out.

Another shot.

Then another.

This one grazed him, slicing across his left arm and again slamming into the dash. He ducked down beside the car. A masked shooter appeared in the side mirror just before it was shot off. Even in the dusty air, smoke now beginning to billow from beneath the hood of his car, he had no doubt who was shooting at him and why.

Mr. P.

Why? Because he was a link to them. A loose end that needed to be tied up.

In one swift move, Patterson slid away from the car and across the mess of broken glass, bricks and pulverized drywall. Exposed wires snapped and sparked as he pushed his way through them. He looked back at the shooter through a crack in the wall.

Mr. P fired again. He had pulled up alongside the curb and was standing behind the open door of his car.

More silenced rounds thudded inside the office. One hit a computer monitor which caused a small explosion. With the little bit of energy he had left, Patterson threw himself through an open doorway at the far end of the office, stumbled down a short hallway and escaped out a back door. Falling into the cold air, he sprinted as fast as his legs would move, crossed N. Irving St. then turned south. When he hit 10th St., he tripped and almost went down, but somehow he stayed on his feet. He ran east on 10th for a block or so. At the sound of screeching tires, he scrambled for a hiding spot. Adrenaline was the only thing that kept him moving forward.

An apartment building—The Reserve at Clarendon Centre—was off to his left. A delivery truck emerged from the garage beneath the building on the N. Highland St. side. As the truck lumbered off northbound, Patterson dodged beneath the metal garage door that was slowly closing.

Made it!

In the dim light, he slowed to a walk until finally lightheadedness overcame him. He plopped down in front of a big SUV in the corner of the garage, chest pounding. For several minutes, he just lay there as still as a statue, frozen in fear, his body rising and falling with each pained gasp for air. Before he slipped into unconsciousness, two words spilled from his bloody, quivering lips.

"I'm alive."

55

HE couldn't believe what he'd just heard. FBI Special Agent Frank O'Neil sat still for a moment while the man's incredible story sank in. It was something out of a spy novel. A Russian man named Mr. P. Stolen military secrets. A laser gun. Yet this was no novel. This was real.

Four hours ago, O'Neil and his supervisor had gone and scooped the man up after their office had received a queer phone call. A staffer at the Urgent Care facility on S. Carlin Springs Rd. in Arlington had called, explained to them that a patient—a gunshot victim—was demanding they call the FBI, said it was vital to national security. The patient had refused to speak any further to staff, not counting of course the colorful expletives and insufferable demands.

So it was that they now sat in an FBI interrogation room, looking across the table at each other, sizing each other up: Special Agent in Charge Trevor Dawes, Special Agent Frank O'Neil, and the man about whom they had been called, to wit, Noel Patterson.

O'Neil looked at the man with a straight face, just waiting for him to say something else. It was a tactic he'd found particularly provocative in eliciting confessions, or at minimum, an incriminating statement or two. Most people were uncomfortable with silence, and therefore felt compelled to fill it with something, anything to get the FBI agents across the table to stop staring at them.

A minute in, Patterson blurted out, "Are we going to sit here all day just looking at each other or what?"

"So let me get this straight. You contacted us because you're afraid they—these Russian friends of yours—are going to kill you? Is that right?" probed O'Neil.

"That's right. And they're not my friends." He frowned. "I know that if I stay out there, they will find me and kill me. These are very dangerous people. Just look at what they've done today."

"I'll be honest with you. If what you say is true, you're looking at some serious jail time. You're in a lot of trouble, Noel."

Patterson shifted in his chair, shook his head back and forth. "No I'm not." He managed a smile. "See, you're going to give me blanket immunity."

O'Neil guffawed. He'd been knocked off balance, which didn't often happen. "We're gonna what? Listen, you just admitted to selling top secret information to the Russians. You think the U.S. attorney is gonna give you immunity? You're delusional if that's what you think!"

Patterson leaned back in his chair, arrogance spread across his battered face. "Oh, I'm not delusional, Agent... Agent...

"O'Neil," he said wanly.

"I promise you I'm not delusional, Agent O'Neil. You're going to give me immunity. And do you know why?" Patterson's eyes grew more enthused.

"Why?" asked O'Neil, folding his arms with indignation.

"Because there's more."

"*More?* More what? More B.S.?"

Interrogation was a delicate art. If you came across too strong, too soon the person would often shut down. Conversely, if you came across too weak or too willing to let details be glazed over in generality, which was usually where the lies or purposefully withheld facts were hidden, the suspect would know he could walk all over the interrogator, maybe even lie with impunity. There was a balance that needed to be struck right from the beginning, until the status quo changed and more deliberative measures were necessary. Most times a conversational tone was ideal while plying subtle psychological control—the offering of a cup of water or meal with strategically timed delivery; a chair that was lower than the interrogator's; spatial relationship of interviewer to interviewee. There were countless ways of exerting subtle dominance over someone during questioning. There were also those that were less so. The important aspect for the interviewer was control. Over the person in front of him and himself.

O'Neil had started off well, but now he was beginning to let the man's arrogance get to him, beginning to lose his patience. When he was with the Seattle PD working narcotics, he had never allowed a drug dealing thug to claim dominion over the interview; that was a cardinal sin for any cop. And he wouldn't let this little bureaucrat-looking scientist puke do so either.

"Listen up, pal, we don't like it when people waste our time. And I really—"

"It's a bomb."

O'Neil grew instantly quiet.

Patterson took a swig from the bottle of water he'd been given and grimaced as his broken nose bumped the side of the plastic container.

"What do you mean, a *bomb*?"

Patterson's eyes moved over his treated wounds. "Well, not really a bomb...at least not yet. An explosive to be more precise. It's state of the art, experimental. Military-grade stuff. Cutting edge even by DOD standards."

"Go on."

Patterson smirked. "Ah, ah, ah. Nice try. I need you to promise me immunity first and then I'll tell you all about it."

"We're not in the business of giving people immunity for crimes such as these without knowing what we're talking about first. It's just not gonna happen, Noel." By using the man's first name, O'Neil was stripping the man of his authority, intentionally reducing his status. Rather than Dr. Patterson, Ph.D., he was just...Noel.

"Fine, then you can cram it where the sun don't shine. I'm not saying another word."

O'Neil settled back in his chair and crossed his arms, glaring hard at the little weasel sucking on his bottle. Finally, he looked over to the man next to him who to this point had been dead silent, studying Patterson's every movement, every chosen word, searching for any sign that would betray his true intentions.

But Special Agent in Charge Trevor Dawes saw nothing that intimated deception. Nevertheless, he casually shook his head and said, "He's full of it, Frank. No doubt he is in a lot of trouble with someone, but this…this story is too unbelievable. We have a lot of other things going on right now. We'll pass it back to the locals, the FBI doesn't have time for shenanigans. What's he really admitted to anyway? Huh? Nothing that would hold up in court, that's for sure. Cut him loose. I got crap to do. I'm not gonna waste any more of the Bureau's time with this weenie. Get him outta here." Dawes icily stood up and started for the door.

Patterson, who to this point had been extremely sure of himself, suddenly wore a mask of consternation. He'd been rattled. His eyes shot back and forth from Dawes to O'Neil and then back at Dawes. He slouched in his chair. "Wait," he said with a whimper.

Dawes ignored him, opened the door.

"Wait! Please!"

Dawes stopped and flippantly turned his head back toward the table. In a dismissive tone, he replied, "What?"

Patterson sighed, his shoulders slumped. "I'll tell you everything. But you have to protect me. You have to promise me you won't let them get to me. They will kill me. Please."

With his hand still on the doorknob, Dawes glared at Patterson. He held the man's gaze for a full eight seconds without blinking, without saying a word.

Beads of sweat formed on Patterson's forehead, his carotid artery throbbed. He started massaging his neck—a sign of extreme anxiety.

Finally, Dawes walked back to the table, snatched up his chair and repositioned it so that it was less than an inch from Patterson's right leg. He sat down and leaned in, never breaking eye contact. Their faces were nearly touching. "No promises. None. Now, is there something you want to tell me?"

56

Tucson, AZ

BY the time Rainey had landed and filled out the paperwork at the Avis counter, it was 4:29 p.m. local time. He climbed into the minivan, threw his backpack on the front-passenger seat and bolted off southbound on I-19. Driving with the A/C blasting away, Rainey recalled his conversation with Doug Creighton. Devonte Reyes was a merciless cartel leader with covert and overt connections with various governments, most notably his own, and, it was rumored, to myriad worldwide organized crime syndicates. Globally, he passed himself off as a successful businessman, and in reality he was, but his was a business of violence and illicit activity against which law enforcement agencies around the world relentlessly fought.

Over the past twenty years, Reyes had ruthlessly ordered the murders of hundreds of government officials and scores of others who'd dared to get in his way. Maintaining the position of president and CEO of Primer Sol Energías and holding other seats of international prominence gave him a warm blanket of legitimacy throughout the world. He financed countless green initiatives in numerous countries, even teaming up with several leftist American organizations to push what was now a global agenda into the political, educational, and cultural discourse. In Progressive circles on both the left and the right, he was considered a champion of enlightenment. In truth, he was a savage in a suit.

Doug Creighton had warned Rainey not to underestimate the depth and breadth of lethality and the vast network of informants Devonte Reyes enjoyed. He'd also cautioned Rainey to be extremely careful in whatever endeavors he and his Delta mates were planning to pursue. If any of them were caught, they would no doubt face an excruciatingly painful death. But Rainey was not someone who could be easily deterred especially when the fate of his nation or innocent lives hung in the balance. He was a Delta Force operator. The word "quit" was nowhere in his vocabulary. Oh, and he didn't bother to trouble his buddy with the minor detail that there were no Delta mates this time. No team. He was alone on this one.

Regardless, Rainey followed Creighton's instructions to the letter. Based on what Doug had said in the e-mail draft—they had previously agreed to communicate via a Hotmail account to which they each had the password—it had taken the deep cover operative years to work himself into Reyes's ranks. If Reyes caught even a whiff of the stink of suspicion, he would execute the man on the spot. Worse still for the deep cover DEA operative, he would have no advance warning, no clue about Rainey's intention to meet, or even who Reagan Rainey was for that matter. But to get that far, he first had to go through the man's handler, Cruz was her name. Abigail Cruz.

Within spitting distance of the Mexican border, Rainey pulled into a parking lot, circled around. There she was. The white, windowless panel van. Decal on the back door, bottom right. The number 6776.

Rainey parked beside it, stepped out of his rental. He knocked on the sliding door three times, then once. The door of the panel van opened. A woman's hand shot out, motioned him inside, then withdrew into the shadowy interior.

Abigail Cruz was a short, slender woman of about forty. She had a button nose, a dusting of freckles on her face, likely from years in the sun, and lustrous black hair—longer in front than it was in back. She wore a fitted, white dress shirt, keenly pressed brown slacks and sensible loafers. Her manner was business-like, professional. She was clearly a very bright and very motivated individual.

Rainey stepped inside and sat down on a milk crate next to a makeshift desk. The van smelled of fast food and perfume. He glanced around making sure they were alone. They were.

His host removed her sunglasses, revealing big, cinnamon-colored eyes. A set of dimples came alive as she spoke. "Abigail Cruz, DEA. You must be Luke Dalton." She extended her hand.

"Pleasure to meet you, Agent Cruz."

Skipping past the formalities, she jumped right into it. "Well, Dalton. Word is you need the skinny on Devonte Reyes and Primer Sol Energías."

Rainey nodded. "I'm not gonna beat around the bush, Agent Cruz, and incidentally, Luke Dalton's not my real name. I'll tell you exactly what I need. I need to talk to Ciro."

"Who?"

"Ciro Martinez. I need to meet with him. Need you to set it up."

Cruz squinted, her discerning, sugary brown eyes noticeably darkening. "Whoa, whoa, whoa. I was told I was just gonna be giving you a general run-down of Reyes's organization. No one said anything to me about a *meeting*. With *Ciro* of all people."

"There's a reason for that."

"Reason or not, I've been Ciro's point of contact for almost five years now, nearly all of his time in deep cover. I can tell you one thing. He doesn't like surprises and he's not going to like you—a complete stranger—all of the sudden showing up for a chat. Frankly, I don't see why that would even be necessary. I don't know who you are, but obviously you have some kind of pull to know what you know so far. But I'm sorry. You're not gonna be meeting with my guy. Go back to your boss and tell him I said so. It's just not gonna happen."

"Agent Cruz, I am fully aware of the danger involved here. Trust me, I will be extremely diligent in maintaining not only his cover, but also his safety as well. All I need is for him to get me close to Reyes and I'll—"

"Yeah, okay," Cruz said sarcastically. "Listen, I'm not sure you fully comprehend what you're talking about or who. Last month, Ciro told me he helplessly looked on as Reyes had one of his own men skinned alive—one of his closest advisers mind you, a man he grew up with—just because he suspected him of meeting with a federal police official and ratting on him. Ciro could do nothing but stand there and watch in complete and utter horror lest the same fate should befall him. This man is even more paranoid than Stalin was, Mr. Dalton, or whoever the heck you are, and every bit as lethal, maybe more so. They call him Carnicero—the Butcher—for a reason. Some of the stories I've heard about him have kept me up at night. I can only imagine what Ciro has to go through day in and day out. I'm telling you with all seriousness, this is no one to play with. We are steadily building a case against him here, but we need more time. So, I'm advising you to tell whoever it is that sent you here, this is a non-starter. Maybe come back to us in a few weeks, after we've had a chance to compare notes, explore all of the options. I am not going to jeopardize Ciro's safety or this investigation just on your say-so. You feel me?" She glared at him.

Rainey nodded. "I get it, Agent Cruz, I do. I can appreciate your position. I actually like how you're standing up for your guy. Nevertheless, I gotta get to Reyes and I need to do it like yesterday. We, and by *we* I mean the United States of America, don't have weeks. Quite possibly we could have but hours. There's gonna be an attack. Someone's gonna hit us hard. Nine-eleven style.

"Now, it's my intention to do everything in my God-given power to stop these evil monsters from ever hurting another single American ever again. That's why I'm here. I need Ciro to get me near Reyes. Then he's out of it. Now, I thank you for your warning, but Devonte Reyes has answers and I intend to get them. You have my word that I will not bring harm to Ciro in anyway. I only need him to get me access to the man, nothing more. *Nothing...more.*"

* * *

The subtle growl in his voice was a tacit indicator that he held authority over her somehow—over her position in government; he was essentially pulling rank. But not through normal means. This man wasn't FBI or DHS. Could be a spook, but judging from his physique and penetrating eyes, he was likely military—special ops or something. Guy seemed fearless. He exuded confidence. Looked dangerous in his own right. In truth, he actually scared her a little. She'd dated a Navy SEAL for a few years after college. It was striking how similar the two of them were.

Obviously, Luke Dalton—or whoever he was—was intelligent. Very. Cute, too. Probably nice as pie under normal circumstances. But right now, he looked down right lethal. Even so, it was ridiculous what he was proposing. To confront Devonte Reyes? Alone? He had to be just plain nuts.

After a few seconds of staring into Rainey's chocolate eyes, searching for any indication of give, Cruz relented. "I have to run this by my superiors."

"We don't have time for that. I need to go now."

Cruz frowned and let out a long sigh, ran her fingers through her hair. "All right, but you must do exactly as I say."

"Absolutely."

* * *

Rainey listened intently as Cruz related strict instructions. Throughout their conversation, he detected a flare of emotion in her voice and suspected that over the years she and Ciro had grown much closer than simple handler and undercover operative.

When they were done, Rainey powered on his phone and pecked out an e-mail message to Pappy, then saved it to the DRAFTS folder.

"Be safe," said Cruz, grabbing his arm. "I'll be praying for you both."

Rainey shook her hand. "Will do. Thanks. I mean it."

57

Nogales, Sonora, Mexico

RAINEY walked across the border into Mexico with relative ease. After two blocks he grabbed a cab and barked out his destination. For all the languages he spoke fluently, Spanish was not one of them. After the cab driver dropped him off, Rainey pulled down his ball cap and immediately turned westbound, crossed over Alejandro Villaseñor, and strode through the Parque Ana Gabriela Guevara. He hesitated for a dump truck to pass. It lumbered along with what he estimated was thirty or so Mexicans standing in the back. Construction workers en route to a job site.

Rainey continued across the Avenida Adolfo Ruiz Cortines, a set of railroad tracks and the Plutarco Elías Calles. After buying two cell phones at the TelCel shop, he grabbed another cab to the Carl's Jr. by the Nogales Mall. He went inside, got a couple burgers and a large bottle of water. When his order was ready, he sat down at a table near the back along a window with a view of the mall parking lot.

He ate slowly as he waited.

He checked his watch then quickly used the restroom.

Almost time.

Ten minutes later, the car pulled into the lot. The driver got out, bent down and examined his face in the side mirror then disappeared inside the Cinépolis. Rainey watched for ten more minutes then got up, dumped his tray and paced calmly over to the car, an old gray Dodge Diplomat. The paint on the roof and hood was faded and the left rear quarter panel looked as if someone had repeatedly beat on it with a shovel. It was perfect.

He reached down and removed a magnetic hide-a-key from under the rear bumper. He unlocked the car and climbed inside. The seats were worn and spongey, the yellow foam cushioning visible in spots. The gear shift on the column was loose and sticky to the touch and the glove box door was missing, as was most of the ceiling liner save for the ragged corner hanging down directly above his head.

He parked on the street half a block away from the hotel. Rainey circled to the rear of the car and popped the trunk. He pulled out the only two things inside save for a bald spare tire: a Samsonite suitcase that had surely seen much of the world and a black canvas duffel bag. He didn't bother to exam the contents of either here. Rainey placed the key back in the ignition and left the windows down, then trotted into the hotel. The car would likely be stolen in minutes. Which was the idea, of course.

In the privacy of his room, he examined the gear Pappy had wrangled up for him through his contacts, in this case a defense contractor friend based in Houston. Rainey wanted to kiss the guy. Whoever he was, the man's attention to detail and sense of quality was top notch. Not only did the Glock 19 and Spectre M4 submachine gun fill his request for a good silenced pistol and sub-gun, they were all but brand new, clean and appropriately lubricated. No serial numbers either. Someone knew what they were doing.

Rainey completed his inventory, finding everything he'd requested and then some. Magazines, ammo. Body armor. ATN Generation 4 night-vision monocular. Extra batteries. Flashlight. Tactical fixed blade. Good to go.

He stood over the suitcase, looking down at the remaining items. *Really hope I don't have to use these.*

To be certain everything was in working order, Rainey stripped the guns and then, after being satisfied they would adequately function, put them back together. This didn't mean he had any doubt in Pappy's guy; he had really come through, but the man, whoever he was, was still a stranger. After all was said and done, it was still his butt on the line out here. Always better to be safe than sorry.

With the gear all set and the mags topped off, all he could do now was wait. He decided to take a quick shower. After that, he downed a couple of Power Bars, a bag of beef jerky, and two bottles of water while he went over in his mind the scenarios that might play out. He knew this was crazy what he was doing...by himself, but he wasn't afraid really. Rather, he was ready to get on with it. Ready to take the fight to the enemy. He was born to do just that.

As he played through several different plans, possibilities and angles, it happened. A verse from Scripture bubbled up into his thoughts—Deuteronomy 32:35:

Vengeance is Mine, and recompense; Their foot shall slip in due time; For the day of their calamity is at hand, And the things to come hasten upon them.

Rainey considered his motives, reminded himself to keep them in check. He would do his best to stop the threat, prevent another 9/11, kill if need be, but not exact revenge. This was tricky to explain, but he understood the concept perfectly.

He believed in it.

Rainey offered a prayer of thanksgiving for God's safety thus far. Hindsight revealed that God had placed a hedge of protection around him. Nothing else could explain how he wasn't already dead. He asked God to comfort the families of the fallen, to heal hearts and bodies of both Americans and Iraqis, and any others caught up in the maelstrom of the most recent battles of the War on Terror. He prayed for a straight and true path to those enemies who still intended harm to innocents. And that Divine Providence would continue to guide him, to help him think clearly and decisively and above all to have courage. In closing, he asked that whatever was to happen that God's will be done.

58

THE lobby of the Hotel Fray Marcos de Niza was crowded with the normal swarms of tourists and businessmen. Ciro Martinez waited patiently but anxiously behind a group of college kids. Judging from their wardrobes, he assumed they all attended Colorado State University. When it was his turn at the front desk, he asked the man at the counter if there were any messages for Luis Garza—an alias he used in his communications with Abigail. The man rummaged around and after a few seconds of apparent absent-mindedness handed over a sealed envelope.

Martinez thanked him and strolled over to the bar, ordered a glass of Corona. When it was finally pushed in front of him, he relaxed his shoulders, cast a quick glance around the bar via the mirror behind the bartender and opened the envelope. Inside was a small piece of paper with the message, "Hurry, honey!" written on it and the key card to Room 395.

Barely a sip gone from his glass, he pushed back on his stool and tossed a tip on the bar. As he waited for the elevator, he continued nonchalantly surveying the people around him, making sure to come across as a man with love on the mind. Soon the elevator spit him out and he skirted down the hallway to Room 395. He was both anxious and curious about the disruption to his normal routine. He and

Abby had known each other for quite some time. He'd deduced early on in their symbiotic relationship that she was both very bright and very much in love with him. Although he didn't quite feel the same way about her, he'd never had the nerve to tell her so.

* * *

It had been close to eight hours since Rainey had left Agent Cruz. He was growing worrisome about the prospect of the deep cover DEA man showing up. Once again he reviewed the local street maps of Nogales he'd picked up in the hotel lobby.

He heard the elevator doors open and like the thirty or so times before, he checked the peephole. This time, based on Abby's description of the man, he was sure it was Ciro. The man was thin and handsome and appeared to be of Mexican heritage. He wore dark brown dress slacks, an untucked Tommy Bahama shirt and expensive leather loafers. A pair of minimalist wire-rimmed glasses was set atop his high cheek bones and closely trimmed beard. His dark eyes were far more alert than those of the other guests stepping from the hotel elevator throughout the evening. The man was definitely anxious, but was trying hard to conceal his trepidation.

Rainey stepped backed away from the door, disappeared into the shadows of his room and listened. Soon came the sound of the plastic key card against the metallic inner workings of the lock. Then a *click*. The doorknob began to turn. The heavy door dragged against the carpet as it opened, closed. The carpet muffled the sound of several slow footsteps.

He didn't want to spook the man, but this was no time to take chances. Rainey held his position in the shadowy corner.

"Abby?" Martinez whispered, standing statue-still before finally stepping further into the roomy suite.

Rainey clicked on the lamp beside him. At the speed of light, the look on Martinez's face switched from curious to mortified.

"Lift up your shirt. Do it now."

Martinez slowly pulled his shirt up exposing his hairy chest and a slight paunch.

"Keep your shirt up and turn. All the way around."

Martinez did what he was told. As he again faced Rainey, his eyes became bloodshot, his forehead glistened in a cone of light projected onto him from the recessed bulb above.

Rainey lowered his pistol, placed it on the table beside him while raising his open left hand. "Relax, Ciro. I promise I'm not gonna hurt you. I had to be sure you were unarmed."

"Who are you? Where's—"

"Abby's fine. She's the one who helped set this up."

Martinez appeared severely disoriented as if he'd just woken up on the surface of the moon.

"I need your help. Actually your country needs your help and I'm afraid time is a luxury we simply do not have."

Ciro wiped the sweat from his forehead with the back of his hand. "Who are you?"

Nothing less than complete honesty would do now. This man had been risking his life for the past five years. He was edgy and deservedly so. "You can call me Luke—it's not my real name, you understand. Right now I'm in the employ of the CIA."

Martinez's eyes narrowed. "What do you mean, 'right now?'"

"It means I'm on temporary assignment. It's a long story. What you need to know is this: I'm trying to prevent a terrorist attack in the homeland. An imminent attack that will dwarf 9/11. The investigation has brought me here."

Martinez swallowed hard.

"Have a seat, Ciro, and please relax. I promise you I will not bring you harm and I'm a man of my word."

After several long seconds, Martinez took a deep breath and replied, "Okay." He sat down gingerly on the corner of the queen-size bed.

"I'm looking for two men who were sent here to link up with Reyes."

Martinez nervously stroked his beard. "Two men?"

Rainey nodded. "Foreigners. It seems that Reyes was to help two foreigners, men of Middle Eastern descent—Arabs—get across the border. These men are strongly suspected of being involved in a plot to unleash something big somewhere in the continental United States. I need to find them, find out who they are, what they intend to do, along with when and where. I gotta stop it. Our window of opportunity is closing quickly." Rainey paused. "Now, you know Reyes. You've spent the last five years or so working your way into his ranks. For starters, what can you tell me about the man or his operation that might make sense in the context of what I've just described?"

Martinez sighed heavily. "Well, I can't tell you much, I'm afraid. Though I can confirm that two men, foreigners as you say, did arrive in Mexico less than twenty-four hours ago. I know this because Reyes told me himself before he left for L.A. He seemed especially conspiratorial about who they were and why they'd come to Mexico. I gently probed him about the matter and he snapped, told me not to mettle, which isn't unusual really, but in this case…something about the whole episode was markedly odd. Reyes told me that they would be gone before anyone knew they'd even arrived so there was no cause for further concern." Martinez tried to smile, but it came out crooked—a result of the adrenaline still in his system. "He doesn't know that I know this, but… A member of his personal security detail, see, is one of my unknowing sources of information. *He* told me that—at the request of someone overseas, he didn't know who— Reyes personally accompanied these two men from the airport to a specific location here in the city, in Nogales, somewhere along the border, but he didn't know where exactly. I was going to report all of this to Abby during our next meeting.

Martinez sat up straight as if he'd just remembered something. "They flew in from South Africa."

"How do you know that?"

"Reyes told me. A little while back, I mean. I don't think he meant to, actually. He'd been drinking, see, and was distracted about his upcoming trip to Los Angeles. As soon as Reyes mentioned it, he seemed to regret it. Ordered me to not breathe a word about them to anyone and so far I haven't. Until now that is."

"Anything else?"

"I'm afraid that's all I can tell you."

"Okay. Now tell me about Devonte Reyes. I need to know everything." The two of them continued in this manner for the next few hours. Rainey would ask pointed questions about Reyes's routine, his tendencies, his vices. Martinez would provide the details he was after. Based on this conversation, Rainey now had a fairly good picture of the cartel leader and his operation.

He also now had a plan.

"All right." Rainey paused, leaned forward. "Ciro, I need to talk to him. To Reyes, I mean."

Martinez guffawed, tilted his head. His exasperation grew in a few short seconds. "You're serious?"

"I'm dead serious."

"You don't understand. No one gets close to Reyes," Martinez chopped the air with his hands, shook his head vehemently. "He has a team of, for all intents and purposes, cartel-variety Navy SEALs around him at all times. All hardened commando types and extremely nasty. Reyes is the head of one of the most dangerous, most powerful cartels on the planet. If you think you can just schedule an appointment with the guy and—"

"I wouldn't dare do that."

"Oh, okay. Well then—"

"He's gonna be the one who schedules it." Rainey grinned.

Dumbfounded, Martinez blinked. "Yeaaahhh, right."

"Listen, you told me that he checks in with his financial guru here in Nogales every morning without fail, did you not?"

"Yeah, but—"

"And tonight he's in L.A. for some tree-hugger fundraiser."

"Yes, but you can't—"

"That's my in. When he checks in with his money man in the morning, he's going to learn some interesting news about his accounts. He's gonna come to me. Why? Because like anyone in his position, he's paranoid. He won't trust using the phone for the conversation he will doubtless want to have. So, he is gonna come to me. And when he does, we're gonna have a nice, little sit-down. Well, I can't promise it'll be nice, but a sit-down we shall have.

"What I don't get, is why the money man operates out of a hole like Nogales and not some place like Mexico City or L.A., New York, even?"

Martinez jerked his head toward the door as several unsupervised kids noisily ran down the corridor outside, their footfalls loud thumps that shook the entire floor. He turned back to Rainey and exhaled. "That's easy. See, Reyes and Jiménez were both born here. They grew up here together. They were both dirt poor as kids, doing odd jobs for the cartel to put food on the table for their families. Reyes was a brilliant student and his abilities were quickly noticed by the cartel. They quietly sent him abroad to all the best schools…U-Penn's Wharton School of Business, Harvard, Oxford. It didn't take Reyes long to put his abilities to use. He rose through the ranks quickly and most importantly from abroad. He lived in Europe for a long time. As time went by, Reyes methodically used his abilities and innate cunning to turn on his masters, the very same people who had created him. For a while there was a kind of a covert civil war within the cartel. When it was all over, Reyes had assumed control and had his own most trusted people in key posts throughout Mexico...and the world.

"Jiménez on the other hand excelled at math, but lacked leadership skills, social skills. He was a nerd. Never good at fútbol or baseball. Not charismatic or good-looking like Reyes. Regardless, Reyes trusts him implicitly. He's been managing the cartel's finances ever since Reyes took control.

"Of course to answer your question: why does Jiménez remain in Nogales? It's because, well frankly, this is his home. No, he no longer resides in a shanty in the *Colinas del Sol*, but what remains of his family is here. And so, at least according to my sources, he will never leave Nogales. Reyes would prefer otherwise, but he doesn't complain since the man has incredible gifts with finance and is able to hide his drug money and above all is immensely loyal. An aside: we generally know about the money and where it is, but DOJ has had a hard time getting cooperation from our international partners. They don't want to buy in to the notion that Reyes is not a legitimate business mogul, but that he's just another silver-tongued, murderous drug baron. But we press on."

Rainey nodded thoughtfully. "I see." He parted the window blinds with his fingers and peeked down to the street. "Can I trust you, Ciro?"

"Can you trust *me*?"

"Can I trust that you will keep all of this secret and not tell anyone, even Abby or your superiors, should it come to that?"

Ciro nodded his head. "You can trust me, Mr. Dalton."

"Excellent. Oh and one more thing..."

59

DEVONTE Reyes launched out of his chair and asked again, this time with much more volume. "Are you positive?!"

"I'm afraid so. It's all been frozen. Flagged for seizure. I've double- and triple-checked. The only—"

The cartel leader batted his glass of liquor from the desk in front of him. The small tumbler shattered as it struck the floor. "This is outrageous! How? Who?! We're talking about *two hundred ninety billion dollars!*" Reyes's blood was boiling. He wanted nothing more than to continue this conversation over the phone, but the truth was that the Americans and their allies were very slick with their communications intercepts. It was far more prudent, safer, to speak to the man in person.

"I'll be there in two hours."

"I'm sorry, but the—"

"Two hours!"

"Very well. I'll be in my office." With a shaky finger Francisco Jiménez carefully pressed the button on the desktop phone to disconnect the call. He looked up at the man next to him under a rapidly perspiring brow.

Rainey made sure the call with Reyes had disconnected, then took the disposable cell phone he had been holding off speaker. The speakerphone had been activated on both his phone and Jiménez's desktop phone during the tense call—Jiménez's phone connected to Reyes and Rainey's phone connected to Ciro Martinez. This allowed Martinez to monitor the Jiménez/Reyes conversation from the safety and privacy of the hotel. Since Rainey didn't speak Spanish he had to be sure Jiménez didn't tip off the cartel leader either by a code word or some other pre-arranged signal. Martinez would know if he did and would tell Rainey immediately.

"So?" queried Rainey, the cell phone now to his ear.

"Nothing," replied Martinez. "He followed the script. And Reyes bought it."

"Okay. Thanks." Rainey powered off the cell phone and pushed it into his pocket. He lowered the Glock then patted Jiménez on the back. "Relax, Frannie. You did fine. You know, you actually exceeded my expectations. Well done. Maybe you should go into acting when this is all over." Rainey smiled ominously at the banker. "Now, listen to me very carefully. Does he usually come into the office alone, or does someone accompany him all the way to your desk?"

Jiménez's eyes fluttered with anxiety, his hands visibly shook in their duct tape bindings. "Señor Reyes's personal bodyguard is always present. He never leaves his master's side. The others stay out there." He pointed with his chin to the reception area outside his office door.

Rainey continued pumping him for information. The trembling man gave up everything: the chair in which Reyes always sat; where the bodyguard stood; the interior layout of the office building; entry/exit points; where Reyes's vehicle would be kept staging.

Rainey had been waiting for Jiménez when he'd arrived for work this morning. Dressed in a sharp navy suit, bright white dress shirt, and a swank, two-tone blue necktie, he had entered the office building on the heels of a few low-level employees after which he'd effortlessly blended into the busy office scenery—associates and clients coming and going from this suite and that. Only two people had approached him. But they'd been easy enough to shoo away. A sudden and violent coughing fit tends to have that kind of effect on people.

Concealing his mini arsenal had been easy enough. The Spectre M4 had hung—still did—along his right side beneath his suit jacket on a makeshift sling that looped around his shoulder. He'd worn the Glock in a holster on his left hip for a quick cross-draw. The rest of his gear he had stowed inside his briefcase.

A simple ruse—something about her car being struck outside— had gotten Jimenez's secretary out of the building long enough for him to slip in and introduce himself to the shocked cartel banker. She'd been so relieved upon her return—it wasn't her vehicle after all—that she'd failed to notice that her boss's door was closed, which in any case meant he was not to be disturbed.

60

CLOSE to two and a half hours later, Devonte Reyes arrived. The secretary dutifully buzzed her boss on the intercom and alerted him to the fact, but Reyes was clearly in no mood to wait for permission to enter. Of the four men accompanying Reyes—his security detail, the largest and meanest-looking curmudgeon of them all followed his boss inside and closed the door, while the other three waited outside in the reception area and took turns hitting on the voluptuous secretary.

Reyes started talking even before he sat down. "Francisco, what is going on? How can all of my accounts be frozen?!" He stared across the desk at the back of Jiménez's high-backed leather chair. "Hey, you look at me when I'm talking to you!"

There was silence save for a muffled grunt. The chair wiggled.

Devonte Reyes swatted the air, a wordless order to his bodyguard to go commandeer the insolent banker's attention. The big man trudged around the wide desk and whipped the chair around. His eyes widened suddenly. Jiménez's mouth and eyes were duct-taped shut. Tears streaked his face, a manifestation of unmitigated fear. The bodyguard immediately went for the large S&W inside his suit jacket.

"I wouldn't do that, said Rainey as he stepped out from a small closet holding his Glock in front of him, its thick silencer stabbing the air like a big gloved finger.

The bodyguard ignored the warning and cleared leather, moving quickly sideways.

Rainey's gun spit two rounds into the bodyguard's head. Before the man hit the floor, Rainey turned the gun on Reyes, who hadn't even flinched, as if he were impervious to such violence. "On your feet."

The cartel leader smiled and remained seated. "I think not, my friend." He flicked a piece of lint, or it could have been brain matter, from his trousers.

Just then the office door flew open and the remainder of Reyes's security detail burst into the room. But Rainey was already poised for action. He dropped the first two with headshots. The third, he clipped in the shoulder as the man rolled wildly into the room. As the guy rose up to fire, Rainey drilled him with two rounds to the chest and one to the jawbone just below the ear.

The wide-eyed secretary shrieked, began yelling frantically in Spanish as she peered in on the bloody mess. Rainey hoisted Reyes up by the scruff of his suit jacket, patted him down quickly for weapons then ordered him to move. He holstered the pistol then gripped the Spectre in his right hand. Rainey pushed the man out of the office, past the frantic secretary who was now huddled in the corner of the reception area covering her head with her arms, crying hysterically.

Rainey shoved the man toward a door that led down several flights of stairs to the employees' parking lot behind the building.

"I don't know what you think you're doing," said Reyes, "but—"

With a quick, powerful jab to the kidneys, Rainey said, "Shut up and move!"

Once outside, he led the man to Jiménez's black BMW 528i, shoved him against the back door as he opened the front passenger door. "Get in."

The man again smiled in defiance.

"Have it your way." Rainey struck the man hard on the side of the neck just below and in front of his left ear which immediately rendered him unconscious. Rainey caught him and dumped him into the front passenger seat. Then as if he were simply running a few minutes late to meet a client, closed the door and trotted around to the driver's seat.

Easy. Easy now. Blend in.

Rainey backed out of the stall and eased into traffic. Once he was a good three blocks away, he turned onto a side street and stopped, patted the unconscious man down for any electronic devices. He removed the man's watch, his belt, his shoes and his tie clip. All were likely locations for a small hidden tracking device so his security team could locate him should this very situation occur. Rainey tossed everything out his window just as the rear windshield exploded and gunfire tore into the car. In a nanosecond, he was standing on the accelerator. After the first turn, he reached over and stuffed his passenger to the floor.

Rainey slalomed through the crowded Mexican streets, doing his best to avoid running over innocent pedestrians while at the same time evading Reyes's goons. He raced southbound on Álvaro Obregón. He weaved through several slow-moving cars, then sharply cut in front of a bus clipping its front bumper. Reyes's men were not as careful in their pursuit, forcing vehicles out of their way, ramming others.

Sliding into a right turn onto Victor Hugo, Rainey destroyed a vender cart stationed on the corner as the mustached man behind it dove out of the way. "Sorry!"

Rainey glanced in his rearview mirror, saw the sedan chasing him take off the driver-side door of a Chevy S-10 pickup parked on the street just as its driver was about to exit. Again bullets sprayed into the BMW from an automatic weapon. Rainey ducked his head and pushed the vehicle even faster. His side mirror exploded and several rounds whizzed past his head and pocked the inside of the front windshield.

His left hand on the wheel, Rainey grabbed the Spectre in his right. He took a quick target glance back, then pointed the weapon around his seat and fired several bursts toward his pursuers through the rear windshield. One of the rounds must have connected, because as he spun right onto Padre Nacho, the first chase vehicle continued straight through the intersection without slowing, slamming into a rock wall at the T intersection. Smoke and dust began billowing from the vehicle. A small explosion erupted under its hood.

After about fifty yards on Padre Nacho, Rainey banged a hard left onto Cuauhtémoc, a narrow alleyway, and again stood on the accelerator. Just as he checked his rearview again, several rounds snapped by his right ear and punched three, four, five holes in the windshield. Rainey glanced over at his passenger. He was still out cold.

Rainey reached behind the seat and grabbed the briefcase from the floor, placed it on the front seat beside him. He popped open the latches then held the lid closed as he deftly cranked the wheel with his left hand bringing the car with a scream of screeching tires onto Calle Dr. Alejandra Silva Hurtado. Because of the speed at which he was traveling, the Beemer slid in a sideways arc into a parked Volkswagen Beetle which allowed the sedan chasing him to gain ground.

Another spray of automatic gunfire. Rounds pinged and thudded into the metal framework of the car, some passing through and around the Beemer and into the Beetle shredding glass and metal alike. As he stomped the gas pedal, Rainey reached inside the briefcase with his right hand and grabbed a fragmentation grenade. He squeezed the handle, pulled the pin with his teeth then spit it out. He stole a glance in his periphery as the chase vehicle's engine growled ever closer.

Rainey pumped the brakes, sped up, then pumped the brakes again allowing the other car to overcome him. At the exact time the other car was shooting past him on the left, he tossed the grenade. It sailed through the other vehicle's open front passenger-side window, bounced off the driver's right shoulder and fell between the seats.

Jamming the brake pedal to the floor, Rainey jerked the wheel to the right.

Boom!

The grenade ripped apart the cabin of the pursuing sedan and everyone inside. The rudderless vehicle continued out of control and T-boned a parked car.

Rainey looked back. *All clear.* Slowing down, he turned right onto General Mariano Escobedo then left onto the narrow, dusty Calle Triufo. Rainey parked behind a white Volvo wagon. He loaded the limp cartel leader into the station wagon and hot-wired the ignition.

Once he got her moving, he steadily worked his way out of the city in a northwesterly direction. Destination? Some place quiet, where he could spend some quality time with the man called Carnicero.

61

THE assassin couldn't believe his eyes. When he first saw the man exiting the banker's office, he was legitimately confused. *Rainey wasn't dead? How in the world could he not be? And why was he here, now? Did he follow me?* That didn't seem logical. *What on earth is going on?* So many questions, so few answers.

Demyan Rostov had decided to trail Rainey at a safe distance and almost lost him and his latest target for good thanks to the bumbling idiots on Reyes's security detail. Amateurs.

With yet another surprising opportunity at redemption, Rostov looked down at his sore left arm. He would not fail this time. It was like Mosul all over again. Two birds with one stone. This time though, he would go for Rainey first.

Rostov squinted into the distance. The station wagon ahead of him seemed to be slowing down. Once he was sure that the car had stopped, Rostov pulled off the dirt road as best he could, tucked in behind some scrub brush and set out on foot, sniper rifle in hand.

* * *

Reyes's eyelids slowly cracked. He squinted. He was lying in the dirt at the base of a Guajillo tree and in the shadow of a man with nothing but purpose on his face, eyes ablaze with intensity.

"Up and at 'em, Devonte. Siesta time's over." Rainey gave the man a good smack on the jaw.

Reyes rolled over onto a knee as if to stand up, but Rainey shoved him back down. Rainey had already shed his suit and tie. He'd changed back into the clothing he'd bought in Philly all right there while Reyes had been out cold.

"Okay, listen up. I've got questions and you've got answers."

"You might as well kill me. I am not telling you a thing."

"It might come to that. Look, I'm not here to discuss cartel operations. All I want is information about the two men who flew in from South Africa." This had been one of the things Fayyad had mentioned at the CIA base, since confirmed by Ciro Martinez.

Reyes's eyes darted up and to the right. "I know of no such men."

"This isn't gonna go well for you, is it?" Rainey fired a round from his Glock into the ground directly between the cartel man's legs, close enough to his genitals so that he could feel the puff of dirt from the round slamming into the parched earth.

"No more warnings. You hear me? Let's start with their names. Who are they?"

"You have no idea who you're dealing with. I will see to it that you die a slow and painful—"

Rainey squeezed the trigger sending a round this time slicing through the man's shoeless right foot. The cartel leader screamed in agony for several long seconds then swung an arm at Rainey's leg, but whiffed.

"I told you. No more warnings."

"I swear. You are a dead man! Your body will be dragged—"

Psht.

Rainey's gun kicked as another ball of lead ripped through the man's left foot sending him into conniptions. He hated the idea of torture, hated all violence really, but there were simple realities that some in America would never understand or appreciate. This was combat in a different kind of war, a global war on terror. Bottom line, it was his job—*his duty*—and that of others like him to save innocent American lives. Period. He had to stop them or thousands of people were going to die, maybe more. He was willing to die for his country and countrymen if need be. Being court-martialed or jailed paled in comparison. It's just how he was wired. Someone had to be willing to do what was necessary, to hunt down evil, confront it and defeat it. It *was* a dirty business, but a very necessary one.

Failure is not an option.

"This isn't a game here, *muchacho*. I don't think you know who *you're* dealing with. Names. I want their names and I want them right now."

Reyes whimpered as he rocked back and forth, holding his bloody feet in his hands. "I don't know their names."

Rainey raised the gun again.

"I don't know their names! Please! They arrived from South Africa. I'd arranged to pick them up for a business associate—"

"Details."

"It was all prearranged. I was only doing what I was asked."

"Who asked you to pick them up?"

"I…I can't."

Rainey again raised up his gun, shaking his head. "Wrong answer." He shot him in the left knee.

The man writhed in pain, cursing and screaming at the top of his lungs. After a minute, with eyes closed, still huffing and puffing, he spoke. "He has many names, but his real name…is Jamil. Jamil ibn Hasan. He is Iranian. He is the one who asked me to tend to them. Please." His breathing was labored, his face drenched in sweat. "Jamil sent them here. Two men, two Arabs, but it was obvious they had been coached to look like Mexicanos. I did not ask for their names. I simply did what I was asked to do. It was… It was just business. You must believe me."

Just business.

Rainey stared down on the cartel leader, his face and eyes betraying nothing as he tried to decide whether to believe him. Reyes seemed to legitimately believe that Jamil ibn Hasan was real. Maybe he was even unknowingly involved in disguising the deception. "What did they look like? And think hard before you answer."

Reyes nodded slowly, his breathing becoming more normal. "Both were clean-shaven with short hair. One was older, sixty or so. His left hand…he was missing some fingers on his left hand. Two of them."

"Which ones?"

"Ring finger and pinkie. Both were completely gone and a section of his hand, too." He pointed to the blade of his palm.

"Go on."

Reyes grimaced with pain, then continued. "The younger man, I'd say was around thirty, seemed anxious and edgy. Very nervous."

"What else?"

"How much do you want, a million? Ten million?! You let me go and I will give you whatever you want. Name your price, man, and it's yours."

"I don't want your filthy money, Devonte. All I want is information."

Tears now streamed down Reyes's face. His eyes were closed, his chin rising and falling against his chest as he breathed. "They spoke to each other in Arabic... I was supposed to see to it that they crossed the border unmolested, nothing more. After I did this—"

"The border. Into the U.S."

"Yes." Reyes was barely audible.

"How? How?!" shouted Rainey, kicking the man's foot.

Reyes roared, his eyes now again wide open. Sweat poured down his forehead, soaking the collar of his expensive shirt. "Through one of my tunnels." Reyes was like a woman in labor, grimacing and sucking in air deliberately as the pain coursed through his body. "I have a vast network of tunnels that lead across the border into your country."

"When and where did they cross?"

"Yesterday. I don't know the exact time. There is an office here in Nogales...on Avenida Internacional. In the basement there is a door that leads to the tunnel. That's where I took them. And that's where I left them. I do know they made it into your country safely. On the other side, the two men were received by some of my associates who were tasked with safeguarding their arrival. The two Arabs were to await further instructions from someone—I do not know who—that would make contact with them there. I don't know what became of them after they left my care. As I said, I was only to assure they safely made it across the border."

"These associates of yours. How do I find them?"

"I'm sure you will find them at the end of the tunnel. They are always there. They are always conducting my business, distributing my products to you cities."

"What else? You said, 'After I did this...'"

"Please. I've already said too much."

Rainey kicked the drug cartel leader's foot again. "Let's go, spit it out!"

After more screaming, Reyes settled back down. He was now crying like a three year-old kid who'd just dropped his ice cream cone on the sidewalk. One of the most dangerous, ruthless men in all the world had been broken. He took a breath and let out a long sigh. "After I sent the two Arabs through, I received a call from someone. A very old friend. We discussed usual things...business, current events. He is in the intelligence business, you see. Prides himself on being well-informed of things going on around the world. In passing, I mentioned to him about the two men and...I didn't think anything of it at the time, but... I got the vague impression that he already knew about them."

"Who? Who's your friend?" Rainey crouched down, leaned in, his face inches from the cartel leader's.

Reyes wiped his face. "It's—"

It was the slightest of movements, but it bespoke volumes. Rainey noticed it immediately, as the man's voice trailed off. Reyes's eyes had darted past him and narrowed for only an instant then slightly widened. As Rainey dove out of the way, he heard a muffled slapping sound as a bullet narrowly missed him and obliterated Reyes's head. Nearly a half-second later came the thunderous report of a rifle. A fine mist hung in the dry, hot air as the cartel leader's body drooped toward the ground.

As soon as Rainey hit the dirt, he rolled behind the closest tree. Reyes's body lay there twitching and convulsing before finally going completely limp, but Rainey paid it no mind. He was already reading the terrain, making the calculations that would lead him to the location of the shooter. *Just a few more seconds... That's all I needed. Crap!* The man's lifestyle had finally caught up with him.

Vengeance is Mine...

Rainey was calm and methodical as he quickly deduced probabilities and angles, trajectory. At least Reyes had given him some indication already with his eyes. Along with an IED, a sniper was the most feared threat a soldier could face. Not being able to see your adversary or his implement was absolutely vexing. It could easily manifest into a gripping paranoia.

Can't stay here. Reyes's men will soon be storming the area.

With a nearby stick he stretched out and retrieved his backpack from the ground next to the cartel leader's body. As he threw it over his shoulder, he stole a quick peek around the tree and then immediately withdrew. A round lodged in the tree right where his head had just been, making a punching sound and splintering a patch of tree bark.

He sucked in a big gulp of oxygen, then using the scrawny trees for cover, all at once turned and ran straight back into the lean woods as fast as he could. When satisfied he was far enough back into the foliage, he began to flank the calculated position of the sniper. Soon, he saw it—sunlight reflecting off the mirror on the door of a dust-covered Chevy sedan. The car was stashed behind some brush.

Methodically, Rainey scanned the terrain. *There. A man.* Not a group of Reyes's men, but a single, solitary man. Two hundred yards up the escarpment tucked behind a grouping of rocks, the man was lying prone behind a long black tube. A scoped rifle. There was something very familiar about the man, even at this distance. He filed it away in the back of his mind for now.

With his lack of cover and the open ground he would have to cross to get off even a crappy shot at the man, his best option was to live to fight another day. Rainey pushed away from the tree he was shielded behind, kept his head down and bolted back through the trees, back toward town. He ran at nearly an all-out sprint for roughly a mile. As he caught his breath and walked along the outskirts of town, it came to him. The man's profile. The elbow brace.

It was him.

The assassin from Montreal.

62

WHEN Rainey finally reached Avenida Internacional and saw the place Reyes had described, he shook his head. A law office? Really? Rainey crossed the street and stood behind an old grass green pickup truck while he surveyed the building and its security. Like many in Mexico, this building had rolldown metal doors and barred windows.

Rainey gazed up to the heavens. The sun was beginning to melt into the horizon. The sky, painted in orange and red and lavender, was glorious to behold.

Scouring the street and his mind in the quickly fading light, Rainey worked through his options. His eyes suddenly sparkled.

Fifteen more minutes until darkness. Fifteen more minutes.

* * *

The men inside tempered their boredom by playing card games and chain smoking. But soon there would be much to do; the next shipment was due to arrive in ten minutes. The man in charge stood and cursed at his subordinates. "Must I do everything around here?" His eyes flitted back and forth between the two men bellied up to the card table.

The seated pair looked at the monitor, specifically the camera feed from out front, then at each other across the table. They exchanged devious, conspiratorial grins from within the viscous cloud, which hung in the room like a London fog. One of them said, "Hector, you need to relax. It's the bracket clamp. Needs replaced."

Hector stomped upstairs, slipped out the back door and trudged westbound in the alley. The truck would soon be arriving and it was his job to make sure things went smoothly here. Working for a man like Devonte Reyes, his life depended on it.

It was the third time now, one of the cameras had tilted backward, its lens now aimed skyward. Maybe Jorge was right. Maybe he should try to relax. The clamps do need to be replaced. Stupid junk clamps.

Hector stopped under the camera and looked up, hands on his hips. He sighed before putting one foot on the ladder peg screwed into the pole. Suddenly, a strong hand clamped over his mouth. He grunted as something hard—a gun—was jammed into his back. The man's whisper was deep and gruff in his ear. "Make a sound and you're a dead man."

Hector's head bounced up and down quickly. He raised his arms as if by instinct. A powerful hand moved quickly from his mouth to his waistline, removed the Beretta from under his shirt.

* * *

Rainey pulled the man into the shadows by his ponytail, keeping his gun pressed against the back of the man's skull.

"I don't know what you think you are doing—"

"Quiet!" Rainey yanked hard on the man's ponytail. "Listen to me. Answer my questions truthfully and you will live. It's that simple."

Hector nodded slowly.

"How many men are inside?"

Although Hector was fearful of whomever it was behind him, he was far more afraid of Devonte Reyes. So, he said nothing.

Rainey delivered a knee strike to the man's outer thigh as he tightly gripped the ponytail in his left hand.

Hector grunted in pain, hinged over at the waist.

"I don't like repeating myself. How many?"

The man groaned. "Two."

"If you're lying, you're gonna regret it."

The man shook his head emphatically from side to side. "Only two. I swear. Me no lie."

"For your sake, I hope so. Move." Rainey held the man firmly by his ponytail and ducked his head behind him, all the while keeping his gun ready to address any threats.

As they entered the room, the two playing cards instantly grabbed for their Uzis and stood. One of their chairs fell over backward.

"Tell them to drop their weapons. Now!" Rainey jerked the ponytail tightly in his powerful grip.

The man's head snapped back. The veins in his neck visibly throbbed, as his body responded to the pain. "Do as he say." Hector's eyes were watering now. His Adam's apple sharply protruding, bobbed up and down as he breathed.

In concert, the men laid down their weapons, their eyes never leaving the unwelcome visitor.

"Two men were brought here yesterday. My interests—"

A throaty engine noise. Loud squeaking brakes. A truck had just pulled in. Heavy doors opened and closed. Through the smoke, Rainey looked at the monitor on the desk. Four men appeared in the alley, two of them carrying large parcels. Each man had a MAC-11 submachine gun brazenly hanging from his torso. One of them walked to the door, knocked twice and paused, then knocked three more times in rapid succession.

"I have to answer it."

"Just be quiet." Rainey's eyes shot back and forth from the monitor to the two men in front of him. He repositioned himself so his back was no longer to the door. He could now keep everyone in sight and still eyeball the monitor.

A cell phone rang inside the room, its happy, upbeat Salsa ringtone starkly out of context.

"Relax. Just ignore it."

"You don't understand," said the man in his grasp.

All at once, the two men in the room both went for their Uzis. Rainey fired two silenced shots from his Glock in less than a second. Both men fell to the ground with bullet wounds to the head. At the same time the ponytailed man attempted to pull free. Rainey released the ponytail and stepped back. The man spun and threw a punch that missed badly. Rainey's right leg shot out—a powerful push kick to the man's sternum. As a consequence of the speed, force, and accuracy of the blow, the drug smuggler flew backward, crashed over the poker table and into a cart. There was a grotesque sound as if someone had clapped their hands. Then a pained scream. The man on the floor, rolled over clutching at his leg, terror splayed across his face as he realized that the bright white thing poking through his lower pant leg was a bone.

Bullets ripped into the room. Sparks flew. Cards danced and jumped on the table. An unopened Coke can exploded.

Rainey dove to the floor, rolled onto his back. The raking gunfire continued. The moment it stopped, two men burst through the door. He waited half a second then raised his gun off the floor and shot the first one between the eyes. He drilled the second man with a double-tap to the side of the head before his first ejected shell casing had even hit the floor.

Rainey picked up one of the Uzis and checked the monitor. He saw the last two guys urgently conferring with each other, crouched down behind a grouping of dented, old file cabinets. They were obviously trying to decide what to do next. He couldn't let them retreat. They might tip off whoever was on the other end of the tunnel. Quickly, he checked to see if the Uzi was charged. It was.

Boom! A loud blast behind him.

His body jolted as if he'd just been kicked in the stomach. The searing, white hot sensation on his left side was immediate. Rainey looked up. The man with the ponytail and the broken leg was sitting up, a pistol in his hands. Gun smoke was wafting from its muzzle. The man's face was white and clammy. The front of his shirt was wet with dark crimson. He'd been gut shot by one of the MAC-11-toting delivery men.

Don't you die on me yet.

Rainey was about to put a bullet into the shoulder of the man's gun hand. But before he fired, the man dropped the gun, groaned and slouched back down to the floor, where he lay motionless.

Rainey turned back to the monitor again. They were still there, frozen with indecision.

He ascended the stairs and burst outside. The men instantly let loose. Rounds ricocheted off of discarded truck wheels stacked in the alley and other debris. Sparks popped like little fireworks pursuing him as he ran. He dropped to a knee behind cover and waited.

One second passed.

Two.

Then another. The silence was deafening.

Now!

Rainey rolled out and ripped off a controlled burst at the rusted file cabinets. The bullets easily tore through the thin metal. There was a pained gasp then one of the men fell forward, crashing into a small square of corrugated sheet metal before rolling face down into the dirt.

One down, one to go.

Rainey scanned the alley. *Where are you? Ah. There you are. Bad place to hide, bro. Concealment, not cover.* Rainey fired a trio of three-round bursts into the rusted 55-gallon drum. Chewed up and bloodied, the man fired harmlessly into the dirt as he slid out.

The basement now smelled of cigarettes and cordite. The man who had been shot in the stomach was sweating profusely, his face was pale. Rainey stood over him and assessed his injuries. He was near death. He had maybe a minute, two tops. Rainey leaned down and in a clear, controlled voice spoke into his ear. "The two foreigners you sent through the tunnel, where were they headed? Who were they to meet on the other side?"

The man's eyes were glassy. His breaths were shallow and unsteady. He swallowed hard. He blinked. He blinked again. "Tun...nel. Tun... Man."

"Hey! Concentrate!" Rainey snapped his fingers twice in the man's face. "Listen. The two men who were here yesterday. Where were they going? Who were they meeting?"

"Don't...know." He was still save for the slow rising and falling of his chest.

"Anything. Is there anything you can tell me? Did you hear them talking at all? Maybe you heard a name."

The man's eyes turned toward the wall then back to Rainey. He blinked slowly, so slow in fact that he appeared to be dead. After several seconds his mouth opened. He let out a shallow sigh and whispered, "Farid." Another sigh. His eyes drooped closed again.

"Go on." Rainey clapped his hands loudly.

"Old man...Farid...left...hand...miss..." He swallowed. "Missing...fingers."

Rainey could smell it. He was getting closer, the scent of his prey growing stronger. He checked the monitor. "What else?"

There was a death rattle. The man blinked again, but this time his eyes didn't open. There was a whooshing sound as the air left his lungs for the very last time.

He was dead.

63

RAINEY gazed around the room. Ten feet in front of him on a folding table was a box of large red trash bags marked with bold, black lettering. In English.

BIOHAZARD – MEDICAL WASTE

It made perfect sense. The drugs outside in the truck were packaged here to look like medical waste then they were humped across the border through the tunnel system. Who in their right mind would dare tear into a bag of medical waste?

Their timetable was probably tight. This would leave little to no time for discovery by the authorities in the event there was a leak somewhere within the cartel.

He went outside and retrieved one of the cardboard boxes from the truck. It was sealed. The label like the graphics on the truck indicated that it contained paper products. Once back in the basement, Rainey tore the lid off. He shook his head in disgust at the sight. Kilos of marijuana, cocaine and heroin in tightly wrapped bricks were stuffed inside, all of it destined for America's streets.

He picked up one of the bricks, inspected it. The tight plastic wrapping had a pink-orange hue. As he turned it over in his hand, he decided on his next course of action.

* * *

The air was stale and damp. He walked quietly, as quietly as anyone could in three inches of water. At least he hoped it was water. The normally stagnant, opaque liquid, now disturbed by his careful steps, bisected the floor like a muddy brook. His gentle sloshing in the cloudy, brown soup made a ghostly echo. He'd been on the move now for close to forty minutes. Whoever was on the other side was doubtless expecting a shipment and he was hoping to use that to his advantage.

His eyes at times followed the bare wire strung up along the ceiling from which dangled light bulbs spaced at equal intervals. The illumination they threw off was adequate, saving him from having to negotiate the tunnel by flashlight. A hose next to the electric line supplied the tunnel with fresh air, i.e. oxygen.

The United States had much to do if it wanted to get serious about securing the southern border. If only the jellyfish in the Administration and both political parties would work together for a change, put a stop to the dishonesty, the circus of pandering for votes. It was their duty to do what was best for America and nothing less.

Pulling on the straps of his backpack, Rainey adjusted their bite on his shoulders. He switched the Spectre back to his right hand and continued on. He needed to reach Job. But how? Through Pappy? He really didn't want to trouble Pappy any more than he already had. His mind raced with a million thoughts all slamming into each other like neurological little bumper cars. With each step, a crude mosaic of divergent images appeared in his mind as if someone were pinning them up on a corkboard. Layering them so that no one image was fully visible. Nika. Vladislav Kozlov. The laser gun. The warehouse. The chalet. The writing on Horst's arm. Mosul. Raji Fayyad triumphantly proclaiming his salvation. Christofer Bracks. Fayyad wide-eyed from the betrayal. Why had Bracks killed Fayyad? Was he the CIA mole? Or was there some other explanation?

Rainey had not yet allowed himself to deal with his grief over the deaths of Boyd, Drummy, and Shane Cassel. To be honest, he was still having trouble swallowing the pain of losing Monster. He shoved those feelings deep into a lockbox in the back of his mind. Closed the lid, turned the key. He would just have to deal with all of that later.

For now he was here, in a tunnel somewhere beneath the United States-Mexico border, chasing down the two men that someone had sent to be martyrs. But where? What was their endgame? How did this fictional Jamil ibn Hasan character play into it? More vexing...how did this all tie to Kozlov's group and the L-97X, the Agency assassinations? He tried to unwind everything in his mind, but it only made his head hurt. He had to stay focused on the here and now. Things would become clear at some point. Had to.

He fingered the left side of his abdomen and the now brocaded patch of Kevlar where he had been hit by the ponytailed man's unsteady shot. He'd been lucky the man's bullet hadn't penetrated the soft shell body armor, luckier still that the man hadn't targeted his head. Then again, no. It wasn't luck that had saved him. It was the unseen Hand of Divine Providence.

64

Nogales, AZ

FOR two hours, Rainey had walked slowly and deliberately every few minutes stopping to perform a quick sensory audit of his surroundings. From his pace, he calculated he was at least a few thousand feet inside the continental United States. He wondered how much further this thing went. At least the air quality was decent and it was nice and cool.

The tunnel ahead of him now doglegged to the right. He progressively edged around the blind curve with the sub-gun raised to eye level, ready to fire. Rainey utilized a technique called "slicing the pie" until he could clearly see what was ahead: a set of rudimentary steps leading upward into a dead end. He silently ascended the earthen steps which rose on a gradual incline of about eighty feet. As he climbed the steps, it became darker and darker. Ten feet from the top, he detected the slightest hint of illumination. Creeping upward, he saw a small crack at the base of the door ahead through which seeped a sliver of light. He moved closer until he was finally right up on the door. Rainey gently touched it with his palm and fingertips. Something about its cold, metallic veneer felt strangely alien.

Suddenly, dampened voices broke the eerie silence. Rainey withdrew, kneeling down on the craggy steps. After two minutes of complete silence, he stalked back up to the door. In the dim light, he felt around its edges. *There. A latch.* Sliding his hand across to the other side he could feel two heavy-gauge metal plates. He flipped the latch open and pushed on the door handle ever so slightly, his weapon up. There was a sucking sound as the sticky rubber gasket extending the circumference of the door gave way. *Amazing.* He couldn't believe it. He was in a morgue...or what looked like a morgue. In front of him were three large stainless steel exam tables, a metal chute connecting one table to an adjacent lower one with a heavy duty sink and a large drain outfitted with some sort of garbage disposal on steroids.

The wall off to his left was covered in neatly hung stainless steel instruments, saws, knives, and other even more menacing tools that were utilized in the performance of postmortem examination. Through a glass window that separated this room from the next, was a wall of shelves stacked with jars and other supplies.

Now the markings on the red trash bags made even more sense.

Rainey carefully emerged through the threshold of the hidden door, pushed it shut, noting the absolutely ingenious intricacy of the workmanship. It blended in marvelously with the sterile, blue-gray tile wall. Even from two feet away, the door was nearly impossible to see. The handle was disguised as a fire alarm activation panel. The room was cold and icy, replete with the odorous stew of formaldehyde and death.

Six long canvas duffel bags were piled along the wall by the tunnel door. Rainey unzipped one of them and saw a bounty of assault rifles, pistols, and machined parts for even larger weapons. He ran his finger over the obliterated serial number of a Bushmaster AR-15. Three more duffels were packed in similar fashion. The remaining two were jammed full of cash—easily four, maybe five million dollars worth.

So Reyes ships drugs up here and the people here send back guns and money.

Suddenly, there were voices.

The muffled baritones grew louder as he zipped up the bags and pushed them back against the wall. He ducked down behind one of the metal tables just as the door swung open; it slammed into the wall with a loud thud. From the number of footfalls, there were at least two

of them. He peered at the reflection in a shiny stainless steel blade
hanging on the wall. *Aww man.* There were four of them. Two were
enormous. *Why me?*

Feet shuffled across the room. The men brought in more duffel
bags, placed them along the wall.

"When are they gonna be here? I'm starved," one of them com-
plained.

"Should be any minute now," said another one. "Don't worry.
They'll be here. Then we'll go eat."

Rainey eased out to get a better look, all the while preparing to
move on them.

"What the—," said a deep voice tinged with expectant violence.

He'd been spotted.

Rainey rolled out and brought the Spectre up to address the
threat. But as he did so a large meaty hand swung down like a
sledgehammer across his forearms. His gun clattered to the seal-
coated concrete floor. The big hand was quickly joined by another,
both of them quickly converging around his neck from behind. The
hands were massive. Thick, fleshy paws—five-fingered vices really—began literally crushing the life out of him. He saw white stars
and black blotches. He would lose consciousness in mere seconds.
After that, his life. He needed to act now.

Rainey summoned up what little oxygen was left in his body. Vi-
ciously, he stomped backward and at an angle on his assailant's right
knee. There was a grotesque *snap* and *pop* as ligaments in the man's
knee must have surely ruptured. The man yelped, but didn't release
his grip. Rather, he only clamped down tighter. The life was being
squeezed out of him. Have to make it stop. *Now!*

The others laughed as they watched their powerful associate
fling the intruder back and forth like a rag doll.

Light was fading, his throat… *Can't breathe.* The stars were getting bigger, brighter. Becoming supernovas. Felt like his head was
being separated from the rest of his body. The warrior spirit within
roared.

Fight! FIGHT!

Rainey brought up his left leg, drew the Ka-Bar on his calf and
with all the power that remained in his left arm thrust it upward and
behind his head once, twice, three times, plunging the knife into the
side of the man's face and neck. The effect was immediate. The huge
hands retracted, began pawing at the spurting afflictions with urgency.

Rainey fell to the floor, sucking in large gulps of fresh oxygen, wonderful, beautiful oxygen. Coughing and wheezing uncontrollably, he blinked his eyes, which were bloodshot and teary. He turned his focus to the others circling him now like sharks. With oxygen storming back into his lungs, Rainey got to his feet and mule-kicked the giant behind him. The big man crashed to the floor in a heap, squirming and writhing in pain as the bright crimson fluid lashed across the floor and up the wall in rhythm with his heartbeat.

Seeing this, the other Mack truck-of-a-man lunged, accelerating toward Rainey with nothing but unbridled rage.

Rainey pulled his Glock, drew down on the red-faced giant and was about to fire, when a third man dove into him forcing his arm down and the gun to discharge. The bullet ricocheted off the floor and slammed into the giant's knee. The big man's arms swung together in an impotent bear hug. He growled as the injured leg buckled under his weight. With nothing to break his fall, he toppled off-balance onto the man already on the floor, who by now was very close to having bled out. But the knee-capped giant wasn't finished. The man rolled onto his side, fished out a .45-caliber J-frame and started firing wild, reckless shots. Even the man's associates had to dodge out of the way. Errant rounds hammered into the ceramic tiles and cinder block walls, ricocheting around the room in high pitched screeches. When the gun finally clicked empty, the man swore, then threw it at Rainey. Rainey ducked and the gun hit the wall behind him.

The big guy started crawling back to his feet, heaving and snarling like a rhinoceros. Rainey stepped forward and delivered a swift roundhouse kick to the big guy's temple that dropped him like a sack of bricks. He was out cold.

Rainey spun back to the other two remaining men just in time to see out of the corner of his eye, a dull metal object rocketing toward him like a missile. It struck him hard across the forehead, a head rest—an instrument used for propping up the head of a corpse during an autopsy. One of the men, leapt into him knocking his pistol to the floor.

On his back and empty-handed, Rainey cracked the man in the head with a few short elbows, gouged at his eyes, then grabbed his head with both hands and began torqueing his neck.

"Stop! STOP!"

Through the warm blood leaking down into his eyes from the gash on his forehead, Rainey stared into the barrel of a nickel-plated Colt .45. It was pointed squarely at his head from no more than a foot away.

He had a matter of milliseconds to run the computations. If he gave up now, they would surely kill him regardless. Truth be told, it was not in his nature to ever give up. Even if he were killed in the process. Rainey was a warrior and warriors never quit. Not ever.

Slowly releasing his grip on the man on top of him, Rainey feigned concession. Then with lightning speed he yanked the man down and with his left shin flipped the guy backward over his head into the man with the gun. The blast was outrageously loud.

He didn't wait to see what had just happened. The only thing that mattered was that he wasn't hit. With his shirt sleeve, he quickly wiped the blood from his eyes. He rolled onto the balls of his feet, darted behind one of the exam tables. He peeked out. The man he'd flipped lay sprawled out on the floor dead.

Rainey crawled next to the large dead man in the corner, picked his knife off the floor and slid behind another exam table.

"You know you're a dead man don't you?! Even if you survive, Carnicero will see to it that you and your *entire family* are gutted like pigs and fed to his dogs. Alive!"

"I find that hard to believe," said Rainey as he turned the knife in his hand, so the blade was at just the right angle. He took a deep breath and let it out slowly, quietly.

"Why is that?" The man was circling around the room trying to get a better angle, trying to locate his surprisingly dangerous adversary—whoever he was.

"Because he's dead, you idiot." With the speed of a cheetah, Rainey jumped up. The man fired almost immediately, but only because his finger was already on the trigger. The round was grossly off target and it cost him his life. The knife thudded into the middle of his chest, the nearly five-inch blade bisecting his heart in two nearly equal sections. The man dropped to his knees, and, as if in slow motion, fell backward to the floor, his face contorted, eyes wide with horror.

Rainey leaned against the counter, grabbed a towel from the shelf above. He wiped his forehead and then held the towel firmly in place for several seconds as he caught his breath. He found his Glock on the floor then went and cleared the rest of the building, locked all the doors and returned to the basement. It wasn't a morgue after all; it was a funeral parlor.

Going through the men's pockets, he found the keys to a gunmetal gray Mercedes GL 500 out front, but nothing else fruitful. Just then there was a soft grunt, like a bear awakening from a long hibernation. Rainey turned toward the enormous man on the floor—the one still living; he was just now beginning to come to. The man blinked his eyes, shook his head back and forth several times as if trying to clear the cobwebs.

"Have a nice nap?" Rainey scooped up the Spectre along the wall.

The man grunted louder this time. With one of his hands, he gently touched his bloody, distorted leg. His eyes shot open. He was completely awake now. "What—?"

"They're all dead. Sorry, Goliath, but it's just you and me now."

"Who are you?"

"Doesn't matter who I am."

The man guffawed, gritting off the severe pain that was surely coursing through his body. "You obviously don't know who you are dealing with. The man I work for is going to rip you apart limb by limb. You're a dead man."

"Believe it or not, that's the third time I've heard that today. You guys need some new material. Listen, Frankenstein, your boss is dead. I don't want to know about your lousy operation. What I *do* want to know about is the two men who came out of that tunnel yesterday," Rainey jerked his head toward the secret door in the wall. "Right now. Everything you got."

The man laughed, cocked his head back in amusement until the pain restored the grimace to his face. "I know nothing." The bitterness in his eyes was evident as was the joy of withholding information from the man in front of him.

"I see," countered Rainey. He walked over to a stainless steel countertop and grabbed the Thermo Scientific Shandon autopsy saw hanging on the wall above it, slid the power switch on. The oscillating blade whined loudly, forebodingly.

The man's demeanor changed instantly.

"Now... You gonna talk?" Rainey waved the earsplitting saw back and forth. Or are you gonna make me use this thing?"

The large man nodded urgently, his eyes wide with anxiety. "Okay, okay. Here's what I know."

65

FOR the past two hours, Lieutenant Roberto Alvarez and his partner Detective Sergeant Terry Kincaid had been sitting bedside to the enormous man. They'd taken turns peppering him with questions about the carnage found several blocks away at the funeral home. Someone had arrived to inquire about services and discovered a blood trail in the parking lot. The police were called. When they'd arrived, they forced entry and then found the dead men and a bloody mess in the basement. A quick check of local hospitals had turned up this guy, a man built like a house. He'd arrived at the E.R. with an obliterated knee and clothing covered in blood. So far, the ugly beast-of-a-man had stonewalled them on every question.

Kincaid was staring at his crime scene notes trying to reconcile the rough sketch he'd made on scene with the man's injuries. Obviously, this was cartel-related. And as usual no one knew anything. Frustrated, they were about to call it quits when a handsome young doctor with trendy eyeglasses and slicked-back, black hair knocked on the door and entered the room. He made a show of checking the patient's chart, then pressed some buttons on the little blue computer that regulated the big guy's IV drip.

"How are you feeling?" the doctor asked in a Latin accent. He seemed to pay the detectives no mind.

"Little better. Although it'd be nice to get some rest without being harassed by these *pigs*."

The doctor turned toward the plainclothes policemen and nodded with an appraising glare. "He's right. This man needs his rest and it's high time you allowed him to do so."

Kincaid was about to respond to the massive man's pejorative, but was held back by Alvarez. "You're right, doc. We'll come back later. I think we could all use some rest."

"Thank you, gentlemen." The doctor smiled. "Perhaps in a few hours, my patient here will be ready to answer your questions, yes?" The doctor looked at the man on the bed who now had his eyes closed in a child-like act of defiance.

"Sounds good. We'll be back up in a few hours."

"Very well."

The large man on the bed watched the door swing close out of the corner of his eye. When he was alone with the doctor, he said, "Thanks, doc. Those guys were driving me nuts. They're like vultures."

"Indeed." The doctor reached into the pocket of his white coat. "They can be so insensitive. Here. This should help you relax." The doctor inserted a needle into the man's IV port. "There you go."

"Thanks, doc," The big man let out a long sigh as he closed his eyes and adjusted his overwhelming frame in the bed beneath him, mindful of his wrecked limb. The strong narcotic blend shot through his bloodstream. Thirty seconds or so passed and he seemed to slip into another state altogether.

"That should be long enough. Feel better?"

"Yes." The man smiled like a happy drunk.

"Good. Now, understand that I can help you keep feeling that way or I can make you feel like you're being eaten alive by piranhas."

The big guy just looked at the doctor, still with a goofy smile on his face.

"I want you to tell me everything. Leave nothing out. If you do that, I will give you more of the good stuff. Fail to do so, then well, let's just say you'll wish you were dead. Understand?"

"Suuuuure."

The large man answered every question the doctor could muster including what had happened at the funeral home. He left nothing out. When he was finished with his questions, the doctor stood back and shook his head then quickly pulled another syringe from his jacket pocket and plunged it into the IV port. "More of the good stuff, my friend." Demyan Rostov removed his blue rubber gloves, balled them up and pushed them into his pocket. "Rest in peace."

As he passed by the nurses' station, Rostov squirted some anti-bacterial liquid into his hands from the dispenser beside the plump charge nurse. Using his charm and good looks, he smiled and said, "Our large patient will be fine with lots of rest. Make sure he's not disturbed for at least a few hours. I'll be back around to check on him."

Inside the elevator, he shed his eyeglasses and mussed his hair. He removed his stethoscope and white lab coat, rolled everything into a tight ball then pushed that into a plastic grocery bag he'd had stuffed in his pants pocket. Rostov maneuvered through the lobby a different person now—a sad-faced visitor distraught over an ailing relative. Once outside in the lot, he discarded his bagged disguise, slipped behind the wheel of a sedan and drove away.

He had an extremely important call to make.

66

Tucson, AZ

THE Lago de Oro was a run-down fleabag motel on W. 29th St. about seven blocks east of Interstate 10. The sun-baked paint was peeling from seemingly every surface of the one-story building. What little paint remained on the once bright canary yellow exterior was now faded and dull. The building contained a total of sixteen rooms that ran parallel to the road except for the very last one, which made the building from above look like a backward letter L.

It was nearly 7:15 a.m. local time when Rainey pulled into the pitted parking lot next door. It was an equally rundown building that seemed to have been sitting vacant for decades. For close to fifteen minutes he sat there behind the steering wheel playing a part. To anyone who might have noticed him, he would appear as if he were merely consulting a large folding map. In reality though he was staring at Room 8 and the vantage points around the motel. He watched for any of the telltale signs of countersurveillance. Deciding it was safe, he walked to the door, placed his ear against it and listened. Nothing but the din of traffic behind him. He gripped the old, dented brass doorknob.

Locked.

The window curtain was closed, but there was a light on inside.

Rainey walked toward the motel office all the while keeping his attention on Room 8. A Hispanic man who looked to be upward of seventy years old stepped out of a room marked Private and stabbed a set of jangling keys into the motel office door.

"Excuse me, sir."

The man started and turned, leaving his keys dangling from the lock. "Ah. *Buenos días.* Let me open up here *y* I get you eh room."

Rainey shook his head. "I don't need a room. I need to know who's staying in Number Eight."

The man tsked and shook his head vehemently. "Oh, es confidential information, *señor.*"

If the situation wouldn't have been so dire, Rainey would have laughed in the man's face. Instead he glared at him, a dark foreboding in his tone. "I'm afraid you don't understand." He stepped closer until he could smell the man's rancor dragon breath, see the deep creases in his face and forehead and the quiver that was now visible in the man's lips.

The old man swallowed hard.

They both stepped into the office. Rainey turned and kept an eye on the door to Room 8 through the office window.

"Heere. Thees es all I half." The man handed him his ledger.

Rainey flipped it open. "This is worthless. There's nothing here for Room Eight."

"Guests are told to sign een, but es really voluntary. You see?"

"How was the room paid for?"

"Cash."

"Who paid for the room? What did they look like?"

The man's eyes widened as he leaned in, supplementing the words he spoke with dramatic hand gestures. "All I know, *señor,* es he was a very large man. *Un gigante.* Hees name... *No lo sé.* I do not know thees."

"All right. You have a key to the room?"

"*Sí.* Heere, take eet. But I theenk they already go. I hear noises very early thees morneeng. Like four sometheeng. A dark car come, *dos* men," he held up two fingers, "they get een *y* they go." The man turned his head quizzically, searching for whatever it was that Rainey's eyes were focused on behind him.

"Excuse me." Rainey brushed past the man. "Does this thing record?" Rainey picked up a device with wires spewing out the back in a jumbled mess.

"*Sí.* Those drug useers…they always steal from thee cars een *mí* lot. But you see now *mí* cameras catch them *y la policía*…they go arrest."

Rainey studied it for a few seconds, turning it over in his hands, examining each side. The box was not connected to the Internet. Recorded video files could only be extracted via the unit's lone USB port with a thumb drive. He'd seen many like this in places like Afghanistan and Pakistan. It was a fairly inexpensive, store-bought surveillance system. The box connected to four cameras with infra-red capability. There was one camera above the front desk, another above the vending machine just outside and two more covering the lot.

"Tell you what. How 'bout I buy you a new one? A better one." Rainey didn't wait for the man to respond. He gripped the wires leading into the box in his left hand, pulled out his knife and cut them cleanly in one abrupt motion.

"*Ay, ay, ay. No es—*"

Rainey held up a wad of cash. "We good?"

* * *

Rainey studied the room; it was empty. He now searched for clues, anything that might aid in the identification of the two men who had been here, what they were plotting and/or where. The two bathroom towels on the floor facing Mecca weren't exactly prayer rugs but they easily confirmed he was on the right trail. For a fleeting moment while he'd been watching the motel, he had considered the possibility that the giant back at the funeral home might have lied to him, but this here was verification the man had been telling the truth.

The air inside the room was a repugnant mix of musk and cigarettes. The ceiling tiles were yellowed with large brown and gray rings where the rain had leaked through the roof and birthed a habitat of mold. An old TV weighed heavily on a small, particle board dresser. The two beds stood weary and unmade.

Rainey walked into the bathroom and almost vomited at the stench. It obviously hadn't been cleaned in God knows how long. Worse still, the last person or persons to use the toilet hadn't flushed their business from the bowl. It was a foul, pungent stew of briny urine, feces, and floating cigarette butts. Squinting, he looked down at the dark-colored iceberg rising out of the yellow-gold liquid. *Nasty. Now there's a weapon of mass destruction.*

Under the worn, '60s-era vanity was a tiny plastic trash can. Rainey stepped out of the bathroom and dumped its contents on one of the beds. With the tip of his knife, he poked through and separated the things before him. Several balled-up tissues, a used Maxi pad—obviously emptying the trash bins on a regular basis wasn't a concern for the motel owner either—and an old syringe. He knifed through some used tissues that were stuck together and then saw it.

A SIM card.

One of the men—perhaps the one named Farid—had doubtless removed it from his phone and discarded it, thinking no one would ever find it. And if anyone did, so what? They would be gone by then.

Rainey carefully collected the SIM card and held it up to the light angling it back and forth. *There. Ridge detail. A fingerprint, or at least a partial.*

He ripped a page from the dust-covered 1998 Yellow Pages on the nightstand and folded it into a makeshift envelope, securing the SIM card inside, then tucked it into his pocket.

Again, he glanced around the room. He looked at the TV, then the remote on the bed, then back at the TV. He powered it on. When he saw the adult channel to which it was tuned, he frowned and shook his head. It didn't surprise him anymore: the fiery indignation of Islamists, their bloviated piety, their propensity for sanguinary violence in response to the slightest perceived insult. And then this.

Just one more example of their complete and utter hypocrisy.

67

"WHAT?!" exclaimed Pyotr Kupchenko into his cell phone as he drove. "How can that be?"

"Apparently the old man had a DVR system installed at the motel after your advance people were there. Seems some local thieves have been targeting the cars in his parking lot. Rainey's got the box and what's more: there is a good chance that one of the cameras might have captured someone or something. You know what that means…"

"Yes, I'm not stupid, you idiot! At some point he is going to surface with what he knows and it's going to ruin everything. We can't let that happen. You must intercept him."

Rostov moved his cell phone from his left ear to his right. "Did your sources get anything back yet on the vehicle he took from the funeral home?"

"As a matter of fact, yes. According to the Mercedes Benz locator, the vehicle is parked in a mall parking lot in Phoenix. But that no longer matters. Sentinel had his people check with all the cab companies in the area. Apparently, a cabbie picked up a guy matching Rainey's description outside the mall. Dropped him off at the Hilton Garden Inn."

"All right, I'm en route."

"Demyan."

"Yes?"

"This time you'd better make sure you do not fail. Kill him or else *you* will be a marked man. Do I make myself clear?"

A pause. "I understand."

"Get Rainey and destroy that DVR."

68

Hilton Garden Inn
Phoenix, AZ

THE hot water felt heavenly melting over his shoulders and back. For what seemed like hours, he just stood there, hands pressed high on the shower wall, his head down allowing the near scalding water to massage his lean, muscular form. Rainey was exhausted and sore. So sore. His body was already worn well beyond its thirty years. Seen more carnage in the past ten years than most men in ten lifetimes. Just a few hours ago, he had placed an anonymous call to the FBI Phoenix Division office from a disposable cell phone in Tucson and arranged a time and place to meet with an agent assigned to the Joint Terrorism Task Force. Rainey had then checked into the hotel under an alias, paid in cash. He'd needed a place where he could shower, get something to eat, and alter his appearance before heading out to conduct countersurveillance of the location where the meeting was set to occur.

The FBI man had been told in no uncertain terms to come alone; Rainey would make sure he did. Once it was safe, he would turn over the DVR and the SIM card and give an account of everything he knew. Everything that Fayyad had told him. He'd simply have to put his faith in the FBI at that point. They had jurisdiction anyway. He would also reach out to Job from the security of the JTTF office if all went well. He'd thought again about going through Pappy, but decided against it. If these people, whoever they were, wanted him bad enough they'd be monitoring Pappy's communications. Maybe that's how the assassin had found him in Mexico.

There was still an empty feeling within his soul. As if he hadn't done enough. He was still no closer to identifying the target, when or how they were planning to strike. Still hadn't discovered who was definitively behind it all.

Rainey turned the knob making the water hotter still. Thoughts of his lost friends crept into his mind. Those who had perished in service to their nation. Not just Monster and more recently Boyd, Drummy, and Cassel but all of those who had given everything they had to give fighting for God and country. Fighting on the side of good. There, standing in the shower in a state of exhaustion and with a gut-wrenching sense of loss, his heart swollen with empathy for the families of the fallen, he wept.

After some time, he collected himself and his thoughts turned to his father. My, how he missed him terribly. He would give anything to have him back for one hour, one minute, one second. Rainey reflected on how his dad's death had affected the trajectory of his life. What would life be like if he were still alive today? What kind of man might he now be? Would he be different somehow? Again, he contemplated how the events of 9/11 had changed him irrevocably. He should have been married by now like most of his childhood friends. Married to Kayla. They would have had children by now, too. He tried to picture her face, what she might look like now. He remembered the last time he saw her. It was before he'd left for boot camp. She was looking up at him with sapphire blue eyes as earnest as a Hallmark card, beaming with heartfelt sentiment, with yearning. Each time he'd tried to explain why he had to leave, she had graciously smiled and said she understood, said she knew America needed men like him. Her love for him was clearly deep. At least it had been anyway. He had hurt her very badly in just up and joining the Army. For that he would feel eternally guilty.

Rainey slowly turned 180 degrees giving the steamy jets of water access to his entire body.

He considered the future. In his soul, he wanted to settle down and start a family at some point. For some reason while growing up, he'd always pictured himself the father of four—two girls and two boys. But how could he be a father doing what he did for a living? There was always the what-if. What if he were killed? He couldn't do that to a child of his own. Not after knowing what it felt like to lose his own father as a boy.

Spinning the faucet dial off, he began to feel sorry for himself then abruptly told himself to stop it. There were plenty of others in the world who had it far worse off than him, in circumstances that were well outside their control. Standing there in the hotel shower, Rainey looked skyward and asked God to forgive him his trespasses, to give him strength, and for someone, someday to love…for someone to love him back the same way that Kayla once did.

All he could think of now was that blue-eyed beauty in the Duke Soccer sweatshirt looking up at him. And him walking away from her to go do whatever it took to kill those responsible for murdering his fellow Americans. Al-Qaeda. He still blamed them. Their acts of cowardice perpetrated on American soil on 9/11 had stirred in him, still did, an intense fire. Those terrorists had taken so much from him. They'd stolen Kayla, stolen his dreams. Indeed, he would never forget. Nor would he ever forget the words he'd whispered to himself sitting there in math class on that fateful Tuesday as the news spread like wildfire. The entire school had come to a solemn, sorrowful stand-still. Each room in breathless silence, tuned in to the shocking events as they unfolded on live national TV.

This is war.

When it came right down to it, even now as his thoughts came rushing back to the present, he still wanted to be the one to wage it against America's brutal enemies. Someone had to.

Rainey toweled off, checked to see if the bandages on his forehead were still there when suddenly he heard something.

Someone was in his hotel room.

69

*C*RAP! His gun was on the nightstand beside the bed. He had no weapon in here, or clothes for that matter. He could see it now, what a way to go: U.S. Delta Force operator on TDY with the CIA, trained terrorist killer, shot dead in a hotel in Phoenix. While taking a shower.

He scanned the bathroom; he'd have to improvise. He removed the pop-up lever from the faucet, gripped it tightly in his left hand. A rudimentary dagger of sorts. He needed something else. A glass tumbler from the bathroom counter. He swiped off the little paper covering and brandished it in his right hand.

Rainey glimpsed himself in the mirror. If only his Delta mates could see him now.

He opened the door and stepped into the short hallway between the front sitting room and the bedroom. His eyes were severely alert, his body ready to spring like a coiled pit viper.

He padded toward the bedroom. The door was half open. Rainey reasoned where an interloper would position himself in the room in order to have the best tactical advantage.

All at once, Rainey burst into the room. And just when he was about to unleash hell on earth, recognition poured over him like a bucket of ice water.

"This how you normally operate when you're away on company business?" The man shook his head with dissatisfaction and a devious grin, eyeballing him up and down. "Are there some new Delta TTPs I'm not aware of. A commando going commando. Nice. I give you high marks for improvisation."

Rainey let out a long, frustrated sigh. "Job, I could have killed you." He tossed his makeshift arsenal on the bed and quickly grabbed a freshly bought pair of boxer briefs from the dresser top. "What are you doing here? How did you even know I was here?"

The confused look on Rainey's face forced a chuckle. Job Jackson uncrossed his legs and stood up. "I would have had you easy, by the way." He picked up one of the empty plates from the tray on the nightstand and tilted it toward his nose, gave it a sniff. "Yikes. Stuff smell's awful."

"I've had worse."

"Yes, I'm sure you have. I know you have." Job settled back down into the only comfortable chair in the room. "Of course, maybe whatever it is you ate for breakfast there will put some hair on that chest."

"Hey. It's like I always say, hair doesn't grow on steel." Job's jabs about his hairless chest were ceaseless.

"By the way, kid, what the heck happened to you? You look like you've been through the wringer." Job studied the array of visible injuries on Rainey's body. The gash on his forehead, now held together with Krazy Glue and butterfly bandages. The vivid red and purple pancake-size bruise on his left side. The neat row of stitches on his leg and upper shoulder.

"You don't want to know. Now are you gonna tell me what the heck you're doing here?"

Job grew serious. "Easy, Ray. We need to talk."

"So talk." Rainey got dressed then pulled on a new pair of Merrells he'd bought in Tucson. "You can start by how you knew to find me here."

"Short version: we intercepted the delivery of the items that Pappy's man supplied. I had a GPS beacon sewn into your holster there."

Rainey picked up the holster and rubbed his fingers over the stitching trying to comprehend how that was possible.

"There's another one in the handle of your Ka-Bar. I know, Ray. Seems impossible."

"How?" Rainey was dumbfounded. "Who?"

"Never mind all that." Job's visage turned grim. He tented his hands under his bottom lip. "Ray, we don't have a lot of time, so I'm gonna cut to the chase."

"I wish you would."

Job ignored the remark. "First, I must say... You are one incredible man. Truly a very special breed. And I couldn't be more proud of you."

"You're not gonna cry are you?"

"I knew when I first selected you that you were special, but... Ray, you are one of, if not *the*, most talented warrior spy America's got. The most versatile by far. You possess an unheard of array of talents from the tactical to the intellectual. Your language abilities are unprecedented for someone with your aptitude for gunplay. You work well within a team, but you seem to thrive working on your own, too. I've never come across anyone like you in all my years, and I'm someone who has been around, trust me. I've always tried to stay objective because you were my best friend's kid, but there is no other way around it. You are *incredible*. And you still have so much untapped potential. If you only knew what I knew..."

Rainey smirked, cocked his head. "You're gonna cry. I knew it."

"Shut up, will ya," snapped Job. "I came here to bring you in. I know about what happened in Mosul and at Kingston Park."

"And?"

"You didn't kill Christofer Bracks; Christofer Bracks didn't kill Raji Fayyad."

"Ah, a riddle. I give up," said Rainey straight-faced as he checked the chamber of his Glock and slid it into the holster under his shirt. He then tossed his knife, the Spectre and extra mags into his backpack and zipped up the pouches, having already made sure everything else was inside. He plopped down on the bed and impatiently stared at Job.

"You can drop the attitude."

"Sorry. I'm just tired. Go ahead."

Job sighed. "The man you killed was Russian SVR. His name: Sergei Nuriyev. We don't have much on him save for the fact that he spent about seven years at a secret training camp in Siberia. Left there fifteen years ago. We lost track of him soon after. Get this: our analysts think he may have been working with the guy who tried to whack you in Montreal. It's complicated, but I agree with their conclusions.

"Yeah? Well, he tried to whack me again in Mexico yesterday. Took out Devonte Reyes, aka the leader of the Sinaloa cartel, instead." Rainey related what had led him to Mexico and everything that had happened since.

"Which brings me back to Fayyad," said Job. "What was it that he told you?"

"He said that his source in the Russian embassy in Doha had come across information involving a plot to strike America. In the homeland. Two Arabs had been selected to carry out the actual attack. They're here by the way...they're inside the border. Apparently, this Iranian, this Jamil ibn Hasan character—IRGC, Quds Force—is behind it all. He's assembled a team of mercenaries, mostly Russian ex-pats, to do the heavy lifting...you know, Kozlov and his people... But here's the kicker: the man's a ghost. Jamil ibn Hasan doesn't exist. Fayyad said he believes it's likely someone high up in the Russian government is the one behind the curtain, no pun intended. Said that when the attack occurs, everyone will be led to believe Iran is responsible. Why or how? He didn't have a clue." Rainey shook his head. "Russia and Iran are allies. I mean, why would the Russians want to frame Iran for a terrorist attack?"

Job leaned back, ignoring the question, the gears of his mind spinning.

Rainey crossed his arms. "So tell me about Iraq. What happened in Mosul? It's like those ISIL twerps knew we were coming. Knew we were gonna try to spring Fayyad."

"It wasn't ISIL, Ray. I've seen the UAV footage. Someone fired an RPG round into the compound. Into a room full of explosives, which we've since learned from the Jonah Team personnel, was where Fayyad had been held. That's why Cassel's dead. ISIL got in on the action after the fact. Someone wanted Fayyad dead before he could talk. What happened at Kingston Park must have been a back-up plan put in place in case you guys succeeded in getting him out. Which you did."

"Not sure I understand."

"Ray, we found Christofer Bracks—the *real* Christofer Bracks. Turns out he was assassinated on a road outside of Baghdad. The man you tangled with at Kingston Park did not work for the Agency. As I said, Nuriyev was Russian SVR. A trained assassin. Incidentally though, for a short time at least, some at JSOC and the Agency—not yours truly, of course—thought you had killed him. Him and Fayyad."

"That's crazy."

"I know. You don't have to convince me. But after KP, I knew... I knew we had our man."

"What do you mean, 'our man?'"

"I mean Roman Lerner." Job nodded. "Perhaps some background would help."

"Perhaps it would, but we'd better get this stuff back to Lynn Street," said Rainey patting his backpack. Lynn Street was another term commonly used by Directorate insiders for headquarters. It was the name of the street in Arlington, VA on which it was located.

"You're right. Let's go. Plane's waiting."

They walked to the door. Rainey removed the chewing gum he'd placed over the peephole and once he was sure it was clear outside, kicked the rubber door stop loose from underneath the door. How exactly had Job gotten into the room? Must have used the balcony.

As both men continued toward the elevator, a door opened at the end of the hall. Rainey's eyes instinctively flitted to the person stepping through it. With a flash of recognition, he yelled, "Gun!"

Then chaos.

70

DEMYAN Rostov opened the door leading to Rainey's floor. Not even a minute ago, he had flashed a photo of his target at the front desk along with a believable badge and a toothy smile. The female guest receptionist nodded enthusiastically and identified the room in which the "fugitive pedophile" was hiding out and additionally provided him a key card for easy access.

He was done playing games. If he didn't finish the job this time, he was going to be in the crosshairs. This Delta Force/CIA/whatever man had thoroughly ruined his professional reputation, embarrassed him. He was consumed with wrath. It was time to end it. Time to be bold. Time to kill Reagan Rainey once and for all.

He stepped through the door, two Mini Uzis beneath his department store blazer.

What the—

Rainey was twenty yards ahead walking directly toward him with another man close behind. There was no hesitation. Like a bird of prey taking flight, Rostov swept both sides of his jacket back and gripped the Uzis. He took off in an all-out sprint with guns belching fire.

* * *

"Back! Go back!" Rainey pulled his pistol and fired. "Here!" Like a magician performing card tricks, he pulled out the key card and held it up for Job, while keeping the older man pressed against his back.

Job snatched it out of his hand and began working the lock.

"Hurry!" implored Rainey as he engaged the assassin, who was now dodging from alcove to alcove, room to room. The man was coming at them with an unexpected recklessness.

"It's not working!"

"Try it again!" Rainey peeked out, was about to fire. The corner of the wall exploded. Rounds stitched up the wall in front of him as he withdrew back into the tiny alcove.

"Okay! C'mon!" Job pushed into the room.

Rainey leaned out and fired three more rounds then turned into the room and quickly shoved the door shut. He picked up the rubber door stop and slammed it into place. Just as he was about to stand back up, the door splintered and rounds began chewing through the thick wood. He dove to the floor.

"Ray! Let's move! Over here!"

Like a spider, Rainey quickly crawled further into the room. A heavy foot thudded against the door which was followed by another spray of automatic gunfire that bored large gaping holes into the thick wood door and the room beyond. Rainey dropped the magazine from his gun and slammed in a fresh one. He turned, partially sat up and fired into the door at the assassin. The man on the other side was grunting with each kick—each one becoming more frenetic. The door and jam were already starting to give way. With each kick, the door clapped open several inches.

A fusillade of bullets ripped through the weakened door. Another kick. Then another. The door flew open. The assassin pushed inside the room with a Mini Uzi in each hand, spraying rounds in disciplined bursts, loud as a pair of jackhammers in a phone booth.

Rainey and Job scurried as rounds punched holes back and forth across the walls. The suite was a haze of cordite and drywall dust.

Job threw open the door to the balcony, the same door he'd used to enter the suite, while Rainey fired off another volley. But the firestorm coming their way was relentless. His Glock was just no match for two Uzis. Bullets were flying everywhere. Rainey swam across the thin commercial-grade carpet toward Job.

People were screaming—horrible, primal screams. There was panic throughout the entire hotel.

Rainey scrambled out onto the balcony. Immediately a shower of tiny daggers rained down on him as the windowed door exploded. He followed Job who had already leapt across to the adjoining room's balcony, a distance of five or so feet.

"Keep moving, Ray! We're outgunned."

He fired again but after only one round the slide on his pistol locked back. He was empty. Rainey spun and jumped for the next balcony. When he thudded onto the landing, Job was already in the air again. He quickly holstered his pistol, gripped his backpack tightly in his left hand, and followed suit, leaping over the railing and clearing the balcony in one graceful, though hurried, motion. Just before he hit the water, he flung the backpack into the bushes behind a row of deck chairs. People outside were screaming, running for their lives as bullets slammed angrily into the textured cement that encircled the large hotel pool.

From the balcony, the assassin continued to rain down bullets, although from this distance his Mini Uzis were far outside their effective range. But he could spray. And spray he did. When both guns ran dry, he quickly reloaded and fired again.

Rainey surfaced with a gasp, looked around. Job was already ten yards away and heading toward the edge, plowing through the clear water like a speed boat. It was incredible. The man's powerful strokes. The graceful way he cut through the water. Rainey quickly fell into his wake.

Reaching the edge, both men pulled themselves out to dry ground and ran in a zig-zag pattern which made it all the more difficult for the assassin to target them.

Rainey detoured only long enough to scoop up the backpack then raced to catch up to Job. They were now sprinting shoulder to shoulder. Shots coughed in the distance behind them. More screams. A fire alarm now shrieked. Sirens blared.

"Your assassin?" Job asked as they ran.

"No, Job. I didn't reuse my towels and the cleaning lady's pissed."

71

ROSTOV withdrew into the destroyed room. He was enraged and demoralized at the same time. He was also hit, twice actually. One round had been a direct hit to the center of his chest. If not for the thick trauma plate in the bulletproof vest, he would be dead. The other round had hit him in the bicep of the same arm Rainey had destroyed in Montreal. Adrenaline masked the gut-wrenching pain that would soon throttle his body.

Before he fled the room, he pulled his belt from his trousers and wrapped it tightly around his arm to stop the bleeding.

Then he ran.

A hysterical guest stepped in front of him as he raced down the hallway. He didn't even slow down before plowing her out of the way. He took the stairs three at a time and was soon on the ground floor. He slipped out a back exit and into the oppressive Arizona heat. Sirens screamed. Too many to count. Tires screeched, mere blocks away. As he disappeared from sight, waves of sharp pain washed over him like hot lava.

Reagan Rainey!!!!!

72

In the Air, Eastbound

THE Cessna Citation X's powerful Rolls-Royce engines droned a quiet song in the background. The men faced one another in the sleek cabin space now seated in a peace that was in stark contradiction to the wild storm of events they'd just left far behind.

Rainey and Job had already stripped out of their wet clothes and put on fresh pairs of socks and underwear along with attire from a smartly stocked supply cabin. Rainey now wore a pair of khaki 5.11 tactical cargo pants and a black long-sleeved T-shirt. Job, pleated khakis and a green Polo shirt—a Greenbriar Foundation logo on the chest. Their shoes were off and drying in a room at the rear of the luxurious jet that was also one of the fastest of its kind in production.

Job smiled briefly. "So…"

"Lay it out for me."

"What happened back there, kid, only confirms what I already know to be true. It's why I came for you. Roman Lerner is our mole. Actually been on my list of candidates for some time. He's a crafty one, that's for sure. But now we've got him."

Rainey squinted. "I don't follow."

"I've had my eye on him and some others for a while. Just didn't have any way of drawing them out."

He was trying to work through it but was having trouble connecting the dots. "Lerner was responsible for the assassinations? I don't get it."

"Indirectly, yes, he was. Fed their names, identities to the person or persons doing the actual killing. Sergei Nuriyev and the guy back there were probably the ones doing the actual wet work. Lerner was integral to all of it. Each and every assassination can be laid at his feet. Montreal, Iraq, Mexico, and now Arizona. Lerner is responsible for it all. Why? That I can't say, that is I don't know, but his days are certainly numbered, I can assure you."

Rainey stared at the carpet. "That explains a lot, but DARPA? That part doesn't make sense to me."

"You're right. The key to that little mystery is Noel Patterson. He is—was—a DARPA employee. Turned himself into the FBI yesterday after some guys tried to whack him. He provides the missing piece. He's how Kozlov's group got on to Dr. Horst in the first place. Patterson confessed to spying for the Russians, said he had once mentioned to his handler—a guy he knows only as Mr. P— what his good pal Eddie Horst was working on at DARPA. Man-portable high-energy lasers. Russians apparently acted on it." Job nodded. "Things are beginning to fall into place."

Rainey massaged his forehead, as his mind worked to make sense of things. He thought back to the beginning. The first lead, the first clue had been Nika. Then it hit him like a hurricane wind. She wanted to be seen by the ATM camera. The facial recognition hit is what gave them their first clue. But that meant... "She's working for you. Nika's working for you."

Job drew in a deep breath, let it out through pursed lips and nodded. "Yes."

Rainey's mind raced now, computing information sets at a feverish pace. "Nika's on the inside. She led me to Kozlov, to Horst. It was all a ruse to draw out the mole."

"Very good, Ray. But it's more than just a simple game of cat and mouse. See, we knew that the Agency mole was clearly responsible for facilitating the assassinations. Something had to be done, something bold yet truly clandestine. Horst's disappearance presented an opportunity. Nika had been inside Kozlov's group a few months by then on an unrelated assignment. She got word to me after she'd discovered Kozlov was being fed info about someone at DARPA. She didn't know that someone was Edward Horst until the last minute. She also didn't know why Kozlov was interested in him until later. Kozlov compartmentalizes everything.

"I ordered her to do what she could to lead us to Kozlov, but without exposing herself, without blowing her cover, and also without spiking the mole's, i.e. Roman Lerner's, suspicions. I can't say how dangerous it was for her—still is. When you actually found them outside Montreal, Kozlov must have gone berserk."

Rainey nodded. "He did. By the way, who was the VIP in the chopper? Nika tell you about him?"

"She mentioned him in one of her communiqués. She didn't know the guy. Said Kozlov only referred to him as *The Colonel*. My guess: he's GRU. From what Nika reported, the Colonel dude was there to collect Horst and his work product. Seems he was gonna fly him outta the country. Probably back to Russia."

"So, this Noel Patterson—this DARPA guy that turned the Russians on to Horst—what else did he say?"

"Nothing that's of any consequence."

Rainey closed his eyes and tried to think.

"In my mind, the one person who ties everything together...Kozlov's group abducting Horst and forcing him to build a prototype, this fictitious Iranian terrorist, the plot that Fayyad's told us about, the Agency assassinations and what happened at Strathcona...is this Mr. P person."

"Strathcona?"

Job was in his own world now. "He's also gotta be Lerner's contact. *Think*, Job! The assassinations seemed random, but...what if they were designed to be that way?" Job looked at Rainey. "Remember our man who was killed in Montreal, Keith Nelson?"

"Sorry, never knew the man."

"Nelly was the Agency's foremost authority on the Russian mafia in Canada, read Vladislav Kozlov. Nelly knew the players, their exploits, how they work, their internal politics, et cetera. What if he was targeted? Maybe whoever's behind all of this was just sort of clearing the chessboard of any possible threats to Kozlov. A just-in-case kind of thing.

"I don't quite know *how* Lerner knew about you guys going to Montreal, but you were definitely targeted. That's for sure. Same goes for Iraq. Lerner explains how word got out about the operation to save Fayyad as well as Christofer Bracks and the location of Kingston Park." Job's eyes moved about the cabin, his thoughts materializing in words. "Roman Lerner's contact. Noel Patterson's contact. Same guy. Has to be. That's who we need to identify. This Mr. P. He is the key. He will lead us to the brains behind everything."

Rainey fingered the bandage on his forehead. His mind was shifting pieces of the puzzle around and fitting them into place. "You planted the stuff to make it appear that Nika was related to Kozlov."

Job affirmed with a grin. "Actually, we used all of that crap a while back to convince Kozlov to bring Nika into his confidence. Surprised you found it. She was working on something else back then but as I said when the Horst business kicked up, I re-tasked her to this operation. The letter, the photos, all of it helped authenticate her bona fides as a rogue former Mossad operative looking for her long lost step-brother. Kozlov—and Lerner obviously—bought it. That took some doing...we have my Israeli friends to thank for that."

"So now what? What about Lerner? He's gotta know that you're on to him."

"Agreed. Surely, he knows that we know about him now. He'll have to go to ground. He'll disappear. At least he'll try." Job shot a sly grin to Rainey before his eyes turned stone cold.

"And this pending attack? The fact still remains that someone is planning to hit us hard, Job."

"You're absolutely right. Our job has only just begun. Thanks to you though we now have knowledge of it. That was a serendipitous, dare I say miraculous, discovery on your part. If you and your Delta friends had not saved Fayyad in Mosul, the intel about the attack would have died with him. When he made it out alive, it in turn forced them to go to a plan B, which further exposed Lerner. Nuriyev killed Bracks outside Baghdad and then took his place at Kingston Park. That's where things began to really turn in our favor, especially when, as you say, Fayyad demanded you be present while he spilled his guts. Nuriyev killed Fayyad and then tried to kill you because of that intel." Job shook his head. "But you survived. Based on what we now know, it's obvious that the Russians are behind everything. There are still many questions that we need answered though. Is this plot the design of the Russian government, a rogue group, or a solitary man? If the Russian government is involved and we confront them, they'll only deny it and begin covering their tracks. Proving something of this magnitude will take some doing."

Rainey went to the bathroom when the phone in the console buzzed. He could hear Job talking into the handset as he closed the door. When he was finished, he returned to his seat and plopped down.

"They are running the name *Farid* through the databases. Not a whole lot to go on there, but we'll see what shakes loose. Can't wait to see what's on that DVR…and the SIM card. Well done by the way. Well done, indeed."

"Can I ask you a question?"

"Of course," said Job.

"Why did you keep us in the dark? You know, the four of us sent to Montreal. Why didn't you just tell us from the start?"

Job rubbed his forehead. "That was my decision. I didn't want to complicate an already complicated operation. I thought that it would only muddy the waters—more than they already were."

"And what about these assassins? There was an obvious chance, a very good chance, that we were going to be targeted. C'mon, Job, give it to me straight."

"I never intended for that to happen, Ray, but, yes, I knew it was a possibility. It's just a fact that this business I'm in, we're in, is a dirty one. There are things we must do at times that are extremely dangerous, and though they are dangerous we still must do them. You have no idea how worried I was about you and the others. I dread each and every time I have to send people into harm's way. I've lost some really good people over the years and it's something that will torment me until the day I die. But in spite of the danger, in spite of the risks, someone has to be willing to confront America's threats, no holds barred. It's what Directorate Twelve was specifically designed to do, Ray.

"In this case, we decided, *I* decided, to ostensibly challenge the threat head on. And while the threat was occupied with what appeared to be a full-on, albeit covert, frontal assault, we would flank it, and drive a stake through its heart."

"I don't know what any of that means, but…" Rainey shook his head. "I just don't see why it was necessary to keep us in the dark."

"Well, if you'll recall, you never were really in the dark with respect to the assassinations. You were briefed on that at the onset. I was adamant with Director Thompson about that particular fact."

Job held Rainey's gaze for a few seconds then opened his briefcase. He pulled out a file, handed it to Rainey. "This is why Kozlov made Horst build him a laser gun."

He opened it, saw a thick report inside. He read the heading in the center of the first page:

TS//SRF//IROQUOIS – Preliminary Investigation Findings
Rainey looked up without saying a word.

Job nodded knowingly. "Strathcona. All I can say is brace yourself."

* * *

He stared out the window, down onto a rumpled blanket of phosphorescent clouds. Through a few breaks in the constant bulk of white beneath them, he could make out the Mississippi River as it slithered back and forth between Arkansas and Tennessee.

He and Job had already discussed what had taken place at the Strathcona Research Facility. Kozlov's group was responsible. How did they know? Nika. She'd alerted Job the minute she could. Job had explained Nika's new orders: recover the stolen Turbo. At all costs. Nika would try to replace the real tubes of Turbo with inert replicas but only if the opportunity presented itself. This would allow them to exploit the situation right up until the point of attack. But Job had been clear, securing the real Turbo was absolutely paramount even if it meant risking exposure...or, as Rainey was sure Nika knew, her life. It was clear to both men that the two Arabs already here on U.S. soil, were going to strike the homeland with the Turbo.

Rainey eased back into his seat. He cradled his chin in his left hand, working through the past week logically. After a few minutes of silence, he looked up. "What if she fails? How do we stop it?"

Job massaged the bridge of his nose. Finally, he looked up into Rainey's penetrating gaze. "I have a great deal of faith in Nika, but if she does fail..." Job swallowed. "We do what you've already been doing. We follow the bread crumbs. And pray."

The secure phone in the polished woodgrain console next to Job buzzed again. He picked up the receiver. "Yes?" Job stared at Rainey as he listened intently. After a minute or so, he said, "Thank you, Eleanor," then gently replaced the receiver.

"What is it?" said Rainey drawn in by the look of disbelief on Job's face.

Job grinned. "Lonnie Conover just came out of his coma."

73

Crystal City
Arlington, VA

THE minute they touched down at Reagan National, Job led Rainey on a quick march to a black Ford Expedition with dark, tinted windows. The driver already seemed to know exactly where to go. Job told the man to step on it and he obeyed without hesitation.

Rainey felt the soreness in his body returning and almost as a matter of habit put it out of his mind entirely. "So, where are we going? You're obviously not taking me to Lynn Street."

"All things in due time, Ray. Almost there."

In less than five minutes' time, the driver was gone and he and Job were walking into the lobby of a sand-colored office building with a brass plate out front that read, "Sharkey & Giles Consulting Ltd."

"Sharkey and Giles?" said Rainey. "What is this place? Where are we?"

"In a moment. You'll see," said Job with a cryptic smile.

Rainey shook his head. He was still trying to come to terms with all that Job had told him in the past several hours. And yet there was still much he wasn't privy to when it came to Directorate Twelve.

"Indulge me with your patience just a bit longer, please, Ray. In a moment, things will all make sense."

"Whatever you say, Job. Whatever you say."

Job approached an unmarked door at the back of the lobby. He looked up at a camera perched overhead. After a second or two, there was *buzz* and a *click* and Job pulled open the door. When they were both inside, Job made sure the door was closed then continued down an unremarkable corridor that smelled of new carpeting. He turned left and bypassed several closed doors, finally stopping in front of one. He swiped a card across a plate on the wall then punched a numeric code into an electronic lock mounted above the doorknob. Someone had taped a piece of computer paper on the door that contained a message in black magic marker, "DS Restricted (Unless You Have Coffee)." Someone else had added below it, "Or Chocolate."

The room was larger than it appeared outside, a kind of make-shift squad room with cubicles positioned along three walls. Four folding tables had been pushed together at the center of the room to form a central platform for various computers and other sophisti-cated electronic hardware. There were people scattered around the room clicking away on keyboards and talking on secure phones. A few of them briefly glanced toward the door as Job and Rainey en-tered. A man sitting at a desk on the far side of a wall-mounted smartboard slid out from his chair and began walking toward them. He was in his early-thirties, had short, blond hair and a neatly trimmed beard. Behind his titanium-framed eyeglasses were a set of intelligent blue eyes. He wore two lanyards around his neck. Dangling from one of them, was a shiny thumb drive. From the other, an ID badge.

"Hiya, Chief. Whaddya got for me?"

Job handed over the backpack of items Rainey had collected in his travels. "Do your magic. And, Spencer, this is priority one."

"On it boss." Spencer Ford spirited back to his desk, calling out to several others in the room who quickly huddled around him.

Job guided Rainey past an empty briefing room. "Spencer's TOG. Technical Operations Group. He and his people are nothing short of amazing."

They went through another door, into a private office. A man in a suit immediately stood up from an ugly, upholstered chair situated in front of a metal desk. He adjusted the cuffs of his shirt. Job brushed past him while shedding his coat. "Ray, I'd like you to meet Ken Thompson, director of the Central Intelligence Agency. Ken, *this* is Reagan Rainey."

Rainey shook the director's hand. "Pleasure to meet you, sir."

Thompson was tall with a commanding presence much like that of a CEO of a highly successful and very high profile corporation, which in a sense he was. He wore a charcoal pinstriped suit and a yellow-gold power tie.

"Pleasure is all mine, Sergeant," said Thompson. "I'm thrilled to finally meet you face-to-face."

Rainey had seen him countless times on TV, in print, and one time in real life during one of the director's surprise visits to Baghdad years ago, but had never actually met the man. He had an endearing quality about him. A sincerity perhaps. In any case, he seemed likeable.

"You're wondering what this is all about. Am I right?" He turned to Job. "Why don't you bring him up to speed."

"Sure. Have a seat. Please, both of you. Ray, what you see here is the special task force component of Operation Dark Special. Everyone here has been working on this operation since its inception. Sharkey and Giles? A front, of course. Although there is a dedicated staff here who actually does consulting work and not just for the Greenbriar Foundation." Job smiled. "I had everyone assigned to DS move here from Lynn Street after what happened at Kingston Park. OP SEC, you know...

"This...this reserved space, is what we in Directorate Twelve anecdotally refer to as the *Greenbriar Room*." Job made air quotes. "Most of our front organizations, businesses, what have you, have them. Some are outfitted with SCIFs. Size and capability vary with each location, but collectively their remit is the same: to fulfill Directorate operational requirements."

"Wow."

"I know. It's pretty cool."

Rainey picked at one of the butterfly bandages on his forehead as he studied the circular crest on the wall, the crest for Directorate Twelve. He'd never seen it before probably because he had never actually set foot in a D12 facility before now. Frankly, he'd never set foot into any official Agency facility. Which was entirely on purpose, of course. His eyes moved across it slowly. There was something unmistakably familiar about it, something overwhelmingly...American.

At the center was a bald eagle, its eyes fierce and resolute, mouth open as if it were screaming at the top of its lungs. The eagle's powerful wings were spread wide. In one of its razor sharp talons, it held a spearhead. In the other, a flaming torch. A small skeleton key hung from a gold ribbon around its neck. An inscription in cursive writing ran the length of the ribbon, a Latin phrase: *Veritas pares libertatem.* Truth equals liberty. Profound yet simply stated.

Whoever designed the crest had clearly intended to make a statement in more than just words. The font was very small. So small in fact, that to read it, he had to squint, lean in. Really seek. Just like in life, he mused. If you searched for truth you would ultimately find liberty, because truth is liberating.

Below the eagle was a navy blue banner that proclaimed, "Defenders of the Free," in decorative gold text. Stamped into the outer ring of the crest, were words of distinction, power, authority: "United States of America – Central Intelligence Agency – Directorate Twelve."

Job was still talking. Rainey stroked his chin and acted like he'd heard every word.

Just then, Sean Vajda—head of the Agency's Clandestine Service—knocked on the doorframe and entered. He took a seat in one of the ugly chairs along the wall. "Sorry I'm late, but I wanted to be absolutely sure I wasn't followed." After he was situated, he grinned at Rainey, gave one of those nods that seemed to sum up a handful of sentiments: Hi, Good job, Thank you, Sorry for your loss, I'm here to help. "So, what did I miss?"

"Nothing. We just got in." Job leaned forward and grabbed a glass jar from the corner of the desk, a gift from one of the funnymen out there working the computers. A jar of Hershey's Special Dark candies. Special Dark...Dark Special... "Chocolate?" He lobbed the bite-size candy over the desk to Rainey and Vajda. Thompson declined. "So?" said Job, looking at Vajda.

"The hammer has already begun to fall. It was just as you predicted."

"Who was it?" said Job clinically.

"Phillip Krut. He's one of Lerner's faithful minions. Keller and his people pounced on him as soon as he entered Lonnie's room. He had two full syringes of succinylcholine on him. Lonnie would have been toast. You saved his life, Job."

"And? Keller get him to talk?"

"You bet he did. Gave up Lerner, gave up everything. The Bureau has been notified. I gotta ask. How did you know they would go after Lonnie?"

Job popped a second chocolate into his mouth. "Because of something that's always bothered me about the attack on the ambassador's residence in Doha, specifically why those animals took Lonnie...only *him*. They just as easily could have killed him along with the others. But they chose to take him instead. Clearly, he has information someone wants. I know some in the Agency and at State still believe that the ambassador was the target, but I'm not one of them. I think Lonnie was the target all along. Once we discovered Lerner was complicit in the assassinations it just seemed logical that Lonnie Conover's ordeal had a bigger part to play in all of this. Or was even central to all of this. What if the other killings were just cover? Obfuscation by design. A needle in a stack of needles, so to say. I'd be willing to bet that he was supposed to have been killed, too. Something must have gone wrong.

"Anyway, all of that got me thinking about what information Lonnie might possess that would have made him a target in the first place. After that, it just made sense to me that someone, maybe even Roman Lerner himself, would try to take him out if he regained consciousness."

Thompson sat there shaking his head. "Unbelievable."

Rainey recalled Job's phone conversations on the plane. After learning about Conover's updated condition, Job had immediately called Curt Keller, the head of Agency security then Sean Vajda and finally Director Thompson himself.

"So why was he targeted in the first place?" asked Thompson.

"Before the attack, do you remember what Conover was working on?" asked Job.

Vajda sat up straight. "Holy cow. Conover was working on a new source, felt he was just starting to win the man's confidence."

Job nodded.

Vajda looked up at the ceiling then closed his eyes. "I should have seen it sooner."

Thompson gazed back and forth at his two subordinates. "What? Seen what sooner?"

Sean Vajda shook his head in frustration. "The guy Conover was cultivating as a source around the time of the embassy attack— *Crap!*—worked in the Russian embassy in Doha. He had to be Raji Fayyad's source, too. He knew that Jamil ibn Hasan didn't exist, knew

Iran wasn't plotting any terrorist attack, at least not the one that we're worried about presently. That's why Lonnie was targeted. Because he knew about everything. At least they thought he did."

Thompson cocked his head like a dog when its puzzled.

"Sir, I spoke to Lonnie, you know, after Keller and his people hauled Krut away. I explained to him what was happening. He doesn't know a thing about any pending terrorist attack. Back around the time of his abduction, he and his source were still in the early stages of their relationship. Lonnie was still trying to identify the guy's motivations although he was convinced he would have been an excellent agent. The guy had really good access and nerves of steel. The two of them were developing good rapport. Lerner would have known all of this, of course." Vajda grabbed a chocolate, folded back the wrapper as he unwound his thoughts for the group. "But what Lerner didn't know was the source's identity. Up to that point, he'd known him only by his code name: Pegasus.

I've since reached out to two of Lonnie's people about Pegasus. According to them, he's vanished. After what happened to Fayyad, he probably got scared and split, or—"

"Maybe he's dead," said Job.

"In any case, I also asked Lonnie about what went on during his captivity. Not a full debrief, mind you, just some quick questions while I was there. He said he remembers the attack and being hustled out of the city. Remembers being interrogated. Remembers the guy who was asking all the questions. Lonnie said he was Russian. Guy only stayed long enough to get the identity of the man called Pegasus. The men in the camp were then supposed to kill him, but several of them—particularly the ones involved in his torture sessions—got violently ill. No one would go near him after that. Then you guys showed up. He said it's a miracle the way things turned out."

"Indeed," said Job.

It made sense now. Pegasus. The source. That's why Nuriyev—the Christofer Bracks imposter—had been so quick to ask Fayyad about the identity of his source. He was trying to verify whether or not Fayyad's and Conover's sources were the same person. So as to identify the extent of the Russians' exposure. Rainey's blood began to boil. The same people responsible for the Agency assassinations, for killing Boyd, Drummond & Cassel, were also responsible for Monster's death.

Adrenaline now surged through his veins.

74

JOB tented his fingers on the desk in front of him. "My people abroad are pressing their sources. One report we received just a few hours ago, from someone deep inside the Russian government, contains something very interesting. Seems it's rumored that Levka Borovksy, is becoming a little erratic, pre-occupied some say. Like he's planning something very big, very off-the-books."

"You think he's behind this?"

"Definitely a possibility, sir," said Job.

Thompson leaned forward, elbows on knees. "So what now? We still face the prospect of… I mean if Nika is not able to secure the Turbo… Job, thousands of people are going to die, maybe even *millions*. What can we do? Do we have any idea where the Turbo is?"

Job pulled out his cell phone and checked the screen. "Unfortunately, we are still in the dark on that. But Nika's good. She'll find it. I'm expecting her to report in soon. Sir, as you know, Kozlov's been extremely careful even amongst his own people."

Just as Job laid the phone down on the desk, it lit up and vibrated. He held up his index finger as he answered it. "Yes?" He was silent, his eyes as intense as Rainey had ever seen them, yet when he finally spoke his voice was calm. "I see. Anything else?" Job's eyes tracked from Thompson to Vajda to Rainey. "Okay. Thank you. Good job. Let me know if anything else comes to light." Job laid the phone back down. "That was Spencer. His people are making progress. The DVR from the motel contains footage of the two Arabs that sneaked across the border, care of Devonte Reyes. Also captured on camera was the guy who picked them up as well as the car he was driving, including a good shot of the tag. Comes back to a holding company based in the Big Apple. Spencer's got some people chasing down leads on the company as we speak. He's running the footage against our facial recognition software now, too. But we may already know the identity of one of our prospective martyrs—the older one. The partial fingerprint on the SIM card you recovered, Ray... We got a hit."

* * *

"I know him. Very well, in fact." Vajda massaged his forehead and closed his eyes. He repeated the name slowly. "Farid Shafiq al-Nasem. We had him at Gitmo for a minute. Dangerous dude. Pakistani Taliban. Smart, brutal. We actually captured him in Afghanistan—Zabul Province—back in 2004 during Operation Asbury Park. But he was repatriated back to Pakistan in early 2007. He's a bomb maker—IEDs, suicide vests, all kinds of crap. Also teaches others how to make bombs. Should have never been let go. We tried to keep track of him and did for a while, but lost him in the FATA (Pakistan's Federally Administered Tribal Areas) in the fall of 2008. Later that year, we got good intel that he was staying at a camp outside Ghulam Khan. We dropped a couple Hellfires on the compound, but somehow he managed to survive. Disappeared again after that. Since then we've received reports that he's been spotted in Iran, Saudi Arabia, even France. Other reports have him pegged as joining up with AQAP in Yemen. But, all of that intel is unconfirmed. He's been very hard to track down.

"Al-Nasem is an old head. In his teens, he fought the Russians in Afghanistan, you know the drill." Vajda shifted in his chair and let his mind work. "Gotta ask ourselves why would he be connected to a martyr mission? He's a bomb maker right? Not usually martyr material. Much more valuable to the cause if he's alive." It was like a light bulb went on above his head. "But maybe—"

"Yes?" said Job.

"Maybe he's in this for...revenge. See, al-Nasem survived the drone strike in Ghulam Khan but his wife and two brothers weren't so lucky. Also, word from our people on the ground in the days that followed, was that al-Nasem suffered some serious burns to the left side of his body. Lost part of his left hand in the blast. But what if al-Nasem's thirst for revenge was co-opted? Russians invent this guy Jamil ibn Hasan out of thin air and through this fiction seek out two men for a special martyr mission. Al-Nasem is getting old, maybe he's finally ready to be a martyr himself."

Thompson chimed up. "What I don't get is how al-Nasem would even know this Jamil character. I mean he's made up, right? Why would he trust someone he doesn't even know? We ourselves didn't have a clue about him until recently."

"I see your point," said Vajda. "But, and I'm sure Job's people are hearing the same thing now, reports in the last few days are flowing in big-time. All of them about a mysterious Iranian terrorist mastermind named Jamil who is supposed to be the next big thing in radical Islam. Blogs, known jihadi websites, even previously good, credible HUMINT and SIGINT sources are picking up all kinds of intel now on what is thought to be an Iran-backed terror plot."

Job agreed. "If what we believe is true, then the Russians are responsible for all the chatter. They're flooding the zone with all kinds of misinformation. Remember Fayyad said that Iran is going to be blamed for the attack. But why al-Nasem?"

"Well, the Russians would have known about al-Nasem. To them, it could be a funny twist of irony to have him do their dirty work in that he fought against them back in the day."

Job nodded encouragingly as Vajda continued.

"Knowing al-Nasem as I do, I'd bet my pension that the other man with him turns out to be a relative of some kind. A cousin, a nephew. Something along those lines. One thing we learned about him from other detainees at Gitmo is that al-Nasem is extremely distrusting of anyone outside his family. Never travels with strangers. Usually only with family members, in fact.

"My point is that al-Nasem might be involved in this plot just for the sake of carrying out revenge for the drone strike."

"Well, regardless of his motivations, he's involved in this. As of right now he's our primary target," said Job looking at his Agency colleagues. "Get your people on it, Sean. I'll put the word out to mine as well. FBI, DHS, state and local cops, too. Put out everything we know about al-Nasem. We need to find him and his turban terrie BFF. Preferably before they link up with Kozlov. Pull out all the stops."

Thompson stood up, looked at his men with purpose. "Do it."

* * *

After Thompson and Vajda had cleared out and Job had issued the appropriate alerts to his people, Rainey eased back down into the battered sofa. "I still feel like we're missing something here. What are these guys planning? And when? Also why?"

"I'm afraid we're still in the dark on that, Ray. Nika will alert me if that information becomes available to her. She's due to check in soon. But you're on the right track. We must ID whoever is behind all of this, who is really pulling the strings...and why. Why is it that a group of Russians have fabricated a terrorist? What is their goal? What's the endgame? And why use the TRB-80, our own experimental stuff? If Levka Borovsky's operating outside the authority of his own government, so be it. But if we assume that the Russians are behind this, I mean, what's in it for them? What is it that has them ready to deliver us a blow of enormous proportions?"

The wheels of Job's chair squeaked as he stood answering his own ruminations. "At this point, I don't have a clue. Payback for what we've recently done to their economy perhaps? It doesn't make sense. Something has them taking enormous risks with enormous ramifications. This operation of theirs is very complex. Their reasons might be equally complex."

75

RAINEY willed away the tension in his neck. He relaxed his mind, allowed his thoughts to incubate. An idea slowly came to him. "What drives the Russians? What always drives the Russians? They want to bring down our way of life. Make us vulnerable. Is it possible that they, or perhaps just Borovsky, if he does end up being the mastermind behind all of this, might be using these unknowing conscripts, the two Arabs, as proxies in order for Russia to reassert itself in the global picture somehow. What better way than to compromise our very own intelligence community, our CIA...our military in the process...by using our own experimental tech against us. First, there would be so much distrust, chaos, turmoil within our own ranks that we wouldn't be able to adequately address available intelligence, subsequent threats. Sources would dry up overnight. I don't think Russia would ever preemptively attack us, but what if that's not their intent, at least overtly. But covertly, what if that's their deal? What if they are setting the table for something, a new power grab. Maybe they are intending to lead us into another military engagement that will occupy our increasingly limited resources and heavily taxed resolve." Rainey looked at Job as each thought he had led to another. "What if they are trying to shove us into a war with Iran? We're already busy with ISIL and other hot spots around the globe. Afghanistan is heating back up despite what the Administration's been saying."

Job sat back down. Leaning forward in his chair, he placed both elbows on his desk. "Interesting. Let's consider that to be the case...in the big picture, but what about the smaller one? The immediacy of the here and now. What would they want to destroy with the Turbo in order to do so? It's quite possible they have two targets. After all, they have two martyrs. And then why use the men from abroad? Why not co-opt people already in the U.S.? God knows there are plenty of them here who are willing to martyr themselves for the cause given the proper means. Or why not just set off the stuff remotely, bypass this whole cockamamie Jamil business altogether?"

Something fell into place inside Rainey's mind. "To frame them. They want there to be a clear trail that we assuredly uncover that will lead us to Iran's doorstep. Surely, we'll find it post-event. Of course, Iran will categorically deny responsibility. But Americans won't believe them. The drumbeats are already starting to sound for us to preemptively engage them over their pursuit of nuclear weapons despite their idiotic claims to the contrary. Maybe Kozlov's group is going to be sold out by Moscow...as being collaborators with Iran. Some wild group of mercenaries or who knows, maybe even converted Islamic jihadis. Do we know what part of Russia Kozlov and his turds are from? For instance, did he once live or work anywhere near Chechnya? I'm just spit-balling here, Job.

"Another possibility... Russians just wanted to get their hands on the Turbo. This whole thing was just a giant ploy to steal it. Laser gun was just icing on the cake. If the Turbo does what that report you showed me says it does, it might be worth the risk to them. They not only steal a sample of it for their scientists to reverse engineer, but all in one fell swoop they get to test it, see the effects of the Turbo. How sweeter than on an old adversary. And Iran takes the fall. Oh and guess what? Iran needs armaments, missile defense systems, blah...blah...blah. Just what Russia likes to sell to rogue nation states. The Russians create a raging demand for their products overnight; it drives up their economy. They win big-time. Maybe a war between us and Iran is a business decision. And just in case we were thinking of striking them—which you and me both know this Administration won't—they could leverage the Turbo against us. Use it to ward off any offensive action from us or NATO even. We're talking end times-type scenarios here.

"I know it sounds far-fetched, but say the Russians want us to rush into a war with Iran, overextend ourselves, our troops, into yet another war with another Islamic country. The Middle East is already on fire as it is now. Another catalyst to rally Islamic nations against the Large Satan."

Job stood up again and paced around the room. "So your positing that the Russians might in some way be pushing us down a path that leads to the United States militarily engaging Iran? But for what purpose? Russia is one of Iran's biggest allies."

"Like I said, maybe that part is a business decision. I don't know. I'm not an analyst. Could be for other reasons. Maybe they want cover to invade Iran, take over the oil fields...under the ruse of helping us battle terrorism. If that Turbo is unleashed on American soil, I promise you, the ramifications would easily be beyond the scope of the U.N. Security Council's influence. It would be grounds for all-out war. Nations would come together and would back America's righteous wrath. A coalition would form to destroy the Iranian military, its whack-job leadership for good. Russia would be stupid to stand against that. Rather they would be wise to do just the opposite: join the party. That would give them at least a plausible reason to swarm into Iran. Once they quote/unquote *secure* the oil-rich areas of Iran, their financial attachment to the Iranian government would be moot. They wouldn't need to be an ally to Iran any longer.

"If the Kremlin takes control of Iranian oil, heck maybe even tries to control the Strait of Hormuz, they might look to expand...move into the old Soviet states...get the old gang back together. It could easily cripple the rest of the world's economies especially if they shut off the natural gas that feeds the European continent. Russia would be able to re-launch a new Soviet empire, perhaps not in the old sense, but in a new economic sense. Haven't we always believed that there is a large contingency within the current Russian leadership that would give anything to capture their former global dominance? Just look at what happened with Georgia in oh eight, more recently with Crimea."

Job rubbed his eyes. "The red embers of communism continue to burn beneath the surface, under an illusion of democracy. Theirs is a gangster government. Everyone knows that. But there are some inside the Kremlin today that pine for the rebirth of the empire. One far more powerful than the last. The Turbo would make them extremely powerful." He looked at his watch. "Listen, Ray, I want to check on a few things, run this by some of the Agency eggheads. And Nika hasn't checked in. I want to have Spencer make sure our commo gear is working properly."

"Here," Job scrawled an address on a piece of scratch paper and handed it to Ray. "Go get some rest. You've more than earned it. It's a little apartment I keep in D.C. Consider it your personal safe house, if you will. I'm the only one who knows about it. If I need you for anything I will call you." Job receded to the far side of the room. Behind a handsome reproduction of Arnold Friberg's famous painting *The Prayer at Valley Forge* was a small safe. He quickly punched in a numeric code then waved Rainey over. "I'll trade you your Glock for this. After all, you don't want that gun on you anymore. It links to too much in Arizona and Mexico. Am I right?"

Rainey accepted the SIG Sauer P229 SAS Gen 2 9mm, slammed a fresh mag into the grip, charged the weapon then shoved it into his holster.

Job handed him several spare magazines. "Listen, that's only for an emergency. You had to do what you had to do in Arizona, but we are on U.S. soil. You know what that means. From now on—"

"Yeah, yeah." Rainey pulled on the parka he'd been given on the plane, stuffed his pockets with the spare magazines. "These Sharkey and Giles folks out front do car rental? I need wheels."

Job tossed him a set of keys. "Black Chrysler 300 downstairs. Call if you need anything. I'll do likewise. And Ray. Remember: I want you to rest."

76

Washington, D.C.

IT was already twenty-two minutes after eight. Rainey gripped the steering wheel and sped out of the underground parking garage beneath the Sharkey and Giles building. The sedan's headlights swept across a stretch limousine as he turned north onto Jefferson Davis Highway. While he drove, he tried to review in his mind everything that had transpired over the past several days. But it was no use. He was so tired. His eyes burned for sleep.

He circled the block then parked in the underground garage of Job's "little apartment." For some reason he'd been expecting a crappy-looking building and a phone booth-size apartment. He should have known. Job always did have good taste.

The Meridian at Mount Vernon Triangle Apartments were elegant and sleek, beautiful living spaces. First-rate all the way. However, despite the amenities and spaciousness, the apartment just felt too abstract. Didn't feel like a home. It did however beat lying in a sleeping bag in zero-degree weather—something he'd done numerous times in the mountains along the Af-Pak border.

After giving the place the once-over, Rainey threw his backpack on the living room sofa and crashed down beside it. He sat there without moving a muscle for close to twenty minutes. He'd stopped at a drive-thru on the way and picked up two big chicken sandwiches which he'd since devoured. *Should have gotten three.* His whole body ached. He didn't know how things were going to turn out with al-Nasem and his tag-along or with Kozlov. Had he done enough? What more could he do?

As sore as he was, he knelt down on his knees and prayed. Rainey wasn't a perfect Christian. But in reality, there was no such thing. If anyone said there was, they were lying. Everyone was a sinner. But each day, he tried his best.

He asked God for forgiveness for the things he'd done which he knew were wrong even if the ends were justified. He thanked God for keeping him alive. In hindsight, the danger he'd survived was nearly impossible to get his mind around now. It was obvious: God had protected him. He asked for strength, for patience, that his nation would be shown mercy. There was an incredible evil out there lurking in the shadows, still threatening America, threatening untold innocent lives. Rainey prayed that the enemies of good would be stopped in time. He shuddered to think of even one kid out there losing a parent or loved one in another terrorist strike, let alone thousands.

He prayed for Nika, for her protection. She was a gifted operator. Brave, too. Rainey asked God to grant him and all of his American warriors the chance to prevent more terrorists from attacking. It was his calling no matter how many times he tried talking himself out of it.

Falling back onto the sofa, Rainey was soon fast asleep comforted in the knowledge that no matter how dire the circumstances ever may seem, God was in control. Always.

* * *

It was the summer of 1993. He was just seven years old. Little Maddie, three years his junior, was in the patch of grass they called a backyard enjoying some midday July sunshine. The Raineys had only recently returned home from living abroad—Germany this time. But Ben had been called back to Berlin, where he'd been ostensibly working in some capacity with the American diplomatic corps, part of a complex assignment on the quintessential frontlines of the recently expired Cold War.

Ray wiped the sweat from his brow with paper towels and surveyed the backyard through the door just off the kitchen. He had just come inside from knocking the soccer ball around with a group of local kids. They'd been juggling in a circle, showing off for each other by executing their favorite trick moves. He loved soccer. It was undoubtedly his favorite sport and the one thing that had helped him acclimate to his frequently changing surroundings and of course make new friends.

He chugged a glass of water and shook his head as he observed Maddie outside now trying to juggle the soccer ball, his soccer ball. Her brown pigtails bounced jubilantly with each movement, shimmering in the sun. Occasionally, she would stop to bend over and push down the end of a Band-Aid on her left knee; it kept curling up. Finally, Maddie ripped it off, threw it down in the grass and went right back to what she was doing. Her forehead wrinkled in concentration, she continued trying to juggle the ball just like she'd seen her big brother doing. She was always trying to be just like him, always trying to do the exact same things he did. It so annoyed Ray, and, as one might imagine among the uncodified laws of family, was a frequent point of contention within the household. Each time he would lodge a complaint with their mother, she would mete out a judicious smile in her usual gracious way, often accompanied by a sympathetic nod or a loving touch on the arm or cheek. Invariably, she would tell him that he should take it as compliment. Somehow Maddie loved her brother so much, she wanted to me be just like him and that's why she mimicked everything he did.

Ray went on watching her as he cooled off inside. Maddie could string three touches together, but kept losing the ball after that. Pretty impressive for a four-year old. He sighed then tossed the soggy, balled-up paper towels in the trash before walking back outside.

"Hey squirt, can I show you something?"

Maddie's big, honey-colored eyes beamed in the brightness of the day, her cute little face scrunched up in absolute determination. She ignored him. She tossed the ball into the air again. One, two, three...the ball bounced off her knee. "Ugh!"

Ray stopped the ball with his foot. "Lean back a little more at the waist and get your legs up higher. Try to strike the ball in the middle of your thigh, not out here with your knee." Ray pulled the ball back with the toe of his sneaker and flicked it up into the air. "Like this, watch."

Maddie stood there taking in her big brother's effortless juggling ability. After he tapped out about ten or so touches alternating back and forth from thigh to thigh, she grabbed the ball out of the air. "I can do it myself, Ray!"

"Fine. Be that way." Ray shook his head and went back inside, a flash of frustration on his face. She could be so stupid. As he closed the door, he turned back, still shaking his head. He crossed his arms. His intense eyes relaxed a little. Maddie was doing just as he had instructed. She was up over five now and counting. Six, seven...

"It's just her way, dear." Sarah Rainey had quietly walked up behind him and swept the moist hair off his forehead. "She wants to be independent, but she definitely watches everything you do. And trust me, she soaks it all in."

"When's dad coming home?" Ray asked, ignoring the pep-talk.

"He'll be home just as soon as he can, dear. He misses you guys, too." She smiled, gently kissed his forehead. "Why don't you go work on some vocabulary until I'm finished with these dishes. Pick up where we left off."

"Why do I have to learn Russian?"

"Because my children are going to be well-rounded. Besides, you're good at it and you're a fast learner. You both are. God has given you guys special gifts. We honor Him by making the most of them. Did you know there are people in Africa and elsewhere around the world who can speak seven or eight languages?"

"Really?"

"Mmm hmm. Your father's one of them."

Ray brightened. "Dad?"

"Yep."

Ray looked at Maddie again. She was still going strong.

"We'll go over your Russian when I'm finished here, then later this afternoon we're going to start a fun new block of American history—a comprehensive study of one of America's greatest heroes. We talked about George Washington before, but what we're going to do this time is delve deeper. We're gonna learn about the truly extraordinary man that he was. YA dumayu, vy budete ocharovany." I think you'll be fascinated.

Rainey's forehead wrinkled up. When he thought he had it translated, he nodded and walked off. As he padded across the living room, he steadily picked up speed then launched himself over the coffee table and onto the spongey sofa. His Russian language text bounced off the fabric and he snatched it out of the air. He flipped the pages until he found the word he was looking for and grinned, realizing he had it right.

He carefully formed the words with his lips, hesitating between some as his young mind recalled the proper tenses and sentence structure, "Vy deystvitel'no dumayete, chto ya budete ocharovany?" *You really think I will be fascinated?*

"YA delayu." *I do. As she placed her hands back into the soapy water, a smile appeared on her face.*

* * *

Rainey bolted awake. It was morning. A shock of unexplained fear coursed through him as he checked his watch. How long had he been out? He wiped his eyelids, blinked several times and squinted, waiting for his vision to adjust.

He looked at the clock on the wall. *9:14 a.m.*

He stood up and stretched, did some jumping jacks, then dropped to the floor and quickly hammered out some push-ups and sit-ups. Once the blood got moving, his brain would wake up. He walked quickly into the kitchen, opened the cabinet and was pleased to see a canister of Maxwell House. It wasn't long before he had a piping hot cup of coffee in his hand.

Rainey leaned against the counter and organized his thoughts. Suddenly, something sparked inside him. A haunting premonition. If these nut-jobs really wanted him dead bad enough, they might just go after Mom or Maddie. Like a distant train getting closer, so the fear grew in his gut. He didn't want to believe that in some way he might be responsible for bringing danger to their doorstep.

They would be easy targets. They had no clue what he truly did for a living let alone know about this particular assignment. Kozlov and the Russians, this assassin who'd been after him since Montreal, they just might try to use Mom or Maddie to get to him. The thought was terrifying.

This would not be over until these people were stopped.

Until he stopped them.

He called Job. His mom was with Iris. Job had already dispatched a two-man security detail to keep tabs on them. The men had just arrived and reported back that Sarah and Iris were fine. *Thank God.* Job had ordered the team to get the two women to a safe house up in Towson and to keep them there until further notice. Job had also sent a team to Maddie's place. The men hadn't checked in yet. They were probably just caught in traffic. The swearing-in ceremony today at the Capitol had some parts of the city in near gridlock.

Rainey realized he was now behind the wheel, traveling at close to 75 mph, well over the speed limit. But his foot only pressed the accelerator further to the floor. As the needle on the speedometer continued clockwise, his sense of urgency ran wild like lava spilling down a mountainside.

He pounded the steering wheel. He'd already tried reaching Maddie by every means he could think of. He'd even tried calling Wes. But all of his calls were going straight to voice mail, his texts unanswered.

She was in trouble. He knew it in his soul.

He had to get to her.

And fast.

77

One Hour and Fourteen Minutes Ago

JOGGING across the street to her building in her winter running garb, Maddie couldn't contain her excitement. All throughout her run she'd been thinking about her man…and breakfast. How fitting it was that she and Wes were starting the new year together, but a new chapter in their lives as well. She was *getting married*. Her overwhelming joy was spread all over her face.

Wes had agreed to meet her at her apartment for a hearty breakfast. Wes made the best omelets. They had been up late last night at his place, talking and making plans. Maddie had decided to leave her job at the Library of Congress and run the studio full-time. After crunching numbers and calculating a budget, she and Wes had found that they could comfortably swing it.

She rode the elevator up to her floor, pulled the earbuds from her ears and continued wiping the sweat from her forehead. She was starved. She would shower and dress quickly. Ah, the perfect omelet and perfect man awaited. Her stomach growled.

Maddie forged down the hallway to her apartment. Sliding the key into the lock, she flipped the deadbolt back, turned the knob and opened the door. She dropped her keys into a square, multi-colored, ceramic dish just inside the door and unzipped her running jacket. A smile on her face, she pressed further into the apartment. Wes was probably hiding, waiting to jump out and plant one on her.

On the small dinner table, a thick, red candle burned amidst a festive medley of pine cones and Christmas greenery. The small flame wiggled back and forth playfully. Sunlight streamed in through the open blinds casting wide, bright lines across the floor and walls.

"Wesley," she beckoned, adding a sexy, come-hither timbre to her voice.

When there was no response, she walked into the kitchen. A wide pan had been set on the stove, a stainless steel bowl on the countertop. There was a whisk beside it. She opened the refrigerator. *I have eggs.*

Her eyes flashed to the clock on the microwave. *8:03.* On the counter, beneath a fresh newspaper, lay Wes's iPhone and keys. She furrowed her brow, turned around just in time to see hands reaching for her.

She fought wildly at first. Then came the painful prick of a needle on the right side of her neck. A tranquilizer dart or something. The room began to spin. The floor rocked beneath her as if she were in a canoe on the high seas. She was falling.

Then everything went black.

* * *

Present Time

The closer he came to Maddie's building, the more his apprehension—no, this was fear—grew. She hadn't answered his repeated calls and texts. He'd tried her cell, her apartment, even her studio. Then Wes's cell. Nothing. Something was very wrong. She was in grave danger.

When he turned onto U St. from 13th, the Chrysler was literally on two wheels. Rainey swerved around a slow driver, ignored the blaring horn and angry curses directed at him and turned into the alleyway on the west side of her building. He skidded to a stop. As he got out of the car, he drew his pistol, pushed it into the large coat pocket on his right side with his trigger finger poised along the frame.

He sprinted up the stairs. When he reached Maddie's floor, the elevator doors at the end of the hall were opening. He quickly assessed its occupants. They were harmless.

After his first few steps down the hall, a young woman in her twenties wearing a low-cut dress and a man easily twice her age emerged from a room on his left. The bosomy woman smiled and made eyes at him while the older man hunched over and locked the door with a jangle of a keys. The look on Rainey's face must have scared her because the woman's demeanor quickly changed. She clutched her companion at the bicep, whispered into his ear and jerked him toward the elevator as Rainey brushed past them.

He drew closer to Maddie's apartment. *No!* Her door was slightly ajar. A tendril of rage fizzed through his tightly pursed lips.

He held the pistol firmly now indexed in front of his chest, ready for anything. Rainey listened as he stood next to her door. Craning his neck, he tried to spy into the room through the cracked door for something, anything that would tell him the door was just an oversight. But this was no oversight. Something foreboding had happened. Maddie was a stickler when it came to her personal security. She would never be so careless.

He brought up the floor plan of Maddie's apartment in his mind's eye. Then like a gust of winter wind, he pushed open her door and began clearing the apartment. He cleared each room until it was apparent there was no one there. Now he switched into analysis mode, soaking up any and every conceivable clue that might tell him where she was. There was no mistaking it. It didn't take a genius to figure out what had happened here.

In the living room, there was clear-cut evidence of a struggle. A potted plant had been thrown, apparently, the soil spilled all over the floor had been tramped through. A woman's—Maddie's—green and gray New Balance running shoe—*shoe*, not shoes—lay by itself on the floor just outside the kitchen. A throw rug was bunched up against the bookcase. Two chairs had been knocked over. A picture frame had been smashed on the coffee table: the photo of Maddie and UFC fighter Ronda Rousey together in a D.C. eatery a few years back. The two were very good friends, trained together from time to time. That photo was one of Maddie's favorites.

This was bad.

His heart stopped. He realized he was holding his breath.

They took her.

Rainey walked into the kitchen, saw the pan on the stove. It looked like someone had been getting ready to cook breakfast. The window blinds were open. He picked up Maddie's running shoe, felt the inside. It was still moist. Must have grabbed her right after her morning run. Rainey looked at his watch. *She hasn't been gone long.*

He fished out the cell phone Job had given him, was about to call him when the cordless phone on the counter rang. He looked at the caller ID. *Restricted Number.*

"Hello?"

"You're a very talented man, Mr. Rainey, to have survived to this point. I must say I am very impressed."

"Who is this?" he growled, the veins in his neck throbbing. His eyes shot around the apartment...at the windows, then he saw it— Maddie's laptop on the table. It was positioned so that the Web cam was aimed at the front door to her apartment.

"Shh-shh-shh. Manners, please, Mr. Rainey. After all, you do not want to anger me. For I hold in my hand the fate of your sister, you see. And that of what appears to be the man she's promised to wed. Now, I know—" The man was calm if not icy. Borderline professorial.

Rainey tapped the space bar on the laptop. The dark screen came alive and a cloaked man appeared. "So help me, if you lay so much as a finger on her, I will hunt you down, no matter how long it takes. I will not stop until you're dead. Do you hear me?"

"Ugh! There you go again. I'm afraid you're not going to like what she will have to endure should you interrupt me again." He paused as Rainey responded with silence. "There, that's more like it. Now, as I was saying, I know you are privy to certain things, certain details relative to recent events. As such, I'd like to propose a trade. Pure and simple. Are you interested?"

"Let me talk to Maddie."

"I'm afraid that's out of the question, but you have my word she is alive, and quite well I might add, considering. Her friend, too. And I promise you they will stay that way as long as you do as I say."

"I need proof of life."

"My word is all the proof you will get."

Rainey gripped the phone so tight his knuckles were chalk white. "What kind of trade?"

"It's very simple. I will free your sister and her friend, here, in exchange for you. Two lives for one. It's a bargain really."

There was no hesitation. "When, where?"

The man on the other end outlined the details of the exchange and hung up without further mention of the consequences should Rainey not follow his orders explicitly. The man sounded as if he were licking his lips, giggling with delight.

Deep within, the rumblings of rage pounded. Thunder before a terrible storm. Like the end of the third movement of the Kraft Timpani Concerto. The adrenaline that throttled his veins coupled with the fear of losing his baby sister made his fingers shake as he dialed Job.

"They have Maddie."

There was silence.

"Did you hear me?!"

"I heard you, Ray. Listen to me—"

"There's no time. I'm going after her. I'm gonna end this. They want me. They're gonna get me."

"Ray, wh—"

Rainey disconnected the call and left the phone on the counter next to the gun Job had given him. He couldn't put Maddie in any further danger. Job would want to put together hasty surveillance and assault teams. With the limited number of people he could trust at the moment outside of Job, he was going to play this safe. His way. He would go alone.

And finish this.

78

Arlington, VA

"I love you, Daddy."

"I love you, too, Maddie. You know, you are looking more and more like your mother every day. You have her eyes and her smile. My, what a beautiful young lady you are becoming. You'll always be my little girl though, no matter how old you are."

Maddie smiled as she regarded her father's strong, reassuring embrace, his smooth, velvety voice and the scent of the pleasant cologne lingering on his neck. She was tucked under his resolute jawline. Her little hands wrapped around his solid frame, she squeezed him tightly, cuddled him and closed her eyes. Here, within the confines of her father's arms, she was undeniably content. It was a heavenly place, ethereal, absolute.

"Maddie." The distant voice of her mother danced across the molecules in the air. Her joyful spirit was so magnificently pristine, rife with the promise of hope, of love, of family. "Maddie. Ben. Time for dinner." A pause, a prelude to a disquieting chill. Something wasn't right.

"Maddie. Maddie! MADDIE!!"

The memory faded away. Slowly, she blinked her eyes and saw the man she had promised to marry kneeling over her, nudging her shoulder with his head, tears streaming down his face. "Maddie, wake up! Please!"

She was groggy. She wanted to return to the vivid memory of her childhood. "Wh... What?" As coherence returned, her eyes regained their focus. "What happened? Where are we?" The tight restraints dug into her wrists, soreness shot through her shoulders from being in the same position for who knew how long.

"I was so worried about you. I didn't think you would ever wake up."

Maddie breathed in steady drags of oxygen, her memory finding its cue as she sensed a pinching pain on the side of her neck where the tranquilizer dart had hit her. "Where are we, Wes?"

"I don't know. I have no idea. They haven't told me anything."

"They? *They* who?"

"I don't know that either. But, I could hear them. Speaking in Russian, I think. From the voices, there are at least two of them, maybe more."

Maddie fought to stand up. She was woozy. While she regained her equilibrium she steadied herself against the wall with her hands, which were flex-cuffed tightly behind her back.

"There! Do you hear it?" Wide-eyed, Wes jerked his head toward the metal grill on the wall. Two men speaking in normal voices seemingly unaware that their conversation was traveling to the floor below via the building's aging metal ductwork.

"Shh. Be quiet," she whispered. Maddie knelt down on the cold cement floor. "If we can hear them, they may be able to hear us."

Their prison was barren. There was nothing to differentiate the four walls save an electrical outlet on one, a thick door on another, and the metal grill at the base of the one against which they were now crouched.

"Oh my gosh!"

"What? What is it?!"

Maddie's eyes were wide, terror-stricken. They began tearing up.

"What? Maddie, please! What did they say?"

Maddie shifted, then rocked forward against the wall. "My Russian is rusty, but I'm certain they said...they're gonna blow up the Capitol Building...during the swearing-in ceremony today."

79

Robert M. Watkins Regional State Park
Prince George's County, MD

FOR what seemed his entire life, even more so since his father had died, Rainey had taken it upon himself to protect his baby sister with unadulterated vigilance. And now he was to blame for her predicament. His warrior lifestyle had dragged her into the danger zone. He hated to consider the possible outcomes. But he couldn't afford to let his mind go there.

The only thing that drove him now was saving Maddie. If she lived, it would all be worth it. He had no desire to die, but if it meant sacrificing himself for his kid sister, he would do it in a heartbeat.

Tiptoeing into his thoughts was an image of the woman he was counting on, the woman who quite possibly held his, Maddie's, and Wes's lives in her hands.

Nika.

* * *

"He's alone. Shall I take the shot?" asked Kozlov clinically into the cell phone at his ear. *Please say yes.*

"*Nyet*. Bring him to me. I want to hear what he knows, what they know."

"Are you sure about that? I can take him out right here, right now. Finish what our friend from Dagestan could not." Kozlov didn't want to sound like he was pleading, but he knew the goal here was to kill the man—the man standing in the crosshairs of his scope. Now Pyotr was changing his mind, diverting from the plan and saying that he wanted to interrogate him.

"I think it better if we first see what, if anything, he is willing to tell us. Right now he has no choice in the matter, he must cooperate. Or else he faces the alternative. No, bring him to me. Rest assured I will make quick work of him. And then we can get back to the business at hand."

"Yes, sir," said Kozlov through clenched teeth. His eyes were still on the man 140 yards away in the clearing. This was a bad idea. Every instinct he had was screaming within. They were playing with fire here. Visually, the man in the crosshairs was the epitome, the very essence of the Main Adversary. Regardless of whether or not the motherland's primary enemy was a historical conscript of truth or fiction, real or the concoction of trumped-up paranoia—the legacy of Stalin and his modern-day acolytes—Reagan Rainey bore the visceral persona of everything he'd always known about elite American warriors. They were confident and strong, superbly intelligent, utterly unflappable and quite simply fearless. He loathed him and feared him at the same time. Against his better judgment and his instincts, he softly relayed the command to his colleagues below. "Take him."

* * *

Rainey walked slowly across the clearing. Out here he was a sitting duck. Someone right now probably had him on the business end of a scoped rifle, perhaps even Vladislav Kozlov himself. Still, Kozlov and his people weren't stupid. If they were going to kill him, he'd be dead already.

They wanted to question him. Would he be able to hold up? It was definitely not going to be pleasant.

Please, Nika, be near.

For five solid minutes, he stood in the same spot just as he'd been instructed to do, motionless, evaluating his odds of success, calculating his ever-evolving, although critically limited tactical options. And beseeching his God in silent prayer.

"Hands up!" The voice was high-pitched, frenzied. A man's voice coarsely flavored with a thick Russian accent.

Rainey obeyed the man's command, moved his hands skyward slowly, deliberately.

"Keep them up! Any sudden movements and you will be shot."

He held his hands lazily in the air as a man wearing a black balaclava emerged from the brush twenty yards away on his right. He held a Steyr TMP along with nearly 100 percent of Rainey's attention. Men like this had itchy trigger fingers.

The man took his support hand off the gun long enough to motion to his partner, in synch two steps behind, a silent order to approach the Delta operator. The second man roughly groped him, searching every conceivable hiding place for a weapon.

He repressed the urge to latch onto the guy, snap his neck, as the tentacle-like arm probed him. "No weapons, no phone. Just like the man said," growled Rainey.

The man who'd felt him up didn't respond except to make a pronounced grunt. Seemingly satisfied the American was unarmed, they bound his wrists behind his back in heavy gauge plastic ties. Mr. Hands then gave him a gruff shove. "Move!"

The two men led him to a game trail that cut through the undergrowth and a thick wood. When they emerged on the other side, a Chevy Tahoe was waiting for them. Mr. Hands stuffed him into the front seat then seat-belted him in. The man with the Steyr stood there still aiming the gun at Rainey's head as if he were doing everything in his power not to pull the trigger. There was rustling in the dry leaves behind him. Then soft footfalls in the dead grass. He craned his neck toward the sound just as another man approached the vehicle from the dense thicket. The third man stalked around the Tahoe with a sniper rifle slung over his shoulder. He said nothing. He secured the rifle in a black case in the back of the SUV over which he then pulled a heavy wool blanket before stepping around to Rainey's side of the vehicle.

The man removed his balaclava and threw it forcefully into the backseat. Vladislav Kozlov. Their eyes met long enough for him to see Kozlov's lethal intent. There was no warning, no preparatory insult. Kozlov struck him cleanly on the right side of the face. He immediately tasted blood. The sting of the man's powerful, perfect punch radiated from his jawbone to his eye socket and across the bridge of his nose.

Kozlov glared at him. *"Dobro pozhalovat' v ad!"* Welcome to hell.

Rainey spit a wad of blood onto the dash of the SUV. *"Vy dolzhny menya. Teper' yee."* You have me. Now let them go.

"I'm afraid your sister's freedom is contingent on your *full* cooperation."

"I have cooperated fully. No one knows I'm here. What more do you want? Now let her go. Both of them. They have nothing to do with any of this."

"We'll see about that." Kozlov climbed into the SUV, turned in his seat and smiled. Then he punched his trophy capture again. The skin on Rainey's cheekbone instantly split and a rivulet of blood began to meander down his face. "Don't worry. If you tell us everything we want to know we will make it considerably less painful for you."

* * *

Kozlov couldn't contain himself. Maybe Pyotr was right. Maybe this was going to be worth the risk. They had him. Finally.

He ruminated about whether or not Pyotr would let him be the one to finish him. He'd definitely earned it. Where Rostov and Nuriyev—two trained assassins—had failed, he would not. He would be the one to taste the sweetness of success. He would be the one to beat him to a pulp, the one to put a bullet in his brain.

Reagan Rainey. Reagan. Ah yes.

He laughed for the first time in a long time. He was going to thoroughly enjoy this.

80

Arlington, VA

AFTER thirty minutes or so, the SUV turned on to Army Navy Dr. They slowed just as an ambulance was maneuvering lethargically out of a driveway in the 1700 block. They proceeded to turn into the very next driveway, which led onto a semi-wooded lot. A big red-brick Colonial Revival emerged. One of the two garage doors on the side of the house opened expectantly. The anonymous man behind the wheel pulled the SUV inside and shut off the engine. All three of Rainey's captors waited until the garage door had completely closed before exiting. The driver and Mr. Hands followed as Kozlov led Rainey through a door and into an anteroom of sorts.

Rainey prayed again that Nika was near.

"Wait here with him, I'll be back in a minute." Kozlov inserted a key into the lock, opened the door and disappeared.

Rainey was about to turn toward Mr. Hands but was cracked in the right kidney before he could eyeball the man. "Eyes forward!"

"Is that all you got?" Rainey said, fighting the stabbing pain in his lower back.

"Don't let him provoke you," said the driver to the one Rainey had dubbed Mr. Hands. "Vlad will—" The man stopped talking when the door swung open.

"Okay. Bring him in," said Kozlov.

Rainey was led into a sparsely furnished living room. Instantly, his heart stopped. Nika was bound to a metal chair in the center of the room next to an empty chair no doubt meant for him. She'd been badly beaten. She looked up with a grimace, eyes full of defiance and at the same time pleading. She grunted her recognition through the duct-tape wrapped tightly around her mouth. Any signs of hope were quickly slipping away.

A man stepped forward and pointed. "Come. Have a seat, won't you?" The man was tall, not necessarily handsome, ordinary-looking, in fact, with closely cropped hair that was in the middle stages of balding. He had an athletic bearing about him but was far from Kozlov's taut muscular form. His nose was sharp and angular and appeared upon close inspection to have been broken at some point in his life, maybe more than once. He walked with a slow confident pace and was grinning proudly.

"Welcome, Mr. Rainey. I've been looking forward to meeting you. My name is Pyotr Kupchenko."

Mr. P.

He momentarily stepped back in front of a laptop on the countertop, as if checking something, then turned his attention back to Rainey. "I must say, you have been extremely bothersome to me and my comrades. Actually, you should take that as a compliment."

Somewhere in the back of his mind he heard his mother telling him the same exact thing. "Where's Maddie? I've done what you asked, now let her go."

"Cht, cht, cht," Kupchenko sighed with feigned drama. "Well, there's a problem with that. You see, I'm just not a man to be trusted. You understand. Frankly, I'm astonished that you so willingly came to us. Glad, mind you, but, well you know…" Kupchenko glanced toward a door that Rainey was sure led to where Maddie was being held. "This I say is true, however: you and your sister will both soon know your maker. Nika, too, I might add. Don't want to leave her out. But before we get to that, I need some information from you." Kupchenko nodded to the empty chair.

Rainey lunged for him. But Kozlov was prepared; he pulled the trigger of the Taser he had trained on the Delta operator. There was a *pop* and then a loud crackling sound as 50,000 volts raced across his muscled torso. Rainey's body seized up, his teeth clenched. He thudded awkwardly to the floor unable to resist the pain or the involuntary muscle spasms.

When the five-second wave of electric shock passed, he rolled over onto his side. "Consider yourself extinct."

Kupchenko laughed. "My, such mettle. You Delta Force guys are impressive. I'll give you that much." He looked at Kozlov. "Hit him again."

After the second wave of electricity passed, Kozlov's driver and Mr. Hands lifted Rainey up and shoved him down into the metal chair. Mr. Hands wound a large yellow Nylon strap around his torso and tied it behind his back. Rainey took a deep breath, widened his shoulders and arched his back in an attempt to maintain some wiggle room.

"Now, I must inform you that due to other commitments, I'm afraid I just don't have the time I usually require for an inquiry such as this, so if you answer my questions truthfully, I promise to make things quick and painless. You see, normally I'm an extremely patient man. It's not uncommon for me to drag out an interrogation for days on end, weeks…months even. I'm sure you can appreciate my dilemma." Kupchenko paced slowly back and forth in front of him.

"I don't get it," said Rainey. "What do you guys intend to accomplish? Yeah, I know all about the Turbo. Blow something up and then what? You know our resolve. You guys want a war, is that it? And by the way, they're not buying this Iranian frame-job. They know it's all just an elaborate ploy. They know who's really behind this." By spouting off, he was hoping to buy himself enough time to come up with a plan.

Kupchenko sneered. "Do they now?"

"You're gonna kill me. I know that. You know that. You might as well tell me what kind of grandiose scheme you whack-jobs are on the verge of loosing upon the world."

The Russian man looked at his watch before pulling out a Walther P99. He stepped closer to Rainey. "Very well. I'll indulge you. In less than fifteen minutes your Capitol Building, your newly elected Congress will be no more. In the blink of an eye." He snapped his fingers. "With them gone, we will be able to deal with your president directly, and of course he with us. He's got strong communist leanings, you know. Though he would never say as much. President Winslow will rally the support of the American people and after it's discovered that Iran is behind the attack, he will be forced to retaliate. In reality, we really don't care what happens after that. America will be so entrenched in fighting the Iranians and the entire swath of Islamic countries, who will doubtless join together in solidarity, they will lose track of our pursuits. A new Russia will emerge. An *empire*. It will grow bigger, stronger than ever before. And we will bury the West once and for all."

"You're Jamil ibn Hasan. You were the one who tried to get Conover to talk."

Kupchenko's eyes narrowed. "See, Vlad, he knows things," he said over his shoulder. "Don't you, Mr. Rainey? You know about the Turbo and Lonnie Conover. My, my. You *are* bright. Yes. I will admit it. You are looking at the man who assumed the role of Jamil ibn Hasan. Masterful work, wouldn't you say? Oh and Conover *did* talk, by the way. Took some time, but he talked. Screamed a lot, too.

"I'll assume then that you know Nika here as well. See, she's been a naughty girl. Very naughty, indeed. It's a funny story actually how we came to learn that she was not who she said she was. Vlad found her snooping around the sticks of Turbo. Apparently she was going to replace them with inert replicas that contained discreet GPS tracking devices. Which is ironic because the ones she and Vlad had fled Strathcona with were exactly that...carefully crafted replicas. See, old Vlad here actually left the real tubes of Turbo by the side of the road, in the brush...for me. Precaution, you know." Kupchenko smiled as if perfectly satisfied with himself. "Nika had us going there for a bit. Eh, Nika?" He spun, struck Nika's head with the butt of his pistol. She closed her eyes, tried to brace herself but the impact was severe. Her head snapped back then fell forward. Blood from the fresh laceration on her forehead ran freely, soiling her shirt and spotting the floor.

Despair began to grip him. Next, they would torture Maddie and Wes and finally him. It was over. He had failed.

Please, God. I need you!

"Such a sad state of affairs really." Kupchenko leaned over the motionless woman, stroked the fair skin of her cheek with the back of his finger. He brushed a lock of stray hair from her face and wiped away a tiny droplet of crimson from her chin. "She was quite beautiful. A shame, really. But, I'm afraid once again you Americans have underestimated us.

"You cannot stop the inevitable, Mr. Rainey. Without your Congress your country will be brought to its knees. For good." Kupchenko smiled broadly and chuckled. "Ah, the perfect irony in all of this, is that while accomplishing our mission we also get to defeat a man named *Reagan.*" Kozlov erupted in laughter behind him. "The two men you've been so earnestly tracking are already in possession of the real Turbo, you see, and at this exact minute are en route to erase the very essence of America's representative government. I'm normally quite a humble man, you should know, but I must say that using men dressed as EMTs driving an ambulance was pure genius on my part." He smirked then turned to Kozlov. "You see, when they get to within a thousand yards of the Capitol Building, the Turbo will detonate and subsequently everything within a six-block radius will be instantly vaporized. Might rattle the windows of the White House a bit. Will definitely topple the Washington Monument."

Rainey looked up from the female operator, her motionless body bearing witness to the formidability of the men in front of him. "It's GPS-activated."

"Like I said, you're very bright. And fearless to boot. Of course, in the event that a technical problem ensues—a glitch or what have you—the men have been instructed to manually detonate the package. And if they should suddenly lose their courage..." He pointed to a cell phone on the counter next to the laptop. "I simply phone it in." Contingencies upon contingencies. It cannot be stopped. It's really a shame that you won't be alive to appreciate the full effect of our plan.

"Now, getting back on point. I'd like to know what loose ends I need to tie off and I'm running short on time. You have survived numerous run-ins with my friends, Demyan and Sergei, which you have no idea, is quite an impossible feat. The first person that I am aware of ever to do so. How many times was it really? It doesn't matter. There was a man with you in Phoenix. I want to know who he is."

Rainey glowered defiantly. He had nothing else to give, except whatever resistance he could muster. He would dig deep and do his best to thwart these men in any way possible, even if it meant he was going to die doing so. Rainey bent forward in his chair and for a moment remained like this. His captors doubtless thought he was going to crack. Then, in a voice that was more of a low growl, he said, "Understand something. I'm going to kill every last one of you."

Again Kupchenko's eyes snapped to the door off to Rainey's right. "I was really hoping you would make this easier on your sister." Kupchenko tilted his head toward Kozlov. Placing one hand on the muscular man's shoulder, he whispered something into his ear.

Kozlov nodded and smiled broadly as he looked at Rainey. Then he walked up to the Delta man. "I'm going to enjoy this."

The blow this time made him nearly pass out. It struck him just above his right eyebrow and split his forehead open with a long, wide gash close to three inches long. His face was quickly streaked with blood. But the pain was nothing compared to the realization that these men were about to perpetrate unconscionable acts of depravity and violence against his sister in an attempt to make him talk.

C'mon! Just a little further.

He continued focusing on the strap below his right hand. Moments ago, he had slipped his left hand free but was still having trouble with his right. He'd dropped the strap at one point, but thankfully no one had noticed the loose knot dangling there behind him. During Kupchenko's monologue, he had been urgently struggling to reclaim it without being discovered.

"I really don't have time to play any more games. I've got to get moving. We all do.

We'll see how much you really love your sister."

81

"They're coming," whispered Wes.

Maddie nodded. They'd heard the thuds upstairs and without knowing why they'd even been kidnapped were preparing for the worst possible outcome.

"Rise and shine, boys and girls." Kozlov banged on the door with his fist then slid back the pair of deadbolts. The big Russian flung open the door and, holding a SIG Sauer P226, stepped into the room. He waved the gun, motioning for Maddie to stand up. "Let's go toots." As she pushed herself up with her back against the wall, he added, "You're going to enjoy this. I know I am. Get to find out what it's like to be with a *real* man."

"Leave her alone. Take me instead!" pleaded Wes. He scrambled over to the larger man, tried to stand.

Kozlov kicked Wes in the face with the sole of his boot, sending him back down hard to the cement floor. "Sit tight guy. You'll get your chance." Kozlov laughed as Maddie walked past him slowly with her head down.

No matter what happened next, she would never give herself over to such a vile human being. Even if he did have a gun, even if he killed her in the process. She'd always told herself if she were ever in a situation such as this, she would never willingly allow herself to be raped, or worse. She would fight with everything in her. She would fight to the death. It was just the type of person she was. She was a Rainey.

Using the sharp edge of the aged metal vent to saw through her restraints had taken no small measure of determination and grit. And dexterity. But she'd done it. She carefully held the white plastic ties behind her back as if she were still bound. This was the moment of truth.

"Top of the stairs. Move!"

The words were barely out of his mouth. Maddie spun and closed the space. She trapped Kozlov's gun against her side with her left forearm and at the same time delivered a stiff punch to the large man's throat, which caused him to lose focus with his grip on the gun. With the speed of a striking cobra, Maddie then grabbed the gun with both hands and twisted it back toward him then toward the floor, raking it out of his grasp. But before she could turn the gun on him, he bull-rushed her. Maddie spun out of the way. As Kozlov shot past her, she brought the butt of the gun down hard on the bridge of his nose, shattering bone. She hit him again on the temple then punched him once more in the throat, this time with more leverage and much more power.

Kozlov grabbed at his damaged airway with his left hand. He grabbed and swung wildly at Maddie with his right.

Maddie dodged his reckless punches, letting him step past her as she struck him repeatedly with the butt of the pistol on the side of his head. He roared with a hoarse voice before finally connecting a solid punch to her jaw. It stunned her for a second. Maddie stepped back, shook her head. She took a step to the side, pivoted.

Finish him!

She kicked the back of his right knee which made him lean to the left. He was severely off balance. A nanosecond later, Maddie delivered the coup de grâce—a switch kick to the side of the head that completely rocked his world, buckled his legs. The redwood of a man collapsed. His head slammed onto the bare cement floor with such force that it likely cracked his skull. His body began convulsing with seizures.

Maddie glared down on him with contempt. She was still angry that they'd been able to get the jump on her back in the apartment.

Wes sat against the wall, a look of shock and awe on his face, as if utterly flabbergasted with the speed and lethality exhibited by his bride-to-be.

Maddie gripped Kozlov's pistol and walked over to Wes.

"Maddie, are you okay?" His nose was bloodied and there was a dark red scuff on his cheek from the heel of Kozlov's boot.

"I'm fine. You?" She quickly cut him free with a knife she'd pulled from Kozlov's pocket.

"If you're good, I'm good." Wes rubbed the scuff mark on his face, then opened and closed his mouth several times, as if checking to see if his jaw still worked. "That's gonna leave a mark."

Maddie looked at Kozlov, then the open door. "C'mon. Let's go."

82

SHE was falling into a deep, dark abyss. Her head was pounding. It felt wet. She was probably going to die. And there was nothing she could do about it. At the very moment Nika had laid eyes on Pyotr Kupchenko—a man to this point known only as Mr. P—she knew it was all over. Knew they were going to kill her. They pummeled her body for hours, but still she kept silent. Kept silent about who had sent her, what she knew, and what she had done. And at the same time they tortured her on the outside, she tortured herself on the inside. It all made frightening sense now. Somehow, Kozlov had managed to pull a switcheroo on her outside Strathcona. He must have left the Turbo for Kupchenko by the bridge where they had dumped the ATVs. *Before he pumped the tire. Yes. That's why he gave me that look in the mirror.*

Even more vexing was that she was captured while switching out a replica for a replica. This had surely been yet another marvelous facet in the first step of Borovsky's master plan. He had anticipated everything, the tubes which had been hidden in the false bottom of the bookcase at the safe house were expertly crafted counterfeits. Simple misdirection. And it worked to perfection.

Something else occurred to her as she rocked in and out of consciousness, still fighting for control of her thoughts: Edward Horst hadn't overheard Kozlov talking about himself meeting the two Arab martyrs. He'd overheard Kozlov talking on the phone to Kupchenko about Kupchenko meeting the two Arabs. Kupchenko had already met with them, turned the Turbo into a bomb.

The worst possible scenario was reality. The Turbo was loose and headed for the Capitol Building packed with America's newly elected legislators eager to be sworn into office.

* * *

Kupchenko turned at the sound of footsteps coming up the wooden basement stairs. The creaking of the old boards seemed to echo throughout the entire house. He raised his gun playfully to his shoulder. "Now you will talk," he said with a devilish grin. "Or Vlad is going to have some fun with your sister…while we all watch. She's quite ravishing, you know." The intent in his eyes was ruthless, repugnant. The footfalls grew louder. "Why here we go—"

The words caught in his throat as Maddie swung around the corner with the pistol held up to eye level. The smile on Kupchenko's face was replaced by shock then recognition. In the time it took for his brain to tell his hand to lower the gun and shoot, Maddie pumped five rounds into him. His body convulsed, contorted. A spray of crimson burst from the back of his head, neck and chest as the Russian man fell backward to the floor.

* * *

"What they'd say?!" barked Mouse straining to hear the radio traffic over the engine noise.

Job Jackson returned a pensive glance. "They heard shots from inside." Job brought his radio to his mouth. "Command to Radical. You are green to go. Repeat. Green to go."

Tonka gripped his carbine in the back seat. As they skidded to a stop, he jumped out, took up a position of cover behind a large oak tree on the lawn.

Five men outfitted in full battle kit emerged from the woods behind the large home. They had arrived mere minutes ago pursuant to Job's orders. Thankfully, Rainey still had the holster on his belt with the GPS beacon sewn into it. Job surmised Rainey had done this on purpose. As a result, they'd been able to track him to this precise location. After he'd received Rainey's call about Maddie, Job decided to act. He'd ordered the launch of a D12 rapid response team. What resulted was a whirlwind of activity that erupted throughout Directorate and CIA headquarters in addition to the Counterterrorism Center over in McLean. The FBI and DHS had been notified, too.

Job had now just given the command to the rapid response team to storm the house.

* * *

The man standing by the door leading to the garage—Kozlov's driver—was just starting to go for his weapon when Rainey finally wiggled out of the strap. In a split-second, he stood up, pushed his bound hands under his butt and sat down hard on the flex-cuffs, which snapped their locking mechanisms.

He was free.

Rainey picked up the metal chair beneath him and swung it like a baseball bat into the man's head smashing his skull. Then just as fast, he turned and bull-rushed Mr. Hands, plowing into him with utter fury. Both men slammed hard to the floor. Rainey straddled the man from the top position and rained down punch after punch on him. The man struggled to block the blows, squirming like a fish out of water. Somehow the man managed to scoot backward. He began to sit up, frantic to get free. In one quick motion, Rainey raised up over him and, with both hands, pressed down sharply on the man's head, forcing his chin to his sternum. The man's neck snapped with a loud crack. Rainey jumped back to his feet and scanned the room for more threats to destroy.

Suddenly, a man with a noticeable limp burst from the back of the house. Yuri Pershin. He sprinted as fast as he could from the hallway, a submachine gun in his right hand. Bullets ripped across the bare walls. Wes jumped for Maddie, shielding her body with his own. Both of them tumbled into an empty room.

Rainey dove over the kitchen island counter and ducked down to avoid the spray-job.

Pershin made it to the front door, swung it open and ran outside. An SUV was sliding to a halt in the street in front of him. Pershin turned the gun on the vehicle and fired. Glass shattered, tires exploded, the grill, fender and entire passenger side were obliterated.

All at once, a choir of jack-hammers loudly proclaimed its presence on the front lawn. The rapid response team.

Then there was silence, save for the ticking of the SUV's engine and the gurgling of coolant as it spilled onto the street from ruptured hoses and reservoirs.

* * *

"Maddie, Wes! You guys okay?!" shouted Rainey.

"Yes! Yes! We're okay," yelled Wes, ignoring the fact that he'd taken a round to the shoulder. He stood up, brushing powdered drywall from Maddie's hair and face.

Rainey looked around the room. He ran to Nika, felt for a pulse. If she had one, the heartbeat thumping in his own fingers made it impossible to tell. "Hang on, girl! Hang on!"

"Maddie! Get on that computer over there and see if you can find a way to disable the geo fence for a device heading toward the Potomac. As soon as it crosses that fence, it's gonna detonate." He didn't wait for her to speak. "I know. Just do the best you can."

Maddie looked at the laptop on the counter. A little blue arrowhead was tracking northbound on a digital map. "They're heading for the Capitol. They're gonna blow up the Capitol, Ray!"

"I know, I know. See what you can do. We have to stop it!"

Rainey flung open the door leading into the garage, ran to the back of the Tahoe and grabbed Kozlov's sniper rifle, an HK MSG90, charged the weapon. He peeked at the ignition. No keys. He didn't have time to search for them. He'd have to improvise.

"Friendly coming out! Hold your fire!" Rainey noticed the man who'd run outside only seconds ago. He was lying in the grass, littered with bullets to the head and chest. Job was hanging halfway out of the passenger side of a shredded SUV. There was a dark, wet spot on the sleeve of his upper right arm. "Chief!"

Job shook his head. "No worries, kid. Just winged me."

Tonka appeared. "Bronco! You okay, bro? You're a mess."

"Nika's inside. She's down!"

"On it, boss!" The big Delta medic took off into the house.

Mouse came trucking around the front of the SUV, fragments of glass embedded in the one side of his face. "Bronco!"

"Mouse! We gotta stop that ambulance, the one that just left here!"

"We didn't see any ambulance."

"Then I gotta book it! Farid and his buddy have the Turbo and are heading for the Capitol. Get on the horn! I'm going after them."

Job winced as he reached for his cell phone with his good arm. "I'll do my best. Just go! There's no time. You gotta stop them!"

He was already off and running when Mouse called out after him, "I'm coming with ya!"

Rainey sprinted across the street, gripping the 7.62mm rifle with both hands, his legs pumping. As he neared the fence that delineated Army Navy Dr. with I-395, he slung the rifle. He climbed to the top, reached over, grabbed the fence below him then swung his legs over in one swift maneuver. Mouse was right on his heels.

Rainey ran smack-dab into the middle of traffic with the rifle aimed skyward and cracked off a round. Cars, trucks—a freight train of traffic—swerved, screeched and slid wildly around him. A tractor trailer jackknifed. Traveling at speeds upward of 70 mph, drivers struggled to bring their vehicles to a sudden, unexpected stop. Horns blared with rage. Several vehicles crashed into each other causing a chain reaction of gratuitous vehicular violence. A pungent cocktail of burnt rubber, antifreeze, and woodsmoke from a nearby chimney permeated the air.

He ran to the nearest vehicle, a white Chevy Caprice station wagon with faux woodgrain sides. It was near the head of the pack and looked relatively easy to negotiate out of the congested tin. The large wagon seemed to be in good condition save for the freshly crumpled front fender.

"Get out! Now! I need your car!" shouted Rainey as the driver, wide-eyed and panic-stricken jumped out and ran away. He and Mouse climbed in. Rainey dropped the gear shift into drive and stomped the accelerator, sending suffocating blue-gray clouds of burnt rubber billowing out from behind the rear wheels of the powerful car.

"We gonna make it in time, Bronc?"

Rainey didn't answer the question. He passed a car on the shoulder while still accelerating. "We're looking for a D.C. ambulance. It's red and white. There are two men inside along with some nasty stuff that could very well level everything within a six-block radius." He checked the rearview mirror, whispered under his breath, "I just pray Maddie can disable that geo fence."

Please, Lord, give me time. Direct my path.

* * *

Mouse glanced over at Rainey. He absolutely loved the guy. They were closer than family. They were warrior brothers. He would die fighting for him if need be. Rainey would do the same for him. It was part of the warrior code, but moreover, it was just who they were. Would today be their day?

He swallowed, but not an ounce of hesitation crept into his mind only a flash of his children's faces and that of his wife, Brielle. Mouse finally snapped the buckle of his seatbelt and stole a glance at the speedometer. It was approaching 120. The vehicle's powerful V-8 engine was screaming, roaring like an angry lion.

God, protect us.

83

"EASY now. We don't want to draw attention to ourselves…yet," advised Farid Shafiq al-Nasem. "Remember what Jamil said, 'Make sure to get nice and close.' And if anyone gives us any strange looks, simply smile and wave. Americans love people in uniform."

Atuf Mu'tamid nodded. He heard his father-in-law speaking beside him, but he wasn't really listening. The only thing his mind could focus on now was the intense hatred he had for America. In a few minutes he would strike a glorious blow to the infidel. Washington, D.C. of all places. The very heart of the demon. He thought of his wife and young children back in Yemen. They'd had a ceremony for him before he set out on this grand odyssey. They would surely be watching today on the Al-Jazeera network feed back home. He had been ordered not to tell them anything about the operation, but he couldn't help himself. They had all beamed with pride when he'd told them what the target was. The Iranian man who'd sent them— Jamil ibn Hasan—had promised to see that they were very well-compensated for his and their sacrifice.

"Turn here," said al-Nasem. "L'Enfant Plaza. Then it's a right onto Independence Avenue. Ha. Indeed. We will deliver your independence all right." Both men laughed anxiously.

Mu'tamid gripped the steering wheel, his palms were sloppy wet. Beads of sweat were already running down his forehead, his cheeks.

Allahu akbar!

* * *

Rainey skillfully negotiated the large station wagon back and forth through the D.C. congestion.

"They're no doubt going Fourteenth to Independence. That's the most direct route," said Mouse.

"Roger that."

Mouse had his left hand on the dash to steady himself as Rainey accelerated back and forth through traffic. He thumbed the safety selector switch on his HK416 making sure that it was set to fire. As soon as they turned onto Independence Ave., he yelled out, "There they are! Two blocks up!"

The wagon's engine growled even louder as Rainey stomped down on the gas pedal. "This is gonna be close. Be ready to bail out. You with me?"

"I'm with ya, Bronc."

He pushed the car as fast as it would mechanically go. As they approached 7th Ave., the traffic signal turned red. "Hang on!"

Both men braced themselves for impact. Rainey kept the accelerator pressed to floor. Cross traffic just started moving as they entered the intersection. A coach bus began to turn into their path. Rainey swerved but the bus clipped the back end of the wagon spinning them violently. Miraculously, Rainey kept control and after one full revolution swung the car back and forth until he regained their heading.

"Get ready," Rainey warned through clenched teeth.

As they drew behind the ambulance, Rainey again punched the accelerator. They flew past the driver's side of the heavy red and white truck. Just past 4th Ave., he slammed on the brakes, causing the car to skid across the pavement. At the last second, Rainey whipped the steering wheel hard to the right then back to the left. The old, oversized station wagon now blocked the two middle lanes of eastbound traffic.

"You got the passenger. Be quick! Head shots!"

* * *

Mu'tamid watched in his side mirror as some maniac driver in an ugly white station wagon raced up behind them and then sped past. "Crazy American drivers," he murmured.

"Step on it, Atuf! They are trying to stop us!"

Mu'tamid pressed the accelerator down under his boot. "They will do no such thing."

"See?! They are stopping," exclaimed al-Nasem as the wagon's brake lights activated and its tires locked up. "Do not stop! Drive around them!" Al-Nasem picked up the medical bag between his feet, slipped his hand inside.

Mu'tamid already had a nervous sweat going, but now his entire face was drenched, his eyes red with bloodlust. The car in front of them skidded to a stop, two men jumped out with long guns. They quickly took up positions on the far side of the car and were now pointing their weapons. Traffic had stopped as panic-stricken motorists sensed something very bad was happening. With cars at all angles, there was no room for him to cleanly drive around the station wagon.

"Ram them, Atuf!" said al-Nasem. He began to apply pressure to the button beneath his fingertip.

Mu'tamid had barely heard his own name, when a wet spray showered the right side of his face. He glanced over and saw the man beside him now unrecognizable, his head split open, body hanging grotesquely in the seatbelt.

"*Allahu akbar!*" Mu'tamid yelled. He rammed the front end of the white station wagon, but in doing so lost control of the cumbersome ambulance; it rocked back and forth on its axels. The heavy vehicle smashed into a Smart car, instantly killing its lone occupant, ramped the curb and clipped a tree, which caused the back end to whip around violently. Bloodied, but irrevocably committed to his goal, he grabbed one of the AK-102s that Jamil had left for them in the cab, climbed over al-Nasem's disgusting corpse, opened the passenger-side door and jumped out. Before sprinting toward the Capitol Building, he scooped up the medical bag like a football, which was no longer filled with anything remotely intended to treat the injured, but rather something meant to do just the opposite: to inflict death and destruction.

* * *

Mouse rolled out his side of the car and steadied his rifle on the roof while Rainey fished out Kozlov's sniper rifle and lined up behind the front wheel opposite the fast-approaching ambulance. Rainey snapped down the gun's attached bi-pod and propped it on the hood, flipped the safety off.

Mouse's gun was the first to break wind. He fired two shots in succession, the first one finding its mark. The second a reiteration of the first.

Just as Rainey was about to fire, the ambulance swerved and then came roaring back across traffic right for them. Mouse grabbed Rainey by the shoulder and yanked him away from the impending collision. The ambulance crashed into the front end of the wagon, which swung around and slammed into them, knocking both men hard to the pavement. The right side of the larger vehicle lifted up and Rainey was sure it was going to flip over, but then it banged back down, bouncing recklessly back and forth on its double rear wheels. The screeching tires and sound of glass breaking resonated throughout the midday revelry. Rainey helplessly looked on as the ambulance plowed headlong into a little golf cart-size car, jumped the curb and slammed into a tree.

Before the ambulance came to rest, he was already on his feet and sprinting at full speed in hot pursuit. He was barely onto Maryland Ave. when a head popped out from behind the far side of the truck. At least one man had survived the crash and was now running on a direct line toward the Capitol Building. Rainey was a hundred yards behind but closing fast.

The man turned around only to see Rainey coming for him. His eyes were wide. He yelled something in Arabic then ran faster.

Rainey sprinted with everything he had left inside him, the weight of America on his shoulders. His legs pumped faster and faster. His face was the epitome of determination, eyes aflame with raw intensity.

Faster, Ray! Faster!

This is it.

The other man slowed to a jog and with one hand began probing the inside of the bag. He was reaching for something.

A button.

A switch.

Rainey immediately put on the brakes, dropped to a knee. He shouldered the rifle, aimed and squeezed the trigger. The weapon jolted against his frame. He prepared to fire again, but there was no need. The man's lifeless body fell forward in a heap as the bag filled with Turbo dropped to the pavement. Rainey ran up to him just to make sure he didn't pose any further threat. He looked over at the medical bag, the ends of several tubes of blue gel were sticking out of the wide-mouth pouch, wires exposed.

He crouched down beside it just as several dark-colored SUVs skidded up beside him with red and blue LEDs flickering, headlights strobing in a wig-wag pattern. A full complement of FBI assaulters wearing tactical gear jumped out and surrounded him. "Police! Drop the gun! Drop the gun!"

"Hold your fire! Hold your fire! Stand down!" yelled Special Agent in Charge Trevor Dawes. The FBI man jumped out of one of the SUVs. "This man's on our side!" Dawes had on a black jacket. On its front and back were large yellow letters "FBI." He strode up to Rainey as Mouse came limping over with his rifle slung.

Rainey appraised the FBI SAC as he handed him the sniper rifle then pointed to the pavement. "There's live ordnance in there. Get EOD here PDQ."

"I know. I know. Your chief called." Dawes shook his head. "America owes you guys big time. But I'm guessing that they'll never know, will they?"

"Know what?" said Rainey.

"That it was you two."

Rainey looked at Mouse then back at Dawes. "We'll know. That's good enough for us," he said straight-faced. "Right, bro?" He looked at Mouse again.

Mouse winked. "No doubt."

Dawes waved over one of his subordinates. "It might sound trite, but thank you. I mean it." He turned toward the Capitol Building then Rainey.

Rainey nodded. "You bet."

As they climbed into the back of the FBI SUV, Mouse smiled. "Looks like your sis came through, huh."

Rainey wiped the blood from his eyes. "Was there ever any doubt?"

A cacophony of sirens wailed from what seemed all over town. Rainey leaned his head back onto the seat, breathed a heavy sigh of relief. He looked up at the Capitol dome, considered the lives of the men and women they had just saved. *Thank you, God. Thank you.*

The FBI agent that Dawes had hailed trotted over. "Yes, sir?"

Dawes pointed to the SUV. "Hospital. Go." As the man turned, Dawes grabbed him by the shoulder. "Not a word to anyone. And nothing goes on paper about them either, you understand?"

The agent nodded enthusiastically as he jumped behind the wheel. "Got it."

"Actually..." Rainey leaned forward, patted the guy on the shoulder. "Just drive. I'll tell you where to go."

"Now what?" asked Mouse as the SUV pulled away.

Rainey slumped back in his seat, closed his weary eyes. "Sleep, brother. Lots of sleep."

84

L EVKA Borovsky sipped at three fingers of vodka as he perched himself on the edge of his desk in anticipation of the big show. He briefly gazed out his window toward the Moscow city center. You wouldn't know it to look at him, but he was exhilarated, anxious with the promise of success. His eyes returned to the plasma monitors affixed to the dark wooden wall of his expansive office.

Any moment now the networks would lose their feeds from the United States Capitol Building. What would follow was a chain of events that would quickly put Russia back on track to becoming one of the most powerful and brazen superpowers the world has ever known. Through the blogosphere, the timely influence of several of his well-placed spies and some carefully crafted leaks, he would go about shaping the narrative so that Western intelligence agencies would have no choice but to conclude the obvious: Iran was responsible. He'd already left several clues that when found would suggest the Russian authorities were on the hunt for a group of rogue expatriates, former intelligence officers, ex-military personnel—a collection of *Iranian agents*—who had been secretly working for Jamil ibn Hasan. For the Islamic Republic. For radical Islam. Though Russia would of course be embarrassed to admit it.

Eventually he would see to it that this rogue group—Kupchenko, Kozlov and the others—was hunted down and terminated along with his spies inside the American government, specifically Sentinel. All in due time. He would send his assassins to quietly silence them for good. Where Demyan Rostov and Sergei Nuriyev had failed, others would not. He had yet to decide whether or not to add Rostov to the list of doomed men or if perhaps he had additional usefulness.

It was perfect. The international community would hold Iran responsible for the brazen attack on American soil and that was the whole point. America would be both gripped with terror and at the same time distracted with their reactionary rage which would clear the way for the second step in his grand scheme. The United States would react by attacking Iran's defense infrastructure, key military assets and locations, enrichment sites. Its very soul. Russia would assist and in doing so would spread its talons deep into Iran, seize oil fields, then push fully into Ukraine, Moldova, and the other former Soviet states. Natural gas feeding Europe would be shut off. Economically, Russia could cripple the West. A new bigger, stronger Russia would emerge. And if the United States and her allies would dare to even think of attacking Russia, they would be very sorry. The TRB-80 would be used against them. The Turbo would be leveraged to keep them at bay. Plans were already in the pipeline to rapidly reverse engineer and mass produce it.

In America, everything would be in complete disarray. The incoming Congress would have spelled trouble in a number of ways for Russia as well as other nations on the global stage. No one more so than Marty Kendall, the Republican senator from Texas, who was likely to challenge President Winslow in the upcoming presidential election and, from what the talking heads were saying, stood a very good chance of winning. He was intelligent, politically fearless, articulate and photogenic, and, perhaps his most dangerous quality of all, he was a born-again Christian. If Kendall won the presidency a lot would change in America and throughout the world.

Senator Kendall's goals included reestablishing a clear focus on true American values, free markets, and traditions of honor and goodwill toward all who endeavored for man's natural right to be free.

And just like the Gipper had, he preached an unmitigated, unapologetic policy of peace through strength.

For Borovsky and those to whom he answered, that just could not be allowed to happen. For these and other reasons, now was the perfect time to dispatch the whole of the American Congress. The old Russian spymaster had been given complete authority to plan, organize and carry out the operation. There had been a few bumps in the road, but momentum was on his side. In a few moments the world would change forever.

The American people would clamor for vengeance. Despite the current president being a naïve pacifist and inherently against the use of America's supreme military might, he would be forced into yet another war, stretching America's military capability even thinner. Americans would be so distracted with the loss of their representative government and their lust for revenge that they would turn a blind eye to anything beyond the feigned assistance Moscow would be offering along with a host of other nations. Then suddenly it would be too late. The whole of the European continent would quickly be within the Kremlin's grasp. With some negotiated help or at least neutrality from China, there would be no one to stop the coming resurgence of a Russian global superpower. The East would be in charge for a change.

Borovsky's eyes gleamed with purpose, his inspired visions were now ready to be played out in the weeks, months and years ahead. Blueprints for global communism that would rival anything Stalin had ever dreamed. Yet everything hinged on this first step. Everything.

Following another swig of his favorite vodka, Borovsky reached across his desk and turned the phone toward him. He was all set. But something happened. Something was wrong. Two networks switched feeds to cameras set up outside. As the footage on which he was fixated chronicled each blow to his masterful design, the excitement and fortitude set deep within his eyes sublimated into absolute fury. Borovsky held his now-empty glass in a death grip. With a sudden *pop*, the small tumbler shattered.

A rivulet of blood trickled from his palm as he stood, his anger reaching the boiling point. He stepped closer to the TV screens, scrutinizing each pixel. The cameras were zooming in and out on the man or men who had apparently laid destruction to everything he had carefully crafted.

With petechiae erupting in his eyes, the tiny blood vessels hemorrhaging like fireworks, Borovsky shouted at the screens while at the same time pounded the dark wood paneling around them. "No!" Seething, he studied the screens, searching for a clue as to what had gone wrong. Then something registered. A recollection that was fleeting at first, but then became more discernible with each passing second. As the cameras quickly zoomed in and then back out on the man holding a rifle, something clicked into place in the old spymaster's mind. The man's face was covered in blood and only perceptible for a split-second at best. But that was all that it took.

That face.

His teeth were clenched so tightly that they made grinding noises. His facial muscles flexed, cheeks shivered with rage. *Yes, that face—* It was a ghost from the past. For he had entrusted Pyotr Kupchenko with many of the operational details of his scheme, but had he known this was the man with whom he was dealing... *This* was the Delta Force operator he'd been told about... *Ben Rainey's kid?*

Borovsky shook his head and huffed. Tiny particles of spittle flew out of his mouth and stuck to the screen in front of him. His plan now in shambles, a hot sensation washed over him: the dread of failure.

85

Seward, Alaska
Two Weeks Later

THE landscape was absolutely breathtaking. There were just no words to accurately describe it. Roman Lerner had been here before during his time on the Teams, but he'd never fully appreciated it like he did today. As he slalomed back and forth on the dangerous winding roads, he continued to gaze in awesome admiration at the clear blue glacial lakes and the blankets of majestic forestry that knitted together to frame each snow-capped mountain. Bleach-white clumps of snow weighed heavily on the conifer branches forcing them toward the ground which itself was hidden beneath an ocean of wind-driven snowpack.

Looking out across the wispy waves of gleaming ivory, Lerner shook his head in wonder as a giant moose emerged along the tree line. The big animal planted its nose deep into the snow and then lifted its head, turning to lazily acknowledge the passing automobile. Its nose frosted with fresh white powder, the moose took a few steps forward and gazed toward the road again before finally meandering off along the trees apparently satisfied in its solitude.

Would that be me someday? Satisfied in solitude?

Lerner cracked his window. The shock of the frigid air struck his sensibilities immediately. Beginning to shiver after only a few seconds, he closed the window. He'd forgotten just how cold it was up here and how concentrated the Alaskan air was with the glorious scent of evergreen.

Resurrection Bay, situated on the underside of the Kenai Peninsula in south-central Alaska, was a fitting name for his launch point. He snickered as he said the name again in his mind. *Resurrection Bay.*

He traveled down Seward Highway, made a left on Port Ave. then hung a right onto 4th Ave. He continued southbound at a pace that would not draw attention, while he scanned the marina. *There she is.* Extending fifty-three feet from bow to stern, the blue and white purse seiner bobbed gently in the calm seawater.

Lerner drove past the marina and then squared the block, checking for tails one last time. He circled the Harborview Inn and glided back toward the marina parking lot. For the past two weeks he'd been hyper alert to his surroundings. Alas, he was certain no one was following him. Not one soul throughout all his traveling had even given him a second look. He was a pro after all, but a pro that was now on the run.

Lerner wiped his prints from every surface inside the vehicle. He'd rented it in Seattle using an alias and fake California driver's license. Before exiting, he tugged a watch cap down on his scalp, zipped up his coat and pulled on a pair of thick gloves. Lerner glanced at himself in the rearview mirror and wished himself safe passage en route to Russian soil.

He placed his fake credentials in an empty potato chip bag along with his car keys and pushed them into a trash can as he made his way toward the fishing vessel. As he boarded, the man standing on the bow, his maritime chauffeur as it were, nodded and pulled in the last of the rope lines from the dock. Lerner nodded back and stroked his face as the chill air made his nose begin to run, his eyes water.

Once inside, he threw his duffel bag on a wooden bench painted a dreadful green and sat down. He glanced around assessing his accommodations and finally let out a long sigh. His shoulders and neck were stiff from the last leg of his drive. For a brief moment, as the waves licked at the hull of the fishing vessel, he felt as if he were again back in the Gulf with his SEAL team readying to launch on a new mission. He looked down at the ragged scar on the back of his hand. Memories of his old buddies, old teammates flirted with his conscience. *That was then. This is now.*

A large, dangerous-looking man with a nasty scar of his own gouged into his face, sat across from him with an AK-47 in his lap. "Relax, Sentinel. You're home free."

Almost forgot. Lerner slipped the disposable phone from his coat pocket. He stood, walked outside and dropped it into the cold harbor water. He had only communicated with his new Russian handlers by text and only from disposable cell phones since he'd fled Langley, aware that his voiceprint would be instantly detected by the NSA. It would have been a carelessly discarded bread crumb to put them on his trail.

As the boat glided out of the harbor, Lerner pulled out his newly bought iPad and sniffed out an unsecure wireless network from a home nearby. He browsed the websites of the *Washington Post, New York Times,* CNN, and Fox News and several other media outlets for any mention of his name or even a veiled reference to someone within the intelligence community being sought in connection with the terrorist strike that had been thwarted in the nation's capital. Sifting through the repetitive chatter and the litany of experts opining about what had happened and why, he found nothing of any consequence.

He packed up the iPad still with a feeling of dread while he considered the efficacy of his decision to sell out his CIA colleagues and his country. The offer had simply been too good to pass up and besides America was already trending downward in a hurry. With the U.S. swirling in a cultural and socio-economic tailspin that was impossible to pull out of, he had to look out for number one. Still, he wasn't ready to allow himself to celebrate his accomplishments just yet. They were looking for him intently and were no doubt pulling out all the stops in their pursuit of information, of answers, of him. He'd committed the cardinal sin for anyone working in the Clandestine Service, let alone for a veteran of the Special Operations community.

Betrayal.

One of the CIA operatives who Demyan Rostov had assassinated had been a former Navy SEAL like him. He'd pulled off a two-for. Two betrayals in one man's death. If the SEALs ever caught him, it wouldn't be pretty. Add to that the Delta Force operators who were killed in Qatar and Iraq directly based on information he had passed on to Kupchenko. There were many dangerous people quietly hunting him. The FBI wanted him brought to justice as did the CIA and Special Operations community, however each respective group had a different definition of the word.

The former deputy director of the CIA's Clandestine Service peeled the latex from his nose and cheekbones, removed the hazel-colored contact lenses and smiled at the man across from him. The disguise, on par with Hollywood's best, had done its job. He was finally pleased to feel his own face. He scrubbed his skin brusquely and scratched several areas he had been dying to itch for days.

The man with the AK-47 handed him a stainless steel cup of muddy brown coffee. It was hot and it was strong. He let the liquid roll down the back of his throat. He could feel it go all the way down into his stomach. Picking at the last of the latex on his face, he contemplated the journey ahead. In a few days, he'd be resting comfortably in a cottage on the shore of the Sea of Japan near the coastal city of Preobrazheniye in the Primorye region of south-eastern Russia.

Lerner mustered a grin as they drifted out of the harbor.

Home free.

For the better part of the first two hours of the voyage, the three men nary said a word to each other. Finally, Lerner with his eyes burning for sleep pulled an old wool blanket down from the shelf beside him and then another which he rolled up like a pillow and stuffed under his head. In a few seconds he was fast asleep.

86

Due South of Atka Island

LERNER awoke to the sound of men shouting. He struggled to hear what they were saying over the noise of the boat's throaty engine. Getting his wits about him, he bolted upright and looked outside. How long had he been out? It was pitch black outside now.

He scanned both sides of the vessel. The man with the AK was standing on the port side deck, his attention attuned to something off in the distance. The man was angrily shouting over his shoulder for the guy at the helm to increase speed.

In seconds, Lerner realized what had the man so concerned. A fast-moving helicopter low on the horizon suddenly raced in, coming dangerously close to the boat then just as quickly looped back out to sea. It was circling, preparing for another pass. Lerner grabbed an AK-47 from inside the wooden bench, charged the weapon and raced outside into the bitter cold air and sea spray.

* * *

Choreographing their approach with the chopper on the opposite side, Rainey, Mouse and Tonka skipped across the waves in the Zo-

diac F470 Combat Rubber Raiding Craft. They were on a direct
course for the starboard side of the stern. Rapidly, they approached
and prepared to board her. As the D12 helicopter drew fire from the
boat's occupants, Mouse quickly reversed the craft's engine and
drifted her into place. As the two vessels touched, Tonka looped a
bow line around the railing. Rainey leapt aboard and immediately
crouched down, gripping his silenced HK416. Then Tonka did the
same. NODs on, they assessed their surroundings. Just as planned,
everyone was focused on the helo. Mouse then released the rope and
allowed the rubber craft to fall away out of sight.

As the chopper banked away, Rainey and Tonka each tossed stun
grenades and quickly shielded their eyes. There were two insane
flashes of white light and a near simultaneous double *boom*. Rainey
and Tonka moved deliberately but cautiously toward the bow as the
fishing boat rocked and swayed.

Rainey's first silenced shots took out the ship captain. The man
lifelessly fell forward over the stainless steel steering wheel and rode
it down to the floor, which caused the boat to turn haphazardly. The
two Delta men on loan to the CIA balanced themselves on the deck
railing as the vessel listed abruptly.

They continued forward along the wet surface. Without warning,
a large armed man suddenly appeared around the corner in front of
them. He was clearly dazed by the stun grenades, but dazed or not,
he was still a lethal threat. Rainey put him down with two quick
shots to the chest followed by one to the head then glanced around
for additional threats. He stepped over the dead Russian as he
pressed on toward his prey: the traitor, code-named Sentinel.

* * *

Roman Lerner's AK-47 had run empty just before he was blinded
and disoriented by the stun grenades. *What is happening?* But in his
gut he knew exactly what was happening. They had come for him.
Lerner yelled for the other men, but neither man responded.

He was alone.

He blinked his eyes several times but all he could see were
splotches of brilliant white. His eyes were literally wide open yet he
saw nothing but the white after-effects of the stun grenades. It would
take minutes for his eyes to adjust to the darkness that enveloped him.

Lerner chucked the AK-47 toward the stern and waited for the thud before he moved in the opposite direction and crouched down against the slick, wet deck. He unzipped his coat and pulled out a Beretta 9mm, took a few careful steps toward the bow. Focusing his other senses, he desperately tried to listen over the clamor of the ocean beating against the prow and the engine's high-pitched growl. But his ears were still ringing, too. Everything was muffled.

As the boat rolled over a large cresting wave, he grabbed the railing beside him, bracing himself as the vessel slammed down on the other side. A spray of seawater lashed across his face. It was so frigid that for a moment he thought he'd been shot in the head.

Lerner cursed under his breath. Keeping himself as low as possible, he sneaked onward below the windows of the bridge. Suddenly, the window just above his head exploded. Shards of glass showered down on him. He dove forward involuntarily before quickly scrambling back to a crouched position. In the very next instant, he thought he detected a small muzzle flash off to his right, yet he heard no report of gunfire. Inexplicably, his pistol fell from his grasp and bounced of the railing with a hollow ping before it disappeared into the rising swell below. Then came the white hot pain. He'd been shot in the shoulder. Warm blood ran down his chest and back beneath his heavy coat. With his left hand, he sought purchase of the railing for balance. His eyes were now as large as saucers, full of rage and terror alike. Still he saw nothing but gleaming white. Thus he couldn't know that Reagan Rainey stood only feet in front of him.

* * *

"Game over," said Rainey as he punched Lerner hard on the chin then latched onto him, lifted him off his feet. He carried him inside the boat's cabin, pivoted and hurled the traitor into the bulkhead on the far wall.

Lerner crashed to the floor upside down, then shimmied up to a sitting position. Blood dripped from his sleeve onto the cold wooden floor. He was panting, grimacing, eyes fluttering.

Tonka cut the boat's engine as Rainey shed his NODs, flipped on the interior lights. "You know what they say... You can run but you can't hide. Oh and by the way, Nika sends her love. She actually wanted to be here for this, but doctors wouldn't clear her. It's a shame, really. She would have loved seeing the look on your face right now."

Lerner finally regained his senses, lunged, for his bag. Inside was a spare pistol. He almost had his hand on it, but Rainey was ready. He kicked him across the outer thigh then delivered a lightning fast knife-hand strike to his forearm that made the traitor yelp in pain. Rainey picked up the bag and tossed it to Tonka.

"I want to know why. Why?! You were a *SEAL* for crying out loud! Why would you betray your countrymen, men and women who have sacrificed so much, for the noble cause of freedom... Because of what you've done, a lot of very good people are dead. Kids orphaned. Have you any idea the pain and turmoil you've caused? Is there any part of you that is sorry for what you've done?"

Lerner was silent. The smug look on his face said enough.

"Well?! What could be worth more than the lives of your fellow Americans? Money? Is that it? Tell me it wasn't for money, you—"

Lerner grinned. "I want a lawyer."

Rainey ignored the idiotic remark. The rage inside him had finally burned to the point that he couldn't stand the sight of the man any longer. Thoughts of his buddies and the other fearless warriors who'd been killed because of this man, their families now left to deal with the heart-wrenching pain of such loss stormed his brain. He thought of all the lives that had been snuffed out as a result of this elaborate plot to push America to the brink of war with Iran. He'd almost lost Maddie because of it.

Rainey had begged Job to let him, Mouse and Tonka finish out the assignment, to complete the mission after Lerner's exfiltration plans came to light. He wanted to look this despicable man in the eyes and tell him that good had prevailed. In truth, a part of him had hoped to see even the slightest glimmer of remorse. But there was none. This man was completely and utterly unrepentant of the pain and anguish he'd left in his wake, of his betrayal of honor and virtue, of his nation's trust. No one would lose a wink of sleep if he now put one in Lerner's forehead, but in the end that wasn't why they'd been sent. More importantly, especially under these circumstances, killing Lerner wasn't right. Rainey was a trained killer, yes, but not a murderer.

Vengeance is mine...

"You know officially no one knows where you up and disappeared to."

"Yeah? And unofficially?" Lerner cocked his head with disdain.

Rainey grinned. "That's up to you." He nodded to Tonka at which time the Delta medic plunged what looked like an EpiPen into Lerner's arm. "Nighty night."

Rainey pulled a device from a pocket on his vest and dropped it on the floor as Tonka radioed Mouse.

After Rainey and Tonka had climbed back into the Zodiac with their unconscious prisoner, Mouse banked them away from the larger vessel and gunned the engine. From another pocket, Rainey extracted a small, black remote about the same size and shape as a pack of playing cards.

Inside the fishing boat, the device on the floor rocked back and forth against the bulkhead, in rhythm with the rolling waves. If someone were to inspect it closely they'd find a thin, blue-colored stick of gel the size of a crayon.

"This is a test. This is only a test," Rainey said dryly. They were nearly ashore by the time the massive fireball obliterated the dark, peaceful night sky. The resulting exothermic gust buffeted them from behind. Soon the darkness and peacefulness returned. A wave originating from the vicinity of the obliterated fishing vessel splashed over the stern of the Zodiac and quickly receded back into the sea. Rainey sat there for a moment along the vacant coast. What would twelve full-size tubes of Turbo have done to Washington, D.C.? There was nothing left of the fishing boat but a burning slick of oil and some matchstick-size pieces of debris that now danced on the surface of the frigid water.

Rainey watched Tonka click on an IR strobe. The black Sikorsky MH-60T Jayhawk was already headed toward them, its rotors thumping in the distance. Within the green glow of the ChemLight clipped to his jacket, Rainey said into his radio mic, "Party of four standing by for extract."

Job leaned forward in his seat, focused on the flashing infrared beacon on the horizon below. "Copy that, Bronco. We gotcha. Be there in a jiff."

Rainey sat there in the blustery cold, his elbows on his knees, chin tucked. None of the operators spoke. He listened intently to the undulating currents out there beyond sight. There was a song in there somewhere.

The approaching chopper was still invisible against the moonless sky. He took in a deep drag of the bone chilling air and considered where he would go from here. He thought of his faith and his family. He thought of America.

Rainey glanced at Lerner proned out there between them, then down the desolate coastline of Atka Island. Next, he cast his gaze in the direction of Russia and out across the sea. *There be dragons.* It was a phrase he remembered hearing in a college geography class once. Despite what some people want to believe, evil does exist. It's real. For sure, it's out there waiting to consume men's lives and souls alike. Yet the God of the universe, his God, master of all and second to none, holds everything in His command.

Thank you, Lord. Thank you.

EPILOGUE

FROM the driveway, Job could hear the clanging of ironwork coming from Rainey's blacksmith shop, could smell woodsmoke floating in the air. Off in the distance, ever so faintly, was the distinct sound of a horse galloping. This is what it must have been like back in Colonial days. This is why Ray loves it out here. It's pure; it's serene.

It's America.

With no answer at the door, Job trekked around back and found Pappy sitting next to a blazing fire framed by a circle of watermelon-size rocks twenty yards off the flagstone patio. He was reading the Bible and sipping hot tea.

"So what do you think?" asked Pappy without looking up, pointing to the far side of the blacksmith shop.

"Looks like he's adding on."

Pappy nodded. "He doesn't sit still, that's for sure. Wants to open up that wall there and build on a big space for woodworking. Says his goal is to be a master craftsman. He's already got the plans drawn up. If I didn't know any better, I'd say he was a young George Washington. That's what he is, you know—a modern-day George Washington. He makes me feel young again, I know that. Definitely one of a kind."

"He's a Rainey."

"No doubt."

Rainey pulled the shop door shut and joined his elders. "So whaddya think?" he said smiling.

Job shook his head. "Ambitious, kid. I must say, you are ambitious."

Rainey shrugged. "Helps clear the mind."

Pappy closed his Bible, threw another log on the fire. "You guys go ahead and talk. I'm going for a walk."

"Thanks, Pappy."

* * *

Once Pappy was out of earshot, Rainey looked at Job. "Any word?"

"We've identified him as Demyan Rostov. Same story as Nuriyev. But I think it's safe to say he won't be bothering you anymore. He's got other people to worry about now. I've heard some things. Seems the Russians are hunting him. By the way, they are denying involvement. The PM says it was all Borovsky, blames him for everything. Obviously, we know otherwise. POTUS is meeting with the Russian president today, so... We'll see how that goes."

"I'm not holding my breath. How's Nika doing?"

"She's getting there. She's kinda like you, kid—can't sit still. She wants to get back to work. Lonnie's doing a lot better, too, by the way. He's still gonna need more time, but I think he's gonna be okay. Maybe not well enough to come back to the Agency, but he'll be able to play with his grandkids."

Rainey pulled out a stainless steel thermos full of piping hot green tea—the same kind Nika had been so keen on in Montreal—and turned to Job. "Want some tea?"

"Don't tell me she's gotten you hooked on that stuff now?"

"Hey, it's actually pretty good." Rainey chucked a thick log onto the fire which caused a small shower of sparks to shoot out. The freshly added wood popped and crackled as he stoked the fire with a long, sturdy piece of hickory he used as a poker. "How's the wing?"

"It's all right, still a little sore at times." Job held his hands out to the fire. "By the way, thought I'd let you know, I just heard back about the last of the wire transfers."

After Roman Lerner's and Noel Patterson's accounts had been tracked down at various points around the globe—banks, safe deposit boxes, etc., Rainey had suggested that the funds be anonymously wired into private accounts for the family members of all those who had heroically died as a result of Levka Borovksy's plan. In addition, he asked that an anonymous letter he drafted be sent to each of them. In it, he briefly, though vaguely, explained the monies as well as his personal sentiments. He concluded his letter with these words:

Ours has always been and will always be a quiet fraternity whose members do not fail to appreciate the danger that exists in the world today. And yet it is that very danger—both known and unknown— that we make it our business to charge toward, to battle, to destroy each and every day. Those among us, who have committed the ultimate sacrifice for their beloved country and countrymen, though no longer here on this earth, live on in our hearts and minds. They live on giving us everlasting inspiration to conduct ourselves with honor, courage, and humility. Their memory fuels a burning desire in each of us to press on, to fight the good fight. And while the loss of these heroic patriots which we share with you is great, the purpose for which they gave their lives is greater. Speaking on behalf of the brothers and sisters they leave behind, of fellow warriors, of silent operators and operatives and others who proudly serve alongside us, I want to communicate to you that they did not die in vain. And in that same regard I want to make known to you that our resolve is unwavering. We will continue on with the mission to protect and defend even till our last dying breath. In doing so, we humbly strive to represent the ideals that faithfully drove our lost members and those that continue to drive us going forward, none of which is greater than a relentless devotion to the enduring hope of freedom, now and forever.

For God and Country,
Your Fellow Patriot

It had taken some doing at the onset, but Job had said he'd make it work and was on board with the idea as soon as Rainey had voiced it.
"And?"
"It's done. Just how you wanted."
Rainey nodded thinking back to the faces of those he'd served with, the men who'd sacrificed everything for America, for each other. He thought of their families. No amount of money could ever come close to compensating them for their grievous loss, but he would much

rather those funds go to the families than being squandered away on the special interests of unscrupulous politicians.

"Hey, I don't think I told you this... You know that medical bag...the one used to conceal the Turbo? Only six of the tubes inside were real, the rest were inert...more replicas. SSE of Kupchenko's computer and other items found at the house you were taken to, led us to the six missing tubes. They were hidden inside a townhouse in Front Royal, another safe house. Boy, you saved us big time in going after Maddie. Otherwise those six tubes of Turbo might have been lost to the Russians. Not to mention D.C. would be in ruins. Talk about lucky."

"More like Providence, Job."

After a few minutes had passed, Job cleared his throat. "Ray, I need to ask you something. Something very serious."

"You want the receipt for your Christmas present so you can return it?"

Job shook his head.

"Sorry. Shoot."

"I wanted to wait until after you had some time to rest and recuperate." A pause. "I want to know if you would be interested in coming to work directly for me, permanently."

Leave Delta? Rainey stared into the flames. After a few seconds his eyes shifted upward over the tendrils of orange, toward the rolling pastures, the woods beyond. The green was starting to return in places. Birds were chirping.

"If you want, you can begin immediately. After some more intensive training that is."

Rainey scratched his bearded face and took a sip of tea. He let out a long sigh, his breath forming a nickel-colored cloud in the air that slowly drifted into oblivion. "It's not her real name is it?"

"What?"

"Nika. It's not her real name." This time it was a declaration rather than an interrogative.

"No."

"Who is she?"

"I'm afraid that information is restricted to only permanent D12 employees and further still to only a few amongst them."

Rainey was stone-faced. He enjoyed the mental calisthenics. He mused how Job had dodged the issue and craftily turned the conversation back to his recruiting pitch.

Suddenly, a cell phone disturbed the peace, its shrill ringtone echoing across the old farm. It was Job's. The spymaster looked at the screen and said, "Excuse me. I have to take this." He walked a few paces away and answered the call. After a few minutes, Job returned, stuffed the phone back into his jacket. "Well?"

Rainey scratched his beard again, crossed his arms. He let out a long sigh. "I don't think it'll work."

"Believe me, Ray, we'll make it work. I need a man like you."

Rainey was staring at the ground adjacent to the blacksmith shop, the large area he'd marked off with white spray paint, wooden stakes and bright orange string. "I think it needs to be bigger."

ACKNOWLEDGMENTS

First and foremost, I want to thank my Lord and Savior, **Jesus Christ** from whom all blessings flow. I am truly blessed.

To my lovely wife, **Jill**, my daughter **Claire** and son **Jackson**, I love you guys! Thank you for your unending support, for putting up with me in my lesser moments and for loving me back unconditionally. You are my joy. As I said, I am truly blessed.

To my parents, **Donald and Diane Harbaugh**, from whom I've learned the value of hard work and sacrifice, learned to be a parent myself. Thank you for being godly parents and for modeling Christ's love to me. Thank you for sacrificing your time and money to see me through thirteen years of Christian school. This book is, I hope, evidence that your investment was sound.

A very special thanks to author **Jan Thompson**. Jan has been a mentor of sorts to me. She's uniquely talented and a humble, joyful soul. I believe God places certain people in our lives, especially at key moments, to encourage, equip and guide us. As far as my life and my writing are concerned, I wholeheartedly believe Jan is one of those people.

I want to extend my gratitude to several others who have provided me with kind words of encouragement, valuable advice and much-needed prayer, to wit, **Mike Dellosso**, **Luana Ehrlich** and **Steven J. Wilson**. Incidentally, they are all authors, too. I urge anyone who enjoys quality Christian fiction to check out their stuff.

Lenny and Amy Luchetti, thanks for being in my corner. Your critical insights and friendship are much appreciated. Lenny, I still find your personal story to be incredibly inspirational. God is good. One of these days, I promise we'll make it out to Indiana.

To **Adam Zimmerman**, for some last-minute technical assistance, thanks, brother.

A giant thank you to the men and women of the United States military, intelligence community, law enforcement community and all those who selflessly serve, and courageously defend freedom around the world. You inspire me. You sacrifice, you give so much of yourselves—physically and emotionally—not for glory or fame, but because someone has to. Freedom is definitely not free. Nor does it come cheap. My heart equally goes out to the families of these folks. You are certainly heroes, too. Their sacrifice is your sacrifice. May God keep you and comfort you.

Finally, to the readers, I say thank you! Thank you for your time and for investing your hard-earned money in this book. You are why I write. You are why all writers write. Know that I will always consider myself a reader first and thus, I will never write a book that I myself would not like to read. Readers rock!

If you've enjoyed this book, please consider leaving a review on Amazon or Goodreads, or simply telling a friend or loved one about it. It really does matter.

For more information and to sign up for my free e-mail newsletter, the Reader Intel Bulletin, visit my website at **DonyJayBooks.com**. and be sure to drop me a line to tell me about your reading experience, your—or your loved one's—military or other type of service, or even just a little bit about yourself. You can reach me through the website. Again, that's **DonyJayBooks.com**.

God bless and keep reading!

ABOUT THE AUTHOR

DONY JAY is a patriot, a book addict, a sports enthusiast and a family man. He loves to laugh and joke around, so it's not uncommon to find him in the throes of planning his own clandestine operation with that aim.

For more than a decade, Dony's worked in law enforcement, the majority of that time as an investigator. In 2010, he set out to write his own brand of spy thriller series—one with a distinctly Christian worldview and a patriotic flair for America...as she was founded.

Dony's partner in crime—er, writing—is a Beagle named Daisy, who prides herself on being able to nap through the loudest, most intense gunfights and explosions Dony can put to paper.

When he's not reading or writing, Dony enjoys playing sports (soccer mostly), being outdoors, staying fit and cheering on the Philadelphia Eagles.

Above all, he is a follower of Jesus Christ. Dony believes the tenets of a rich and rewarding life are faith, family and freedom. In that order.

He resides in south-central Pennsylvania with his wife and two very active kids.

Made in the USA
Middletown, DE
20 January 2016